W9-BMA-489

GOOD GIRLS

BOOKS BY GLEN HIRSHBERG

The Book of Bunk

The Snowman's Children

American Morons

The Two Sams

*Motherless Child**

The Janus Tree

*Good Girls**

*A Tor Book

GOOD GIRLS

GLEN HIRSHBERG

A TOM DOHERTY ASSOCIATES BOOK

NEW YORK

This is a work of fiction. All of the characters, organizations, and events portrayed in this novel are either products of the author's imagination or are used fictitiously.

GOOD GIRLS

A Tor Book
Published by Tom Doherty Associates, LLC
175 Fifth Avenue
New York, NY 10010

www.tor-forge.com

The Library of Congress Cataloging-in-Publication Data is available upon request.

ISBN 978-0-7653-3746-7 (hardcover)
ISBN 978-1-4668-3442-2 (e-book)

First Edition: February 2016

Printed in the United States of America

0 9 8 7 6 5 4 3 2 1

For Kim, Kate, and Sid,
with a murder ballad and hiding places

It is not often given in a noisy world to come to the places of great grief and silence. An absolute, archaic grief possessed this countrywoman; she seemed like a renewal of some historic soul, with her sorrows and the remoteness of a daily life busied with rustic simplicities and the scents of primeval herbs.

—Sarah Orne Jewett,
The Country of the Pointed Firs

GOOD GIRLS

1

In the heart of the hollow, at the mouth of the Delta, the monsters were dancing. Their shadows slid over the billowing green walls of the revival tent, rolling together, flowing apart. To Aunt Sally, rocking and smoking in her favorite chair in the shadows of her pavilion tent out back, their movements seemed hypnotic, lulling, like nimbus clouds across the moon, rainwater down glass. They kept her company, the shadows did. They were all the company she had ever kept or needed. Looking past the hollow down the mossy bank, she could see the moon out for its nightly stroll down the slow-sliding surface of the Mississippi, through the clustered cattails, the swamp roses, and spider lilies. As she watched, the moon seemed to turn, as it did every night, and nod in her direction.

Howdy, neighbor. Mind if I smoke?

Almost peaceful, *Aunt Sally thought.*

Except that someone—one of the younger monsters—had gotten hold of the stereo in there, under the big tent, and unleashed some of that shuddering rumpus music. Thunder-and-swagger music. It didn't last long, Caribou saw to that. Just long enough to put a big jagged crack right down the center of the evening. Break the mood. Remind Aunt Sally just how far from peaceful she'd been feeling lately. How very, terribly bored.

Probably, she thought, she should try to remember some of the younger monsters' names, although the truth was, she couldn't imagine what for. Had she even known their names when she'd made them? She couldn't remember, now, but suspected she had. All she could *remember with any certainty was the surprise, every time, when it did happen. When they sat up after she had finished, patting in wonder at whatever holes she'd torn in them. And she remembered her delight for them, or maybe simply for what she'd done. She'd always assumed she would understand what made it happen, someday: the transformation instead of dying, or after dying. Some of it, she knew, was simply that she'd* wanted *it to happen. But she never had quite figured it out. Neither had Mother, or any of the very few others who'd achieved it, accidentally or otherwise. And the fact was, Aunt Sally had stopped worrying or even wondering about it a long, long time ago.*

Should she tell Caribou she had taken a secret liking to a little thunder-and-swagger music from time to time? The idea—the look of horrified disbelief, of shattered sensibility she could already envision on his gaunt, luminous sickle-moon face—made her smile, faintly. At least, she was fairly certain that she was smiling. According to Caribou, her mouth never moved, these days, except when she was Telling, doing Policy. Not even when she ate.

The music reverted to old, familiar favorites. No drums, no guitars, just a piano and a muted trumpet loping and leaning, ducking and bobbing. Victoria Spivey moaning and sighing, surrounded by snakes. That song, too, had sounded like shuddering rumpus back in its day, when Victoria Spivey had played it. Way back when Aunt Sally used to dance, too, instead of sitting out back watching the dance. When she did for herself, instead of for others. Back when she and Mother used to light out for the shacks, the little towns, the helpless husbands and sad, hungry boys, on the best, most memorable nights. The two of them twisting and spinning, in a sweatbox-cabin full of people who sweated and spun wherever she and Mother spun them.

She did miss that, sometimes. Occasionally. The doing for herself. More, she missed Mother, although that word—"miss"—wasn't the right one. Aunt Sally did not "miss." She simply remembered.

And because she remembered, she wondered, from time to time, exactly where Mother had gone and got to, now, with that weedy little monster she had somehow made—how had that happened? Why *had that happened?—and then gotten herself addicted to. Foolish Mother. Gone these so many years. How many, now?*

Aunt Sally blew smoke through her motionless mouth, the cloud of it closing over the starlight, spreading thin, dissipating. In the cattails down-hollow, frogs bleated, cicadas sawed. All the night creatures, humming their hunger. She watched the tent, the shadows on its rippling walls. Too many shadows. For the first time since . . . oh, when? That year the Riders came down here, created some rumpus of their own, got the whole countryside so stirred up and boiling and ripe? *For the first time since then, Aunt Sally found herself musing on the world out there, just on the other side of the cane fields and pecan trees. Full of people to set spinning. Not that they'd spin any differently than the ones here did.*

How many of the dancers in that tent, she wondered, watching the walls, actually were hers, were creatures she had made? Caribou, of course, but the others? Any *of the others, come to think of it? Maybe she couldn't remember their names because they weren't hers, after all. Maybe all of hers—and there hadn't been so very many, truly—had long since left her side. The thought jarred, even alarmed her, a little.*

Was that true? It could be true.

Drawing her shawl tighter on her cold, cold arms, Aunt Sally pushed her bare feet into the night-wet grass and set her chair rocking. Had Mother been her last? Sometimes, Aunt Sally forgot she had even made Mother. Certainly, she hadn't meant to. What God There Was—which was what she had always called whatever God there is—had apparently sensed that she needed a companion, was going to die of boredom or loneliness without one. And for once, What God There Was had shown mercy, fulfilled a wish she hadn't realized she was wishing.

Or else—more likely—He'd sat up there in His hollow, outside His own tent, watching the shadows He had made. He had gazed down the years and seen a new opportunity, a whole new sort of suffering he could inflict on His *long-suffering Sally: He'd give her a companion. And then her companion would leave her.*

So in the end, was any of it her doing? His?

Either way, it had happened. She had been bored, lonely, both. So bored and lonely that she could no longer imagine herself before or after boredom or loneliness. And then she had found Mother and made her.

Maybe that was what happened in those moments. Maybe the changing really was caused or catalyzed simply by need, when the need was strong enough.

Or maybe when the need was most reciprocated? Or did the process require a specific sort of need, at a specific time? Or was it chance? Luck?

Policy?

To herself, rocking in the grass, watching the moon vanish downriver, Aunt Sally snorted. Smiled. Thought she smiled.

Where was *Mother now? Still chasing her Whistling fool, no doubt. And Aunt Sally had to admit it: her fool really could Whistle, and also sing. How many years could singing and Whistling fill? More, apparently, than sitting in her chair, just there, beside Aunt Sally, rocking together, listening to the cranes and alligators in the swamp. Watching their children grow.*

The flap at the back of the revival tent parted, and Caribou emerged, white as moonlight, long as a river-reed, eyes round and dark and skittish as a deer's. He stopped a moment before approaching, settled his white tails-coat on his hanger-thin shoulders, straightened his bow tie. To Aunt Sally's surprise, he had a companion in tow. She'd seen this one before, of course, but not for a while. She thought she might have known his name, once, but hadn't the slightest idea of it, now. What did it matter?

And what could he possibly want or wish for that Caribou would believe she might acknowledge or grant?

"Tuck your shirt in," she heard Caribou say.

His companion—bearded, in a flannel work shirt that looked warm, to Aunt Sally, comfortable, yes, she liked that shirt—mumbled out of his drunken mouth. But he risked a single glance in Aunt Sally's direction, caught sight of her, and did as he was told.

How long, Aunt Sally wondered, since she had even spoken to any of them but Caribou? Were they stopping coming to her? Forgetting she was out here, even? Surely not. But the nights did keep stretching out, now, spooling away down the grasslands, slow and muddy as the Mississippi, bored by their own movement, moving anyway. With a sigh, she waved a hand at Caribou, the sign to approach.

"Your stocking's down again," Caribou said to her as he stepped out of the moonlight, under her canopy, into her circle of shadow. And Aunt Sally sighed again, this time in something like contentment. It was Caribou's voice, more than anything, that she enjoyed. That impeccable tone. Groomsman, servant, grandson, lover, all at the same time. Her lily-white Man of the South, who did whatever she told him.

It had bored Mother, that tone. Mother liked her lovers louder, or full of music.

"So pick it up," she snapped.

Caribou's mouth twitched—in delight, controlled de-

light, he knew she preferred his exasperation—and he started to raise one of his ridiculously long arms in protest. Then he dropped to one knee to fix her stocking. Aunt Sally smiled. Thought she smiled. She ignored Caribou completely, pretended to focus on his companion. Silly devil-goatee beard, big fat bruise on his pasty-white cheek, as though he had been fighting. Abruptly, she did remember something about this one: he had a tattoo of a wasp on his neck. There it was, when he dropped and tilted his head to keep from looking at her too directly, seemingly crawling up his throat toward his ear. Right where she had told him his dream said he should get it. Gullible, pasty goatee-moron.

"Aunt Sally," he said, all respectful and proper, the way Caribou always told the ridiculous ones they had to be. "We're hungry. And tired."

Again, she sighed, feeling Caribou's fingers crawling up under her skirt, reattaching her stocking. Lingering, not lingering? He liked her to wonder. She liked him to wonder if she did.

"So you're speaking for all of them, child?" she purred, and whatever Caribou's hands were or weren't doing under her skirt, they stopped. He looked up from under his elegant, artfully gelled swoosh of blond hair, like a baby anticipating a story.

Well, Aunt Sally couldn't resist that. Never could. She smiled—thought she smiled—at the wasp-goatee man, and patted Caribou on the top of the head, let her fingers spread along his scalp, through all that beautiful, beautiful blond.

"It has been awhile," she said.

"Yes," said Wasp-goatee, all mesmerized. "We were all saying so."

"And the nights do get long."

"So long." The moron's voice, his whole body, quivered.

"And you think it's time for a Party?"

Under her skirt, Caribou's hands tightened on her thighs. Then they started sliding up. He couldn't help it, poor boy. He was so utterly hers, always had been. He gazed up at her from way down deep in his hypnotized deer-eyes. "Yes," he said. "Aunt Sally, let's. It has been so long."

"It has," she said, and closed her legs. She shoved Caribou back, hard, on his haunches, and grabbed the gaze of the goateed one, held it until he started to sway. "A Party. We'll need some guests."

"Guests. Yes," said the goateed one.

Once more, Aunt Sally thought of Mother. She wondered if she could get word to her, somehow. Invite her to a celebration, in honor of her return home. Preferably without her Whistling fool, though she could bring him, too, if she had to. Either way, maybe Mother would come. Maybe she would stay this time.

Aunt Sally smiled. Thought she smiled. "Good. Well, then. In that case." She stretched out her own beautiful long-fingered hands, nodded at Wasp-goatee. "Come here, son. Tell Aunt Sally what you've dreamed."

2

Rebecca, come *on,*" Jack said, leaping free of his spinning chair in mid-spin to alight in front of her. He spread his arms, grinned, and the suction-cup dart sticking out of his forehead waggled like an antenna. "Do the thing."

Beside Rebecca in the next cubicle over, Kaylene's stream of muttering intensified. "Come here, little Pookas. Come here, little Pookas, comeherecomeherecomehere . . ." Her fingers punched repeatedly at her keyboard, and out of the tiny computer speakers came the twinkling music and popping sounds that accompanied so many of Rebecca's nights working the Crisis Center, as Kaylene's Dig Dug inflated and exploded her enemies.

"Comeherecomeherecomehere SHIT!" Kaylene, too,

leapt to her feet, joined Jack in front of Rebecca's desk. Her beautiful black hair had overrun its clip, as usual, and poured over her face and shoulders.

"Tell Rebecca to do the thing," said Jack, grabbing Kaylene around the waist and glancing over his shoulder. "Marlene, put the book down, get over here."

"Rebecca, do the thing," Kaylene said. "MarlenePooka, don't make me come over there."

In the far corner of the room, where she always set up so she could study but never stayed, Marlene sighed. She stood, straightened her glasses, put a hand through her red-orange, leaves-in-autumn hair. Not for the first time, Rebecca felt a flicker of jealousy about Marlene: too much work ethic *and* hair color for any one person. Especially a person who could barely be bothered to comb all that hair, let alone care about it, and who also knew when it was time to put the *Advanced Calculus and Cryptography* textbook down and come help her closest friends bug her other closest friend.

Then, as always, Rebecca's jealousy melted away as Marlene took up her position, linked arms with Jack, and grinned down at Rebecca, still seated at her desk with the Campus Lifeline Crisis Center manual she knew by heart tucked right where it belonged against the special blue Campus Lifeline phone, complete with idiotic life-preserver logo. Rebecca watched them beam down at her. Jack and the 'Lenes.

For an awful, ridiculous second, she thought she was going to burst into tears. Happy tears.

"Rebeccccaaaaa," Jack chanted, and the suction-cup

dart on his forehead bobbed, whisked the tears away. "Read our minds . . ."

"Okay, okay, okay, stop waggling that thing at me." Controlling her smile, Rebecca glanced across their faces. Her eyes caught Kaylene's.

"Do. Your. Thing," Kaylene said.

"Fine. Stop thinking about her," said Rebecca. "She's safe now. Mrs. Groch's looking after her. And she's got you, now. She'll figure it out."

"*Fuck* you, Rebecca," Kaylene said, and burst out laughing. "How do you *do* that? I haven't said one word about the Shelter tonight. I don't think I've said a word about it this whole week. I don't remember saying one thing to you about—"

"She's a witch," Marlene said, through her perpetually exhausted Marlene-smile. "Do me."

It took Rebecca a second, only because she wanted to check herself, make sure. Then she shrugged, nudged a strand of her own mousy brown bangs out of her eyes. "Too easy."

"Oh my God, you bitch, you've got Twinkies," Kaylene said, broke free of Jack's arm, and dove for Marlene's backpack. Marlene started to whirl, give chase, but there was no point. Kaylene was already elbows deep in Marlene's backpack, shoveling aside organic chem textbooks, notebooks, calculator, tissues, until she came up with the crumpled pack in her fist. Strawberry flavor, tonight.

"Really?" Kaylene said, straightening. "You weren't going to share these?"

"Actually, I wasn't even going to open them, I don't think. They just . . . called to me out the PopShop window."

"Well, now they're calling me." Kaylene tore open the package and offered Marlene a piece of her own late-night snack. Marlene's perpetual and permanent late-night snack. The secret, she claimed, of all-night cramming.

"My turn," said Jack, putting his hands behind his back, standing at a sort of parade rest in his baggy shorts and blue bowling-team button-up shirt, with the dart sticking straight out from his head.

"You look like a unicorn," she said, and Jack's green eyes blinked, then flashed in his cookie-dough face. *That* was what he actually looked like, Rebecca thought. Not a unicorn, but a cookie. Purple-frosted, with spearmint leaves for eyes.

Over his shoulder, through the floor-to-ceiling windows, she could see the black gum trees melting into their moonshadows along Campus Walk. The light from this room was practically the only light in the quad, which didn't seem particularly strange at 1 a.m. in East Dunham, New Hampshire, in early August, with the great majority of UNH-D students still elsewhere for another few weeks. And yet, tonight, the dark looked deeper out there, for some reason.

Because I am so aware of this island in it, Rebecca thought, and felt herself fighting back tears again, grateful tears. *Because I am so happy I washed up here.* She glanced into the corner, saw Marlene's hair spilling into Kaylene's, red into black, as they elbowed each other and fought over strawberry Twinkie crumbs. Then they were up, laughing,

Kaylene making biting-mouth motions over her fingers like a Ms. Pac-Man, burbling like a Dig Dug.

"Well?" Jack said. "Come on. What am I thinking?"

Focusing on the dart in Jack's forehead chased the tears, instantly. But as soon as Rebecca lowered her gaze to his eyes, she blushed, without knowing why. Without wanting to think why.

"Come on," said Jack.

Quietly? Nervously? Was that a little croak?

"Rebecca. What am I thinking?"

On the desk behind her, Rebecca's computer pinged. Out of the corner of her eye, she saw Joel's name pop up in its seemingly personalized, permanent chat window. Poor Joel.

"You guys go on," she murmured, not quite meeting Jack's eyes again. "Go play."

"That isn't quite what I was—"

"You weren't thinking Human Curling? Tell me you weren't thinking Human Curling."

"Human Curling!" Kaylene whooped, dragging Marlene back between cubicles toward Jack.

"I can't," said Marlene. "You guys, it's two weeks until school." But she was only protesting out of habit, Rebecca thought. Duty. She was hardly even trying, tonight.

"Kaylene, let go."

But now Jack had Marlene's other arm. And there they stood in front of her. Her Crisis Center shift mates. Her every-single-day cafeteria meal buddies.

Her friends.

"Someone's got to man the phones," Rebecca said, ignoring the pings behind her as Joel tapped out his lonely messages from the kitchen worktable at Halfmoon House. He'd be sitting in no light, at this hour, Rebecca knew from long experience, from so much shared insomnia at that table in that house at these hours, the only sound the wind whipping leaves down the cracks in the gutters, owls in those trees, loons on the lake. Poor Joel.

But why would he be poor? Why did she always feel bad for him? Certainly, he *never seemed to.*

"Rebecca," said Jack. "This is your Captains speaking."

"Jack and the 'Lenes," said Kaylene.

Even Marlene joined in, smiled tiredly. "Jack and the 'Lenes. Come on, Bec."

"Not tonight," said Rebecca, and wondered if she sounded as happy as she felt.

"Oh, it's tonight," said Kaylene.

"It's tonight, it's tonight, it's tonight," Jack chanted. "Why won't you come? Seriously. It's the middle of summer. It's the middle of the night. It's the middle of East Lake NoAssWhere, New Hampshire. No one's going to call. And if they do, they'll just get forwarded to the Hospital center. To, you know, professionals."

"Who aren't their peers."

"Is it a money thing? How about if tonight's on me? Rebecca, seriously, I know you don't have—"

"It's not a money thing," she said, too fast, and half-honestly. There was always the money thing, of course. But that wasn't the reason. How could she even explain the reason?

Was there even one?

Only Joel. And the phones, which were supposed to stay manned at least another hour. And the fact that this feeling—this *accompanied* sensation—was still new in her life. And wading around too much in it—or setting out across it—felt foolhardy. Dangerous. Like testing fresh ice.

"You take Crisis Center rules pretty seriously, don't you?"

"So do you, Jack. Or you wouldn't be here."

"The rules are not the Center."

"*We* are the Center," Kaylene said, and grinned at Rebecca. And . . . *winked? Gestured with her chin toward Jack, and his ridiculous dart?*

Then, somehow, the 'Lenes were shutting down their desk lamps, and Marlene had packed her backpack, and they were out the door, arms around each other's shoulders, doing their leaning thing, first to one side, then the other. Their voices echoed down the empty corridor as they stomped and leaned their way down it, fluttered up staircases and sounded the silent classrooms overhead.

Jack, meanwhile, had shut down his computer, collected his supplies. But he'd dawdled, doing it, and now he paused once more in the doorway, his face half in shadow, the only remaining light coming from Rebecca's lamp. He folded his faintly pudgy arms across his pudgy chest, which made him look twelve, like someone's little brother, or else like a jester. A harlequin. And also like Jack.

"Is it me?" he said. "Is it my rad thrift-store blue bowling shirt?" He plucked at his pocket, with the name *Herman* stitched across it. "How about I man the phones, and you go Human Curling with the 'Lenes. You could use it. They're good for you."

"They're good for everyone," Rebecca said.

As if on cue, both 'Lenes appeared at the windows, on

the path, standing together, joined at the hip. When they saw that she was looking, they did the lean. One side, the other. Kaylene beckoned, calling Rebecca out, into a world Kaylene was so obviously sure she belonged in.

And therefore, did? Rebecca wondered. *Was that all it took?*

"So it is me," said Jack.

"It really isn't."

Unfolding his arms, Jack waved his fingers in front of Rebecca's face as her computer pinged again. Joel, seeking contact. Jack's fingers continued to wave in her face like a mesmerist's. "*Rebeccccaaaaa. You are getting very hungry. And thirsty. And Curly. You want to come play Human Curling with Jack and the 'Lenes.*"

When Rebecca just sat, arms folded over the logo on her UNH-D hoodie, and smiled, he lowered his hands and stared into them, as though baffled that his spell hadn't worked.

"Maybe tomorrow," she said.

"Tomorrow," said Jack. "You're coming tomorrow. Plan on it. Book it in your Rebecca-Must-Plan-Everything-Years-in-Advance book."

"I might," she said.

"You just did." Jack thrummed his dart, and it vibrated at her.

"Someone could really take that the wrong way," Rebecca said.

"But not you, apparently." Sighing, he smiled sadly—as sadly as Jack knew how, anyway—and left.

She watched the windows until he appeared. Instantly, the others adhered around him like charged particles, forming a nucleus. Kaylene glanced up once more at Rebecca, scowled, then waved. Jack waved, too, but over his head, without looking back. Then they were off, crossing from shadow to shadow down Campus Walk toward Campus Ave, where they'd skirt the forest, the edges of the little subdivisions full of tiny, mostly subdivided shingle houses, many of them empty for the summer, and make their way, at last, to Starkey's, which had to be the only non-pub within fifty miles still open at this hour. They'd eat Mrs. Starkey's awful canned-pineapple pizza, drink a pitcher of her Goose Island Night Stalkers: cranberry juice; white grape juice; seltzer; some rancid, secret spicy powder; and gin. And then, if Mrs. Starkey was feeling friendly, or else Jack waggled his magic fingers at her, she would give them the keys to the rink in the giant shed out back, and they'd grab brooms and push-paddles out of the cupboards in there and Human Curl to their hearts' content.

It's an orphan thing, she muttered inside her head, standing there in the dark. She was talking to Jack and his unicorn horn, but the phrase was Joel's. Just one of the thousand things he had taught her during her four and a half years under his and Amanda's foster care at Halfmoon House. *That reluctance. That inclination toward solitude. You either have to learn to pay it no mind, or learn to mind it enough to do something about it. One or the other.*

Like most of the things Joel and Amanda had taught her—most of Joel's things, especially, she had to admit—that idea had made more sense back when she'd lived with them. Had seemed so comforting. It made less sense these days, or maybe just seemed too simple, not at all helpful, now that she lived on her own, had a little rented room she called home, even if it didn't feel like home, yet. Not in the way she'd always assumed—been told—her own room would feel.

Stepping closer to the giant windows, Rebecca flicked on the lamp on Marlene's desk. And voilà, there she was, out there in the world. At least, there was her reflection superimposed over the path: little Chagall girl in a blue UNH-D hoodie, more pale-faced and mousy brown than glowing blue, but floating, anyway, up amid the lower leaves of the gum trees, her narrow face tinged green by the grass, blue by the moon.

Flicking off Marlene's lamp, she watched herself vanish, then retreated to her own desk, pulled up a chair, tapped her sleeping computer awake.

RebeccaRebeccaRebecCaCaCaCaRebecca. Her name scrawled, and was still scrawling, across Joel's chat window, as though he were tagging her screen from inside it.

Hiya, Pops, she typed.

Instantly, the scrawling stopped. The ensuing pause lasted longer than she expected. It lasted so long that she actually checked her connection, started to type again, then decided to wait. Around her, the whole building seemed to settle. Rebecca could feel its weight, hear its quiet.

Please don't call me that, Joel typed. *I'm not your dad.*

I know. Don't be ridiculous.

I know you know.

So don't be ridiculous.

Pause. If she closed her eyes, Rebecca could see him there so clearly: his coal-black skin even blacker against whichever filthy white work T-shirt he'd worked in this particular day, the light from his laptop the only light in that long room, at that long wooden table. His wife gone to bed hours before, without bothering to tell or even locate him. His current foster kids—just two, right now, though he and Amanda generally liked to keep four at Halfmoon House, because that helped it feel more like a boarding school, which was exactly how Amanda wanted anyone she brought there to think of it—upstairs in their beds, possibly sleeping, possibly sneaking reading or headphone time of their own now that Amanda-chores and schoolwork were over.

On the lake, less than a mile away through the woods, there would be loons, Rebecca knew. The night-loons.

How's Crisisland? Joel typed.

Empty, Rebecca answered, but didn't like how the word looked. She deleted it, started to type *Serene* instead—which wasn't quite right, either, just closer to right than "empty"—but Joel was faster.

SMACKDOWN??!!

Joel's enthusiasm worked like Jack's wiggling fingers, but was even more powerful, or maybe just more practiced. Or familiar, and therefore comfortable. And yet, what Rebecca typed back was, *How're my girls? How's Amanda?*

Tiring. Fine. SMACKDOWN??!! And then, before Rebecca could respond: *I mean, the girls are tiring. Testing us. Amanda's fine. I guess. Hardly saw her today, as usual. Working hard. Trudi still mostly talks to her socks.*

Trudi was the newest Halfmoon House resident, one of the youngest Joel and Amanda had ever decided to bring there, barely ten.

She'll come around. You'll reach her, Joel. You always do.

Hey, R: maybe you could take her out rowing when you come tomorrow? Or—take her Human Curling!

Surprised, Rebecca straightened in her chair, her fingers on the keys. She thought about Amanda. Amanda would most definitely not be encouraging—or allowing—Rebecca to do any such thing with Trudi.

You know Human Curling? she typed.

I invented Human Curling.

Liar.

Okay, I didn't. But you have to admit, I could have. It's something I would have invented if your man Jack hadn't.

Which was true, Rebecca thought sadly, staring at the screen. Human Curling was exactly the kind of thing Joel would have invented—and played, with everyone—if he'd had time. Or a wife who played with or even enjoyed him. As far as Rebecca had ever seen, Amanda just worked and taught her foster orphans how to survive the hands they'd been dealt and made rules. Like the one about seeing things clearly. Calling them what they were. And so, *not* calling Amanda "Mom" or Joel "Dad."

Meanwhile, all unbidden, Rebecca's fingers had apparently been typing. And what they'd typed was: *Jack's not my man.*

Too slowly, again, she moved to delete. Again, Joel was faster.

A man after my own heart, your Jack. I do like your Jack, by the way. Fine man, your J—

SMACKDOWN! Rebecca typed, already opening the game site in a new window, calling up a string of letters for them to unscramble, make words from. *READY?*

What, for you? I don't have to be ready for you, Rebecca. I barely have to be awake.

Rebecca grinned. Middle-of-the-night Joel. Checking in

on his former charges, as he did almost every night, and which he had promised he would never stop doing until and unless he was sure they didn't need him anymore. Talking trash to his computer in the quiet dark of his house. As alone as she was.

Can you feel it? she typed. *That rush of wind? That's me, surging past you.*

You can't win, Rebecca. If you Smack me down, I will become more verbose than you can possibly imagine.

Laughing, she typed her name into the left-hand SMACKER 1 box on the game site, waited for Joel's name to appear next to SMACKER 2. Then the scrambled letters appeared, that awful, thudding cartoon hip-hop beat kicked in, the robot-Smackdown voice said, "*Lay 'em down. SMACK 'EM.*" And they were off. She got three words right off the bat, then a fourth, was typing a fifth, her fingers flying, when she realized her phone was ringing.

The Crisis Center phone. The one on her desk.

Joel, I've got to go, she typed fast into their chat window, and then closed it. She couldn't have that open, didn't want to risk distraction. He'd see eventually, whenever he looked up. He'd know what had happened.

And anyway, her phone was ringing. First time in weeks.

Rebecca had been working the Center too long to rush or panic. She allowed herself a moment to get centered and comfortable on her chair and in her head. Out of habit, her eyes flicked to the Quick Reference charts pinned to the cubicle walls, with their ALWAYS DO and DO NOT EVER lists, not that she needed them, or ever had, really.

You're a natural, Dr. Steffen had told her, the first time she'd left Rebecca alone on a night shift. *The best I've ever seen, at your age.*

Switching off her lamp, settling into the dark, Rebecca picked up the receiver. When she spoke, her voice was the professional one she had mastered, had hardly had to practice: neutral, friendly, comforting, and cool. Anonymous. Almost exactly like her regular voice, she thought, then squashed that thought.

"Hello," she said. "I'm so glad you called. To whom am I speak—"

"But should I?" said the voice on the other end. Sang, really. And then it made a sound.

Whistling? Wind? Was that wind?

Rebecca straightened, found herself resisting simultaneous urges to bolt to her feet and spin to the windows. Run from the room.

What the fuck?

"Should you have called?" Rebecca shushed her thoughts, commanding herself to relax as she leaned into the phone. "Of course you should have. It's great that you called."

"So it's going to get better," said the voice.

Was that a question? It hadn't sounded like one. And . . . shouldn't that have been her line?

One last time, Rebecca glanced at the Crisis chart. Then she turned away from it, relaxed in her chair. She was a natural, born for this if she'd been born for anything. "Starting right now," she said.

Again came that sound on the other end of the line. Wind or whistling. Then, "I think so, too. Maybe you're right. Maybe it's time."

"Time?"

"Is it good, do you think? Dying?"

Rebecca pursed her lips, made herself relax her hands on the tabletop. "Where are you?" she asked.

"High. Close."

To the edge? To her? How would he know where he was calling, and why would she think that?

High, as in on drugs? Or in the air?

"The end. Lonely Street," the voice whispered.

No. Sang.

"Is it beautiful there?" Rebecca heard herself say. Then she was staring, astonished, horrified, into the darkened windows, the shadowed summer leaves over Campus Walk. "I'm sorry, that was a really stupid question. What's your—"

"It *is,* actually." And he sounded surprised, her caller. Small, lonely, and surprised. "You know, it really is beautiful here. Hear it?"

Rebecca clutched the phone, watching the window as though it were a teleprompter that would tell her what the ALWAYS DO answer to *that* might be. *Hear what?* Nothing about this conversation was going in the direction it was supposed to.

But she was sure of one thing, or almost sure: this guy wanted to talk more than jump. Or whatever the hell he had been thinking of doing. So that was something. She would talk.

"What makes it beautiful?"

"The roofs," he said. And he made a whimpering sound.

This time, Rebecca actually lifted the phone from her ear and stared at it. She wondered, briefly, if this were a pop inspection, some new Crisis Center supervision thing

Dr. Steffen had invented. Then she decided it didn't matter. Either way, she had a job to do.

"Roofs." Nodding, though she had no idea at what, she leaned forward on her elbows. "That's fantastic. What about them?"

"How far they are from the ground. The beautiful ground, where my Destiny would have walked with me." Then he whistled, low and mournful.

It was like a song, almost, less what he said than the way he said it. Sang it. *Was that why she had tears in her eyes?*

"Listen. Why don't you tell me your na—"

"And they're all peaked! The roofs are. They have little attic rooms underneath, under the peaks. I just saw a little girl in one, with a night-light. She looked so alone up there in the middle of the night."

"Yeah, well. Story of my life," Rebecca murmured—as though she were dreaming—and realized she was blushing. *Jesus Christ, was she* flirting, *now? Maybe she'd better stick to the chart, after all.* "But no one has to be alone. Really. I should know. And I'm here with you."

For answer, she got footsteps. Her caller, walking across whichever roof he'd picked to climb out onto. Then he whistled again, and went silent. As though . . .

Abruptly, Rebecca whirled in her chair, banging her knee on the desk as she took in the empty carrels surrounding her, the long, dark Crisis Center room, the linoleum corridor beyond it where the lights hadn't flickered and nothing had moved.

Nothing at all.

On the other end of the phone, she heard neither whistle

nor whimper nor breath. Swallowing her panic, keeping it out of her voice, she said, "Are you still there?"

"I think she's gone to bed. Our little girl, in her attic room. All my girls have gone to their beds." And there was that whimper again. Rebecca was almost certain he was crying, now.

"Except—" she started, but he overrode her.

"Except you."

And suddenly—again—Rebecca had no idea what to say. Also for no reason she could understand, she wanted off of this call. And that made her feel like shit, and also rallied her. This guy wasn't creepy; he was desperate. "You know," she tried, slow and gentle, "one thing I really have learned, talking to people who phone here: no matter how bad you feel, no matter what you think you've done, it's never too late to—"

"My Destiny killed my Mother."

Rebecca stopped talking. She sat in the chair and waited. But her caller said nothing more. This was nothing new, she told herself, nothing she hadn't dealt with before. So often, what the callers said didn't make sense. And yet, the sense was there, if you listened. And the sense didn't matter much, anyway. Not at the crisis moment.

And so, when she sensed it was time, she said, "I guess destinies do that to mothers. Sometimes." She was leaning on her elbows again, pressing the phone against her ear, her mouth to the receiver. It was almost as though her lips were resting right against her caller's ear. Her words didn't even feel like words she would say; they were someone else's words, pouring through her. "At least, that's what I've been told. It's what people told me about mine."

Then she jerked, twitched her shoulders in alarm. *Never, ever, insert yourself into a Crisis conversation.* DO NOT EVER rule #2, right there in bold at the top of the chart.

"Then my Destiny's mother killed her," said the caller, and Rebecca gave up even trying to make sense of this conversation. She just listened.

But there was no sound in her building, and none on the other end of the line. The black gums waved silently out there, in a breeze she could neither hear nor feel.

"And yet, it's a beautiful street," she heard herself say.

To her relief, the person on the other end of the line whistled again; this time, there was no mistaking that sound for wind or anything else. "Yes it is," said the voice. "You're right. Again."

"On a beautiful night."

"So beautiful. Yes."

"Full of people worth talking to, staying up late."

This time, the silence felt different, seemed to yawn open against her ear: he-just-jumped silence. Panicking, Rebecca scrambled to her feet.

But he hadn't jumped. "You're very good at this," he said, and then he said something else. "What you do."

Or, *Oh, you'll do?*

Rebecca pushed out the breath she'd been holding and closed her eyes, gripping the phone as if it were her caller's hand. A hand she had somehow, in spite of all the mistakes she had made, managed to grab. "Tell me where you are," she said. "I can have someone with you in five minutes. There are people just waiting to help. People who really want to help. Let me . . ."

The caller whimpered again. Unless that was giggling. Hysteria setting in.

"Will you let me send them?" Rebecca asked. "Please?"

"I'll come see you," said the caller.

And then he was gone. Rebecca could tell. He hadn't hung up, just wasn't there. Which meant he really had gone and . . .

"DON'T!" Rebecca shouted, grabbing uselessly at the edge of her desk. She waited for the *splat*. But none came.

And yet, her caller was gone. *Had she just babbled some poor guy right off a ledge and out of the world?*

Her eyes flew to the window, Campus Walk, the trees out there. Her own shadow, barely visible among them.

She'd lost one. Failed somebody, in the most brutal way one person could fail another.

She didn't bother second-guessing herself or hesitating. She punched the speed dial on the Crisis phone and called the police.

3

(THREE WEEKS EARLIER)

The most immediate problem, Jess realized, swaying, somehow staying on her feet as sea wind blasted through her and scoured her bloody face with spray and sand, was her ribs. Every time she started forward or shifted Eddie in his baby blanket against her shoulder or just breathed, something else inside her popped: cartilage, or more bone, as though she were stepping on Bubble Wrap.

Catching movement to her left, she turned, too fast, her ribs not just popping this time but pulling apart, and she cried out. Again. She was hoping to see Benny stirring, pushing himself up out of the sand. Instead, she saw three seagulls, their feathers gray, not white, in the misty, moonless shadows under the creaking Ocean Beach pier. As she watched, helpless, they hopped closer to Benny. One of them shrieked as though demanding breadcrumbs. Or—worse—as though calling in flock mates so they could all feast together on Benny and the body of Sophie's son.

Jess's free hand flew to her mouth, and she bit it, held her skin in her teeth to keep from screaming more, or just to have something to bite. She didn't want to glance toward the shadowed pillar just beyond Benny, where Sophie's baby lay like a discarded doll. But she did, anyway.

There he was where he'd been flung, against the post where the monsters that had come for all of them had dashed out his brains: Sophie's Roo, with the seagulls and crabs creeping toward him, not ten feet from the spot where Natalie had fallen.

From the spot where Jess had blown the top of Natalie's head off.

Biting almost *through* her skin, Jess screamed into her palm, let her bloody hand drop to her side, and remembered Sophie. Finally, slowly, she turned that way.

Sophie was still perched—if that was the word—where she'd landed after plunging from the pier. The only thing propping her upright was the sand, certainly not the one leg at that insane angle behind her, which didn't even look attached to her anymore. Her other leg was nowhere in sight. But her brown eyes kept blinking, slowly. Then they stopped blinking. One of her hands lay outstretched toward Jess, but palm down, as though she were trying to pull herself forward.

Sweet sunshine-Sophie, Jess thought, biting back another scream. *Sunshine-Sophie, who made my daughter laugh.*

Who made my daughter . . .

Then Jess was staggering forward, jostling Eddie, who stirred, started shrieking, and Jess cuddled him as best she could against her shoulder but kept moving. Her ribs, she realized, could not be broken, at least not all of them. They hurt—horribly—but they were letting her walk. By the time she neared Sophie, the gun had already risen, as if of its own accord. She glared down into Sophie's face, which wasn't sunshiny anymore, wasn't even Sophie, really, and maybe hadn't been for a long time, even before all this had started. Maybe that was how she and Natalie had wound up the way they had in the first place.

A few feet away, Jess stopped, the gun half-lifted. Eddie still screeched, and worse, he squirmed, but he was settling, slowly. Jess waited for him a little longer, but she kept her eyes on Sophie.

Sophie, meanwhile, just stared back. *In disbelief,* Jess realized, surprised, because of course she knew every one of Sophie's expressions. *In horror, and wonder, at what I've done. At what I just made myself do.*

This time, when the shudder came, it wracked her ribs so hard that Jess thought she could feel them crossing over each other, banging together inside her like badly shipped oars. The pain almost drove her to her knees.

But it didn't.

In wonder, she thought. So they could still wonder, these creatures. That was good to know. Crouching agonizingly, she laid Eddie in his blanket in the sand. He squirmed but made no sound. Only when she looked up again, her eyes now level with her target's, did she realize that Sophie wasn't looking at her at all. In fact, she had never been. She was looking beyond Jess toward the other blanketed bundle, in the shadows of the pier. The bundle that had been her son. The horror, wonder, and disbelief on Sophie's face were for him.

"That's right," Jess snarled, the taste of the words like bile in her mouth. "That's what you've done."

How had she imagined Sophie might respond? With a heartbroken cry, or a laugh? With a lunge, maybe, except on no legs, because the one in the sand was no longer part of her, either; Jess could see that, now.

But Sophie—the stump that had been Sophie—did none of those things. She didn't even seem to hear. She just kept watching the blanket under the pier. She wasn't even blinking.

Because she was dead? Really dead?

But Sophie wasn't. Jess knew that only because she also knew, with absolute certainty, that life would not give her even that much mercy. She would not be relieved of the necessity of acting, even after the action she had taken. That just wasn't how her life had ever worked.

Fuck that, she thought abruptly, and jerked the hand that wasn't holding the gun up to her cheek. She pressed her palm into the splotch where her daughter's blood was drying and crusting in the sea-spray. There were little shards scattered through it, and some gooier bits, too, gray on her fingertips when Jess made herself look at them.

With a whimper, Jess rubbed the whole mess into her face, smearing it over her cheeks and nose and forehead, painting herself with it. Not like a warrior. She just wanted to hold on to it, somehow, to *absorb* it, because soon there would be nothing left. Her cry not only sounded birdlike in her ears but *felt* that way, too: automatic, instinctive, anguished. Helpless.

She stood up, raised the gun, pointed straight down into the top of Sophie's skull, and clicked the safety back. But she didn't shoot.

Why not?

She knelt again. Sophie continued ignoring her, watching the birds encircle her own dead child. Jess shoved the nozzle of the gun hard into Sophie's forehead.

That, at least, made her look up. She blinked as though coming awake, became aware of the gun. Jess saw the moment Sophie understood. Just as Natalie had, right before Jess had pulled the trigger.

"Good," Jess said.

Except that the expression on Sophie's face was not Natalie's. Natalie had been . . . *grateful? Relieved? Sad beyond the power of human beings to express?* Partly, Jess knew, Natalie had been grateful. She'd still been herself, still Jess's daughter, right to the end. Jess would hold on to that conviction all the way to her own grave.

But Sophie—*this* Sophie—just looked scared, and also as though she had something to say.

"Well?" Jess shoved the gun deeper into the cleft between Sophie's eyes. "Speak up."

When Sophie gurgled, though, Jess almost dropped the gun, scuttled back. *How could that thing—half a thing—make sound? Be living?*

Of course, she knew the answer to that: it wasn't living. Not really.

But it was pleading, working its mouth. Sophie's mouth.

Trying to get shape around sound once more. And there were tears in its eyes, on its cheeks, unless that was sea-spray. *Same stuff,* Jess thought crazily. *Just salt water.* She clutched the gun, felt the crust on her own face, heard the awful, ravenous birds, stared down into the face of the only best friend her daughter had ever known.

"Wait here," she said, and somehow pushed to her feet. Collecting Eddie, she nestled him against her shoulder, as far as she could from the bruises all over her midsection. Sophie's eyes followed her every move.

Turning her back, gnashing her bottom lip, Jess stumbled across the sand toward the pier, snarling birds away from Sophie's Roo, and also from Benny, who—*oh, finally, one positive thing*—was waving at them himself. He was still lying prone, his arm-sweeps so weak that he wasn't even startling the gulls, let alone deterring them. His arm itself seemed boneless, too limp, like washed-ashore kelp stirring in a breeze.

But it was stirring. At this moment, that was enough.

For the first time since she'd fired the gun, Jess's own tears spilled down her face. She sketched a wave, almost smiled through her gnawed, bleeding lips like a little girl. *Who'd just murdered her daughter.* Benny hadn't seen that, she realized. He had been unconscious by then. Would she tell him? Over dinner tonight, maybe? *So, hon, here's what you missed . . .*

Somehow, the thought of that conversation—the insanity of it, the fact that she already, absolutely knew that was going to happen—drove her forward. Stumbling into the shadows, hearing the ocean hiss as it crawled up the beach, she pocketed the gun, crouched, waited for her ribs to stop stabbing her, resettled Eddie yet again, and scooped up the bundle of bones that had been Sophie's Roo. She glared the seagulls back, started to stand, and then, on impulse, peeled back the blanket so she could see this baby's face. She wanted to remember it. Someone had to. And now, she would never forget. Any more than she would forget her own child's.

The one she had shot in the head.

George, she realized abruptly. *George William.* For a month, she'd been calling this kid Roo because that's what his mother had always called him. For a month, Jess had cared for him, loved him, assumed she would raise him. She had learned his laugh, which was so different from little Eddie's: a set of short, snapping firecracker bursts, shiny-loud. That laugh had made Eddie giggle, and Benny. And Jess, also. Constantly. Every time. And yet, only now had she remembered his real name. Because only now, when he was gone, did Jess realize how much she had let him feel like her own, from the first second Natalie and Sophie had left him with her, trusted him to her.

She was whimpering again, grinding her teeth to keep from collapsing. To somehow keep from collapsing.

"Good night, little William George," she was whispering, almost singing as she clutched the baby's motionless body against her chest next to Eddie, who kept squirming away, kicking her in the ribs. Lowering her head, ignoring the battering, she just kept taking, nuzzling the blanket, cooing, "Good night, Little Roo," as though he were a stuffed animal.

Only when she'd finally gotten both kids—that is, one kid and one corpse—settled against her body and managed to stagger to her feet once more did she let herself look at

Benny again. To her relief, he was sitting up, though slumped over. One arm hung wrong, and one foot pointed way too far out to the side. His bent head rested on his left shoulder, and his crazy white hair was flying everywhere. He looked like a Mr. Potato Head—a fuzzy one—with all the appendages slid into the wrong slots.

"Come here," he said, and lifted his not-broken arm maybe three inches off the sand. With a sob, she went to him, squatted slowly, and allowed herself one long moment. She put her face in Benny's hair and breathed it in, while Eddie wriggled gently between them. Benny's hand rested cool and surprisingly steady on her hip. His other, dangling hand had found the top of Eddie's head and started stroking it, calming him down. So that hand still worked, too.

"Okay," she whispered, blew out breath, sucked in more, tasting sand and Benny's hair on her lips. Along with Natalie's blood. "Okay."

That next hour, or however long it took . . . those next tasks . . . Jess would never understand how she managed them, or how Benny managed to help. All she would ever know, for certain, was that the tasks got done. She and Benny did them together. They dragged Natalie's body across the sand, somehow bumped it up the steps to the boardwalk, across that to the trunk of Jess's car. Somehow—without screaming, either one of them, from pain or from heartbreak—they hoisted her inside. Then, while Benny sagged against the bumper, Jess spent some time arranging her daughter. Making her comfortable. Weeping over her. Eventually, she took Sophie's Roo and tucked him into Natalie's arms. She let her hand rest for one more moment atop her daughter's hands, atop the dead child. Then, her mouth moving, she'd closed them in.

Night, babies.

Sleep tight, my brooding, beautiful, shining girl.

In all that time—on the beach, on the boardwalk, by the car—were they seen? Certainly, Jess noted other figures in the pre-dawn mist: a homeless man squatting against the seawall next to the stairs; an old woman with a little dog on a leash way down the beach, both of them just watching the water from right at the tide line, like yesterday's sand castles left for the sea. But no one came over to see what Jess and Benny were doing, and no one helped, and no one called the police. It was as though the marine layer had thrown a blanket over everything, turned each living, moving thing into its own shadow. At some point, Jess remembered the decapitated kid back in the condo where she and Benny and their children, who weren't their children, had lived for the past few weeks. She briefly considered what to do about that, her hand on her screaming side, and eventually decided she could do nothing. She wasn't going to drag *that* body to her trunk, and even if she could, she wasn't going to lay it next to Natalie. Nor would she be dealing with the *other* body down on the beach, the big woman who had broken Jess's ribs. The woman Jess had stuck scissors through, which had barely affected her at all.

The woman Natalie had ripped and chewed to pieces.

No. That one, Jess would leave for the police to sort out. Would they track her and Benny down someday? she wondered vaguely. Did anyone here know their actual names? These weeks of hiding—of hunkering down in a burrow she and Benny had made, with just themselves and their own for company—had come surprisingly easily. In some ways, the condo-time in this place hadn't felt so different from the trailer-years with Natalie in North Carolina after Joe died, except now she had Benny with her. One thing the police *would* find was the Twitter page the homeless kid had been accessing just before Jess had bashed his forehead halfway in with a frying pan. Which had happened just a few minutes before the big woman had removed the kid's head entirely.

The monster's Twitter page. The asshole in the sombrero who had started all this, or at least brought it to Natalie and Jess's door. *Well, good,* she thought. Maybe the police would go find *him*. Although, God help them if they did . . .

Somehow, as dawn broke, Jess got Eddie fed and mercifully, finally, to sleep, then clicked him into his car seat. Leaving Benny in the passenger seat, because Benny could no longer move, she forced herself to go back to the condo, started bringing out their very few possessions. That didn't take many trips. She didn't try arranging or packing anything, and obviously, the trunk of the car was off-limits, so she mostly just chucked clothes and necessities in the well under Eddie's feet and on the seat beside him, and laid a coat over Benny like a patchwork blanket. He was in so much pain, now, that he could no longer even open his eyes; he just leaned into the door and whimpered.

When she'd finished in the condo, turned out the lights, drawn the curtains, locked the door—buying them time, though she had no idea for what, or even whether that was what she should be doing—Jess returned to the car once more, stumbled around to Benny's side, and watched him breathe. She wanted to kiss his forehead but needed to conserve energy, rest her rib cage, because she still had one more job to do. Eventually, she simply laid her hand on his shuddering back and let him weep.

She, on the other hand, appeared to be done weeping, at least for tonight. In truth, she felt remarkably close to the way she remembered feeling on the day Joe had finally given in to the mutant cells rampaging through him and closed his eyes for good. Except with at least one or two cracked ribs.

Soon, she would do what she always did: get to it, climb behind the wheel, flee this town. She would save what she could. She would take care of the children.

Child.

Soon.

"I'll be right back." She breathed, counted three, and pressed her fingers into Benny's clammy, twitching shoulder. "Don't die."

Straightening caused something else to rip inside, and she cried out, clutched her ribs—which hurt them still more—then grabbed the roof of the car and held on to that. When she was sure she wouldn't fall over, she slid the gun from her pocket, checked the chamber, and clicked it back into place. Then she turned, one last time, toward the beach.

To get back down the wooden stairs, Jess had to clutch the splintering banister, lower one foot, edge the other alongside it, and she had to watch her feet to make them move. And so there was a single moment, as she reached the sand and the first flickers of actual sunlight flared in the marine mist like searchlight beams, when she looked up and thought Sophie had gone. That she'd somehow scuttled away like a crab, leaving her severed limbs behind, or else buried herself under the beach. In that instant, Jess almost hoped it was true, that Sophie really had gotten away, despite what her lurking presence might mean for future visitors to this grim little swimming spot. Because Sophie really had been Sophie, once, and not so long ago, either. And the sparkle in her laughter had put even her Roo's to shame, had flared so brightly that it had warmed not just Natalie's world but Jess's, too. Sometimes.

But of course, Sophie wasn't gone. She was propped, tilting, exactly where Jess had left her, just a little farther out from the pier than she'd remembered. Glancing up, Jess noted the pier's wooden railing, sagging but unbroken, and realized that Sophie hadn't, in fact, fallen after the monster in the sombrero had dismembered her; she'd been chucked overboard like garbage, or chum.

And now she was watching as Jess stumbled toward her across the sand, step by agonizing step. Her eyes never once blinked, as far as Jess could see. Instead, they seemed to be looking everywhere at once, almost frantically, as though lapping up every last drop of this night, this world where her child had very briefly lived.

Well, drink up, sweetie, Jess thought savagely, ignoring the pain, making herself stand straighter. Again, the gun rose from her side without any conscious direction, drawn toward Sophie's skull like a magnet. Jess almost shot her without even stopping. But she couldn't quite do that. Instead, she went all the way over, right up within arm's length, then closer, still. Vaguely, and with no particular alarm, she realized that she was putting herself in danger. If one of those seemingly dead hands lashed out, yanked her off-balance, got one of her ankles within range of those teeth . . .

Leaning over slowly, she drove the muzzle of the gun through the matted mass of Sophie's hair, pushing it all the way down to the scalp, so hard that she felt the scalp depress.

"Good night, Sophie," she choked out, not looking away, never for one second letting herself look away, which was why she almost screamed when Sophie twitched to life, her lips suddenly squirming over themselves like a snakes' nest poked awake.

"Don't," Sophie said.

Jess's finger froze on the trigger. Not because of the croaking voice, which sounded nothing like the Sophie she had known. This voice was mostly wind. Wind in a seashell.

Nor, God knew, was it the look on Sophie's face that halted Jess. *Was that even an expression?* Sophie's lips kept squirming, and muscles all over her cheeks quivered, as though that face were actually a Sophie mask, and whoever was under there was trying desperately to pull the mask tight, get the face straight.

No. What stopped Jess was the word itself, and the tone in which it was spoken.

A little like a warning. But more like a bid, at an auction, as though this were a contest, or a negotiation.

"Why on earth not?" Jess hissed. If anything, she pushed the gun down harder.

Sophie's answer was too long coming. And not because she was gathering strength or, obviously, breath, but because she was thinking. *Scheming,* Jess thought. She was almost positive Sophie was scheming.

Almost.

"Help," Sophie finally said.

For an answer, Jess dropped to her knees. Ignoring the pain, she glared right into Sophie's so-familiar brown eyes, which were no longer familiar. All that shine in them was gone, or maybe just scummed over, now, like stagnant water. Despite Sophie's condition, Jess braced herself, expecting a rattlesnake-lunge, and kept the gun planted in Sophie's skull.

"Is that a plea or an offer?"

She really was asking, because she really couldn't tell. Not that it mattered at this point. Less than two hours ago, Jess had murdered her own daughter. And her daughter had still been herself enough to know why, to *want* it to happen. Or at least to welcome it. Compared to that, pulling the trigger on this thing would be like smacking a wasp.

And yet, Jess hesitated. Worse, she had to resist an urge to sag forward and pull Sophie's stump against her and hug it.

Then Sophie spoke again. And this time, she said the only word that could have saved her, in a voice that was awfully close to Sophie's voice, after all. Mangled, shredded, but unmistakably hers. And she said it with no tears, no histrionics, and only a hint of hope. The last hope, Jess knew from experience. The one it was impossible to let go of while any part of you was still you, even when you knew it was too late.

"Willy?" Sophie said.

Before Jess even realized what she was doing—certainly before she'd thought it through, because it was crazy, and also so painful that she was howling behind her clenched teeth—she had pocketed the gun, turned around, grabbed stump-Sophie's outstretched arms, and hoisted her off the sand like a backpack. She wasn't the only one howling, she realized; Sophie, too, was whinnying in pain or panic or grief or God knew what, right in her ear. In fact, Sophie's mouth was practically *covering* Jess's ear, filling it with pleas and whinnies and curses, and even as Jess staggered yet again toward the pier and the wooden stairs, she was waiting for those teeth to snap shut, rip her ear clean off, so Sophie could drive Jess into the sand and finally, mercifully, finish her.

But Sophie just cursed and whinnied and went on whinnying. And somehow, right as actual day-heat rose from the sand and brushed over them, Jess reached the bottom of the steps, then flung Sophie off to thud, spine-first, against the planks and cement.

This time, she allowed herself five long breaths. Every time her lungs inflated, the jagged edge of at least one rib on her right side threatened to slice through her skin or her lung or both. Maybe it had already sliced. But the air stayed in when she sucked at it. And it came back out, the way air generally did, except right now she was noticing. Tasting it.

Instead of attempting to hoist Sophie's stump onto her back again—instinctively, Jess knew that would be the one insane thing too many for her tortured frame—Jess took one of Sophie's arms by the wrist. Sophie stopped whinnying long enough to look up, wondering.

"Give me the other arm," Jess said.

Sophie stared at her. "No," she said. And then, "Why?"

With a grunt, Jess leaned down and snatched Sophie's other arm. Then she moved up a single step, yanking Sophie behind her.

Mostly, during that ridiculous, hellish ascent—all of eight stairs, maybe ten feet, through pain-fireworks so blinding that at one point Jess really did believe her eyes had just exploded—she thought of breathing, and nothing else. But two steps from the top, right as she decided she might make it after all, she felt herself float, for a single moment, blissfully free of her skin into the air. She gazed down at herself and the half of her daughter's best friend that she was dragging. And what popped into her head was her own voice, from twenty years ago, reading to Natalie about Christopher Robin dragging Winnie-*ther*-Pooh, bumpety-bump, down the stairs.

This is just like that, floating-Jess thought. *Except up, instead of down. Dragging Sophie-ther-Hellthing.*

After that, there were no thoughts of any kind until they reached the car. She was about to open the back when she realized Benny was *already* in back, drooping sideways away from the door, one hand holding Eddie's. And that was definitely right, definitely better. Propping open the front passenger door, Jess lodged Sophie's stump in the seat and started leaning across to buckle her in. She hadn't even realized that Benny was watching until he spoke.

"Jess. Are you fucking kidding me?"

"Benny," she said, "I need you to shut up." She yanked the seat belt as tight as it would go. Sophie started to topple forward, so Jess had to catch her, shove her back.

"You'll have to . . . lean the seat," Sophie mumbled.

"You shut up, too." But Jess found the lever, tilted the seat back. The seat belt wouldn't sit right; it rode up high on Sophie's breasts and crossed the bottom of her chin and the edge of her mouth. Instead of straightening it, Jess gave it a yank, then glanced at Benny. "I love you. Don't say a goddamn word. Either of you." Then she staggered around to the driver's side, letting one finger trail, so softly, over the top of the trunk in which her daughter lay, and half-fell into her own seat.

They were out of the lot, past the end of the boardwalk, picking up speed as the mist melted before them into the wet, orange morning, when Sophie said, "Turn around."

Jess slammed on the brakes, sending the car skidding sideways onto the shoulder of the street. She started to swing her head toward Sophie, but too fast; the movement brought tears back to her eyes. Or maybe those were already there, had never left. "I said shut up. I said not one word, or I swear I'll kick you out so fast you'll—"

"Turn around," Sophie said, spitting out her seat belt like a gag and turning her own head, which was the only thing she *could* turn. Her stump-thighs looked bloody on the seat but dry, the blood mostly crust. Tendons twitched at the wound openings, making Jess think of those tubeworms that live on hydrothermal vents. Impossible things, that could not—*should* not—be moving, or living.

"Why?"

"Jess. Please. Go back right now and get my goddamn legs."

4

Around 2:00 in the morning, still slumped beside her desk and staring at the phone, Rebecca realized she hadn't actually asked the 911 dispatcher to call her back. She had just assumed that someone would, that she was part of the team of late-night people she'd never actually met but who watched over the town together, saving others from themselves or each other.

Part of the team. What, in her entire life, would have led her to assume that?

She picked up the Crisis Center phone, then put it down. For at least the fifth time, she raised a hand to her right ear, which still tingled painfully. It had been tingling ever since her conversation with her caller, as though scorched.

No. As though freezing. Frostbitten, almost.

Is it beautiful there?

Had she really said that to a man standing on a precipice, staring over the edge of the end of his life?

Lonely street. That's what he had sung, or said. And that was all she'd been able to tell the 911 dispatcher about where he was. The woman on the other end had shouted at her, at that point, told her to stop babbling.

But Rebecca had been babbling inside her own head ever since, replaying the entire phone call but jumbled up, her own comments shuffled into her caller's, shuffled again. As though rearranging the words might change the ending.

She picked up her cell phone, now—this was her own business, not the Crisis Center's; she'd done all the damage she could for one night under *that* persona—and started to dial 911 again. Then she stopped again. This wasn't an emergency. The emergency had already happened. She had, in fact, helped cause it. This was just Rebecca, age twenty, in over her head, needing to know exactly what she'd done.

Nudging her computer awake, she Googled the non-emergency front desk number for the East Dunham police station. But of course, dialing that got her only the automated answering service, which instructed her to call 911 in case of emergency, or to please try again during normal business hours. She snapped her phone shut and stared into its little window until it went dark.

Next, she clicked on her chat window, typed *still there??* and waited. But Joel didn't answer. That surprised her. The fact that one of his girls was facing an emergency—even if the emergency wasn't hers, and even if she wasn't technically one of his girls, anymore—should have been enough to keep him right where he was. In fact, she was surprised not to find her screen filled with her name. With his typings of her name.

Only then, as her chin sank into her hand, did Rebecca realize how tired she was, how little she'd been sleeping, lately. Joel had taught her a little too well, in that regard. She wondered where he was: down by Halfmoon Lake, maybe, sitting on one of the overturned rowboats in the muck and reeds, or possibly puttering on one of his projects in his shed out back. Or maybe he was right where she'd left him, chatting with and challenging random Smackdown opponents online and listening to one of his crazy Internet radio stations on headphones, while his current girls and his wife slept. The only thing she couldn't actually imagine him doing was sleeping. He just couldn't seem to do that, as far as Rebecca had seen, until there really was no one in his world left to check on or play with.

No. Wherever he was, he was awake.

Pushing herself upright, Rebecca opened her phone, and just as she hit Speed Dial 1 and Send, she caught sight of the clock in the corner of her computer screen.

3:22? How had that happened?

Twitching in her chair, Rebecca fumbled with the phone, hit End, prayed she'd cut off before Joel's phone had rung or even logged her call. She didn't want him to see that she'd needed him. Not at 3:22. Partly, that was pride, and partly, she knew that the sight of her name, when he saw it, would worry him out of his mind.

Abruptly, she glanced over her shoulder, staring around the empty Crisis Center, out the giant windows onto campus. The black gums had swallowed their shadows, now, and stood still and dimensionless in the inevitable, unearthly, small-hour light Rebecca always dreaded most. If she was awake for this light, she always knew that meant that she would not sleep at all. This, she thought, was the real midnight: dead center between night and morning, part of neither; the moon gone, the sun absent, the light so flat that the world went flat, as though all air and movement and blood had been siphoned out of it, leaving everything just leaning where it had been left, like rakes in a garage, props in a prop room for a play that had long since ended. Or never started.

4:03?

With a cry that came out startlingly loud—and therefore felt reassuring—Rebecca smacked herself in the face, then did that again. She shook her head and dragged the Crisis Center logbook to her. Fishing a pen out of the desk drawer, she let herself pause only long enough to bite the inside of her cheek as she considered. In the *Calls Taken* column, she wrote, "*Unidentified, singing man in obvious confusion and distress, from a rooftop somewhere in the vicinity.*" She noted the time in the appropriate box and took one more very brief breath as her pen hovered over the *Actions Taken* section before writing, "*Discussed roofs. Convinced him to jump.*" Then she crossed that out and wrote, "*Called 911.*" Then she slammed the logbook shut, powered down her computer, locked up the Center, and fled Mooney Hall.

Just as she hit open air, the Clocktower bells erupted, and Rebecca stopped in the center of Campus Walk, threw back her head, closed her eyes, and let the peals rain down on her. She stayed in that position even after the ringing was over, letting the echoes reverberate in her ears, clearing them, drumming out the whistling she'd been hearing all night, through the hours she had somehow brooded away. Even after she opened her eyes, the echoes continued misting down, seemed to settle like dew on her face and the leaves and the just-mown grass.

It was already morning. Almost. Morning really was coming.

And that was that why she had always loved the 4:15 Clocktower bells so much. A lot of UNH-D students hated them, especially the ones who lived on campus, and a few started petitions every year to have them silenced. And no one Rebecca knew had ever offered a satisfactory explanation of how or why or even when the tradition had started, or whose idea it was to unleash a cannonade over the empty streets of East Dunham, New Hampshire, exactly once a night, exactly at 4:15 a.m.

But Rebecca had been awake at that hour far too often in her life. And hearing those bells had never failed to soothe her. They signaled the end of the nothing-hour, the return of shadows, movement, voices. Already, with day not even broken, she could feel the August air warming on her skin. Glancing down, Rebecca was surprised to see that her hands were still shaking. She lifted her palms and turned them in front of her face, fighting the feeling that these weren't even her hands. They were too flat, stripped of sensation. Nothing-hour hands.

. . . a little girl . . . with a night-light . . . alone up there in the middle of the night . . .

Here it went again: the conversation with her caller, replaying and replaying, threading itself through her brain like cassette ribbon.

Because she knew it was her caller's *last* conversation?

Jamming her hands in the pockets of her light summer hoodie, Rebecca started down Campus Walk, past the stirring gum trees. She thought maybe she should go home to her one-bedroom basement apartment and sleep at least a little, because she wouldn't have another chance until at least nine tonight. But she knew she wouldn't sleep, anyway. Not after this Crisis Center shift, and not in that room, with the water heater clanking and the Rudzinskis' babies burbling and chattering upstairs and the two cardboard boxes full of photos and old sweaters and cat toys and paperback Penguin classics that constituted the Complete Collected Mementos of the first nineteen years of Rebecca's life sitting half-opened, still completely packed at the foot of her futon. Not under the window fan that passed for her air-conditioning, which clanked and stuttered and chopped the air into whispers. She wondered what that fan would have whispered to her tonight—what it would have done with the conversation she couldn't seem to eject from her brain—and stopped to watch a robin hopping around what looked like a fallen nest at the foot of one of the trees. And so she was already still when the man stepped around the trunk and grabbed her.

With a yelp, Rebecca twisted, wriggled loose, shoved her palms into the man's chest, and only then processed who he was.

"Oscar?"

Her shove had barely even moved him. But his arms retracted immediately to his sides. Rebecca caught her breath, saw the horrified expression on Oscar's sweet, grooved face, and almost burst into tears. Instead, she balled her quivering fingers into fists, steadied her breathing, and called herself back to herself. From wherever the hell she'd apparently been, this whole damn night. "*Lo siento mucho,*" she said.

"*En al,*" he answered immediately, tapping his red campus maintenance uniform right over his heart, in the center of his name tag. "*Lo siento.*"

She shook her head, wondering how she'd managed not to see him, since he had appeared almost exactly where he always did, at the end of Campus Walk, in the midst of his rounds. Tonight, though, it felt more like she'd conjured him from some nothing-hour shadow, a sort of Oscar-faerie, trash bags at his feet as he stooped for wrappers or cigarette butts, the top of his uniform already unbuttoned to the surprising morning heat, tuft of black-and-gray hair swept sideways over his scalp and matted with dirt. *Like Santa Claus,* she thought, and not for the first time. Exactly the sort of Santa an orphaned Jewish girl might indeed invent: bone-skinny, groove-faced, and arriving not on Christmas Eve but every single night, bringing nothing anyone wanted. But taking away all kinds of things no one wanted.

"*Hola,* Oscar," she said.

"*Hola, Señorita Rrrrebec.*" As always, he grinned after rolling the *R,* knowing that would make her grin back. And here she was doing that. She could feel it.

"*Como esta, Oscar? Es su hija sienta major?*"

Right on cue, Oscar's grin widened. But this morning, it took a split second too long. And because it did, Rebecca saw clearly, understood properly for the first time in all the five-minute exchanges she'd had over the past three years with this man: that smile *always* came late, and took too long. In a way, Rebecca supposed she had her Crisis Center caller to thank; it was that conversation that had ignited every sense she had, as though she had just awoken, having sleepwalked her entire life away until right now, so that today, she not only noticed Oscar's hesitation but understood what it meant:

Oscar's daughter was not here. She had never been here. Oscar's daughter was in Guatemala. And all the thousand things he'd told Rebecca these last few years were made up, or maybe remembered, or imagined, or experienced from afar, culled from letters or carefully timed, parceled-out cell phone calls.

So much for her fabled intuition. Jack and the 'Lenes would have been astounded.

"*Sí, sí, gracias,*" he was saying as he picked up the trash bags, "*ella quiere . . .*" Then he stopped, because she was touching his arm, squeezing his wrist once before letting go. "*Ella es asi. Gracias, Señorita Rrrebec.*"

He didn't tear up or anything, just stood there smiling. His smile settled her, some, though it did little to calm the next shockwave of guilt. Of astonishment at her own myopia. He'd told her once—several years ago, before she'd officially enrolled at UNH-D but was already working triple shifts at the food service—that she was often the only person who spoke to him during his entire 3 a.m. to 11 a.m. shift, or after that, either, most days. And instead of sorting what that actually meant, Rebecca had indulged in a pride that embarrassed her, and that she'd tried to dismiss. And felt, still. She felt it even now, standing beside him, knowing what she knew.

Abruptly, Oscar lowered one of the trash bags off his shoulders, stepped forward, and the smile vanished from his craggy face.

"Es tu molesto?"

"I'm okay," she said, too quickly. She had to get out of here, find somewhere to get herself settled. "I have to go, Oscar. *Besa a su hija para mi.*" Even as she said the words—the same words she always left him with—she wondered if she should. She no longer liked the taste of those words in her mouth: rubbery and flaccid, like old gum. Leaning up on tiptoes, she kissed Oscar on the cheek, lingered just a moment in his heat, the smell of garbage and leaves and cigarettes and pears that was simply *him,* to her.

Then she was walking away over the grass, not looking back, not letting him see. Because he wasn't *her* father, or Santa. And he had his own daughter to miss and worry about.

She did note, in some corner of her churning brain, the movement behind Oscar. In the shadows of the Clocktower's arched stone doorway, someone had stirred. But as she hurried away toward her room or the lake or maybe—though it was too early, even Joel and Amanda were probably still sleeping—Halfmoon House, she hoped only that whoever was in there would be thoughtful of Oscar. She hoped they would acknowledge his presence, or at least have the decency to clean up their own mess.

5

In her tent amid the reeds, in her sleep that wasn't sleep, was instead a sort of succumbing, the only succumbing she had ever allowed herself or would ever, Aunt Sally listened for the day-music. It seemed a long time coming on this suffocating late-summer early morning, the muddy river just out of sight down-bank thick as sap, silent as it slid past, the reed-shadows on the tent walls lolling like ripped-out tongues licking soundlessly at the air or each other. There were days—whole decades, even—when Aunt Sally had willed herself, during pre-dawn hours, into a sort of stillness beyond sensation or sleep, so that she was no longer herself or even self at all, but an absence in the shape of herself, like dead grass.

But this was not one of those days. And in truth, she

hadn't had one of those days in some time. Lately, upon bedding down, she had found it harder than ever before to find that still spot. The Mississippi heat wasn't helping (not that it warmed her, or ever could, but at least sometimes, in past years, it had been a weight). It also wasn't the source of the problem. And now, all on their own, her fingers had found their way inside her wool nightgown to alight, trembling like those feather-white seedpods that blew, all summer, down the southern wind, at the tips of her sliding, heavy breasts. And as soon as she became aware of her fingers, they started moving, sliding open, pinching closed, teasing, tugging. Opening again. Floating down the curve of her ribs to her hips. Calling her out. Waking her up.

She could hear the others just settling into their rest all over camp. Her monsters. Another night, and whatever they'd done to waste it, safely behind them. The anticipation of a special night, the first Party in ages, luring them into dreams, about which they'd be eager to tell Aunt Sally once they woke up, so that she could perform Policy, tell them their futures, guide their fortunes.

Of course, she could tell them that now, she thought, as her fingers traced slowly over her thighs. But what would be the use—or the fun—in that?

Somehow, though, the knowing did set her tingling, awakened her still more. Her fingers curled all the way between her legs, and just as they slid home, Caribou switched on the music.

His wake-her-up selections were usually so intuitive, so nasty-tasteful. But today, of all days, he had gotten it impossibly wrong, gone all mournful just as her whole body shuddered to attention, wanted to play. *Worse, he'd somehow dug up that stupid whining spiritual, that mewling to What God There Was, hymn to some "home" no one she'd ever known had been to or seen.*

"Sometimes I Feel Like a Motherless Child." If there was a less *appropriate musical accompaniment to her current mood, Aunt Sally couldn't call it to mind. Grunting her frustration, she stopped what she was doing and sat up.*

At least the song reminded her of Mother. Actually, it reminded her of a specific argument they'd had, right out there in their rocking chairs while their monsters danced. A long time ago, now.

"You never feel like that?" Mother had asked, smoking one of her damn-fool cigarillo things while the song played.

"You going to fill up," Aunt Sally had answered, gesturing at the cigarillo. "Keep sucking that stuff down, and you can't really push it out."

That had made Mother smile. "Then I'll be smoke. Just imagine where I could float off to, then."

"Not 'home,'" Aunt Sally snorted. "Tell you that much."

Mother had just sat, smoking, singing along in her dry-gravel rumble. And after a long time—the nights so long, then, so slow they seemed to spread across years, the way Aunt Sally had read nights did for parents on porches, watching children in yards—Mother had said, "You really never feel like that? Like a motherless child? That doesn't speak to you?"

"I never think about my mother one way or the other."

Mother had turned, then, looking surprised. That was why this argument was memorable: it was one of the rare times either of them had surprised the other. "How can that be, Sally? Considering who you are, what you come from. How can that be?”

And Aunt Sally—daughter of a slave, granddaughter of a slave, thrice-raped child of a raped child of a raped child—had drawn herself up, stared Mother down. “I think about my father sometimes. I think about him a lot, actually. But my mother? Turns out she was of no account whatsoever.”

She was thinking about her father now as she slipped out of her nightgown. For the first time in she couldn’t even remember how long, Aunt Sally dipped deep into her traveling trunk and withdrew her dancing dress, with its orange flowers. She slid that over her head, down her body, smoothed it as flat as it would go. The dress still fit her like a sheath except up top, where it couldn’t quite contain her. Aunt Sally gazed down at herself, at once pleased and taken aback: yet again, though for the first time in a long while, she had forgotten how much younger she looked than she was, or felt. And now that she remembered, she also regained awareness of just how much wake she threw out there, in the world beyond this tent, once she got herself up and moving.

Here I come, *she thought, half-said, to her father, long gone. To no one in particular. To everyone she’d ever met, or would ever meet.*

The tent flaps parted, and Caribou’s blond head appeared. He was in the middle of speaking but stopped when he saw her.

“That’s right,” she said. “Remember me?” She considered yanking him inside, pulling up her dress, shoving his mouth where her hands had been. But she knew, from

experience, that even his mouth wouldn't be warm enough, or warm at all. He was useless that way.

"I brought you something," he said, all hoarse.

Aunt Sally grinned, even gave him a little handclap. In most other ways, Caribou had proved as useful as anyone she had ever had in camp with her. Downright industrious, sometimes.

"You going to stand there talking about it, or you bringing it in?"

More gracefully than Aunt Sally would have thought possible, Caribou glided—even while ducking and holding his silver serving tray aloft—through the flaps of her tent. Straightening, he laid the tray atop her traveling trunk and, with a flourish, lifted the cloche covering the white china plate in the center of the tray.

Aunt Sally shook her head appreciatively, then decided Caribou deserved better. She stepped forward and kissed him full on the mouth, pressing the full weight of her breasts into his ribs, the way she knew he loved, could hardly bear. "How do you do it?" she asked, just as Caribou dropped the top of the cloche and tried encircling her with an arm, and she danced back. "I never will understand."

"Just a snack," he mumbled, trying to get his hands back to his sides and his pants re-straightened and settled. His deer-eyes twitched. She watched him—let him—raise those eyes to hers. "Thought this might keep you from getting peckish before the party."

They gazed together down at Caribou's gift: a square of forearm, gnawed so neatly clean at either edge that it could have been sawn, and might have been. The skin so fresh that Aunt Sally imagined she could still feel life-heat rising from it, so marbled with vein and thick with juice that it looked fit to burst.

"When do *you do this?" Aunt Sally teased. His finicky habits embarrassed him, which amused her no end. Some of them never did get used to eating with others, or to the mess.*

Caribou lowered his head. But that brought his eyes back to her chest.

Aunt Sally laughed, gesturing at the plate. "What on earth did you do with all the rest of—"

"EXCUSE ME, BABY."

The voice seemed to burst from the very air, fill the tent like a 4th of July firework. Aunt Sally actually flinched in surprise.

"EXCUSE ME, BABY," *it said again, its tone sassy, feminine, mid-London-ese.*

Not until the third repetition did Caribou suddenly straighten, flush, and reach into his pocket. He pulled out his phone, and it purred in his hand. "EXCUSE ME, BABY."

Aunt Sally put a hand on her hip, grinning her amazement. "That's your . . . what do they call that? Ringtone?"

Lifting the phone to his ear, Caribou muttered, "Been so long since anyone called, I forgot I'd done that."

Aunt Sally had already stopped listening, though. She was too busy eying the meat on the plate. How long had it been, this time, since she had last eaten? Did even hunger fade, eventually? And if it did, she thought—with no panic, but real curiosity, and maybe even a twinge of excitement—what would be left? What came after hunger?

Then the meat was on her lips, in her teeth, her tongue curling around it, drawing it in and in. She didn't even realize she had closed her eyes until she opened them and found the phone in her face.

"It's for you," Caribou said.

Aunt Sally stared at the phone, then Caribou's wide, unblinking eyes. With a scowl, she squished the meat between her teeth, sucked down the juice and just a bit of rubbery tendon-pith, and spit the husk onto the floor of the tent. "Clean that up," she said, and took the phone.

"Aunt Sally?" said a voice she recognized immediately, and disliked as intensely as ever. Mother's whining, whistling fool.

"Where's Mother?" she drawled, licking her lips clean.

Then she just listened while he whined and whimpered and told her. When he'd sniveled his last, babbled something about making his way back down to see her and Caribou and everyone sometime, as if they were all his family, or anyone's, and finally shut up, Aunt Sally stood still for a few extra seconds. The news he'd imparted lodged in her stomach. It didn't move or spread, just sat there.

Mother. Gone for good, this time.

Eventually, she said, "That all you called for?"

Just like that, he wasn't whining anymore, was done with this conversation. And Aunt Sally knew her instincts had been right. She knew exactly why the little whistling shit had called in the first place. And for the third or fourth time tonight—and here, the night just getting started—she experienced something very like a genuine shudder. This one surfaced in her shoulders, her knees. All over.

He had called because he wanted *to. The scary little*

bastard. He had called because he'd thought being the one to tell her this news might be fun.

"You come anytime," she said. "I'll always be waiting." Then she disconnected and handed the phone back to Caribou. He took it, but seemed not to know what to do with it.

"Aunt Sally," he murmured. "Are you . . ."

"I made a list," she said. "For the Party. Things we're going to need. It's a long list."

For a moment, she thought he was going to do something truly stupid, and also ill-advised: touch her hand, tell her he was sorry. But he really did have better sense than most—almost all—of her monsters. Possibly, he loved her, in his way. Definitely, he knew when to be afraid.

"I'll go as soon as I'm done here." He knelt to scoop up the meat-skin she'd spit at his feet.

"Not you," she said. "Send the others."

"They don't generally take to going out during the day."

"Well. Tell them if they'd rather, they can stay here with me." She waited until he looked up and noted the expression on her face. Then she nodded. "Take them the list, send them on their way, and come back. I've got a special errand for you, my dear." She reached out and touched the hair on his carefully bowed head. It always felt so soft, so cold, even in the dead heat smothering the late-summer Delta, like strings of melting moonlight. She let her thoughts alight, once more, on Mother. On riding out these Mississippi nights with Mother. On never doing that more.

With a sigh, she lifted his chin, let him stare up at her. "You see, 'Bou . . ." she cooed, loving how he twitched, "it turns out, this time, that I've *had a dream." She ran her tongue across her teeth, felt the slickness on them.* Yes, *she thought.* Tonight, there would be a Party, like no Party before it. And when that was done, and tonight was over . . .

Well. Maybe then—if she got her idiot monsters to do what she needed them to—maybe tomorrow, there really might be something else.

6

Oscar, too, noted the movement in the Clocktower. Partly, this was because movement was rare at this hour on the UNH-D campus, at least in summer. Partly, it was old habit, a holdover from decades ago, from endless summer Xela nights wandering the city squares in the moonshadows of the mountains. He could still hear the trombone-blats and church bells, the drunks burbling to themselves as they spilled from bars, late-night kids shouting to each other over ice cream cones, street musicians trilling on ocarinas, sawing fiddles, thumping drums. The city, back then, had seemed endless, a teeming jungle complete with canopies, mating cries, movement everywhere even though there weren't so many people, really, especially late, when he'd most loved to walk. Always, then, he'd had

Nahia on his arm, smelling of sweet rum and cinnamon-chocolate, smiling silently, the way Nahia generally did, pressing her wonderful weight against his upper arm, in her blue blouse. Nahia's blouse was always blue, almost black under the late-early stars. Probably, it was always the same blouse, though he either hadn't noticed or hadn't considered that, then.

So full of sensations, those days. So full of people, all of them gone from him or just gone. Nahia had long since ridden her river of drink into her grave. Before she died, she'd ensconced their Carlota with her mother and aunt in the little house with the goats in the small dirt yard. Somehow, to Oscar, that made Carlota seem even farther away than the thousands of miles and the years of his being here had. To his daughter, he knew, he was just that voice on the phone from some imaginary North, thick with smoke. The voice of a man who sent money for her schooling and her horse, and said he loved her, though he'd last seen her when she could barely walk, couldn't talk, and her mother had still been alive.

"Bring a fresh bouquet to Vanushka when you visit your mother's grave," he would instruct her, always, at the end of their perfunctory conversations. Carlota always promised that she would, or assured him that she already had, that week. And Oscar would hang up imagining the gypsy woman's grave in the Xela cemetery, bestrewn with his daughter's flowers, every one of which—so Xela's matriarchs had always told him—brought wanderers a step closer to home.

In the days between those calls, Oscar did his work and smoked his cigarettes and spoke to virtually no one—

except Rebecca, the orphan from the Crisis Center who seemed to have adopted him, for some reason—and watched the campus from deep inside himself, the way an indoor cat stares out a window. He noted everything, still. He could even feel himself leaning forward, sometimes, tensing before settling back. Like an indoor cat, he knew that whatever was out there, in *this* world, for *these* people, he could never reach it.

And so, though he noted the shadow detaching itself from the deeper shadows of the arched entryway of the Clocktower, he reacted only by dropping his cigarette into the grass at his feet, grinding it out, then scooping up the butt with the stray leaves and dumping it all into his garbage bag. Even when the shadow left the gravel of Campus Walk and started across the grass in his direction, Oscar assumed it would simply glide over and past him, the way shadows did in this place, this other dimension he had only recently realized he might never escape. He tied the top of the garbage bag, hoisted it to his shoulder, started forward, and so walked right into the outstretched hand that stopped him in his tracks. Fingers splayed themselves across his chest, their touch so cold that they stung, even through his uniform, like the paintball pellets the fraternity boys shot at him and all the other maintenance guys during Rush Week.

Oscar looked down at those freezing fingers, then up at the person attached to them. The fingers stayed on his chest.

"That girl," said the boy who'd stopped him, from underneath his sombrero. "Tell me about her."

Not a boy, Oscar decided, but slowly; his thoughts felt glacial, as though clogged with ice. This guy was thin like a boy, and taller than Oscar, but his voice was older—old, really—despite the eagerness in it. Also, his mouth looked too round, too dark under the shadow of that sombrero, like an open manhole. The eyes stayed completely hidden in the shadow of the hat, which wasn't even a sombrero, really. Machine-made American approximation.

"You know her," said the man. He wasn't asking. "Is she as . . . I mean, of course she is. Right?" And then, to Oscar's astonishment, the man whistled. The whistle melted into a tune, a *cumbia,* of all things. Oscar knew it but couldn't place it, though he remembered some of the words, or one word, anyway.

Jacarandosa. Person of grace.

His response was instinctive, powered less by protectiveness of Rebecca than longing for his daughter, grief for his wife, and it almost came quickly enough to be convincing. "*No habla Ingles.*"

The whistling man whistled to the end of the chorus, and when he reached that last, long note, he trilled it like an ocarina player, or a bird. The sound sizzled straight into Oscar's veins.

Then the man smiled, tilting back his head so Oscar could see his eyes. "Come on, now," he said. "You poor, lonely man. You'll see. It's so much better when you share."

And Oscar knew—even before his killer knew—that he was going to die.

7

In another hour, Rebecca figured, she could head for Half-moon House. Her shift there didn't officially start until noon. But maybe Amanda would allow an exemption to the ban on overnight stays for former residents—part of the Amanda Plan for Orphan Self-Sufficiency—and let her sack out on the cot downstairs in the "guest" room. That room, after all, had been a staple of Rebecca's chore-list for years, and was always kept hospital-clean and freshly flowered in case a long-lost or newly rehabilitated relative of one of the current residents showed up to visit. And Rebecca wouldn't technically be staying overnight, anyway, just . . . taking a nap. Recovering.

Even if Amanda refused to lift the ban, she'd almost certainly let Rebecca take up her familiar seat at the end of the grooved, warping wooden worktable in the kitchen to fold sheets and sip homegrown peppermint tea while Amanda washed and cooked and folded and scrubbed counters and ignored her. Sooner or later, Joel would finish his morning outside-chores, wander in for his coffee, smile at her or stick out a tongue at his wife's rigid back, and wink. Then he'd head off to the stairs to yell his daily wake-up absurdity to Trudi and Danni, his current not-quite-daughters. *There's a hole in Nantucket, dear Danni, dear Trudi.* Or, *Freight train, gone so fast. Ate my spaniel, kicked my . . .*

Just remember, Amanda would say after that, maybe not right away but at some point, perhaps in the middle of a conversation later in the morning, the chill in her voice like an ice cube dropped down Rebecca's back, *Halfmoon House is not your home. It never was. It's a* path *to the home you'll make on your own, one day.* Hers would be a less kind but more bracing awakening than the one Joel offered. And that was exactly the sort of awakening she needed today, because the voice in her head—her caller's voice—kept threading through her thoughts. It wasn't even his words, just his voice, lilting and smooth, sticky as a spiderweb.

In the meantime, here she was at Halfmoon Lake. She'd barely noticed leaving campus or cutting through the forest. She had hoped, vaguely, that she might find Joel on his tipped-over rowboat, legs to his chest, chin on his knees, watching the dawn. But if he'd been here at any point last night, he was gone, now.

In the center of the lake, a lone family of loons glided through the morning mist toward the stripe of light that wasn't really daylight, yet, just a pinker patch atop the gently rippling water. The woods behind her weren't exactly still but almost silent, the leaves shuddering in place like restless sleepers. Rebecca sat down on top of Joel's overturned rowboat at the edge of the reedy muck that passed for the swimming beach. She listened to leaves, the lapping water, her caller's voice.

I'll come see you. That's what he'd said. That's what she was murmuring to herself, now. She knew she was doing it, but she couldn't seem to stop, didn't even seem to want to. The beat of it was weirdly comforting, or maybe just insistent. Irresistible.

I'll come see you.

On the lake, the smaller adult loon—the male—rose up and flapped its wings, its feet almost leaving the surface of the water before it folded back into its resting state as though it had never so much as stirred. Then he was gliding, not even crying out. Ever since she could remember, Rebecca had loved that particular loon behavior even more than she loved loon calls: the rising up, as though reminding everything around them—including themselves—that they were free, could just *go*. And then the deciding not to, the electing to stay.

I'll come see you.

The metal of the rowboat felt slick under her fingers, against her jeans. Cool, but not cold, like sweat on skin.

I'll come see you.

The woods hushed still further, except for the footsteps. Startled, Rebecca glanced back, put a sneaker on the ground.

Whoever that was, he wasn't close, possibly all the way

back at the top of the path at the edge of town. But he was heading this way. Of course, anyone using that path would be heading this way. Fifty joggers a morning did that.

And yet Rebecca was standing, now, holding still, leaning toward the leaves, ready to vault the rowboat and run. *Why?*

But she knew why: the conversation in her head had finally come untangled, stopped layering itself over itself, so that she could hear what her caller had *actually* said, right at the end, for the first time.

Not *I'll come see you.*

I can see you. That's what he'd said.

Tripping on the bow of the boat, Rebecca stumbled through the muck that sucked at her shoes toward the smaller path to her left, the one toward Halfmoon House. Her eyes never left the opening in the trees from which she'd emerged, except once, to look up into the branches, which was even more ridiculous, except that her caller had been up high last night, on some rooftop, looking down. *At her?*

She saw nothing but froze to listen as the footsteps pounded closer. *I'm being stupid,* she thought. Then she bolted into the woods. Right as she hit the tree line, one of the loons let loose, its call erupting overhead and triggering birds all over the trees, all at once, as though she'd blundered through a trip wire.

Those sounds, though, were anything but alarming to Rebecca. They were, in fact, part of her every-morning sound track: Clocktower bells, stirring town, the birds of Halfmoon Lake. She made herself stop again, just out of sight, to watch the beach. A few seconds later, the runner appeared, and he was just a runner, a bearded professor-type in a hoodie. Very possibly, he *was* a professor in a hoodie, someone she probably knew by sight if not by name. She didn't let the man see her, and she didn't step out of the trees until he'd circled back onto the town path and pattered off. But her breathing eased. By the time she'd made her way through the denser stretch of woods back to the outskirts of town and the long, dirt lane that curved away toward Halfmoon House, she was almost strolling, and she'd stopped glancing over her shoulder, although bits of conversation continued to roil in her head.

People worth talking to, staying up late.

I can see you.

Well, she thought, and this time, she almost smiled. Her ruefulness felt habitual, practiced, utterly familiar: *I bet that's thrilling for you.*

Halfmoon House nestled amid carefully clipped hedgerows at the lip of the woods, in its own nether-zone between the trees and town, located in both but not quite part of either. Reaching the end of the lane, Rebecca caught her first glimpse of the flaking red roof, the white clapboard shingles fading to beige but somehow solid. The whole place reminded her of a fallen birds' nest. She saw a shadow detach from the porch, long and work-gloved despite the heat, bucket in one hand and Bluetooth radio in the other as it moved around back toward the henhouse: Joel, gliding into his morning. He hadn't seen her. It didn't matter. She had seen him. That was enough.

Crossing the lawn, sidestepping the creaks on the front steps that she knew so well to avoid waking the girls upstairs—although Trudi, she suspected, was probably awake, already donning the sock puppets to whom she did the lion's share of her speaking, at this point—Rebecca slipped into the house. She moved through the foyer to the kitchen and sat herself at the long wooden table, which was already piled high with morning laundry still warm from the dryer. Wordlessly, she plunged her hands into the fabric, grabbed some socks, and started matching and folding. She could hear cans and pans being banged around in the pantry, but several minutes went by before Amanda emerged, blond hair already yanked back into that brutal ponytail that made her look twenty years older than she was and seemed to stretch the corners of her wide, blue eyes and pull her thin mouth all the way flat, as though she were perpetually walking into wind.

A solid minute of silence went by before Rebecca said, "Thought I'd stop in on my way home from the Center." Amanda, of course, hadn't even nodded acknowledgment or said hello, and wouldn't until she saw a reason to. Most mornings, Rebecca didn't mind; sometimes, Rebecca not only admired but almost loved this woman's reserve. With just her silence, Amanda created so much space for everyone around her. And space and silence were exactly the commodities the children she cared for—fresh from other, failed foster homes or government institutions or overzealous or abusive or incompetent relatives, sometimes still reeling from the separate tragedies that had orphaned them in the first place—had had the least, and needed most.

But this morning, Rebecca very much wanted to communicate, say anything—to anyone—that wasn't what she'd been saying to herself, endlessly, for hours. Even more, she wanted someone familiar to answer back.

"I didn't expect you until this afternoon," said Amanda, splashing oil into the pans. Half-turning, she slid a mug toward Rebecca without seeming to have paused to heat or fill it.

"And yet you have tea for me." Rebecca lifted the mug, and fresh mint smell wafted into her nostrils, opened her up.

"You work here, you get tea."

"You so much as set foot here, you get tea."

Amanda nodded. "There you go."

From outside, where Joel was, came the end of some chugging, tilting '50s train song, and then, as it faded, a girl's voice. Or—woman's. Girl's? Two different voices? "*Before* heart . . . *grow* . . . *QUEEN COLD* . . . *old* . . . " Then drum smacks, ringing guitars, a new song with another '50s rocker guy yelping about thinking it over.

Whatever comfort Rebecca had just started to feel drained from her. She glanced toward the open window. "What kind of DJ is *that*?"

For once, Amanda actually stopped working long enough to look where Rebecca was looking. "Tell me about it. It's his latest Web find. He listens all day." She gestured toward the stairs. "Freaks the girls out, I'm not kidding."

"How do you even learn to talk like that? What *is* that?"

But Amanda was back to business, pulling a bowl of batter out of the industrial fridge, lining up mugs for the morning serving. "What are you doing here, Rebecca?"

Immediately, Rebecca resumed folding socks, as though justifying her presence. "What do you mean, I—"

"Don't you have your nanny thing this afternoon? Aren't you supposed to be at Jess's?"

"Yeah. But not until five."

"And you're on here at noon. Right? And you worked at the Center last night?"

Oh, I worked all right, she thought, lifting a hand halfway to her face before she realized she was still holding a sock. *Want to hear what I accomplished while I was there, Amanda? You'll be so proud . . .*

"What'd you say? Rebecca?"

"Amanda, I have to tell you something. Please. Last night, I—"

"How many jobs are you working right now?"

At least the question choked off the murmuring in Rebecca's head. Automatically—as though she still lived here, and had no choice but to answer—Rebecca upped her folding speed. She finished the socks, started on the dish towels. "Just the three. Here, the food service, nannying for Jess."

"Plus the Crisis Center. Four."

"That's volunteer."

"You need a hobby. Or a guy."

That actually did it. Rebecca burst out laughing. "Look who's talking. You never even—"

"I have a guy," said Amanda, dead-flat, and Rebecca blushed.

Right on cue, Joel strolled in. When he saw Rebecca, he stopped, cocked an eyebrow at her, and glanced at his wife. He held up his Bluetooth speaker just as the song it was playing ended. There was a pause before the girl-woman voice erupted again, all cut up and stuttering this time, as though in the midst of being strangled.

"*Buh— . . . cat-dah . . . TONGUE!*" Then a gunfire-burst of guitars obliterated her.

"Joel, my God, what the hell are you listening to?"

He just grinned through his bristle of dark morning beard. His skin seemed even blacker than usual under its sheen of sweat or dew. His kinked, curly hair glistened, too. Abruptly, he stuck out one long arm and folded Rebecca briefly against him. He kissed the top of her head and drew back to set the pail of fresh eggs on the counter next to his wife.

"It's 'Tongue-Tied Jill.' "

"That's the DJ's name? It's accurate, I guess."

"That's the song. Charlie Feathers. Classic."

"But what's the show?"

"You mean the finest radio program in the history of the world, ever? Seriously. I'll send you a link."

"It's creepy."

"It's from outer space. From some whole other planet. And it plays *the* best shit."

And with that, off he headed for the foot of the stairs to yell or sing whatever ridiculous thing he'd come up with today to wake his current girls to their morning routine. Back when she'd lived here, Rebecca had kept a list of Joel's wake-up hollers. She still had it somewhere, tucked into one of those paperbacks in the boxes at the foot of her futon.

"Rebecca, aren't you way early?" he called over his shoulder. "You look good, by the way."

That comment didn't surprise Rebecca. Joel said something like it almost every time he saw her, or any of his former wards, whether it was true or not. What surprised her was Amanda's murmured, "He's right, actually."

Rebecca was even more surprised to find Amanda eying her, even while flipping pancakes with her spatula.

"That's ridiculous, Amanda. You have no idea how ridiculous—"

"It's true. It's like you've settled in behind your face or something. Now, if you could only learn to get some sleep, you'd—"

"I lost one last night," Rebecca blurted. The words came out clipped, chopped up, like the scary radio-lady's.

Amanda didn't put her spatula down or anything. But for one moment, she stopped using it, just stood there. "What do you mean?"

"A guy. A caller. A jumper. I could hear it in his voice the second he started talking. I knew he was serious. Or . . . that he was different. That this was something weird and real. He was so freaky. I mean freaked-out. Oh my God, Amanda, he was saying the craziest things. It was like he was already comfortable with his decision. Like the decision was made. And I couldn't . . . I botched it so badly. I couldn't find the words to say. I said everything wrong. I panicked. I—"

"You're sure he jumped?"

Looking straight at Amanda was like getting a faceful of ice water. That gaze stayed so still. It wasn't exactly calming. But it was cooling.

"No. I'm not. I'm pretty positive I didn't help, though."

"So. Worry about that."

"What about him?"

"How many times have I told you, Rebecca? Since the

first day you came here, when you were what, thirteen? Worry about you. Worry about what you can control."

"Yeah, thanks, Amanda. But today I think I'll worry about the guy who died."

For a little longer, Amanda stayed motionless at the stove, like a bird on a branch. Then she set her spatula on the counter and moved the pancake pan off the heat. "You're a good girl," she said, went to the yellow cord-phone mounted on the wall, and dialed it. "Hi, Dawn, it's Amanda," she said into the receiver, and Rebecca realized whom she'd called: Dawn Ripinsky, daytime desk officer at the East Dunham police precinct and former Halfmoon House resident, who'd left—"graduated," as Amanda insisted they call it—the year Rebecca came.

"You at work yet, Dawn?"

No *How's your fiancé?* or *Haven't seen you in ages.* Unlike her husband, Amanda didn't seek lasting relationships with the children she had cared for. She did not play Smackdown with them in the middle of the night. What she wanted, as she'd stated to Rebecca just the once, on the day Rebecca had somehow found the nerve to challenge her about it, was much more valuable, as she saw it, and much harder: she wanted her charges so competent, so ready to confront whatever came for them (not to mention what had already come), that they never once felt the need to come back. That's how Amanda would know she had done her job.

"Good," she was saying into the phone now. "Let me ask you. You have a suicide last night?"

Rebecca held her breath and waited. When Amanda just stood there, she whispered, "Well?"

But Amanda only waved a dismissive hand. "Uh-huh," she said. "Yeah. Rebecca, you remember her? One of ours. That is, she used to be. She's the one who called it in, from the Crisis Center on campus."

Rebecca's hands twisted in the towels on the table.

"Okay. Thanks." Hanging up, Amanda returned to the stove. It was all Rebecca could do to keep from grabbing her and spinning her around.

Amanda, on the other hand, had already resumed sliding pancakes onto plates, while footsteps and laughter reverberated upstairs. Whatever Joel had hollered this morning, Rebecca had missed it while concentrating on Amanda's phone call. Pipes clanked in the walls, then gushed as the upstairs sinks and showers started.

"There was no jumper, Rebecca."

Rebecca let go of the towels. "They're sure? How do they know? They found the guy?"

"Nope. But no splatter."

Rebecca winced.

Amanda never so much as turned around. "What they did find, apparently, is the phone he called you from. He laid that right back where he stole it."

"He stole the phone?"

"Off old Mrs. Tangee's dresser. The librarian at the downtown branch, the public one, you know her? Apparently, this guy slipped in a patio door of her condo sometime after ten p.m., when Mrs. Tangee had turned off *Law and Order* and gone to sleep, took the phone, walked around East Dunham or up on some campus building roof or wherever until at least a little after one—"

"How do they know that?"

And there it was, the only thing that could stop Amanda from moving about her business: stupidity, from someone she had at least partially raised. She turned and stared at Rebecca until Rebecca figured it out and said, "Oh."

"Right. So. Sometime between whenever you were done with him—"

Nice, Rebecca thought, and very nearly said. *Considerately put, very gentle. Thanks, Amanda.*

"—and five-twelve a.m., when the police finally got the callback number and called it and woke Mrs. Tangee up, this guy waltzed back into her condo, returned the phone, and vanished the way he'd come."

"What?"

"That's the best they can figure it. That's all Dawn has got."

"That's . . ." Rebecca started, but realized she had no idea what to say. Amanda finished the sentence for her.

". . . not the behavior of a guy about to kill himself?"

"No," Rebecca said. "It isn't." The information should have been comforting. Instead, an all-new shudder spread from her shoulders to the tips of her fingers, from the base of her neck all the way into her feet. "It's more like a stalker."

I can see you . . .

"Rebecca, go home. Get some sleep. Really, kiddo, you need to sleep."

Only then did Rebecca realize she'd already resumed folding. The habit was simply ingrained; it was the price of Amanda's company.

"You should be relieved," Amanda snapped. "Why aren't you relieved?"

Blowing out a shaky breath, Rebecca turned her head to either side, slowly, as though wetting her hair under a spigot. She could feel the sting in Amanda's rebuke. It felt wonderful. Amanda *did* care, in spite of herself. She always had. This was how she showed it.

"You're right," Rebecca said, folded one last towel, set it square atop the pile she'd made, and stood.

"Does that mean you're relieved?"

"It means I'm sleepy. I'm going to go sleep."

"Rebecca, let this go. Listen to me. You can't do the kind of work we do if you're going to—"

"I will if he will," Rebecca murmured. Out the window, the trees reddened in the early morning sunlight. Her next shiver came quietly.

I can see you.

"I don't know what you're talking about," Amanda barked. "Do I know what you're talking about?"

"Nope," said Rebecca. "And I don't, either." She stood to go and stopped, abruptly, with her hands on the table.

What had Amanda just said? ". . . the kind of work we do . . ."

We *do. Her and me.*

For quite possibly the first time since she'd picked up the Crisis Center phone maybe six hours ago, Rebecca felt herself relax, felt warmth spreading through. "Thank you, Amanda," she said quietly. Carefully. "Tell Joel . . ." But there was nothing she wanted Amanda to tell Joel. She just liked being around Joel, part of his games, in earshot of his holler. "Don't forget, I can only work until five today. Then I go to Jess's house." She moved toward the back door.

"Is Jess really renting *that* house?" Amanda asked, stopping Rebecca with her hand on the knob. "She's really living in the burned-out house?"

Surprised, Rebecca turned. The question itself was reasonable enough, a question any sane person might ask about such an apparently sane and sound person as Jess. What made it remarkable was that Amanda had asked it, was displaying active curiosity about a tenant or employee. Or rather, that she was displaying curiosity so openly that another employee could see it.

"Have you ever been to that house, Amanda? It is one disturbing place. It's—"

"I wasn't thinking about disturbing, Rebecca, I was thinking about filth. And lingering smoke stink. And faulty wiring, and flaking walls and lead paint and unstable floors."

"It's not really like that. I mean, they've cleaned it up, mostly. There's nothing actually flaking or unstable. It's just . . ." Rebecca's voice trailed away as understanding dawned. "Oh," she said then. "Ha." Naturally, Amanda was neither nervous for nor curious about Jess; she was being judgmental. And not gently so.

"She has a baby, doesn't she?"

"Well, yeah, Amanda. Hence my nannying there."

To Rebecca's amazement, Amanda blushed. Maybe. Certainly, her flour-pale cheeks reddened.

"What happened there, anyway?" Rebecca asked, at least in part to save Amanda embarrassment. Amanda-embarrassment wasn't anything Rebecca knew how to deal with. "Do you know the story?"

The question both erased the color in Amanda's skin and earned Rebecca her second are-you-really-that-dense? look of the past twenty minutes. "A fire," she said.

And for the second time, and more easily, now, Rebecca laughed. "Yes. Thanks. I mean, what else? Was anyone hurt or anything? It was right before I came, right? So, at least six or seven years ago. And no one's lived there since?"

"No one was hurt," Amanda said. "Not that I know of. Why?"

"Because I am the girl you"—she very nearly said *raised,* but reconsidered just in time—"mentored. And I bought almost everything I learned here, and I think you know it. So this is me, talking, and not the freaked-out, earlier-this-morning me, either."

"Okay. Good. And?"

"And I'm telling you, Amanda. That place is haunted."

8

(THREE WEEKS EARLIER)

The entire next day, they drove. At some point during that scalding midmorning, an hour or so after the air-conditioning in her Sunfire finally gave up its decade-long death rattle and died, Jess thought she should probably get food, or at least coffee. But she didn't need either; Eddie's screaming in the back kept her plenty awake, and Benny just slept. She did stop briefly at a pharmacy for gauze and bandages to wrap her ribs and a thousand-count bottle of ibuprofen gel caps, which she gulped eight of—knowing better, knowing the body couldn't even process that much drug at once—before she'd even reached the counter.

Then it was back to the swelter inside the car, the traffic-choked road north. Eddie kept screaming, and Benny stayed unconscious, one hand sliding off his abdomen to rest against Sophie's bloodied legs, which lay atop the pans and stuffed suitcases. In the front, next to Jess, Sophie mostly tried to curl away from the sunlight streaming through the windshield and windows. But there wasn't much of her to curl, so all she could really do was press against the door. Jess could tell the sun hurt her, saw the tears sneaking down her face. The girl made almost no sound, though, and never said a word.

Not only did Jess have to give her credit for that, she was also grateful for it. This way, with Eddie shrieking and the road spooling away and away toward nowhere in particular, none of them had to think.

Right at dusk, she swung them off the Beltway onto a two-lane road winding through trees into low hills. They passed a sign proclaiming the place to be *Concerto Woods,* and a mile or so past that, she spotted a rutted track spoking away into the shadows. Jess bumped them down that and parked under a gnarled, towering oak that seemed to stretch its branches over them like a canopy. For at least the sixth time since morning, she got out, unhooked Eddie, rocked him and fed him his bottle and some Cheerios and a jar of greenish mush. She kept herself turned three-quarters away from Sophie, her eyes on the forest but her ears pricked. The air smelled of pine resin and sap, old animal scat and wet earth. Living-thing smells.

"*Sssh,*" she heard herself saying as she swung Eddie back and forth, both the gesture and the sound automatic, instinctive. So, too, the burping him, the extra pressure on his back so he could feel her loving him. Little Eddie. Natalie's boy. The last of Natalie.

Finally, as the vanishing sun sucked the daylight over the horizon behind it, Eddie settled. He stopped hiccupping and complaining. When Jess lowered him to look into his face, he even smiled, or seemed to. His gurgling might have been a laugh. After that—for perhaps his very first time without a mother—he slept.

And for one moment—and one, only—Jess felt almost peaceful.

Settling the child back in his seat, she pushed Sophie's feet sideways so she could get at the paper bag of food she'd salvaged from the condo. One of those feet was, insanely, still in its flip-flop, and the flip-flop kept dangling over the lip of the bag until Jess stripped it off and chucked it out of the car. She rummaged, eventually coming up with some celery and a jar of peanut butter. Returning to her place behind the wheel, she forced herself to eat one entire stalk. Beside her, Sophie seemed to unfold, to the extent that she could, into the evening.

"Benny," Jess snapped, harder than she meant to, more fiercely than she could control. "Benny, wake up."

Eventually, he did, rolling fully onto his back, jerking his hand off Sophie's legs and then crying out at the sudden movement before tucking the broken arm Jess had attempted to sling against his ribs. Judging by his wooziness, Jess was pretty sure that in addition to his busted arm and ankle—or ankles—he probably had a concussion. It occurred to her, too late, that she probably should have kept him awake.

She peanut-buttered a stalk for him, turned, knelt on the seat, and leaned over the back. She had the celery clutched in her teeth like a dagger so she could help Benny arrange himself. Eddie woke up and burbled. Jess actually removed the celery from her mouth to ask Sophie for help. And that's when she realized that Sophie's head was already turned in her direction, her teeth maybe two inches from Jess's left breast.

Jess straightened so fast that she banged her head on the overhead light and cried out. That set Eddie screaming again. Jess ignored him, dropped the celery, kept her eyes locked on Sophie and her arms raised and crossed uselessly in front of her.

Sophie didn't lunge or bite. In truth, she'd barely moved, except her head, not that she had much else left *to* move.

But she was watching, all right. Quite possibly smiling. She knew what Jess was thinking. Even more—Jess was certain—Sophie wanted her to think it.

For a long moment, the two of them watched each other while Eddie screamed and Benny moaned. Then, with a sigh, Sophie looked down at her lap or, more accurately, at her hands, which were playing with the thready, dangling red bits at the tops of the stumps of her legs.

"Ooh," she said. And, "Huh."

At least Jess felt alert again, now. Carefully, she edged her arm over the seat until she could stroke Eddie's face. In her lap, Sophie kept doing . . . whatever she was doing. But she was watching Jess, too, her head cocked, brown eyes ringed by lack of sleep—*did she even need sleep, now, or was that a permanent state?*—but huge, like a raccoon's. The thready bits at which Sophie picked were still wet, apparently. At least, they sounded wet.

When Sophie saw where Jess was looking, she grinned. "Celery, huh? Never understood it."

"How's that?" Jess had neither meant nor wanted to respond, was still too rattled by how close she'd let Sophie get. *Almost everything we do,* she thought, *is absolutely automatic. We think we act. But we mostly watch ourselves act.*

"Crunch, stringy bleah, dribbly-juicy insides, swallow. It's like gnawing a bone." Then, when she saw the look on Jess's face, Sophie laughed and grinned wider. "Actually, it's nothing like gnawing a bone."

"Oh my God, you horrible, monstrous little—"

"Joke," Sophie said, and to Jess's surprise, she actually shrank back, put up her hands, palms out, like a little girl. Like the little girl she'd been right up until the moment she'd become no one, or this new thing.

"I have never gnawed a bone," Sophie assured her. "Nor do I have plans to."

Jess started to answer but instead inhaled a mouthful of the stink just starting to seep from the trunk. Her first impulse was to gag, which sent fresh pain shearing across her ribs, as though she'd ripped herself along some hidden perforation.

Her second impulse, once she'd recovered, was to weep, but she didn't do that.

Her third was to get up, go around back of the Sunfire, pop the trunk, and just crawl in, curl around her daughter and Sophie's son, and let herself sleep.

Instead, she grabbed the steering wheel and caught sight of her arms, striped and streaked where the sun had baked her daughter's blood into her skin. "Okay," she breathed, tasting that smell, feeling the whole horrid, unimaginable day just past melting into her. "Okay." Keying the ignition, she backed the car out from under the oak and up the path and returned them to the road. Instead of turning toward the freeway, though, she aimed them deeper into the forest.

Amazingly quickly—she always had been bright, so much brighter than her teachers or her mother or even Natalie had realized—Sophie understood what was happening. "Wait," she said. "Jess. I want to bury my Roo by the beach. Not in some lonely, stupid woods." She was sitting up straight in the seat now that the sun had gone, her blond hair frizzed and kinked and full of sand, twisted into knotty dreadlocks. Her too-round, sunshine face seemed different, almost frail, younger than Jess had seen it look for years and years. For a moment, Jess couldn't figure out what was causing that effect, and then realized: no freckles. How could there be Sophie with no freckles?

Mostly, though, the difference was those raccoon eyes, the *nothingness* inside or behind them. *God, you can really see it,* Jess thought, then thought maybe she was making that up. She sucked in more sickening air. That, she realized, might be her last physical experience of the child she had birthed and raised.

"Go ahead," she snarled, and returned her eyes to the road.

A few minutes later—all at once, as though a switch had been flipped—night dropped on the forest. In the car's headlight beams, the trees looked painted onto the dark, utterly motionless. Not a single other vehicle passed them. More than once, Jess's eyes flicked to the rearview mirror, but Sophie was always looking out the window or else over her shoulder at the trunk where her baby lay.

Unless she was looking at Benny?

They passed a series of rust-riddled white signs announcing the *Pimlico Post Pavilion Expansion Project,* and then a long stretch of sagging cyclone fencing around what looked like a completely abandoned construction site. Jess noted a lone bulldozer, some scattered stacks of discarded lumber, three filthy blue Porta-Potties with their doors swung open to the dark. Just as they came to the edge of the site and the end of the fence, Jess saw the wheelbarrow.

Which so much depends upon, she thought, half-chanting the lines to herself: some poem Natalie had loved in high school. She was already slowing the car before realizing she meant to. Gravel kicked up under their wheels, drumming the undercarriage of the Sunfire like little fingers. They stopped under yet another rusting sign: *Concerto Woods Development Authority. Future site of Pimlico Pavilion Oaks. Country comfort, urban sophistication, 3 and 4 bedrooms, from the low $500k's.* The words were filmed over with at least a year's worth of muck and dried sleet.

Jess looked back over her shoulder, making sure. The wheelbarrow was leaning up on its wheel against the cyclone fencing. And there really was a gaping hole in the wire, right next to it.

For once, she thought. *Just this once, life was going to be kind.* A sort of kind. It had taken her whole world, her husband, her daughter. But it had left her a wheelbarrow.

Even from the car, she could see that the thing was crusted with rust and bird shit. Silvery spiderwebs glinted in its handles like bows on a birthday present.

Sophie said nothing. Once again, she already understood. Together, they watched the site. There were more junk piles of wood in there, collapsing mountains of dirt, another Porta-Potty. Way back where the forest floor sloped down, they saw some kind of tractor or bulldozer, parked sideways. But there were no lights, no sounds, no sign of a night watchman or of anything worth watching. Some of the trees were oaks, some black cherry. Jess recognized those from road trips up this way with Joe, in the first year of their marriage. Their one year as just a married couple, with no one but themselves. Those days almost unimaginable, now.

"Pimlico Post Pavilion," Sophie murmured. "My mom brought us up here once, when I was like ten. To see Fleetwood Mac. She said Stevie Nicks was her soul sister."

"Stevie Nicks," Jess murmured. That wailing, coked-up, little gold-dust fairy. "Perfect."

Sophie's voice dropped lower. "What are you saying about my mom?"

Raising a hand to her forehead, Jess squeezed her eyes and was surprised by the moisture she found there. She'd thought she was past that, for now.

"I liked your mom, Sophie. In spite of herself."

The second she stepped out of the car, Jess knew she'd found the right place. Partially, the feeling came from the trees. They just *felt* like Natalie, even if Natalie had never seen them. Also, the Post Pavilion had to be somewhere nearby, maybe right over that hill down there, which meant Natalie would hear—or at least be lying near—music on summer nights. More than anything else (except her life, and her child), Natalie would have wanted music.

And in addition, there was *that.*

Knockknockknockknockknock. Knockknockknock.

The sound came from everywhere, bursting out in

unpredictable rhythms all over the woods. In their trailer in North Carolina, when Natalie was a little girl, she had sometimes punched her mother awake to listen to that sound; she'd even done that into her teenage years. Every time, Jess would grumble, pull her close, and they'd lie there together in those too-short, nearly silent times before their neighbors flooded the world with arguments and Twisted Sister and Rush Limbaugh.

In truth, those probably hadn't actually been the happiest moments of Natalie's life. But they really might have been the happiest of Jess's. And given the current circumstances, that would have to be close enough.

"Anyway, you're not really around to argue, are you?" Jess snapped, under her breath, at nothing. At the knocking summer air.

Leaving Benny to watch Eddie, she slipped through the hole in the fencing, collecting shovels and a tarp and a pick. She placed the shovels and pick in the wheelbarrow, wiped the handle of the barrow with the blood-soaked bottom of her blouse, and wheeled everything back to the fence opening. The whole time, she felt Sophie watching. Eventually, Jess forced herself to meet that raccoon-gaze. Once again, she had a choice to make, and no good options. But leaving that thing here with her man and Natalie's child was out of the question, so really, there was no choice whatsoever.

Returning to the car, she opened the door so Sophie could half-drag, half-spill herself onto the ground, then let her follow as best she could back to the fence. Only after Sophie had somehow scraped through the twisted chain-link did Jess squat, suck in breath to steel herself, jam her hands into Sophie's armpits, and hoist her into the wheelbarrow. Sophie went in sideways, clunking against the tools and the sides as Jess straightened. She grabbed at her screaming ribs as if her hands could help. Meanwhile, Sophie managed to tilt upright so that she stuck up out of the well like a jack-in-the-box, her blouse also streaked with blood, her shoulders and breasts raked with scratches, as though she'd been snatched up and then dropped by a bird.

"Not one word," Jess breathed. "You hear? And I don't care. Legs or no: if you're coming, you're helping." Then—biting the indentations her teeth had already gouged in her lower lip to help her keep from screaming—she got the barrow up on its wheel and nudged it ahead of her down the track the workmen had left into the woods.

Even if she'd wanted to, she knew she couldn't have made it very far. But as it turned out, she didn't have to. Leaving the construction site, they jostled down a root-riddled path, up a gentle rise to the top of a hill, and there, spilling out below them, lay the whole of Pimlico Valley. Beech trees and chestnut oaks shaded the hillsides from even the moonlight. Swatches of night-mist stretched between the trunks like hammocks. Far below—farther than Jess would have expected—the shingled roofs of the too-perfect houses and bungalows of the Concerto Woods planned community floated on their culs-de-sac. Beyond those, the Pimlico Post Pavilion amphitheater opened its wide white arms to the woods, as though the stage itself was about to erupt in song.

For a long moment, Jess almost forgot or maybe just let go of how she'd gotten here, why she'd come, even who she was. It was as though she were floating in a hot-air balloon, watching the world from the edge of space, with all the needs and hungers and terrors of all those living things down there reduced, simply by distance, to light.

Then, in the towering sweet gum to her left, a woodpecker let loose. The sound rattled Jess like a factory whistle, calling her back, once more, to work.

"Stay here," she told Sophie.

"Funny," Sophie said. "Good one, Jess." Then, as Jess started back toward the road, she called, "Wait."

Jess turned and waited.

"I actually think I *can* help."

Jess's laugh might have come out a bark, but it was a real laugh, nonetheless. "Now, who's funny?"

"Me," said Sophie. Moonlight glowed in her mouth when she grinned. "Always."

And that was true enough, Jess supposed. Certainly, it had once been true enough.

"Also helpful," Sophie said.

Returning to the barrow, Jess dragged the shovels and pick from under Sophie, banging her again against the sides in the process. Every new movement made Jess grunt or whimper. But she never stopped moving. If she did, she worried she might never start again.

When only Sophie's stump was left, she turned the barrow, and back they went to the parked Sunfire.

Bad ankles and arm and all, Benny had to hobble and hop around to help drag Natalie and the child she now cradled out of the trunk. The work of centering the bodies and rolling the tarp Jess had found proved too awkward and too painful—for all of them—to allow Jess more than a quick, final glance at the ruin of her daughter's face. But there wasn't much face to see, and most of that was hidden by long black hair studded with bits of skull.

So that was some mercy, anyway.

Somehow, Jess and Benny wrestled the tarp up and into the wheelbarrow. Then Jess turned to lift in Sophie, too, but was startled to find her swinging herself forward along the ground with her arms, lifting her leg-stumps and her ass slightly off the dirt with each new lurch, like an orangutan. As she passed Benny, she patted his calf.

"Nice work, fluffy man," she said.

"There's probably room for you in here," Jess said, gesturing at the tarp.

But Sophie never even turned around. "I got this. Feels *good,* actually. Whew." She twisted through the opening in the fence and started across the construction site, her stumps churning up clouds of dirt in her wake.

"I don't even want to think about what that means," Benny murmured, leaning on the car, breathing hard, watching Sophie scuttle up and over a stack of metal piping. Abruptly, he sagged sideways, and Jess had to jerk out her arms and catch him, which set her ribs shuddering and stabbing again. She doubled over against Benny's chest, pinning him upright. The car alone supported them both. Eventually, when he could, he slid his arms around her. "Oh, Jess. My God. What—"

"Ssh." She tried to round the end of that sound, make it softer than she knew it had come out. Eventually, after a long time, she slipped from his arms and eased him back into his seat next to Eddie. "I can't talk now, Benny. I just can't."

"We have to talk. Sooner or later. Jesus Christ."

Jess grabbed his eyes and stared him silent. "About what? What, exactly, do you imagine there is to say?"

She expected no answer, and got one immediately. "How about, I'm so sorry, Jess? Or, I love you, Jess? Will those do, for starters?"

Those will do, she thought, swiping savagely at the wetness that spilled yet again down her cheeks. *There really is no bottom to this well.* She didn't kiss him, mostly because she couldn't imagine leaning over any more than she had to. But she let him see her cry. Then she turned, got the wheelbarrow up and rolling, and followed Sophie toward the woods.

Mostly, on this final trip—the last she would ever take with her daughter—Jess sang to herself, the trees, the bodies in the tarp. The songs were the ones she'd sung to Natalie, and also the ones Natalie had sung to her. She didn't keep track, and in some cases couldn't even remember which was which anymore. Jess had never affixed songs to moments the way Natalie had; Natalie was more like her father, that way. Jess just sang.

Found a Peanut. Both Sides Now. That whiny newer one teenage-Natalie had always walked around crooning, about being human and needing to be loved. Like everyone else does.

Everyone else does.

When the woodpeckers knocked, she stopped singing and listened to them. Let her daughter listen to them. "*Do you hear?*" she whispered.

At which exact instant did Jess forget about Sophie?

It didn't matter, she would decide later, when she made herself go over and over those next moments. What mattered was that she *had* forgotten. She had let herself love, and grieve, and break, and hum. And so she got caught completely by surprise when Sophie dropped from the low branches of the black cherry tree she'd scurried up—like a spider or a bobcat—and landed on Jess's back and sent her shrieking and sprawling. The wheelbarrow tilted forward, and the tarp with Natalie's corpse in it tipped halfway out, actually propping the barrow in position. Incredibly, Jess got her hands down, even as her wrapped ribs crunched together, and Sophie didn't have her balance right, either; she landed farther forward on her stumps than she'd meant to, and that allowed Jess at least to roll over onto her back before Sophie scrambled over and squatted on Jess's stomach, her hands grabbing Jess's wrists and pinning her arms to the root-riddled dirt.

If she'd been sure her body was still capable of bending, Jess probably could have bucked Sophie off, although the grip in those fingers was ferocious. But in the moment, with this hellthing atop her, Jess couldn't think of a single reason to do that.

Sophie leaned down. Her round, freckle-less face hovered over Jess's, blank and gigantic and remote as the moon. Her raccoon-eyes sparkled in the dark. When she spoke, the air she moved—it wasn't an exhalation, just air with sound riding it—stank, but Jess couldn't have said of what. Although what occurred to her in the instant was . . . *emptiness . . .*

"Just what," Sophie said, "were you thinking to do with my Roo?"

"You want the truth?" Jess managed, as her own breathing slowed, quieted. The fact that she *was* still breathing almost seemed the most perfect, defiant response she could make. "The awful truth?" *Because it* was *awful, no matter what Sophie had become, or might have become, or was on her way to becoming*. "I wasn't thinking of your Roo at all."

"Well, I was. And I want him."

"You want him."

Sophie nodded.

Jess's smile felt more barbed and vicious than any she had ever aimed at anyone. She'd never even imagined such a smile could fit on her face. "Sure, hon." And with that, she pushed Sophie off. She was only a little surprised that Sophie let her. She gestured at the wheelbarrow. "Help me get this thing up."

Together, Jess tugging the handle while Sophie pushed from the ground at the tarp with Natalie's body—which was holding Sophie's Roo's body—wrapped in it, they righted the barrow. Wincing and gasping with every step, Jess pushed it over the top of the little hill, up to the edge of the patch of soft dirt she'd found between two yards-long ridged roots of the giant sweet gum. Then she let everything fall sideways, and the tarp thumped out onto the ground.

"Now help me unroll it."

They did that together. The second Natalie's body appeared, Jess bent forward, ignoring the pain. With surprisingly little pressure or effort, she freed the little bundle from Natalie's arms. A gentle tilt, a push on the tiny backside, and the baby was free of Natalie's grip. As easy as sliding a record out of a sleeve. Straightening, grunting as her tortured ribs rang, Jess cradled the bundle one last time. This boy had been hers, too, briefly, after all. He'd been hers, at least a little bit, all his too-short life. A tiny part of her wondered why Sophie hadn't already ripped him from her hands. Jess wouldn't have faulted her for that.

But when she looked up, Sophie was just watching, waiting, with her arms out and her lips flat and no expression Jess knew in her eyes.

"Here you go," she whispered, to George William, to his mother, and held out the child. Sophie snatched him away and clutched him to her breast.

For a few moments, Sophie leaned over her child, murmuring and cooing. Then she seemed to realize Jess was watching and turned away, even managed to edge deeper into the shadows of the sweet gum. That gave Jess a little more time to sit with her own daughter. She didn't coo or murmur or even hum, now; she just listened to the woodpeckers and held Natalie's icy, lifeless hand. One last time, and one time only, she let herself look at her daughter's face. The lips were still there, and still so expressive: slightly opened, turned down, and yet, somehow, almost smiling. That distinctive Natalie-expression. The ghost of it, anyway.

Eventually, with a start, Jess realized that the sky was starting to lighten. Letting go of Natalie's hand, she stood, picked up the shovel, found the softest dirt she could, and took some time settling into the least painful work position she could devise. Then she began her long, slow dig at the ground. She could have made Sophie help, or at least asked her to. Possibly, Sophie could have done that, just using her hands. But Sophie was with her baby. The baby she had abandoned to Jess's care, and come back for too late. And Jess . . . Well, Jess was with her baby. The one who had abandoned *her.*

That isn't fair, she thought, as she dug, rested, wept, dug some more. But she kept thinking it.

"Why here?" Sophie finally said, when Jess had been stopped for some time.

In fact, Jess had just realized that she was probably finished. Looking up, she was again surprised—and again, nowhere near alarmed enough—to find Sophie at the lip of the grave. Somehow, silently, she must have sidled closer. Above her head, through the massed branches, Jess noted the pink-tinged whiteness just spreading at the horizon, like the pressed-in quick at the bottom of a nail.

"We can't keep them in the car," she said, with no emotion in her voice and none in her heart, either, right then. "And I'm figuring, no matter how far the Concerto Woods Development Project develops, if it ever does, they're never going to come up here and move this tree." She gestured at the Pavilion far below. "Also, there's music."

By the time she'd clambered awkwardly out of the grave, Sophie had laid her bundled boy gently against a root and moved to help. She took Natalie's feet, straightening her friend as Jess prepared to roll her into the tarp for the last time. Then, abruptly, Sophie turned, took up her own child again, kissed him on the forehead, and slid him back into Natalie's arms, which of course had stayed folded, as though waiting for him.

"I thought you wanted to bury him by the beach," Jess said.

"He's better off with Nat."

"You've got *that* right." The words just flew from her mouth, and Jess regretted them immediately. Kind of. She saw the look that crossed Sophie's face, too, and braced for another lunge.

But Sophie stayed put, still staring down at her best friend, her baby boy.

"How could you do this?" Jess blurted out. "How could you let this happen? Either one of you. You were *good girls*, Sophie. You were such . . ." She smashed her teeth together, grabbed the shovel. Too late, she realized Sophie might take that as some sort of threat, when all Jess was actually considering was jamming the handle into her own mouth to keep in all these words, the thousands and thousands of them massing at the back of her throat. If she let them loose, she thought she might never get them stopped. They would spirit her straight off her feet and off this hill and drown her.

If Sophie had responded—if she had so much as looked up—Jess would have unleashed it all. She wouldn't have been able to help it.

But Sophie just gazed at her son, and sometimes at Natalie's shattered face. And after a long, long while, Jess felt her churning insides subside, at least temporarily. The words didn't so much evaporate—they would never evaporate, she would never be rid of them—as recede. They would drown her from the inside.

"You were such good girls," she whispered. She allowed herself a single sob, and turned once more to the task at hand.

It took less time and pain than Jess expected to drag the bodies those last few feet and drop them into their grave. Without being asked or even reacting to the light that was sifting through the branches, now, raising instant and ugly red rashes down both of her exposed arms under the bloody ruin of her dress, Sophie immediately started scraping up dirt with her hands. Jess used the shovel. In what seemed no time, they'd filled in the hole together.

The moment that was done, and the mound of dirt patted close to flat, Jess turned, threw the shovel downhill into the shrubs, and turned toward her Sunfire. She would have offered Sophie a ride in the wheelbarrow, but Sophie had already swung herself around and was moving back up the path, with no grace but surprising speed. Jess wasn't certain, but she thought she could hear Sophie whimpering as she scuttled forward, fleeing the light and the grave of her child and her lifelong best friend.

Of course, that sound could also have been Sophie grunting as she gained control of her movements, started to marshal the impossible, astonishing strength in her hands and her shoulders.

When Jess got back to the car, Sophie was leaning against it, up on her stumps, peering into the backseat at Benny. Again, Jess was reminded of a raccoon. The way Benny was staring back, on the other side of the closed window, reminded her of an indoor cat with its back up: magnetized, riveted, unable to look away, shuddering with a threat it could never make good on. Whatever noise Sophie had been making in the woods, she'd gone silent, now.

"You know what," Jess said, "I can't have you sitting next to me anymore. I'm sorry."

With what felt like the last strength in her entire body, she nudged Sophie away, opened the door, helped Benny once more to his feet and eased him into the front seat. Not until she'd got him buckled in place did she remember that if she put Sophie in back, she'd be sitting next to Eddie. And that was not going to happen, ever. And so, stumbling and shaking, Jess returned Benny to where he'd been.

All that while, Sophie hunched in the shade by the cyclone fence. Her mouth moved, but she wasn't saying anything. Jess thought maybe she was singing, now. Saying good-bye to her Roo, the same way Jess had said good-bye to Natalie. Maybe she was.

"Are you finished?" Sophie asked, when Jess finally stepped away from the car. Then she swung forward and pulled herself up into the front passenger seat. When she tried to buckle herself in, she almost tipped face first into the dash. "Shit."

"I'll do it," said Jess, leaning over. "Sit still. Don't touch me."

Sophie waited until Jess was bent all the way over, then poked a finger into her shoulder blade. "I touched you."

"Sophie, I'm not kidding, I'll dump you in the fucking woods."

"Maybe you should."

Seat belt in place, Jess straightened. "See, that's the difference between us. Right there. You're my responsibility, now. I might not want it. But I will never, ever forget it."

"Right," Sophie muttered. " 'Cause you're a *good* girl."

"You're right. I am. I was. I thought I was."

"Me, too," Sophie said. And then neither said anything more.

Several times during their slow wind down the Concerto Woods road out of the trees and into the day, Jess imagined she could feel Sophie's gaze on her. But when she flashed her own eyes to the rearview mirror, she kept finding Sophie with her head turned—farther than it should have been able to go, like an owl's—so that she could look in the back. Toward Eddie, or Benny.

Benny was lying down, legs scrunched up against Eddie's seat, so Jess couldn't see his face. But he was awake, and he was looking back. She could tell; she could hear it in his breathing. She started to say something, realized she had no idea what that would be, and then Sophie filled the silence for her.

"Hey, there, not-so-big boy. Not-so-big Jesus-God *hairy* boy. Wow, Jess. It's like you fluffed him or something."

"Shut up, Sophie."

"Poofed him. *Popped* him. Were you two always an item? Have you been a secret thing all these years? Did Natalie know? I had no idea. I thought—"

"I will hurl you from this car, Sophie. I will suspend you from the branches and leave you for the squirrels."

"Leave the squirrels for me, you mean?" said Sophie, quietly.

That was the moment Jess came closest to doing it, to slamming on the brakes and kicking Sophie out the door. She imagined tossing her severed legs after her like luggage. If Sophie had been smiling, Jess almost believed she would have done it.

But Sophie wasn't. And Jess didn't.

Eddie stirred, started to squawk, or maybe he was simply saying hello. Good morning to the world without his mother in it.

"Benny, give him Cheerios, okay?" Jess said. "Talk to him. Please? Don't let him scream anymore."

Benny grunted and gasped as he pulled himself into a

sitting position and worked the Cheerios baggie out of the side pocket of the child seat.

"Sssh," he said to Eddie, and "Oh, really? Same to you," and, "Wait, Eddie, watch this."

Jess had no idea what it was he wanted Eddie to watch. But she was so grateful, in that instant, for the hint of laughter in Benny's voice, which wasn't fake or forced, just buried in the rubble of the last month of their lives. Which had also been their only month as an actual couple.

Don't, she told herself. Told Benny, in her head. *Don't let* me *scream anymore.*

Behind her, through a mouthful of Cheerios and his own fingers, Eddie laughed.

They were all but out of the woods, now, within view of the turnpike on-ramp. Full daylight burst through the windshield, and Sophie curled as tightly as she could against the door, trying to tuck her arms inside her dress, then behind the stump of her torso. Even so, she saw the last billboard at the same instant Jess did. And for one more moment, she stopped squirming, went still.

August 22nd, the billboard proclaimed, in red, white, and blue letters spangled with glitter that winked in the sun. *Live at Concerto Woods. Sing along with the Archies reunion tour!!*

Sophie looked at Jess. And Jess was sure, this time, that she saw tears in those raccoon-eyes.

Then Sophie burst out laughing. "Oh my God," she cooed. "Your daughter is going to *hate* that."

9

God, it really was like sticking his hands in a hot tub, the Whistler thought, turning his wrists first one way, then the other in the holes he'd punched in the maintenance man's rib cage. That was because of the heat, of course, but also the occasional spurty jets that pumped new waves of warm over his poor, pallid skin. That warm never lasted long, and it was already cooling, now, the light in this man's lonely eyes flickering as the Whistler watched. Oscar, *the man's shirt said, on the stained pocket over his heart. Well, Oscar wasn't fighting very hard, hardly even seemed to be paying attention to his own ending. Some of them were like that; they wasted their deaths the same way they had their lives, imagining where they'd be next, regretting where they'd never be again.*

"You know, I didn't even mean to," he told the man, this Oscar, turning his wrists gently, nudging aside bulgy bits of shuddering organ, tendrils of shredded cartilage until he found what felt like a solid carapace of unshattered bone. Wedging his forearms under that, the Whistler held the man upright so he could die on his feet.

It was true. He hadn't meant to do any killing tonight, or any anything, really. A few hours ago, he'd just been wandering the streets of this nothing town yet again, sneaking into backyards, peering in windows, sliding into houses for what fun there was in sliding into houses. He'd lurked in a couple of people's closets while they slept, because that was always at least a little fun. He'd just crouch in their clothes, Whistle low into their dreams, maybe pet their animals. Take a key or ring off a nightstand. Tonight, he'd taken a phone. For the eighth or ninth night in a row, he'd wound up walking this leafy little nowhere of a campus, wandering into dormitories and classroom buildings, climbing the Clocktower, listening to his own echo.

But then, through giant windows he'd somehow missed every other time he'd strolled here, he'd caught sight of the four of them: the boy with the plastic dart stuck to his forehead, the laughing Asian girl with lightning for eyes, the pretty pumpkin-faced redhead with her rounded bookworm shoulders. And the little still one, just sitting there among them, laughing and singing like the others, and yet so immediately, obviously separate. *Just sitting in her zip-up summer sweater, brown hair back but not too far, brown eyes wide open,* so *wide open, like bird-chick mouths. Eyes that would swallow whatever the world brought them; they wouldn't be able to help it.*

That made him want to bring them something.

How long had he watched? He didn't know. Why had he taken a flyer off the door? He just had, and he'd taken it back up the Clocktower with him, and he'd stood amid the gears of the clock, in one of the belfry slits, so he could feel the air. It had seemed so still down on the grass. But up there, wind hurtled and hissed and rushed and whistled.

Are you lonely? *the flyer read. And he was. He truly was.* In need? Overwhelmed? Scared? Unsure what to do? If you ever are . . . or just want someone to talk to . . . we're here. We're always here. Weeknights 8:00 p.m.–midnight (or later). Weekends 8:00 p.m.–2:00 a.m. (or later).

On the spot, he'd taken out the phone he'd stolen from that old woman's dresser. But he hadn't called the Center, not right away. First—finally—he'd called Aunt Sally and told her about Mother.

And that had *been fun. A sort of fun. Ruthless, imperious Aunt Sally, who'd never done anything, much, who sat in a tent but deemed herself Prescriber of everyone else's fates. Aunt Sally, who'd never understood him, or music, or even Mother.*

Yes. Hearing her silence had been fun.

And yet, the moments after he'd hung up . . . those were confusing. When, exactly, had he slid a foot through the slit in front of him? When had he turned his hips and just edged forward, and forward some more, until he was half-way out in the whipping air, leaning over the campus into the night. The wind grabbed at his hat, tugged at his waist the way it did at birds' wings. It wanted to fill him, pull him out to play. He came so close to leaning just that last bit more, unfurling at long last. Mother gone, his Destiny gone, no hunger to speak of, nowhere to go or be.

Why was he even here? Because he'd followed his Destiny's mother, his Destiny's murderer. But why had he done that? It seemed she should be something to him, mean something or other to him, though he couldn't think what.

The truth was, he had never once, in his first life or this one, had to decide, on his own, what to do next. How did people decide such things?

He hadn't even gone to a club or performed any music, he'd realized, then. He hadn't so much as sung to himself, *let alone Whistled to a crowd.*

But here was all this air, and it *was whistling, tousling his hair, nuzzling him, wrapping him in its wild arms. Sad little Whistler-shadow, up here in the air, so close to free. A single, sliding step from free.*

That was the moment he'd looked down and seen the Center again, darkened by that point. Just the little Still One remained, limned by her computer light: already an angel, and she hadn't even met him yet.

And so he'd called there instead. And he'd heard her voice, felt her opening to him even through the phone. She hadn't been able to help it, as he'd known she wouldn't. Not with eyes like that.

People worth talking to, *she'd said.* Staying up late.

Magical. A magical creature, same as him. And she'd been so right. He would show her just how right she was.

Starting now, *he thought, as Oscar the maintenance man stopped twitching at the ends of his wrists, went motionless, sagged forward. Poor dead Oscar-fish, who'd almost made it to another morning.*

Morning. In the fascination of this night, the tingling sense of awakening, the Whistler had actually forgotten what time it was.

"Come on," he said, withdrew his hands, settled Oscar against him, and dragged him across the grass toward the alley at the edge of campus where he'd left his truck.

Most mornings, these past weeks, he'd driven well out of town, way out into the empty, wondrous woods. But there wasn't time now, and anyway, he didn't want to be far from town anymore. He wanted to be near his new, Still One, and all the sights and splendors he would bring her. So he turned down a lane, juddered between birch trees and sugar maples onto a path. Branches scraped the sides of his truck, battered at his windows. He found a clearing, deep in shadow, and parked there. It was nowhere Mother would have stayed: too much like a campground, either too close to people or not close enough. For today, it suited the Whistler fine.

Except that it didn't. He tried closing his eyes, pulling the silver blackout sunshade across the windshield and windows, curling up on the seat. He tried turning on the radio, but there was no radio worth hearing, here. He tried murmuring into the quiet, imagining upcoming conversations. But that just made him hear his new, Still One's voice.

People worth talking to . . .

And so—knowing there wasn't enough shadow, not this close to town, knowing it would hurt—the Whistler popped his door lock and stepped out once more into the air.

Where was he going? Nowhere, of course. There was nowhere to go, *nothing to be done, nowhere that wouldn't hurt for him to be for hours and hours, yet. And yet, he couldn't stand the thought of another day alone and bored in the truck. For almost the first time since the night she died, he thought of Mother. As he did, he stepped around front of the Sierra, wandered a few steps ahead, and stopped, startled. Then he held absolutely still.*

Where had those *come from? How lost and distracted a Whistler was he, that he hadn't noticed them?*

Just on the other side of a thicket of bramble-hedges, in a clearing already bathed in scalding sunlight, sat a circle of old trailers, sinking into the dirt. Triangle, really, there were only three. Pretty quickly, the Whistler realized there were no people in them. One was tipped forward off its base, its windows bashed in, its front door leaning open into the dirt. One had an American flag painted all along the side, only the flag had so many rust stains (or rust holes) riddled through it that it was barely recognizable. The third one's roof sagged so deeply into its walls that it looked half-folded-up. Like a giant's discarded briefcase, *the Whistler thought, liked that thought, and laughed. Maybe he would bring his Still One here. Show her things. Yes, perhaps he would.*

Maybe even tonight.

That was almost enough. Shivering his pleasure, humming, the Whistler started to turn back toward Mother's truck. It was impulse—instinct—that drove him instead deeper into the woods. He drifted, desultorily, along the path he'd found, which was so overgrown that it might never actually have been *a path, not for people. Surprisingly deep, these woods turned out to be. In these pines, he was humming, all but Whistling, inside his head. Where no sun could ever shine. Any moment, he thought he'd come to some spot too overrun with branch and bramble to pass. Instead, he came to the road.*

He must have walked some way, he realized, farther than he'd imagined. There, maybe three hundred yards to his right, was the edge of this nothing town, that gas station, the brick pizza place with the strange hulking barn-structure out back, which always seemed to be breathing when the Whistler passed it. Certainly, it hummed.

Daylight nipped at his exposed wrists, his cheeks, even under his hat, even back here in the shadow of the evergreens and maples. It really was time to go back, curl up in the truck with whatever music he could find, and sleep, and wait. He was just about to do that when he glanced left—up the road, away from town—and saw them.

It seemed so unlikely, amazing, delicious. It was almost enough to make him believe *in Aunt Sally's damn fool nonsense. Policy. Fate.*

Except that he hadn't told anyone his dreams. No one had led him here. That is, he had led himself here. And now he could see them.

They were kissing. There, on the bench, under the little fiberglass overhang that constituted a bus stop. That is, the raven-haired one, all elbows and laughter, was kissing, and the boy—who still had his plastic dart suctioned to his forehead—was lolling away, or just lolling. Maybe he was too drunk to respond. Maybe he just didn't love this girl, not the way she clearly did him. Or maybe, *the Whistler thought, shivering with the pleasure of the idea,* he loved another.

Oh, yes. The Whistler thought he knew whom this boy loved.

Better and better. More tingly by the moment, these two were making him. Shrinking deeper into the melting shadows at the tree line, the Whistler watched. A logging truck lumbered past, blocked his view, revealed it again. The Asian girl had given up or gotten tired and slid sideways into the crook of her not-lover's arm. The boy stroked her hair, looked up the road, looked right into the woods—almost right at *the Whistler—but saw nothing. His ridiculous dart waggled like an antenna, as though it could sense the lurker in the shadows, even if the boy couldn't.*

That made the Whistler want to clap his hands and laugh. He checked the road toward town, saw no more trucks coming, no one moving down there, everything shuttered and dull and dumb and quiet. In all the world, there were just these two, in the pink and hot new morning. All alone, with no one to sing for them.

Surely, *he thought,* someone should do something about that.

And without thinking further—knowing it would hurt—he slipped from the shadows and stepped out into the early-morning sunlight.

10

"Oh my God, you're so *annoying,*" Kaylene said, burrowing closer against Jack's side, tilting her face to the morning sun so it could start to bake the booze out of her.

"Oh my God, I'm so sauced," said Jack.

"You are the Boy of Annoy. You're like a Pac-Man ghost."

"A sauced Pac-Man ghost."

"I move away, and there you come. I move toward you, and there you are. You're just there. Period. Always. Boy of Annoy."

"That's why you love me."

"No, it isn't." Kaylene squeezed her eyes shut and let

herself feel it. She let Jack hear it, just this one and only time, if he was listening.

When she opened her eyes, she saw Jack running a hand over his face. He accidentally dislodged the dart off his forehead, and it landed in his lap. "I'm pretty drunk," he said, and licked the suction end of the dart to reaffix it.

"Uch. I'm trying to decide if it's the sight or the thought of what you just did that's making me want to puke."

"It's drinking while Human Curling. I really have tried to talk to you about that."

Kaylene snorted, poked him in his pudgy side, and sat up. She wished, briefly, that she was *more* drunk. That either of them was.

"Actually, it's you and Rebecca."

"There is no me and Rebecca."

"That's what's annoying. That you feel that way, both of you, and yet neither one of you will—"

"I'm sorry," he said, dart thrumming as he looked down at his hand, which was now holding her hand. "I really am, you know."

"*That's* why I love you," said Kaylene, and let go of him. She put her own palms to the bus-stop bench—wet with dew, warming to the morning—started to stand, glanced toward town, and froze.

It wasn't so much the guy standing there, but the fact that she knew instantly, could tell from the way he stood, that he'd been there some time. He was right in the middle of the road, not twenty feet away. There'd been no car, no bus. *Where had he even come from?*

"Um. Jack?" she said.

The man in the road pushed the sombrero back on his head, took a step forward, and smiled.

Everything went wrong at once. Sound, for one; suddenly, Kaylene realized she couldn't hear the woods; she couldn't even seem to hear herself breathing. She was pretty sure she'd gasped. But she hadn't heard any gasp.

Also, her mouth had pursed, as if her lips were mirroring the Sombrero-Guy's, which had also pursed. It was as though they were kissing, from fifteen feet away.

But he wasn't making kissing noises, or motions. Even when his tongue snuck from his mouth, he wasn't suggesting. He was wetting his lips. He started to whistle. *That,* she could hear.

And the sensations that caused . . .

As though her nerves had erupted through her skin. If she looked down, she thought, she would see them all breaking into the air, shimmering and seething on the surface of her like mackerel.

As though everything inside her was dancing, swaying. Except her. *Unless this* was *her?*

As though everything she'd felt in the past twelve hours—her crush on Jack, her love for her friends, her guilt, her exhaustion, the sheer glee of being here, being her, *being*—had been sucked into that sound, that melody he was making, which was one she knew and couldn't name, had never actually heard. But no, she had heard it, knew it well, and it was ridiculous, certainly not a melody that had ever done this to her before. *The words just coming out wrong. So he'd have to say he loves me . . . in a song . . .*

And now, she was crying—*crying!*—as the Sombrero-Man started forward. Swaggered, really, though he did keep tugging his shirtsleeves down, almost seemed to be trying to stuff his hands inside them, and he was doing something awkward and not swaggery with his head, scrunching it down in his collar, tipping and re-tipping that ridiculous hat like a sun umbrella. Still, he whistled, came forward. Kaylene felt one of her legs draw up on the bench in front of her, felt her arms encircle it and *hold on,* as though it were the post of a pier in a hurricane. Also, her lower lip was pulsing, right in the center; she half-imagined she could see the exact spot beating, blinking, like the little light on top of a buoy. Most of all, she heard that whistle in her ears, burrowing into her brain like a siren or a baby's cry, pushing her away, pulling her to it.

He'll have to say he loves me . . .

She was vaguely aware, as the Sombrero-Man reached her, that Jack was squirming, bouncing up and down like the little boy he was, forehead-dart quivering. He was making some sort of sound, too, definitely a complaint, a protest, though it didn't seem to have words, and it didn't amount to much.

Good, she thought. *You squirm for once.* Then she thought maybe Jack should get off this bench and get out of here, for his own sake. She thought he should run.

Then she thought she should.

Somehow, one of Jack's hands had found its way to her shoulder. For one moment, Kaylene was impressed by this. Then the Sombrero-Man was before her, blocking the sun. Gently, as though brushing away a seedpod, he flicked Jack's hand off, bent forward, and slid his own fingers over the front of Kaylene's T-shirt, up her breasts to her throat.

Briefly—or maybe for a while, she had no idea—he just

stayed like that. She could feel her pulse against the webbing of his thumb. *I'm so warm,* she thought. And it really was amazing, remarkable, feeling her own life beating. Not soft, either. Punching.

He was leaning in, now, the Sombrero-Man, his lips spreading. With no particular emotion, just a sort of interest, Kaylene wondered if he was going to kiss her, bite her, or whistle into the hollow of her neck.

But he did none of those things. He froze instead, his lips inches from her skin, her seething, surging skin. His shadowed eyes were open, glittering, right in front of hers. But he wasn't looking at hers.

Because he was locked on Jack?

From her unique vantage point—at once in the moment and beside it, in her own skin and in these others'—Kaylene watched it happen, to both of them. Jack had finally gone still, and now he just stared in dumb, useless panic—unless that was a challenge?—out of the blue of his irises. Several seconds passed before he blinked, lowered his head. Poor, pathetic little wolf, bowing to the better wolf.

That was interesting, Kaylene supposed. But not nearly as interesting as what was happening to the Sombrero-Man. His hand had slid farther up Kaylene's neck, closed over the beating part. Every time Jack glanced at that hand, the Sombrero-Man tightened his grip, just a little. Just enough so that Kaylene could feel it, and Jack could see it. Also, the guy's ridiculous mouth kept spreading wider.

Was that a grin? Kaylene wondered, listening to herself rasp. She also wondered, with the exact same detachment, if she was going to die. But she was thinking more about the Sombrero-Man's grin at the moment he finally closed her windpipe shut, slid sideways across her, and kissed Jack full on the mouth.

Even as she strangled, started to twitch in the monster's hands, Kaylene couldn't get her eyes off his face. It was the way his eyes widened, glancing back and forth between Jack and her, drinking them in. Marveling. Discovering.

Like a scientist or a surgeon, the Sombrero-Man poked his tongue into Jack's mouth, which opened to meet it. Kaylene could see that Jack was screaming—in his eyes; he wasn't making any sound—and she could also feel him flowering, right there beside her, unfolding against the Sombrero-Man's other hand, which had slid into his crotch.

Maybe that wasn't screaming at all, Kaylene thought. *Maybe that was yearning.* Kaylene thought she could have told him a thing or two about yearning.

And that thought woke her up. She started to kick, tried to scream, but nothing came out. She tried to pummel Jack in his ribs, wake him, too, except he was already awake. Maybe. He seemed to know full well what was happening, what the Sombrero-Man was doing to Kaylene. And yet Jack went right on kissing him anyway.

It was her kicking, she thought, that brought the Sombrero-Man's attention back to her face. And then she suspected it wasn't.

He's watching me watch, she realized, as the road and the trees and Starkey's Pizza and the morning sun winked in her vision, went dark, went light, and her fingernails scrabbled wildly at the world she was leaving, did not want to leave. *He wants me to see.*

His lips had come off Jack's, but just far enough so that

Kaylene could see Jack strain forward, try to reclaim them. The Sombrero-Man watched her watch that, too.

The last thing she saw before consciousness fled her was the electrified smile on the monster's face, and the last thing she heard was his whistling.

11

Rebecca awoke sticky and sweating, her threadbare sheets clinging to her legs like bits of cobweb. She glanced toward the clock, through the shafts of dusty sunlight diving down into her basement room, and blinked in surprise: 11:42.

Actual sleep. Hours of it.

Peeling back the sheet, she sat up into the hot air streaming like blown breath from her clanking window fan. For a few moments, she stayed put, staring into the fan's face with its bent blades lurching around and around, its gray, scratched frame with *Kenmore #1 Summer* etched into the brow.

"My number-one fan," Rebecca murmured for the first time in a while, leaned forward, kissed the on-off switch, and stopped, abruptly. Air buffeted her chest, pushed past her. She held still and listened.

But all she heard was what she always heard: the fan clanking; the Rudzinskis' baby whimpering out its colic upstairs. No one had whispered. Even the whispering in her head had gone.

And no one had died. No one had jumped, as least as far as she knew. No one was coming to turn her out of this room for her failures, send her off to her next not-home. Last night, she had made mistakes, the way people do, every day. And she'd admitted them, done what she could about them, and then come back to her bed and gotten some sleep, so she could get up and get on. The way she did.

She'd spent the afternoon fulfilling her duties at Halfmoon House. For the first couple hours, Amanda set her sweeping out the pantry and cleaning the upstairs bathroom. Rebecca suspected that that was indeed intended as punishment, not so much for last night's crisis call as for obsessing too much over it. For showing up here afterward instead of going straight home—to her own home, the one she'd made by herself—to sleep. Around 3:00, having finished with the toilet and the floor, she came out of the bathroom with her bucket and sponges and caught Danni, the older and more vicious of the two current residents, crouching in the hall outside little Trudi's door.

Poor Danni, was Rebecca's thought, watching the teenager lean closer to the keyhole, her waist-length blond hair spilling all over her back, hiding her face. *Too smart for her own good. Lonelier than most people imagined it was possible to be.*

And, most days, nasty as fuck.

Which was very likely why Amanda and Joel had held off filling the other two beds, Rebecca realized. Danni needed too much minding. They would never, ever send her back to whatever orphanage they'd found her in. But they would also never let her hurt anyone else in their care.

For a few months this past spring, Rebecca had actually felt like she was forming a connection with Danni. She'd introduced her to Smackdown online, Danni had shown her Minecraft, and they'd secret shared eye rolls and sighs about Amanda. But then Trudi had arrived and given Danni a target.

Even from the bathroom doorway, Rebecca could hear the little girl in her room, murmuring and chirping away to herself, though less loudly than she used to; at least she'd listened to Rebecca about that. She was saying something about leaves, about leaping into leaves. Then came a high-pitched, half-whispered "*Waaaaahhhh* . . ."

Snorting into her hands, Danni stood, started slowly turning the doorknob.

"Get away from there," Rebecca snapped. She'd meant to say it lightly. Danni still needed her, too, or needed someone, anyway. But right now, Rebecca's own priorities were absolutely clear.

Danni didn't flinch or even seem surprised, and she didn't step away from the door. Instead, she turned. Under the cascading hair, she was grinning. "The Loon's at it again," she mouthed, pointed at the door, and pulled her too-small pink T-shirt down, glancing at her own breasts as she did. The gesture was still self-conscious, at least, and would probably stay that way a little longer.

Laying her bucket against the wall and her sponges in the bucket, Rebecca edged forward. She kept her voice low and tried to warm it up. "She's playing, you mean? Putting on a play to entertain herself? Being creative, the way brilliant girls like her do? Like you probably did?"

"She's talking to her socks."

Trudi's door burst open so hard that even Danni flinched back, stepped sideways. And there Trudi was, kinked hair pulled back, Amanda-style, into hard braids at either ear, so that the part along her scalp looked like a half-open lid, something you could pry up and climb into. She had her hands—encased in yellow socks—on the hips of her thrift-store jeans, the ones Amanda bought in bulk and kept in clean, tight stacks, separated by size, on shelves in the basement coat closet. The pants had too many pockets for a nine-year-old, or anyone, and too much torso; they made whoever wore them look—and feel—like a cartoon character. Sponge-orphan Square-butt.

"Better than talking to you," Trudi spat.

Rebecca burst into applause. To her surprise, Danni did, too. In that instant, she was once more what every kid who'd ever come here had been: just another kid who'd never been a kid, no one's daughter, maybe no one's friend. Rebecca stopped clapping. She wanted to gather both these girls to her.

But she was no one's mom. Not even anyone's caretaker.

"Come on, Rebecca," Trudi barked, marching past her down the hall toward Amanda, who had just come up the stairs. "We're going out."

Rebecca watched the little girl's receding back. The white scratches Trudi still gave herself in her sleep slanted through her black skin like leftover scrawl on a badly erased chalkboard. Amanda didn't touch or say anything to the little girl as she marched past. She just stepped out of the way.

"Well?" Amanda said to Rebecca. "You heard her."

"I'm coming, too," Danni said, generating an impressively defiant tone as she faced Amanda's folded arms, even though she knew what that stance meant as well as Rebecca did.

"In a couple hours, maybe," Amanda said. "When you're done with the work I'd have Rebecca doing if I could trust you to take care of other people, yet."

Danni opened her mouth, actually gathered breath for a response, before Amanda lifted a warning finger. The finger waggled in the air between them.

"Ah-ah," Amanda said.

In her day—which, Rebecca supposed, was still this day, since she was still here—she would never have dared test that finger, despite the fact that she actually considered herself tougher than Danni. She still wouldn't.

And so it startled her when Danni erupted into a stutter. "Luh-luh-luh . . . *LOVE ME!*"

Only after she'd snatched up the sponge bucket and sauntered down the hall did Rebecca realize she wasn't quite talking back, and she certainly wasn't pleading. No. She was, in fact, singing. Not only that, but Rebecca knew whose voice she was imitating, and where Danni must have learned that particular annoying tone.

Amanda had recognized it, too. "I hate that radio show," she murmured to Rebecca. "I honestly hate it, I don't know where Joel finds these *fucking* things, or why he likes them."

If Danni's stuttering was startling, Amanda's swearing

was positively alarming. Even with Trudi already downstairs and headed for the front door, Rebecca stayed rooted, trying to remember if she had ever once heard Amanda curse before.

"It . . . really is really weird," she said eventually, remembering the voice Danni had just mimicked pouring out of Joel's speaker, lurching up- and down-register: teenager, temptress, babbling baby, sometimes all those things in the space of a single word. *Buh— . . . cat-dah . . . TONGUE!*

And now, the memory of that voice stirred her memory of that other's: her caller, from last night. The whistler from Lonely Street. "I better go after Trudi," she said, more loudly than she needed to, just to fill her ears with sound.

"Don't let her go by those trailers. I don't know why she keeps going down there."

But of course, by the time Rebecca got outside, Trudi was already halfway across the lot, pointed exactly that way. She stomped past the barn where Joel probably was if he was out here right now, headed straight for the trail that cut through the heart of the woods, right past the campground where those tipping, collapsing trailers hunkered in the same spots they'd occupied since Rebecca had first come here more than a decade ago. Probably, they'd been there long before that.

"Hey," Rebecca called. "Trudi, wait."

If anything, Trudi sped up, barging through the evergreen branches into the forest. Swearing to herself, Rebecca followed. By the time she reached the tree line, Trudi had vanished completely. *Luh-luh-luh . . . Love Me,* Rebecca thought—almost hummed, in her head, to drown out the other voices—and pushed through the needle-pines and grabbing pricker branches after the little girl.

She caught up right at the edge of the clearing where the trailers huddled around the campsite's blackened fire pit, and only because Trudi had had the good sense to stop there. When Rebecca reached her, she was crouching almost *inside* a pricker bush. Thorns rested against but apparently did not penetrate her skin, like half-retracted cat claws. Rebecca crouched beside her. The little girl didn't say anything or even acknowledge Rebecca's presence.

"What?" Rebecca whispered. She reached out a hand to touch Trudi's back, then decided not to. Rebecca herself had never liked those automatic grown-up's touches—the ones Amanda never gave—that were meant as reassurance but probed like a dental tool, tugged like a leash.

"Ssh," Trudi hissed.

So Rebecca shushed, and they crouched together. For the first time that afternoon, Rebecca noticed the heat, which was high-summer humid and had long since permeated her skin, slicking it with sweat. Three minutes outside, and she already felt like a puddle of popsicle left on a counter. Midges rose and swirled, sipping at her ears and the corners of her eyes. Except for those, and the fire ants hurrying around and under her feet, swarming the pricker branches and nearby tree trunks, nothing moved. Even the single squirrel Rebecca spotted had draped itself along the lowest branch of the nearest evergreen like a pelt hung out to dry. A pelt that had hung out itself. Rebecca slapped at her neck, felt that familiar wet squish, the midge she'd just killed not so much smearing as drowning.

Quite some time passed before Rebecca realized she was

looking anywhere but into the clearing. The truth was, she didn't like this place any more than Amanda did, and never had. She made herself look.

It was just as she'd remembered: the crumbling fire pit, still blackened all the way around and inside the rim, but possibly crumbled even more, now, like the mouth of a forgotten well; the curled, colorless drifts of dead leaves that always seemed deeper and denser around the pit, as though they'd been gathered rather than blown there, ages ago. As though neither squirrels nor birds nor time nor wind had disturbed them since.

Worst of all were the trailers themselves, angled together as though they'd been circled, their windows shattered or shot out, some of the openings covered over with warped, fire-blackened wooden boards. The trailer on the left, the one she'd always hated most, remained tipped forward almost off its blocks, its front door hanging open, nearly touching the ground, like a hand extended to break a fall. Instead of wooden boards or cracked glass, the windows on that trailer were barred with chicken wire, suggestive of some abandoned circus-train car, the one for big cats. Sometimes, as a kid, she'd found herself imagining that those cats might still be in there, curled and starving in the heat, trapped where they'd been left, tails whapping. Just waiting.

"Why do you come here?" Rebecca whispered.

"It's *scary,*" Trudi whispered back.

"Right. Exactly. So why come here?"

It was less the ferocity of Trudi's I-just-told-you look than the way her braids jiggled that caused Rebecca to laugh. And it was her laugh that woke the clearing.

In a blast of breeze—*was that breeze?*—the leaves in the center of the trailers stirred, flapped, and settled right back where they'd been. The bent-wire antenna atop the tipped-over trailer waggled as though warning, or beckoning. The open front door edged farther open, drifted almost shut, and it occurred to Rebecca that this place almost certainly *was* inhabited, at least sometimes. It was probably the best squat in town, especially in summer, when the Salvation Army/UNH-D shelter closed down.

"Why are you clutching me?" Trudi snapped—still whispering—and Rebecca looked down at her arms, which had encircled the little girl.

"Why are you letting me?" Rebecca whispered back, and Trudi squirmed free. For one more moment, they stared together into the clearing. Only then did Rebecca understand, at last, why Trudi had stopped here today instead of tramping through on her usual march to the lake, and why both of them were whispering, and what was wrong.

Tugging at the little girl's shoulder, she started edging back. "Trudi. There's someone here."

"What?"

But Trudi knew, even if she hadn't figured out exactly how or *what* she knew. Rebecca could see it in the uncommon curl of her shoulders, and also the fact that she was edging back, too. Following a grown-up's directions, for once.

"That truck," said Rebecca, still retreating, hoping the *shush* of her feet in the leaves was less loud than stepping and crackling would be. She gestured past the trailers to the far side of the clearing where the sugar maples and evergreens crowded together, closing out the light almost completely.

The hulking black Sierra over there had been tucked so deeply into the clustered branches that the pine needles seemed to have assumed its shape, blanketing it like camouflage netting. Rebecca could see just enough of the windshield and driver's-side window to know that they were all the way tinted; even if she'd been standing right beside that cab, she couldn't have seen inside it or made out who was in it.

"You mean that pickup? Wasn't that here?"

"I don't think so, Trudi. Come on."

Grabbing the girl's hand, Rebecca stood and tugged her away up the path. She started to jog, felt Trudi glance back but not resist, and then she heard the footsteps.

Not their footsteps, but someone else's, off to their left. Steady, and gliding.

Squirrel, she thought furiously, except it couldn't have been. There was no scurry-scatter, no stop-and-start; this was more of a trot. And whoever was in there, trotting, was maybe ten feet off the trail on the other side of the wall of evergreens. When Rebecca accelerated, the footsteps did, too. Like something stalking, moving ahead of them, now.

Fox?

Nope. Whatever it was, it was bigger than that. A big thing, moving light.

Bear?

"Rebecca, wait."

"Trudi, come on."

"Rebecca, there's someone in that tree—"

"Oh, *shit,*" Joel said, tripping on a low branch and spilling out of the evergreen where he'd been hiding directly in their path. As he fell, he twisted sideways to protect the Bluetooth speaker in his hands. He landed hard and lay there a second with his back to them as Rebecca yanked Trudi to a halt, heart flailing under her ribs, beating its wings. *Like the loon on the lake,* she thought, grabbing hold of the thought, using it to anchor her. *Reminding itself it can go, but deciding to stay.*

Rebecca breathed slow, made herself settle. Joel rolled over on his back and looked up at them. He was grinning.

"Spider races?" he said.

Trudi glared, looking ready to lunge forward and jump on him. Joel laughed.

"What the hell are you doing, Joel?" Rebecca barked. But barking made her feel like Amanda, and anyway, she didn't seem to want to bark, anymore. She fought for control of her own smile and lost.

"Did I scare you?" Joel asked.

"No," Trudi said.

Rebecca shook her head as a shiver rippled through her. "Why are you even out here?"

Sitting up, Joel dusted dirt and pine needles off his work shirt and the top of the speaker. Then he gave the speaker a pat, as though it were a lapdog. "Following you, of course. I'm Blair Witching you."

"Why?" Her skin had slicked again, or slicked more, and the shudders weren't quite done rippling through her. But Joel was here, casting his spell, shedding his light where light was most needed. *Out of sight of his house, where it isn't even wanted,* Rebecca thought, but that thought confused and alarmed her. She pushed it aside.

"For fun. Why else?"

"You're not funny."

"I'm a little funny. Wait, Rebecca, are you mad? Are you actually scared right now? In these woods? After all the years we spent wander—"

"Joel, there's someone in the clearing."

Joel stopped grinning. "What?"

"She's not lying," Trudi said, and Rebecca had to give it to the kid; *she* didn't sound scared at all.

"Someone who shouldn't be, you mean? As in, not a homeless person or—"

"How would I know?" Rebecca snapped, more at her own thoughts than at Joel, and as she did, she glanced over her shoulder again down the empty path. "There's a truck. A big black one. I've never seen it there before."

"Someone *drove a truck* in there?" Pushing to his feet, Joel looked past Rebecca toward the clearing. Abruptly, Rebecca felt thirteen years old again. All she wanted to do was grab Joel's hand, the way she'd grabbed Trudi's, and pull all three of them out of these woods and back to Halfmoon House.

"Joel, let's just—"

"Do you want him gone?" he said, and his grin resurfaced. "It sounds to me like this guy should be gone."

"I want to do spider races," said Trudi, crouching over a stump near where Joel had tripped, poking at a web with a stick. "I think I've got mine."

"Joel, whatever you're thinking, no."

But Joel was already walking straight past her and back down the path. As he went, he pushed up the sleeve of his shirt, reaching for the iPod he kept strapped to his biceps and switching on the speaker.

Lonely Street, Rebecca thought abruptly, catching her breath as last night's whisper bubbled up in her head again. It was as though that whisper had been lurking in her ears all along, holding its breath, biding its time.

I can see you.

"Joel," she called, as he fiddled with the iPod. "Joel, I mean it, don't. Please, please, please, just leave it alo—"

"BOYYYFRRIEEND!" screamed Joel's speaker, in the voice of that girl-woman from the radio show. Then it screamed again, higher, as Joel strode straight into the clearing, stopping in line with the tipped-over trailer, right beside that broken, barely open door. He hoisted the speaker above his head and aimed it into the bushes at the black truck. Snapping-finger sounds crackled from it, and the crazed girl-woman shrieked again, and then again, faster and louder, like a genie pouring out of a bottle.

"BOYYYYFRIEEND," she screamed. *"Back . . ."*

12

He woke up wild, his legs banging the bottom of the dashboard and the body next to him and his head caroming off the steering wheel as he jolted upright, eyes shooting around the cab, which was dark, close, shadowless, motionless. In a daze, he squinted into his own gaunt face in the rearview mirror. Memory, delicious memory, flooded through him.

First came the sensation—sensations—of kissing the dart-head boy. In all these years, he had never thought to try that. So interesting that he hadn't. At first, it had felt like kissing a gorse bush, all bristly-dry, and then suddenly: There! The hidden burrow, all warm and wet behind the lips. And there! That little pup that lived inside, that so-familiar softness, that heat the Whistler could not generate, could only appreciate in ways they *never would, wafting up from this boy's guts as though from the center of a volcano. It hadn't filled the Whistler—it could never fill him, he could not hold it—but it had reminded him, yet again, of what warmth felt and tasted like.*

Interesting. Yes.

But the kiss hadn't been nearly as interesting as the Asian girl's reaction while he did it. Of course, that might have had something to do with what he was doing to her *at the same moment. But she'd been watching, too. Oh, yes. He could still see her eyes bulging out of her plum-colored face like seeds as he squeezed and squeezed. All that amazed panic, and—this was the best part—it wasn't even mostly about him, or even about dying. It was about her would-be lover kissing her killer, screaming through his open teeth while she clawed uselessly at her hold on this world.*

That girl had seen, *even through her filming eyes. She'd understood what was happening.*

And that had been more than interesting. The astonishment in that poor girl's face—the sheer primal anguish, as everything she thought she knew about love and people she loved fell away with her breath—had positively electrified him.

In fact, it had thrilled the Whistler so much that he hadn't even bothered killing her. He'd danced away instead, skin burning in the sunlight, back into the woods to his darkened truck to dream of the two of them resurfacing inside themselves, looking into each other's faces. What on earth could they have seen there, said to one another?

That's what he'd been dreaming about, surely. And the dream had been delicious.

So why was he awake?

Swaying to the echoing guitars, he glanced toward Mother's seat, which had mostly been his seat when he'd traveled with Mother. His new companion just leaned into the door, slumped in the dark. Around the rim of the blackout shades, the Whistler could see daylight pouring even through the snarled branches in which he'd hidden the truck. And yet he was conscious, tingling, swaying to the guitars.

Guitars?

Spinning to the door, he grappled at the handle, jerked it, and froze again, processing.

It wasn't the music that had woken him. The music was out there, all right; he wasn't imagining that. But it wasn't what had lured him from his dreams. Slowly, he reviewed the last few moments. His mouth opened in astonishment.

Yes, it was true. He was astonished.

Was it possible? How *was it possible? He had seen the trigger pulled, the head exploding, that firework burst of white and bone and teeth and red. He'd watched his poor Destiny fold, ruined, into her mother's lap. And he'd known, in that instant, that he really had loved her, hadn't he? Poor, murdered Destiny. How marvelous they could have been together. And what a poor, bereft Whistler he'd become in that moment, just like in the songs. He'd loved her tender, loved her true, hadn't he? And that explained why he was dreaming—or imagining—that he was hearing her still, hearing her voice, whole weeks after her murder.*

Yes. That was it.

He actually had himself convinced, momentarily. Removing his hands from the door handle, he let his shoulders sink back into themselves and his head tip once more toward the seat in relief. And then he heard her again.

"BOOYYYYYYFRIEEENND!!!!"

This time, his hands positively flew to the door, fumbling, tripping over themselves, his body resisting the orders from his brain because it knew that going out there was going to hurt. With a snarl, he yanked the handle, kicked open the door, and staggered from the truck. Branches clawed at him, and a shaft of light raked like a fingernail down his wrists. He flung up his sleeve and plowed forward toward the clearing.

"Oh, shit!" *someone said, out there. It wasn't his Destiny or even a woman. But there were women with that man, or* a *woman, at least, and also a girl. The Whistler could just see them.*

"Joel, you moron," *the woman said. Laughing? Were they laughing?* "Run!"

And the Whistler, in his confusion, thought he knew that voice, too, though he couldn't place from where. But that voice had also been in his dreams. Lunging, he burst through pines and prickers into the light.

Pain seemed less to crash down on than blaze up in *him, in his face, his wrists, his ears, and not just the exposed places but all over his body. Everywhere the light touched or probed, rashes raised themselves like bites. As though the light itself were biting him. Several seconds passed before he could get his eyes all the way open; when he did, he was sure he would see himself smoking, melting.*

Instead, he saw sun, and daylight colors: deep-pine green, cirrus-cloud white, blinding blue. Even his assailants—three of them: a man, a little girl, a waify young woman—

were just fleeing blotches of color: flying pink dress, blue work overalls on black skin, plain brown hair spattered with sun.

So much color.

The Whistler's heart broke. It did, it surely did.

Falling back into the shadows, he hunched against his truck without climbing into it, his eyes lapping the light, the world in light, sucking it down, as though he were a cat stealing milk. But even here, all the way back in the branches, light hurt. And so, with a mournful sigh, he hoisted himself back into the cab of the Sierra and closed his burning eyes to rest.

Almost immediately, he opened his eyes again. He'd seen what he'd seen, all right: the guy, the girl, the not-quite-girl-anymore, racing away. He'd also heard what he'd heard: his Destiny's voice, he was almost sure of it.

It had sounded so, so like his Destiny's voice.

Also, he knew what the other voice had been, now, and where he'd heard it, and where he'd been: last night, atop the campus Clocktower, listening through the stolen phone, the whistling wind. That was the voice of his new, Still One, who very likely had no idea, yet, that he had met her friends.

Glancing at the mirror, the Whistler checked his greasy hair, finger-combed it, smiled. He felt so much better, all of a sudden. Not only that, he felt hungry. In fact, he realized, he'd been *hungry for days. It was just as Mother had always admonished him, and she really had been a decent sort of mother, all in all: "You're still such a child," she'd cluck, wiping his face clean with one of her lavender-scented handkerchiefs. "Never once stop Whistling and dreaming long enough to recognize you need to eat."*

So that was one more thing to do tonight.

But not the only or the most important thing. Not even close. And these other things Mother could never have understood, even if he could have found the words or the Whistle to explain them to her. It would have been . . . like explaining music to the deaf. She simply didn't have it in her.

Or, he thought—and this thought actually startled him, and made him sad—maybe her problem had been that he *wasn't in her, wasn't her Destiny, never had been, and she hadn't figured that out until the very end. Although, without question, she'd known at the end.*

And now, here he was smiling again. What a sweet, complicated day to be alive for, and in. What a wondrous town, full of dart-horned boys and their blackberry-mouthed would-be lovers, who would never be lovers. Who looked at the Whistler, saw in an instant what none of the others—not Mother, not Aunt Sally, none of them—had discovered. Had seen what he could and should do, for and to them, and opened their blackberry mouths wider still. So he could fill them.

They wanted to play. They all did, and some of them even knew it. And he was hungry, and lonely. And he'd been so very bored for so very long. And his new, Still One was waiting for him, though even he wasn't quite sure what he'd do to, or for, or with *her, yet.*

So. Tonight, in just a few hours, when the light went, he'd come out to play. Then they'd all find out together.

13

It was at least a little Amanda's fault, Rebecca thought just a few hours later, stumbling away from Halfmoon House with that dry-ice reprimand still crackling in her ears and her hands clutched to her chest and her mouth tingling, buzzing with words she'd never imagined she would actually say, had really said, could not unsay.

Had she really just said that? Did she even believe it?

They'd poured back into the yard, she and Joel and Trudi, riding the waves of surf guitar thundering from Joel's Bluetooth speaker, and washed up sweating and laughing at the long, wooden table in the kitchen. "Malts," Joel declared, setting down the speaker and abruptly, with a glance around him, lowering the volume. Then, just as abruptly, he turned it back up. "This calls for malts. Rebecca, to the pantry."

Hoisting Trudi onto his shoulders—and Trudi let him, and she actually laughed, succumbing for the first time to the Halfmoon House magic, which was mostly Joel's magic—he swayed back out the door toward the shed. He would come back, Rebecca knew, with the special-day sundae glasses Amanda let him trot out only on birthdays and rare celebratory Saturdays, and also one of the family-size cartons of generic French vanilla he kept in the industrial freezer. Rebecca, meanwhile, did as instructed, ducking into the pantry to remove the front two rows of Amanda's everyday spices—the basil and oregano, peppercorns and rosemary, all in their identical green jars in perfect alphabetical order—to the treat-powders behind them. All of those were Joel's, and just shoved back there: two mismatched tins of strawberry Quik; an Ovaltine canister Rebecca suspected was the *same* Ovaltine canister that had occupied that particular spiderwebbed corner since *she'd* lived here; a lone king-size Hershey bar; and all the way to the left, fresh and unopened and impossibly free of webs or dust, as though Joel had conjured it into being by calling its name, a single jar of milk shake malt.

She emerged from the pantry with that perfect sour-grain taste already on her tongue, and she was thinking, for some reason, about Jack and the 'Lenes: Marlene and her *True Detective* mags tucked inside her organic chem textbook, her riot of red hair and too-loud laugh; Kaylene and her leggings and K-pop crushes and Pac-Man backpack and reproductive rights crusades and surprising smiles that split her pouty mouth wide open; and Jack, with his fake mustaches and his beer gut (which was actually a milk gut, although he had indeed drunk more beer lately) and his incessant teasing and coercing. All three of them perpetually drawing her closer to them, out into the world. They'd all taken root right in the center of Rebecca's life, before it had even occurred to her that she *had* a center, or a life. And now, here they were in her mind, dancing and 'Lening.

In her ears, she could still hear that voice from last night, the one on the phone, from Lonely Street, coiling through all these other, happier voices that buzzed inside her like summer bees. But it didn't poison them, couldn't poison them, because these were *her* bees, from her hive. This was the hive she belonged to, had helped make.

Just another twenty-four hours, she was thinking, shaking her head. Just a crazy, full, careening sort of day. A normal day? Was that what she'd just had? Was this her life settling into place around her? And accelerating? She opened her mouth, started to shout that she had the malt, what was taking everyone so long, when she heard the murmuring. With her free hand on the worktable, Rebecca stopped, malt half-extended in front of her, and listened.

"Those trailers?" Amanda all but hissed, just outside the open screen door, her voice low, laced with warning. "After all those times I've told them—*we've* told them—not to go there, you just *took* them?"

"I didn't take them," Joel said, and from his sigh, Rebecca knew exactly how he was standing and what he was doing, even though she couldn't see them out by the foot of the stoop-stairs from where she stood. He was giving her the oh-come-on-Amanda smile, reaching for his wife's hand. "I *found* them there."

"And having found them, in a place we've repeatedly told them, for their own safety, they are never, ever, *ever* supposed to go, you and your new playmate—"

"By which you mean the woman on the radio? My music?"

"How about, the woman you devote infinitely more of your time and affection to than me?" Amanda snarled, and Rebecca swayed in place, almost dropped the malt jar.

"Oh, for Christ's sake," Joel muttered. "Keep your voice down, please. Not in front of the—"

There was a scrambling, and a "Trudi, wait" from Joel, and a "goddammit."

Then Trudi exploded into the kitchen, racing for the stairs. Instinctively, Rebecca stepped into her path, putting out her hands as she knelt. But Trudi just aimed a furious kick at Rebecca's arms and darted around her. Rebecca heard her hurtling up the stairs, heard Danni say, "Whoa, who let the—*ow,* shit!" Then doors slammed, one after the other.

Rebecca stayed where she'd knelt. Any second, Amanda would appear, somehow yanking her ponytail even tighter, grunting at Rebecca to get up and go get Trudi. Eventually, when he'd recovered from his latest lashing, Joel would follow, waving a pack of paper napkins like a makeshift surrender flag.

This time, though, neither Amanda nor Joel appeared. They stayed in the yard and went right on arguing.

"You found them by the trailers," Amanda said. "And instead of telling them both off—that little girl's going to get herself hurt, and you know it, she doesn't listen, and Rebecca, of all people, should know better—instead of telling them off, or just getting them the fuck out of there, you, as usual, decided—"

"To enjoy the moment. To have a little fun with our girls."

Whatever Amanda said next, she said quietly. Rebecca couldn't hear it. Not until Amanda said it again.

"They're not *our* girls."

"Right. Got it. They're not our girls. Just the girls we're raising. Yes, Amanda, I decided—"

"That it would be funny. That's pretty much your prime criterion for decision making, isn't it?"

"Well, yes. Maybe it is. Sometimes. And you know what? It *was* funny."

"You think everything's funny, or should be. Don't you, Joel?"

Suddenly, Joel had a new tone, too, one Rebecca had never heard him use. She stood, almost went straight out the door and down the steps to hug him, since she knew his wife wouldn't do it.

"Most things," he said. Almost whimpered. So softly.

"And there it is, isn't it? There's the difference between us. Because I don't think almost any of it is funny, Joel. I don't think I ever did."

"Maybe that's why we're such a good team."

Somehow, the sigh Amanda unleashed next alarmed Rebecca even more than Joel's broken pleading. The Amanda Rebecca knew did not sigh, certainly not like that: as though something had been ripped out of her, yanked free like a knife from her heart.

But unlike her husband, when she spoke again, she sounded exactly the way she always did: flat and controlled. "Are we,

Joel? Have we ever been? In any way? Is that how you read the messages our lives together have given us?"

And that—finally, absurdly, after all these years in these people's house, in their lives and their company—was when Rebecca understood. It had taken her only seven years to register why Amanda and Joel treated each other so distantly, and why they'd built this place and spent their days doing what they did, collecting other people's orphaned children and preparing them—ruthlessly, on the one hand, joyfully on the other—for living alone.

As much as her caller from the night before had rattled Rebecca, gotten in her ears and her dreams, he hadn't reduced her to tears. *Oh, Joel,* she thought, wiping at her face, wondering how even the ruthless world she'd been introduced to all too soon—at four, on the night her parents didn't make it home to the home she couldn't even really remember—could be ruthless enough to deprive these two people of *that.* Of children. And then—precisely because they couldn't have children, and had wanted them so badly—of each other.

Amanda was coming. Her steps were firm, unmistakable, taking her straight up the grooves she'd worn in her stairs toward her kitchen, her pre-dinner tasks. Rebecca didn't want to face her. She just couldn't, not yet, not knowing what she knew now. She could already imagine Amanda's reaction to anything Rebecca might say, so vividly that Amanda might as well have already said it:

"*Seriously, Rebecca the Caretaker? Rebecca the Legendarily Empathetic Observer? You really just now figured this out?*"

Her first instinct was to head upstairs, because that's

what she had done when she'd lived here. It was also possibly the right thing to do now. She could stand outside Trudi's room—which had once been her own room—and knock quietly, over and over, until Trudi let her in. She'd calm the little girl down and tell her not to worry, because there really wasn't anything to worry about. Not from the masters of Halfmoon House. Not for the girls they harbored here.

Instead, keeping her head low, Rebecca slipped past Amanda, out the back door into the late-afternoon murk. The sun was a smear of yellow across a sky the color of unprimed canvas, and the trees seemed to sag beneath the watery weight of the air. It was time for her to go, anyway; she was due at Jess's house in half an hour. She glanced around for Joel, figured he'd retreated to his shed, and started fast across the grass. Gnats materialized as though they'd been hiding in her hair. Their whine sounded like a leak in her head, as though some of her was escaping.

Are we, Joel? Have we ever been?

Then, abruptly, there he was under the live oak at the edge of the yard, with a rake in his hand that he'd picked up somewhere, having apparently forgotten the malts he'd promised Trudi, the spell he'd been stopped from casting, in mid-cast. He was just standing next to the path with his chin halfway down on his chest and his head tilted sideways and his eyes half-closed and the rake in the long grass like the blade on an oar: the ferryman of Halfmoon House, forever rowing his rescued charges back and forth to and from the world he'd left, without ever meaning to.

What Rebecca did next was not only unplanned but almost unconscious; it just happened. Striding straight up to

Joel—the only father-type figure she had ever considered a father, and still quite possibly her closest friend—she grabbed him by the sweat-soaked shoulders, caught his downturned eyes with her own, and said, "Joel. You should leave here. While you still can. This is . . . You've been so good to me. You both have. But she's killing you."

And what stunned her most, immediately afterward, as her mouth snapped shut and she realized what she'd said and how badly she'd overstepped and how little she actually understood about this man, whom she loved, and his icy wife—whom she also loved—was the way Joel just sagged into himself. His head folded into his neck. His arms seemed to swing off the joints in his shoulders and dangle, and his legs twitched, went slack. It was as though he were a scarecrow she'd unpinned from its cross, set free, and so transformed back into raggedy clothes and straw, with nothing in them.

"Oh, Bec," he whispered. He was gazing at her as though he were an old man, as though she were a little girl. "You really need to . . ." But he couldn't seem to finish that sentence, or didn't want to.

Rebecca had already fallen back a step, was waving a hand in the air as though she could wipe away what she'd said, erase the whole last five minutes of her life and start them over. And the worst part was, her brain had already completed his sentence for him, and it went on completing it, over and over.

Leave. Joel was going to tell her *she* should leave.

At least his voice had been gentle. Amanda's, on the other hand—which came from the steps, where Amanda now stood just outside the door with her arms folded and that gaze locked on Rebecca like a rifle sight—was anything but.

"Quite enough of *that,* I think," she said.

Rebecca sucked in a horrified breath, but Joel recoiled as though he'd been shot. As though he'd been the one who'd said his wife was killing him, not Rebecca.

"Amanda, she was only—"

"Shut up," said Amanda, and Joel did.

Then she just stood there in the shadow of her house: a small and pale woman, a single string of hair stuck to her cheek like a strand of web she'd walked through, faded button-up work shirt crisp under her apron, starchy and yet shapeless as a hospital gown. Rebecca wouldn't have thought it possible for Amanda's eyes—or anyone's eyes—to look *more* remote, but they did, now: emotionless as a bird's, blue as a lake. And empty.

"You should go," Joel said, at Rebecca's elbow. He no longer sounded gentle, or even like Joel. "Really. Get out of here."

Tears blurred Rebecca's vision again, gummy and awful. She could neither blink them out nor get them to fall. At her sides, her hands were shaking. And in a totally different way, her lips . . . her mouth . . . good God, her mouth . . . which kept betraying her . . .

"Amanda," she managed, "I'm so sorry. I didn't . . . I don't even know what I . . ."

"Yep," Amanda said, almost to herself, and cocked her head. Like a bird, again. "But of course you wouldn't, really. How could you know? You've never really had one of your own."

For one ridiculous moment, Rebecca thought she meant

a *man,* which was almost funny, and true enough, in its way, not counting her one and only high school guy, Darren, who'd lured her out for a handful of sweet orchard nights that last summer before he went off to Dartmouth and never came back.

But Amanda didn't mean a man, and she was almost talking to herself, now. "Not a real home, I mean," she murmured, and Rebecca almost staggered in place, grabbed her own ribs, her fingers splaying across them as though plugging holes.

"Don't," she said. "Please don't."

"So you have no idea what losing one costs." And with that, Amanda turned and disappeared back into the house.

Rebecca swayed, heard herself make a noise—half whimper, half calling out, though even she wasn't sure to whom—and by the time she got control of her throat again, smashed her tears flat with her eyelashes, and looked up, Joel had gone, too. She caught just a glimpse of his back, the rake driving into the ground and propelling him forward as he vanished into the woods. For a moment, an entirely different, disconnected panic rose in Rebecca. *Not there,* she thought. *Don't go back in there.*

Then she was stumbling away from Halfmoon House, down the lane toward town. Her whole body throbbed with guilt and confusion, and her eyes kept filling, no matter how furiously she blinked.

"So you have no idea what losing one costs . . ."

What had she done? Rebecca's arms still encircled her own chest. Her breathing came in ragged gasps, though she wasn't exactly crying. Every motion she made drew air across the nerves in her ears, set them tingling all over again, ringing with words—her own, Amanda's, her midnight caller's—and also with whistling. Her caller's whistling.

What had she done?

She barely even registered that she'd made it back to Campus Avenue, and so had to stop momentarily to get her bearings. She looked right toward the bank and the Lutheran church and the movie theater, left down the block toward Starkey's, the bus stop, the road north that wound all the way through the woods, up Maine into Canada. For the thousandth time in her life, she thought about turning that way and just setting off. She could simply flag the bus when it passed, climb aboard, and disappear. It would be so easy, would hardly be noticed.

But she wasn't going to do that. Not even if Amanda wanted her to. Not even if Joel did. She had promises to keep.

Prying her arms from her body, clamping her mouth shut, and shaking herself as free as she could get from these last horrible hours, she turned toward Jess's house. When the figure stepped out of the shadows of the bank building and grabbed her, she was too tired even to scream. Then it spun her around, and her first thought was Joel, and her second was the guy from the trailer, whoever that had been who had flung open the door of that black truck in the bushes as she and Joel and Trudi fled.

"Rebecca," Jack said, gripping her so hard that she half-thought he might hoist her in the air, throw her across his shoulders, and make off with her.

She tried to wrench free and failed. Her heart was flailing, and she sucked breath out of the sodden air, which felt like breathing through a pillowcase.

"Jack?"

He looked awful. Pizza sauce—at least, Rebecca hoped it was pizza sauce—streaked the entire left side of his bowling shirt. It was the same shirt from last night. He still had the dart, too; the suction end was sticking out of his pocket like a broken-off antenna, over the cursive *Herman* stitched into the fabric. His hair, face, everything about him seemed rumpled, as though he hadn't slept in his own skin. As though he'd left his skin last night, and now he couldn't get himself properly settled.

"Did Kaylene call you?" he said.

"If you let go of my arms, maybe I can check."

Glancing down, Jack registered surprise—or something even worse?—and dropped his hands to his sides. "I'm sorry."

"What's going on?" Rebecca fumbled in her pocket, pulled out her phone.

"So you haven't talked to her?"

"I turned it off so I could sleep." She pressed the End button and keyed in her passcode. "Wow. She called like twelve times. I forgot to turn it back on. God, Jack, is she okay, what—"

"We were drinking," he said. "A lot."

Weirdly, it was the panic in his voice that calmed her. This, it turned out, was the middle of a crisis, and therefore her most familiar place, the closest thing she had left to a home, maybe the closest thing she'd ever had. She clung to that idea as though to the trunk of a tree.

"There was this guy. We were—*she* was—Rebecca, she was kissing me, and I was sloppy drunk when he showed up, and—"

"When *who* showed up?"

"Right. Exactly. That's what I'm trying to tell you. I don't know who he was. I don't even know what happened. I can't quite remember. But I know he . . . he was grabbing Kaylene, I mean *hurting* her, and I wanted to help, I tried to help, but I couldn't even figure . . . I mean, I was passing out . . . I think . . . and I think she thinks . . . but I—"

"Jack. Is she all right? Tell me she's all right." Even Rebecca was surprised by the evenness of her tone. To her amazement, her calm was spreading, settling not only her but also unfolding over Jack like ice across a lake (and suddenly, she understood something else about Amanda, about why she was the way she was, but she filed that thought away). He quieted and stood there a few seconds, just breathing. He hadn't quite been looking at her this whole time—he'd aimed his eyes over her shoulder, or down at his feet—but now he met her gaze.

"That's what I'm here to tell you," he said. "*She* is all right. And I'm not."

"You're not okay?"

"Huh? No. Wait. Kaylene's okay. Although I think she actually thinks I . . . Anyway, she's fine. And I'm . . ." He grabbed her arms again, as hard as before. "I need you to know I'm not."

"Ow. Jack, you're—"

"Rebecca, I'm so, so not. I mean, it'd be okay if I was, and I guess maybe I could be, or I could have been, except I *can't* be—"

"Jack, could you please let go and—"

"—because I'm way too into you."

Everything in Rebecca went from calm to numb: her arms where Jack was clutching them; her mouth, which had taken to blurting out thoughts she wasn't even sure she was having; her ears, where Amanda's parting words still rang like reverberations from a gong.

"What?" she said.

Then Jack did the thing Jack did best, the thing she loved him for: he smiled. The smile looked desperate, too young, helpless, and all the more endearing for that. "Whoops," he said, sounding so small. "I didn't mean to just announce that."

For a while, they stood together on the sidewalk. The late-afternoon town-traffic—mostly bikes, the shop owners locking their doors and heading behind their buildings for their cars—rumbled and buzzed around them. The weak, too-warm daylight weakened further without getting cooler, tinting toward gray. *I should kiss him,* Rebecca thought, and her cheeks flared as though she'd lit flames under them. But she made no move to do that. He didn't, either, didn't seem to want to right this second, despite what he'd said. And she was still sorting through this whole insane day. And whatever she was seeing in Jack's eyes right now, it wasn't just hope or affection or attraction or relief.

Was that fear?

In the end, what she told him was, "You look like I feel."

"Let me come babysitting with you."

"What? No, I don't think—"

"Jess won't mind."

"You know Jess? How do you—"

"I asked her."

"You *asked* her? When did you even . . ."

There it was again. That helpless, instinctive Jack-grin. A shaft of light, with the dust of everything else dancing inside it. "I'll be back," he said. "I'll meet you at Jess's. I'm going to get us food. And Operation."

"Operation?"

"The game. The board game? It's perfect for this night. No one can take *anything* more seriously than it needs to be taken while putting someone's spleen back in their liver."

"I don't think that's where spleens go."

"Clearly, Rebecca, you have not played enough Operation in your life. I have a cure for that. See you in a bit. Bye."

Just like that, he was gone, head down, gaze lowered as he burrowed straight across the street toward campus and his room, leaving Rebecca in the dimming twilight, hands lifted halfway to her ears. It was as though the summer gnats had found a way in there, laid eggs, and now her whole head erupted in noise, in words, her own, her caller's, Trudi's, Jack's, Joel's. Amanda's.

. . . because I'm too into you . . . what losing one costs . . . people worth talking to, staying up late . . .

Launching herself forward, Rebecca crossed Campus Ave and continued toward the cul-de-sac where Jess and her family had rented their house. She kept wanting to put her palms over her ears, as though that would help, and the third or fourth time she actually started to do that, she realized she was still holding her phone. She glanced at the screen.

Twelve missed calls, all from Kaylene. What had Jack said? "*I'm not. I can't be. I think she thinks . . .* " And why had he looked so scared?

She glanced around, hoping to catch sight of Jack, call him back to her so she could ask what on earth had happened. But Jack wasn't on the sidewalk or across the street. At the mouth of the path toward Halfmoon House, the evergreens trembled like just-closed curtains. Jack lived on campus, though; he wouldn't have gone that way.

Raising the phone again, Rebecca finally registered that she was seriously late. "Shit," she said aloud, and hurried down the block, jamming her phone back in her pocket and willing everybody in her head to *shut up*. All she wanted was to get to work, get her work done, get Jess's baby settled. Then maybe she could figure out what the hell was going on with her and, seemingly, everyone around her. Put her spleen back in her liver.

I'm way too into you.

Her heart hurt, and it just kept pounding.

Late though she was, she stopped, as usual, at the foot of the steps leading up to Jess's porch and took a moment to stare up at the house. It was, in truth, just another two-story clapboard structure, pale blue, essentially identical to all the other clapboard structures in East Dunham and in towns a hundred miles in any direction. The only things that marked it, externally, were the splotchy patches—and Rebecca was convinced there were more of them every time she came, spreading like a rash—where the blue paint had crumbled away, revealing wood that couldn't actually be as blackened as it appeared. And it really was her imagination that the place seemed to be melting, somehow, sagging at the corners and spreading into its own foundations. It had been inspected multiple times. Rebecca knew because she'd asked, and also because she'd gotten to know Jess. And Jess would never have settled her son here, otherwise.

But Rebecca wasn't imagining the sounds. She could hear those even from out here. In fact, she could hear them more clearly out here: that whispering with no words, like wind trapped in the rafters; that rustling and settling; scratch-and-skittering. At least she wasn't hearing any thumps, today. Not yet, anyway. There weren't thumps, most days, although Rebecca had heard more than one over the course of the past few weeks.

"Squirrels," Jess had said dismissively, the first time Rebecca had asked. Actually, that had been the second time. The first time Rebecca asked, Jess had said, "Hear what?"

"Squirrels in your attic?" Rebecca had prodded. "You're good with that?"

"Squirrels. Mice. Whatever. It's not my house. Don't go up there. It's not safe."

As opposed to Halfmoon House, at the moment, Rebecca thought. *Or the Crisis Center. Or her own head, which was the only place she'd been* certain *was safe for most of her life; the one place she'd truly thought she knew.*

Operation, she thought. And, *What have I done?* And, *Jack . . .*

She was still standing there, half-listening to the house, hands crossed over her heart, when the front door opened and Jess appeared. She'd just come out of the shower, apparently, and as usual, hadn't bothered drying her hair, which drooped, limp and dark, down her neck into the collar of her button-up shirt. She had her functional tan work bag—not even remotely a purse—slung over one small, sturdy shoulder. Her pale face looked grooved, as though she'd just been crying. In fact, Jess always looked like she'd just been crying, though Rebecca had never actually seen her do it.

"Rebecca, where have you been? A-mad-da's going to kill me, come on, I'm late. And Eddie's been crying for you. Get in here."

"A-mad-da," Rebecca repeated. "That's . . . the best nickname I've ever heard." She'd thought she was about to smile, but the smile didn't come. Tears came.

"Rebecca, what on—"

"It's okay," she said. Jess had to go. And inside the house, Eddie was crying. And it really was possible, Rebecca realized, that he was doing that for her. Sweet little boy. Jess's sweet, lonely little boy.

Blowing breath—and guilt, and hurt, and words, and noise, and whatever else she could rattle loose—out of her mouth, Rebecca nodded. "I'm coming," she said, and started up the stairs.

14

(THREE WEEKS EARLIER)

That whole day after they left Concerto Woods, during their endless, shadeless crawl up the freeways, Sophie crouched as best she could against the passenger door and kept her suffering to herself. But after the eighth or ninth stop so Jess could once again feed Eddie, cuddle Eddie, try once more to shut the poor kid up, Sophie couldn't take it anymore.

"Please," she said, modulating her voice, trying her best to sound like she remembered herself sounding. As far as she could tell, she got pretty close. "Jess. Can I sit in back? I'll be good. I promise. I mean it."

"No." Jess buckled Eddie back in his car seat. He was hiccupping, fussing, but not screaming right that second. That was something, anyway.

"Why not?"

Still leaning into the car, Jess reached out to brush Benny's bushy head with her fingers. Then, for the first time since leaving the grave they'd dug, she looked at Sophie.

"Why?" Her voice came out absolutely steady, not a trace of waver. She didn't even wipe her face as more tears poured down it.

Sophie started to whimper, but curbed that immediately. This was Jess she was talking to. "More shade. Hurts less."

"Then definitely no," Jess snapped. But she paused there, bent at the waist like a tipped-over tree that hadn't quite been chopped through. Almost, though. She had a hand on both of her boys and her eyes closed.

In another life, Sophie thought—the one she'd had a month ago—the sight of Jess like that would have broken her heart. Even now, the words bubbling up in her brain seemed to come from some primal place, somewhere so fundamentally Sophie *that not even her own son's death could drown it. Let alone her own.*

I'm so sorry. Mom.

That's what she thought, and didn't say.

Letting go of her boys, Jess pushed upright. "Know what? Fuck it. I can't stand you next to me anymore." She moved fast around the front of the car and yanked Sophie's door open. "Unbuckle."

Sophie did, then stuck out her arms like a little girl asking to be carried. Jess just stepped back, arms folded. Gingerly, Sophie swung down from the seat onto the gravel shoulder of the road, into the merciful shade of an overhanging oak. Only then did it occur to her that Jess might have parked in this spot on purpose, to give Sophie shade. Was that possible?

From the look on Jess's face, Sophie doubted it. As a matter of fact, Sophie now wondered if Jess was about to leave her here. Maybe that wasn't such a bad idea, all things considered. She pictured herself hanging out in this spot awhile, until evening, then leaning out of these shadows to hitchhike: a tree stump with thumbs and teeth.

Abruptly, she laughed.

Safe in the shade, she watched Jess half-lift, half-drag Benny to the front. He wasn't going to be any more comfortable up there than she was, Sophie realized. She watched him settle, try to squirm into a position that didn't hurt, find none, and give up. There he sagged, Jess's sweet and fluffy lawn-gnome of a man, all buckled in and helpless. He was looking not at Jess but around her, at Sophie, as though he thought she might eat him. As though at least some of him wanted her to. He couldn't help that, of course. Poor, hurt little lawn-gnome man.

"Hop up," Jess directed, pointing Sophie into the space next to Eddie's car seat. "You so much as touch my kid—"

"Natalie's kid."

"You so much as look at him—"

"You think I'd hurt Eddie? My dead best friend's son? My dead son's best friend? The one friend he got to have in his entire life?"

"You touch him, I'll burn you alive. Got it?"

Grinning, Sophie knew, was a bad idea, a rebellious-teen impulse, the kind of snotty response she'd always trained on her own mother, never on Jess. But at that moment, she couldn't help it. "So. His side, my side. Got it." She clambered back in the car.

"Good."

"Sure thing, Mom."

"Don't call me that."

"Hey, Mom," Sophie said, as Jess yanked the seat belt as tight as it would go across Sophie's chest. "Got a spare top? This one's a little"—she flicked at one blood-soaked shoulder with a thumb and forefinger—"crusty."

Jess just slammed the door shut, went around back this time. But she stopped on the other side, opened that door, kissed Eddie, then rummaged in one of her duffel bags and flung Sophie a T-shirt without looking at her. The shirt was a Walgreens special, Sophie would have recognized it anywhere: pastel peach, scratchy cotton, no doubt bought half price, or maybe half of half price, given Jess's employee discount. It had probably come off the exact same rack where Jess had gotten almost all her own clothes and most of Natalie's, at least before Natalie discovered Goodwill and decided she had taste, and that taste mattered.

My clothes, too, *Sophie remembered,* when my mother was too horsed up to bother, which was most of the time.

"Thanks, Mom," she said once more, to the slamming door, with only a little of the irony she was sure Jess heard, if she heard Sophie at all.

Sophie unbuckled long enough to peel her own blouse off her skin. It came away with tiny popping sounds, as though she were unzipping. There was still dried blood all over her body. But the gouges and bite marks the Whistler had left in her shoulders and breasts were already healing, on their way to gone. She ran a hand over her ribs, which were cold in the open air but broiling in the spot where the sun lapped against them.

Then the car was moving. And Benny was looking at her again, using the mirror; he was also desperately trying to avoid looking at her, trying so hard that the veins in his neck had popped up in his skin like winched cables. On impulse—after all, it was torn and bloody, too—Sophie unhooked her bra and slid it down her arms. Smiling, she lowered Jess's shirt over her head, taking her time, stretching high. It was way too small, of course, and had never before in its cheap-shirt life been filled the way she filled it now. Hideous little poor woman's shirt, scratchy on her skin, and yet impeccably clean. How, even in these circumstances, did Jess keep everything she owned so clean, like new skin?

And right then, for the first time since the graveside, Sophie felt absence in her arms again, and on her chest, in all the places where her Roo had rested.

She glanced sidelong at Eddie, whose eyes were open, drinking in the trees and the sky. Already, he was turning as watchful as his grandmother, though nowhere near as silent.

Goddamn you, *she thought, the words a rifle blast aimed at everyone, all of them, everything. Then the moment passed, and the sun seared into her neck, and Sophie hunched as low as she could go and closed her eyes.*

Every time the road turned, sun splashed across her arms or her stumps. It never even soaked into her skin, just sizzled atop it like oil on scorched pavement. Finally, she couldn't take it anymore, unbuckled again, and somehow slid down the door until she was flat on the seat. Out of desperation, for distraction, she reached out, shoved aside one of Jess's clanking bags of crap, found her legs, and started stroking them. They were cold, and even crustier than the rest of her. She'd been stroking for some time before she realized she could feel *herself.*

Not her legs under her fingers, but her fingers on her legs, shooting off tingles everywhere they touched. That sensation transfixed her for so long that she didn't even notice right away that Jess was talking. But Jess was, and once she'd started, she couldn't seem to stop.

She was telling Benny everything, Sophie realized. Trying to explain what had happened on the beach, and why she'd murdered her daughter. That was certainly interesting, in its way, worth listening to, and became even more so when she looked up and caught Benny stealing another glance over his shoulder at her. This time, he looked mostly terrified, like a little boy eying the lioness at the zoo. He looked away the instant he realized she'd noticed. But a few seconds later, he did it again. And that was an amusing new game, something else that took her mind, for just a few more seconds, off the sun pouring in the driver's-side windows, searing the open ends of her stumps without cauterizing them. Eventually, Sophie squeezed her eyes shut again, forced herself still, and made herself listen to Jess, because listening—to anything—was so, so much better than feeling.

Also it really was remarkable how much Jess had right, how much she'd intuited or maybe been told. Maybe she and Natalie had had one last confab-gossip session back on the beach—Natalie always had told her mother way too much—right before Jess shot her in the face.

It was Benny, though, who got off the best line. He did it with a Jess-like directness, though in a shakier voice.

"What are you going to feed her, Jess? She's going to have to eat, you know. Sooner or later. We can't just stop at a pet shop and buy her crickets."

That made Sophie laugh out loud, which caused Jess to glare into the rearview mirror. Benny turned again, too, and so, sun and all, Sophie rolled up on her hip on the seat, propping on one elbow as Jess's tiny top inched up her side.

"Don't look at her," Jess snapped. And then, to Sophie, she added, "Shut up. Lie down. How long?"

"What? I didn't say any—"

"How long until you have to eat?"

"Oh. Hmm," Sophie murmured. But she didn't say anything else, because suddenly, she couldn't. Instead, she was transfixed by the memory—specifically, of the smell—of the mini-mart where she'd eaten last. The place where she'd . . . Finished, as the Whistler had put it. She'd been covered in blood then, too. Her own, again, just like now. Although some of the blood, that time, had belonged to the deer that Natalie had plowed through with the GTO. The reek she was remembering now was mostly that, but also old Slurpee, reheated hot dog meat. And the counter guy, even from across the store, air-guitaring away to "More Than a Feeling" in his logo-less uniform cap, at the moment she'd caught his eye. After that, he hadn't air-guitared much; mostly, he'd fluttered like a butterfly in a net as she'd beckoned him around the counter, eased him to his knees, rested him against her thighs. She'd been able to smell him then, all right, as she'd gently removed his cap, smoothed his hair, which was thick and dark. "You are lovely," she'd whispered

over him, again and again, like a blessing, right up until the moment she'd ended him. Drained him like a Big Gulp.

Was this remorse she was feeling now?

Shouldn't there have been more of it?

"Sophie. How long?*"*

"Not for a while," she said softly, her fingers on her severed legs and her eyes on the seat back. "At least a few weeks. I think."

"Okay," said Jess. "That's how long you have to live. Or convince me you should."

"Right. Got it. Thanks, God."

"That's right. That's exactly how you should think of me. Except that I am kinder than any God you will ever meet."

Probably true, *Sophie thought, and this time kept her grin to herself.* Because I will never meet Him.

That was the last time any of them spoke until well after dusk. Even Eddie apparently slept. A canopy of shadows slid all the way over the car and stayed there, and Sophie opened her eyes. She could feel her skin, hands, her whole body unfolding into the twilight like one of those ghost-white, gorgeous plants at the nursery where her mother had once managed to hold a job for three years straight: night-blooming jasmine, night queen flower.

Her hand had never left her legs, but now it stretched all the way down to her poor battered knees, and so bumped against the paper bags Jess had stashed against the seat back. The car was crawling through traffic, barely moving. If she lifted her head, Sophie could see the reflection of Jess's face glowering in the windshield. Benny's face seemed to have frozen in a rictus smile. Possibly, he was mulling everything Jess had told him. Possibly, he was just in pain. Possibly, he was still trying to keep himself from turning around again.

The paper bags clattered quietly when Sophie rustled them. Her fingers crawled over their open mouths, slipped inside.

"What are you doing?"

You really had to give it to the woman, *Sophie thought.* She missed nothing. *"You're amazing, Jess. You really are."*

"Sophie, what are you doing?"

"What is *all this?" Digging deep, Sophie pulled a handful of cassettes out of the nearest bag. "Whoa."*

"Get your hands off those. Those are Natalie's things. They're all I have left to remind me of—"

"I made *these for her," Sophie snapped, and it was as though she'd wrung Jess's neck, the way that woman gurgled to silence. Sophie held up a tape, opened the case, slid out the J-card. "I made these," she whispered. Then she whistled. "Man, look at this playlist."*

"You didn't make all of them," Jess muttered.

That was true, as it turned out. The next tape Sophie examined was labeled NATALIE AND JOE, 1989. *And the next:* NATALIE LADY JANE GRAY, 2002, *whatever that meant.*

Sophie dumped those cassettes back in the bag and returned to the J-card she'd found. She'd written out these song titles more than a decade ago, drawn the little yellow and purple flowers along the border. A lifetime ago, as it had turned out.

Two lifetimes.

Not including her Roo.

Shaking her head hard, she made herself focus on the

playlist. Her voice came out almost as a taunt, and she didn't care. "Seriously, Jess. Listen to this progression. 'Eve of Destruction,' followed by 'Radiation Vibe,' followed by 'Heart of Glass.' I was thirteen *when I made this mix. Natalie was the music snot, but* I *should have been the DJ. I could have—"*

"Why?*" Jess erupted, pounding the steering wheel and stomping on the brakes as she swiveled all the way around. Horns blared behind them, but Jess paid no attention. "I mean it, Sophie. Explain it to me. You were* good girls. *You were* such *good girls. You took care of each other. You took care of your responsibilities. You made your mistakes, and then made good worlds out of them. How could you be so reckless? How you could you do that? How could you do it to your* children*? In the backseat of Natalie's fucking car? With a total stranger?"*

"He was a pretty hot stranger," Sophie murmured. Way down under her ribs, something new was sprouting, called up by the heat in Natalie's mother's voice.

"That's what you've got, Sophie? That's your response? He was hot?"

"Well, he was. At least, I think he was. To tell you the truth, I have trouble remembering. So did your daughter, by the way."

"Great. Thank you, Soph. Appreciate that. It's a comfort to know that both *of you were too smashed even to notice the moment that defined the rest of both of your lives. And your children's lives. And my life. And the people you hurt or are going to hurt and—"*

"I wasn't that smashed," Sophie said. The song titles on the J-card beat against her eyes, buzzed in her ears like

whispered words through a tin can. "Come on Eileen." "Sisters of Mercy." "Cat Scratch Fever."

Okay, that last progression was a little weird.

Horns honked. Lights from the turnpike tollbooth up ahead crawled over the hood toward the windshield. Sophie saw a gray-haired cashier leaning out of her little enclosed capsule, peering down into each passing car.

Abruptly, she scrabbled upright, shoving at the seat in front of her. "Holy shit, help me get my legs."

"What?"

"Are you kidding? Jess, what do you think that woman's going to see? You want to explain this to her? Give me my fucking legs."

"Help her get her legs," Jess snapped at Benny. She stopped the car dead again, ignoring the cannonade of honks as she leaned sideways, pretending to rummage for cash or something.

Somehow, Benny struggled out of his seat belt, gasping in pain as he got himself twisted around and up on his knees. "I can't reach," he said, stretching his arms over the back.

"Me, either," said Sophie, trying to balance on one arm so she didn't tip all the way over and roll into the well on top of her legs. Her head hit Benny's. "Jesus Christ, hurry up," she said. She felt his breath on her shoulder as both of them lunged forward. His head practically buried itself in her chest. For one moment, both of them were almost laughing. She was actually *laughing.*

Then her left leg popped up, as though it had taken action on its own, and settled in her hands. She slid it into place, turned it slightly, felt the tendons catch. They didn't hold—not yet—but bumped against each other, almost seemed to clamp together. Like garter-belt straps.

"Ooh," she said.

Benny had her other leg, now; he jammed that into her chest as though it were an oar and she an alligator.

Which she had been, come to think of it, remembering her night with Natalie in the Okefenokee.

And that had occurred all of three nights ago? Four? How was that even . . .

"Hurry," Jess hissed.

Ignoring that, Sophie slid the right leg home, settled back, and closed her eyes. Jess was leaking again. It really was more like leaking than crying. Sophie could tell she was doing it by the way she was murmuring, the phrases she kept repeating like little prayers: "You were such good girls. Such good girls."

"Wipe your face," Sophie whispered. "Smile."

"Don't you tell me what—"

"Sssh. Oh."

Sometime later, as thunderstorms rolled out of the dark over the raked fields around them, Jess parked at an Arby's. While she was inside changing Eddie and getting food, Sophie popped the lock on her door, slid out of her legs—which hadn't reattached, though she thought now that maybe, eventually, if she could lie still long enough, they might—and swung down onto the pavement. Throwing her arms wide and tilting back her head, she waited for the world to drench her.

For once, it obliged. Fat drops of rain filled the too-warm night. Sophie let them gush through her hair, down her neck into Jess's shirt. For no good reason, she remembered another thunderstorm, one she'd spent lying in her pull-down bed at the back of the one-room studio she and her mother had rented the summer after they had had to sell the trailer. All through that storm, she'd lain quiet, listening to her mother fuck some shadow who would never have a face, not even for her mother. I am—*we* are—barely even here, *Sophie remembered thinking then.* We are drums for the rain to sound, ears to hear it.

"What are you doing?" Jess snapped as she raced past, shielding Eddie from the rain with her coat. "Stop it."

Sophie opened her eyes, and only then saw the farmer guy in the parked pickup beside them. He was a remarkably cute farmer guy, with dark hair all crisscrossed like a bird's nest, eyes silvery and shiny as the streetlights at the edge of the parking lot. He was staring through his open window at her. At the stump of her. Her stump-ness, it was clear, mattered not in the least to him, and wasn't what he was staring at.

"Whoops," Sophie said, and gave the farmer-guy a smile slow and shy and genuine enough to hurt him.

Jess started the car. "Sophie, if you don't get in here right now . . ."

"Sorry," Sophie called to the farmer, gesturing over her shoulder. "Gotta go."

But just as she swung herself back into her seat, Jess shut the engine down again. Then she started smacking the steering wheel. She used her open hands at first, both together, but then her fingers curled into fists and stopped moving in unison and simply pummeled the wheel, unleashing staccato horn blasts that sounded increasingly like chickens being strangled as Jess went on hammering.

"SHIT," she was saying. "Shit, and shit, and shit, shit, shit."

"Jess," Benny tried.

"SHIT," she snarled, and slammed a fist so hard into the center of the wheel that she cracked the plastic.

"Jess. Hon, you need to—"

"I need a job. *That's what I need." She wasn't really talking to Benny, and certainly not to Sophie, and the sight of Jess like this caused Sophie a surprising pang of . . . something. Sympathy, almost? Maybe? Because apparently, Jess was as alone inside herself as Sophie felt. Had always, every second of her life, felt, except when she'd been with Natalie.*

You, too, Jess? *Sophie wondered.*

If that were true, maybe she and Jess were more alike than either one of them would ever have wanted to admit.

"We need fruit," Jess blurted.

Benny almost laughed at that, but caught himself. "Fruit?"

"And dental floss."

"Yes, but—"

"We need money, Benny. We're going to run out of money so fast. And we need a place to stay. We can't just run. We can't just stick Eddie in a car seat for the rest of his childhood until he goes to college or runs away. We've got to . . . restart our lives. Somehow."

Thunder boomed. Eddie squawked, screamed, and Sophie reached out and touched his little hand. His squirmy little hand.

And Jess saw that, noted it in the rearview mirror, opened her mouth to tell Sophie to get off. But she didn't.

"You're right," Benny was saying, in that stupid man-voice caring men always thought would help. Not that Sophie had known too many caring men, but the ones she had all used that stupid voice.

"We can't go home, Benny. Ever."

"I know," Benny said. And then, "Why not?"

If Jess had been paying any more attention, Sophie was pretty sure she would have punched him at that point. But she was still staring into the rain, fists still poised over the steering wheel she'd cracked, as if daring the wheel to heal itself.

"I have to . . . find us somewhere. Like, now. Get us on a schedule. Find Eddie a school. Get up mornings and . . . have breakfast."

"Breakfast?"

"Put on clothes. Find child care for the baby. Go to work. Jesus Christ, Benny, how do people actually go and do *that?"*

Finally, she went silent. Her fists fell open, and her face dropped down into them. Sophie watched for Jess's shoulders to start shaking, but they didn't.

Because she couldn't allow it, Sophie realized. Even now, clinging to the splintered debris of her life, Jess could control her responses. Because she was Jess. Because she had no other choice.

Going out in the rain had been a mistake, it turned out, because now Jess's top was wet, and Sophie was freezing. Complaining to Jess about that at this particular moment, Sophie decided, was probably a bad idea. She kept silent, held Eddie's hand, and shivered.

"Okay," Jess said, and lifted her head. She leaned over,

kissed Benny on the mouth, and turned around. Sophie jerked her hand away from Eddie's. But Jess looked only at the child, who was no longer screaming. "Ssh," she said. And then, "Okay. One thing at a time. Let's . . . we'll find somewhere. We just will. Today, tomorrow. Somewhere small and sweet. Where we can be small and sweet."

Sophie watched Jess hold on to that thought, swing from it like a little spider on the first strand of a newly restarted web. She watched Jess brush Eddie's face, not even glance at Sophie's, turn away, squeeze her man's fuzzy hand, and start the car. She let Jess drive them all the way to the edge of the parking lot. Then she said, "He'll come for you, you know."

Jess's whole body bucked, as though Sophie had leapt on her back again. Her hands came off the wheel, waved in the air, and Sophie thought of little spider legs. Poor little Jess-spider, who knew nothing else to do but spin webs in corners that could not hold them.

"Who, Sophie? Who will come?"

"Who do you think? You're not a moron."

Mostly, Jess had control of herself, now. She'd gotten her hands back on the wheel, and her mouth had stopped twitching. But not her eyes. Not yet. "Why would he do that? He won't. If he was the slightest bit interested in me, he could have killed me right there on the beach."

Sophie considered that, and shook her head. "Don't think so. Nope. That wouldn't have been . . ."

There was a pause. A long one. Benny, horrified, was crouching against his door, watching both of them, so paralyzed by it all it was as if he wasn't even there. Eddie was wriggling in his car seat, agitated by the thrumming engine without motion, the perpetually rising voices. And for Sophie—just for one, insane second—it was almost like being back in Jess's trailer again, gossiping about boys, bitching about teachers or Sophie's mom, drowning out the drone of Jess's perpetual baseball games on the radio with their taunting and their arguing and their laughter.

Minus the gossiping, of course. And the bitching, and the baseball games, and the laughter. And Jess's daughter.

Abruptly, she turned, staring straight into Eddie's eyes. There was no doubt or even mystery about it: she could see *Natalie's ghost—or her spirit—or just* her*—in there. There she was, whole and hard and bright and Natalie. And for that instant, all Sophie wanted to do was grab Jess's hand, tug her around, let her see this, too. Share this sight with her.*

"How do you know he'll come?" Jess whispered, sounding almost as if she felt it, too, this closeness, this memory of closeness, whatever it was Sophie was almost sure she was feeling.

"Actually, Jess, in all honesty, I have no idea what he'll do."

"That's what I thought." Jess started to turn away.

"But even if he doesn't," said Sophie, stopping her as surely as if she'd grabbed her by the throat, "are you really just going to leave him out there? That monster? To do . . . this?" She started to gesture, then couldn't even decide where to direct the motion: Toward her severed legs? Broken Benny? Orphaned Eddie? Back the way they'd come toward Concerto Woods, where their children lay buried? "Are you going to let him do this to somebody else? You, of all people, are going to let that happen?" Her last and

deftest comment came as an afterthought. "Is that what good girls do?"

This time, Jess barely even looked up, though she appeared to be crying yet again. "Right. Good idea. Having lost my beautiful daughter, I should risk her son in some crazy . . . What are you even . . . Sophie, we can't fight that. And you know what, I don't even believe you want to. You're up to something. We cannot fight that."

"You can't," Sophie said. "I can."

Jess did look up, then. She pointedly avoided meaningful glances at Sophie's severed legs or their stumps. She didn't laugh, either. Classy Jess. "Even if you could. Why would you want to, Sophie? Is that really what you want?"

"Want," Sophie murmured. Such a small word for the force that seemed to drive everyone Sophie had ever known to destroy anything they'd ever had. In her lap, her hands went on toying with the cassettes she'd found, each one imprinted with Sophie-and-Natalie music. With Natalie's voice.

"I don't know about want. But I have a plan."

Her eyes stayed locked with Jess's. In spite of their separate and shared griefs, their fury at each other, they were right in this moment, now. Like poker players, *Sophie thought. Like conspirators, even lovers, almost. Enemies, maybe.*

Like mother and daughter?

"A plan," Jess said, sounding nothing like a mother. Not Sophie's mother, anyway.

Sophie felt herself grin. Felt the nastiness in it. "You're not going to like it."

15

Long, long after he had come—with a shuddering violence Caribou had forgotten was possible—Aunt Sally went on rutting atop him. Caribou would never have dared complain, and didn't really want to, anyway, though this hurt, *now, twisting and bruising him in all kinds of places. Bracing his back against the floor of her tent, he kept the smile pinned to his face and his eyes open the way she always ordered him to. Fucking Aunt Sally had always been more like weathering a mountain storm than lovemaking, whatever that was. Certainly, he had never mistaken anything in what they did together for love. But there was awe in it, at least on his part, and wonder, too, of the most life-affirming, childlike sort, as he stared up into the majestic, unattainable slopes and couloirs of her, the glacial slides and gullies and terrifying drop-offs. Even writhing, Aunt Sally remained remote, alien. Caribou simply crimped his fingers into whatever handholds she'd decided to allow him today and clung.*

When she was finally finished, having driven him, it seemed, halfway into the earth, she slid to the side but didn't lie down. Like him, she was barely sweating despite the heavy summer evening. Soon, they would be shivering in their nakedness. They'd been shivering mid-act, Caribou realized, like icicles rubbing together, shooting off splinters of ice but no sparks or heat. Aunt Sally gazed down at him. Occasionally she did this, though rarely for so long or so intently. Sometimes, when she did, he almost felt as though he really was important to her: the moon in her vast night sky. Her only light. Of course, his was a borrowed light, a reflection, and so truly, even that came from her. She was his—the whole camp's—black sun, a still-seething dead thing forever collapsing inward.

But she shed light, nevertheless.

They listened together to the cicadas and cranes sounding the dusk. The other monsters were already gone, Caribou having roused them and sent them scurrying, on Aunt Sally's orders, into the surrounding towns for Party supplies: barbecue; booze; music; folding chairs; Bibles, because Mississippi guests, especially, felt reassured seeing a few of those strewn about; greasepaint; other, stranger items, unique to this particular event, that Caribou had never seen on an Aunt Sally Party list before.

He'd also given them her singular, explicit command: tonight, and tonight only, under no circumstances *were any of the monsters to invite any guests. They were also not even to consider eating, not so much as a snack. Today was a day of fasting, apparently. The fasting before. Aunt Sally hadn't bothered saying before what, and she hadn't needed to. The monsters had erupted out of camp the second Caribou dismissed them, barking and eager as hunting hounds.*

Also stupid as hunting hounds, and just as oblivious. Not that Aunt Sally had offered him the slightest clue as to what she was thinking or planning. He knew only that she was doing those things. Lying at her feet now, looking at her face, he felt another awful tremor rock him like an aftershock. Abruptly, her head was beside his, her magnificent mouth at his ear, and a brand-new, little-girl voice he had never heard from her before crawled up inside him.

"Excuse me, baby," she said, mimicking his ringtone. Then she dropped into her own voice. "Sleep some, now. Do tell me what you dream." And just like that, still shuddering, he slid out of consciousness.

When he awoke, he was alone in the tent. Patting around with his hands, he found his dress slacks, slid them on, donned his shirt and started to button it, and froze, experiencing a momentary explosion of panic. She's gone, *he thought.* That *was the plan. She'd finally vanished, left them to fend for themselves, and they would never see her more.*

He would never see her more.

But even as he stumbled to his feet, pushing through the tent flaps and outside, Caribou spotted her silhouette. She was down the bank by the river, still and solid as the cypresses she stood among, a tree no kudzu vine would dare embrace. Unless she invited it to.

"Well?" she called without turning. Her voice, this time, was deep as owl-hoot, filling and rounding the air.

Caribou finished buttoning his shirt, tucked it in, straightened his hair, and assumed his proper posture: straight spine, bowed head. He approached carefully, with a respect born of fear so deep and old, it verged on love. It really did.

She wore a black sheath dress Caribou had no memory of having seen before. This often happened with Aunt Sally. She almost never left her tent, and yet, new clothes or accessories seemed to sprout on her whenever she required or—more rarely—wanted them. He stopped a foot or so behind her, far enough to her left so she could just glimpse him out of the corner of her eye. Always, even with him, Aunt Sally liked her monsters where she could see them.

"I dreamed," he told her, after a silent while. When she didn't stop him, he continued. "I think I dreamed . . . of logs."

That earned him a snort, which smoothed into laughter. "Logs. Really?"

"Why is that funny?"

"I'm just always surprised when it works," she said. "Policy."

"You divined Policy. You brought it to us."

"I made it up." Aunt Sally stopped laughing, but slowly. She watched the river. Trees fanned around her like courtiers. It would not have surprised Caribou in the least to learn that she could command those, too, if she wanted, along with her monsters, maybe the owls and alligators. This was her Mississippi, after all. Her country. The one that had made her. The one she was making.

Just like any other good American, *she'd told him once, when he'd made some similarly inane observation directly to her face. And then she'd laughed.*

"What does it mean, then?" Caribou asked. "My dream. Dreams about logs."

"I'd have to consult my book to be sure. But"—Aunt Sally turned, eyed him up and down—"I'm pretty sure the book says logs mean strangers at a party. "

"You're joking."

"Is that what I do? Is that what you think?"

Caribou knew better than to answer, or to back away. It took some effort, but he held his ground. "And my lucky numbers? Our *lucky numbers, since it's your party?"*

"Four. I think. That I really will have to check."

Four. *Caribou let himself stare openly, for one moment, at Aunt Sally's back. "That's . . . there are only seven of us in camp right now, Aunt Sally. Can we afford . . . that just seems . . . wasteful?"*

She said nothing, and she didn't turn around. Caribou thought she might have been smiling, but he could only see her profile. As often as he had sometimes let himself imagine that he knew her, he did not know her. He never had.

Even so. Four guests, for seven monsters.

"Isn't that a little dangerous? And decadent? And . . . unnecessary? Why risk so many?"

Perhaps Aunt Sally shrugged; perhaps that movement was just tree shadows stirring in what little wind there was. "I'm only telling you what Policy tells me, my young reindeer buck. I am merely the messenger."

"But as you just said, ma'am." He hadn't expected to call her that, never did it on purpose. It happened when he was afraid. "You made Policy up."

The sigh, this time, definitely came from her, and there was a note in it that caught Caribou completely off-guard:

a Bessie Smith moan—of defiance? resignation?—and also a laugh, all at the same time. "Just because I made it up, doesn't mean I don't believe it."

"Believe it?" Caribou snapped, knew he should shut up, but couldn't. "Believe what? A dream of a cow means it's your lucky day? A dream of your cousin, and you're about to get sued? You do not believe that."

Aunt Sally turned, and he rocked back, then curled his toes into the dirt and his hands against his sides and held tight. He wasn't afraid. At least, not for the usual reasons. This time—for that single moment, only, the first in all the time he had known her—Aunt Sally herself had looked . . .

The thought was strange, so surprising that it almost wouldn't come, took forever to come, was triggered by the droop of her mouth, the new shade of blankness in her eyes, like dulled curtains in a room that no dusting could ever clean.

For that one instant, Aunt Sally had looked like an old woman.

"Maybe I made Policy up," she said. "Or maybe it came to me. Did you ever think of that?"

"Came to you? Like the Ten Commandments?"

To his amazement, Aunt Sally exploded into laughter. And that *made her look like a little girl. She moved like one, too, positively skipping up the bank to his side to pat his cheek, kiss him on the mouth.*

"Call it a vision, 'Bou. Or a belief. Or a story I made up. Either way, it's something to live by, isn't it? Maybe even something to live for. *What more can any of us living things ask of the world we inhabit? It's the greatest gift I've ever been given. Or given."*

"Not quite the greatest," Caribou said, and for once, he knew that he had said exactly the right thing.

Aunt Sally grabbed his hand, held it tight, and beamed. It made him feel like her son—which he was, of course—and also her babysitter—which he also was. And her lover. Eventually, with a tug on her wrist, he brought her face around to his again; there it was in the moonlight, as dark as he knew his was white; the negation of him, and the thing that had made him.

"Four guests, Sally. Are you sure?"

"Are you saying that's too many for poor Caribou to procure? Given all those systems and contacts you've spent all these years developing?"

He bristled, exactly the way he knew she wanted him to. But he didn't smile; smiling would have ruined the moment, drained it of its intimacy, or whatever this was. "Of course it isn't. It just seems . . ."

"That's why I want only you bringing them, hon. Not the rabble. Only my dedicated, detail-oriented Caribou."

"Okay," he said. He let go of her hand, already running possibilities in his head. The truth was, he did *have sources in mind, locations he had never actually used or planned to use, places he'd been saving, though he'd never quite imagined for what. He was already on his way back to the tent to consult his files and find his shoes when Aunt Sally stopped him.*

"Oh, and 'Bou? Baby?"

He turned, and there was that new look again: Bessie-on-the-bottle, close to the end, except this Bessie was smiling about it. And it was the smile, even more than the dreaming look in her eyes, the tone in her voice—like a grandmother, now, a grandmother in an old folks' home whose family no longer came—that alarmed Caribou most of all. Excited, and terrified him. Never, not once, ever, had he heard Aunt Sally sound small. Almost loving. And at the same time . . . hopeful?

Yes. That, most of all.

" 'Bou? Hon. Make sure most of them are children."

16

Before Rebecca even made it through the front door, Jess had transferred Eddie and his blanket and his squishy orange pretend-baseball and his pacifier to her arms and spun off again. "Where've you been, Bec?" She was already back in the kitchen, checking the temperature of a just-microwaved milk bottle against the skin of her arm, touching the tip of a wooden spoon to the pot of spaghetti sauce on the stove, dealing plates onto the counter, including one, as always, for Rebecca. There were no lights on, as usual; Jess seemed to prefer just the twilight slipping between the half-drawn curtains.

"Is Benny awake?" Rebecca asked, getting Eddie adjusted in her arms and smiling down at him. She gave him the little baseball. He jerked his arm and threw it on the floor and hiccupped, or maybe giggled. "Hello," she said to him, this baby she barely knew, who had been crying for her.

"I'm pretty sure." Jess passed Rebecca again, collecting her summer shawl and a grocery bag full of cleaning supplies off the leaning little coffee table and switching off the baseball game on the radio. Instantly, as though to fill the void, something upstairs rustled, settled. A whisper whipped past up there, like a gust from a fan, stirring the shadows on the blackened walls at the top of the stairs. "Make sure Benny takes his pain meds, okay?" Jess gestured toward the steps. "Actually takes them. Watch him do it."

"He always says he doesn't need them."

"Yeah, well, I say he's in pain."

Jess had dropped her stuff by the door and returned to the kitchen once more to dump noodles in a colander. "Sauce isn't quite done. Check it in a minute." Then she was out of the kitchen, down the hall. Moments later, she returned to the nearly bare living room, her ankle-scraping skirt belling with the wind she made, expelling it, which made her look like a jellyfish, always tilted forward toward her next task with her head just slightly down, brown curls washed but flat against her ears and neck, her face never quite visible.

So like Amanda, Rebecca thought yet again. *How could there be two of them in the same town?* Tears spilled so fast onto Rebecca's cheeks that for a second, she wasn't even sure she'd cried them. She bit the sides of her tongue as her shoulders shook. Absently, she bounced Eddie in her arms. Eddie reached for her hair, tugging it like a bellpull to get her attention. And abruptly, still crying, Rebecca realized the difference between Jess and Amanda, or A-mad-da, as Jess called her—to her face, no less—whenever she felt Amanda needed the prick:

Jess wasn't mad. Jess was broken.

She was also standing—had actually stopped moving, for a whole breath—right in front of Rebecca. "All right, what's wrong?"

Here was another difference, Rebecca thought. Amanda would have noticed, sure, but she would never have asked. According to the Amanda mind-set, whatever was wrong was something to get over.

"I've had kind of a . . ." Rebecca started, wiping at her eyes with one hand, and realized with a start that Jess was looking right at her. She'd even let Rebecca see her whole face for a second: those high, hard cheekbones, devoid of makeup but still shiny, as though water poured constantly over them; those deep-set blue eyes, also shiny, also hard, like crystals.

Looking away, Jess snatched up her work bag, her grocery bag, her keys, touched Eddie's forehead, and glanced over her shoulder, up the stairs toward the room she shared with Benny. As if in response, something up there sighed or sang. Jess ignored that and returned her gaze to Rebecca. "Well?"

Rebecca shook her head, lifted Eddie and kissed his forehead before settling him on her shoulder. "It's been a really crazy twenty-four hours."

"Not good enough," Jess snapped.

"What?"

Nudging Rebecca aside with her hip, Jess started out the door, but she was still talking. Commanding, actually.

"When I get back, you're staying. So any other plans you've got, move 'em."

"Um," Rebecca said, bouncing Eddie in her arms. "Okay." In truth, now that she thought about it, Jess was not like Amanda at all.

She was even sadder . . .

"Good girl. Tell Jumping Jack Flashypants he's going to have to wait."

"Oh. Hey, Jess, I meant to tell you about that, I didn't ask Jack to ask you to—"

"That third spaghetti plate on the counter is for him. Tell him to eat something healthy, you can tell he eats too much crap just by looking at him. What?"

"Huh?"

"Stop staring. What are you thinking?" Abruptly—almost shyly—Jess smiled.

Just as quickly, she gulped the smile down. For a long moment, she stood frozen, her mouth a hard line, the tendons in her neck tight. Then she darted forward and kissed Rebecca on the cheek.

Before Rebecca could respond, Jess was down the steps, moving fast toward the sidewalk, still talking.

And also shuddering? Was she *crying, now?*

"Benny's meds, Rebecca. Make him take them, okay?"

This time, the ceiling actually thumped, as though a whole family of squirrels had dropped out of the evergreen outside and through a hole in the rotting roof.

"You're not hearing that?" Rebecca called.

"It's Benny."

"What, he's dancing, now? On his half-healed broken ankles? Seriously, Jess, could we have this checked? Or get an exterminator? Eddie's going to wind up picking up mouse-poop or . . ."

At the edge of the tiny yard, Jess turned. Apparently, she wasn't crying, after all. Not with tears, anyway.

"We," she said, softly.

Rebecca had no idea what to make of that. But she realized, in horror, that she'd done it again: hurt someone else she cared about, somehow.

"I mean, I could take care of it for you. Call somebody, or something. Will you let me call somebody?"

"Kiss your sweet, ridiculous guy for me," said Jess. When Rebecca kissed Eddie, she added, "Oh, yeah, him, too."

Which meant she'd meant Jack? Rebecca blushed.

"Take Eddie up to Benny when you bring Benny his dinner. They're so good for each other."

"Okay. Although Benny barely talks to me." In Rebecca's pocket, her phone buzzed. *Jack,* she thought. *Or maybe Joel?* Still bouncing Eddie, she fumbled for it.

"He's had a really bad time, hon. And he's in pain. Trust me. As for the rest . . . Rebecca, are you listening?"

That tone was unmistakable, was the Amanda-tone, and stopped Rebecca grappling with her phone. She looked at Jess, who nodded toward the house's second story.

"As for the rest. You leave it be." Then she was out the gate, down the block, heading straight across Campus Ave into the woods, along the lane toward Halfmoon House.

Maybe to clean up the mess Rebecca had left there?

That was a pathetic, hopeless hope, Rebecca knew. Although if anyone could possibly do that, it would be Jess. Her phone pulsed again. She glanced down into the ID window and saw Kaylene's name yet again. With a sigh, she glanced toward the kitchen and saw the three plates laid at the edge of the counter, in the spot where Jess apparently ate whatever meals she ate, just standing there, alone.

Settling onto the sprung, rust-spotted couch, which was the only place to sit in the entire downstairs other than the floor, Rebecca rested Eddie on her hip and answered her phone.

"Aren't you at the Women's Shelter?" she said, before Kaylene could even speak. "Don't you have work?"

"Rebecca, finally, where have you *been*? I've been calling and calling, there's something I have to tell you and—"

"I got kicked out of Halfmoon House," Rebecca blurted, and Kaylene gave one of her Kaylene-squeaks and went quiet. She really was the most satisfying person Rebecca had ever met to surprise, mostly because she was still—and always—so ready to *be* surprised. "Actually, that's a little melodramatic. But . . . Kaylene, I said something so stupid. It just came out. Amanda was trashing Joel, again, as usual, for daring to make us all happy. And he was just standing there, and he looked so pathetic, and she can be so mean. And I couldn't stand it."

"What did you *say*? You mouthed off to *Amanda*?"

"I told Joel he should leave her."

"You . . . *what*?"

"And she heard."

There was a long silence, broken only by Eddie's gurgling and tugging at Rebecca's hair. Rebecca had been on too many fraught phone calls—was too well trained in the art of fraught phone calls, and was also too much her weirdo, intuitive self—not to recognize panic on the other end of the line when she heard it. Or, in this case, sensed it, since she wasn't actually hearing anything.

But what did Kaylene *have to panic about?* "Hey, Kaylene. What's—"

"Did we all drop acid last night, Rebecca? Together? And someone forgot to tell me?"

That should have been funny. But there was something new in Kaylene's tone—a sourness, a sadness—and it alarmed Rebecca as much as anything else in this whole, insane day. "Kaylene, what the hell? What's wr—?"

"Have you talked to Jack?"

Rebecca groaned, and Eddie squawked. She tickled his stomach as she talked. "He was waiting for me on Campus Ave when I fled Halfmoon House. He—"

"What did he say? Rebecca, you have to tell me. Because it was really weird, and—"

Again, Rebecca had to fight down alarm, quiet herself. "He said you were kissing him."

"Yeah. That's completely accurate. *I* was kissing *him*. And I'm sorry. I'm really, really sorry."

"Huh?"

"*Huh?* What do you mean, *huh*? Rebecca, please, this is hard. I don't even know what . . ."

Kaylene's voice trailed off, leaving Rebecca staring straight ahead at the empty walls. For the first time in the three years they'd known each other, and for no reason she could pinpoint, Rebecca wanted to hang up on Kaylene. In her lap, Eddie had balled his fists in her shirt and was pulling himself to his feet. Cocking the phone against her ear, Rebecca took hold of his hips, tickled him there, felt as much as saw the grin burst out on his face. She lifted him, held him in the air, and looked right into his eyes.

"Rebecca? Did he tell you the rest? Because as bad as I feel about what I did, because I know you two—"

"There is no *us two,* Kaylene. Not yet. You didn't do anything to me. Except be honest with me, and be my friend." She kept her eyes on Eddie's, tilted him one way, the other. Making him happy, sometimes, was as easy as pushing the stomach on one of those Tickle Me Elmo dolls. And there was his laugh, loud and unabashed as birdsong. So comforting.

"Okay," Kaylene said, after a shorter pause than Rebecca somehow expected. "You're . . . amazing, Rebecca. You're a really good friend. And that's why you have to listen, right now. Are you listening? I'm at work, I only have another minute."

"I'm right here," she murmured, tilting Eddie, bringing him to her shoulder, tapping his back, keeping her focus at least a little bit there to keep from focusing too hard on Kaylene's voice. Because what was coming out of the phone barely sounded like Kaylene at all.

"Okay, look. I was drunk, so was he, so it's possible I have this wrong, okay? As a matter of fact, I don't even . . . Rebecca, there was this guy."

"The one who came out of the woods?"

"Wow. Wait. So he did tell you?"

"He told me a guy came out of the woods. He wanted me to know that you were okay."

Abruptly, Kaylene snorted. *Or sobbed?*

"Kaylene?"

"Shit. Oh, shit. He *is* a coward. I knew it."

"Hey."

"Just . . . hang on, okay?"

Rebecca set Eddie on the floor with his back against the couch, then joined him down there, rolled his ball to him. Eddie gurgled and pushed it back in her general direction. Kaylene stayed gone a long time. Then she was back.

"Okay. Listen. First of all, the kissing really was nothing, okay? It was all me. My fault. We got wasted at Starkey's last night, and we stayed out too long."

Rebecca's skin itched, and her heart hurt, and even though she had slept better last night than she had in months, twitchy dreams and all, she just wanted to drop her head back onto the couch's lone cushion and close her eyes.

But Kaylene made that new sound again: snorting or sobbing. And whatever that represented—*hurt? confusion? betrayal?*—Rebecca wasn't sure she could take more of it right that second. Her eyes drifted toward the chipped side table next to the couch where Jess kept her bills stacked and categorized in a cheap wire organizer. The table had one drawer, and for once, Jess had left it half-open. Pinning the phone against her jaw, Rebecca reached into the drawer and drew out the single framed photograph in there.

At her feet, Eddie began to squawk, yanking at the ankles of her pants. He threw the ball across the room. In the kitchen, the stove-timer beeped and went on beeping. Near her ear, hovering like a gnat, Kaylene was talking again. And upstairs, Benny—sounding gravelly, growly, much more agitated than usual—shouted, "Jesus, Rebecca, are you here? Is anyone down there?"

And yet, for just a moment more, Rebecca stared at the

photograph: two teenage girls in summer twilight, emerging fully clothed in jeans and tank tops out of the ocean, onto dark, cigarette-strewn sand. The one on the right glowed red-blond in the last of the sun, had her outside arm flung wide and a horizon line for a smile. The other had eyes the exact bottomless blue-black of the darkening sky around and above them, and her wet, black hair streamed behind. She was hip-checking her friend but also holding her hand, both of them rumpled and laughing, as though they'd just poured out of a car after a long drive and not even bothered shedding or changing clothes. Or else they'd just emerged from the sea on new and unsteady legs, like mermaids.

"God, Rebecca, *please*!" Benny shouted, and Eddie squealed and started to sob. Rebecca laid the picture on the couch, kept the phone pinned between her shoulder and jaw, scooped the baby into her arms, and stood.

"Kaylene, I'm so sorry, I've got to call you back. I've got to go."

"Rebecca, are you fucking kidding? I'm at work. And I've been trying to get you all—"

"I'll call you back. As soon as I can. I'm sorry. I promise."

"Rebecca, WAIT. One second. Are you there?"

She was moving toward the kitchen to shut off the timer, had already bounced Eddie back to relative peacefulness. She'd meant to hang up, but hadn't. "I'm here," she said.

"Just . . . tell Jack we love him, okay? That I still do. That whatever the hell that was last night . . ."

"What? Kaylene, I swear I'll call you as soon as I can.

I love you." She dropped Eddie into his high chair and grabbed the phone and hit End.

What the hell? she thought, moving automatically to remove the sauce from the heat, switch off the alarm and then the stovetop. The old electric burner rings sparked, flared redder, then went dark.

Where was Jack, anyway? When would he come? What hadn't he said, that Kaylene was about to? Nothing, surely, that could unsettle either one of them more than the things he'd already said.

Like, *I'm too into you . . .*

She was plating spaghetti, letting everything churn in her head: Jack, and Kaylene's voice just now, and Amanda's icy reprimand—or kiss-off—and Joel's slumped back as he vanished into the woods; the woods themselves; that black Sierra near the abandoned trailers; the photograph she'd just found in Jess's drawer; the total absence of chairs in this house, because, as Jess had put it when Rebecca asked, "It's just me, right now. When there's someone down here to sit with again, I'll sit."

And under it all, that voice, last night's caller's voice, whispering over the drums of her ears like air from a fan he'd set blowing inside her:

I'll come see you.

I can see you.

Knocking. Someone was knocking.

Almost dropping the dripping colander in the sink, Rebecca turned. She touched Eddie's hand as he stretched for her, murmured, "Hold on, baby, I'm right here," and hurried back into the living room. "Jack," she was calling, hand already stretching for the front door, when she stopped. Held still.

Nothing. There had been a knock or at least a noise, she was sure of it. But now there was silence, or almost silence, just . . . the ghost of a song? The reverberations of a single chord, as though heard from the window of a passing car?

Or maybe *actually* heard from the window of a passing car? Certainly, there was no one on the porch. She knew that even before she opened the door and checked.

I hate this house, Rebecca realized, staring around at the barren living room, the scraped walls with their smoke stains. Her second realization hit harder, and disturbed her even more. *I love Jess. Poor Jess.*

As in, loved her in the same way she had loved Amanda, once? Maybe even more? Because in all of three weeks, Jess had given Rebecca a stronger inkling of what being someone's daughter might be like than either Amanda or Joel had allowed themselves or her? Or because making Rebecca feel that way only seemed to make Jess sadder?

Rebecca closed her eyes and thought of Jess's face: those eyes, clear blue as lake ice, always dry but rimmed in red. Then Rebecca thought of the photograph from the drawer, the smiles on the faces of both of those girls and the eyes on the dark-haired one, which had struck her so forcefully because they were so familiar. They weren't Jess's eyes. Not quite, though close. They were more like . . .

Mouth opening, Rebecca turned back toward the kitchen, the child in there, who stopped squawking the second she looked at him. With a grunt, she shut down her thoughts and returned to her duties. She draped a dry noodle across

Eddie's high-chair tray and another across his forehead, so that he laughed and tugged it free of his face and split it in his fingers. She dumped sauce over the spaghetti on a plate, stirred it, poured a full glass of the disgusting sweet tea both Benny and Jess drank by the vat, and put glass and plate on the tray Jess had left waiting on the counter. Donning the baby sling Jess had left draped over the sink, she dropped Eddie into it, grabbed the tray, and headed back across the living room, past that photograph she'd left faceup on the couch. There they were, those mermaid-girls, staring up from their years-ago beach into the dead air of this house. *I have understood nothing,* Rebecca was thinking as she ascended the stairs. *About anyone. Ever.*

But she was learning. Finally. Today, alone, she'd learned more than she ever wanted to know, perhaps, about Jack and Joel, Amanda and Jess, Eddie and Kaylene, maybe even herself. The new knowledge felt hot inside her, rising in her ribs, as though her ribs were electric-burner rings she'd switched on at last. She was gulping for breath as she reached Benny's door. She knocked with her foot.

"Finally," Benny said.

Nudging open the door with her shoulder, Rebecca edged into the bedroom, which was bare as the downstairs: an iron-frame bed with a drugstore reading lamp clipped to the headboard, an overhead lightbulb with no shade or fixture, a nightstand with three Raymond Chandler paperbacks piled on it. Right in the center of the bed—sideways, as usual, twisted up in the sheets, even though he couldn't really move his legs in their half casts—lay Benny, scowling the way he generally did when she came in with his food. His ropy shoulders sagged under his wifebeater. Prematurely white hair spilled out all over him like down from a ripped-open pillow.

"Hi, Benny. Brought you something." She turned so he could see the sling, and so Eddie could see him.

Eddie gurgled. Immediately, Benny's smile caught, flared, blazed out of his train wreck of a body. "Bring that here," he said.

Laying the tray on the nightstand, Rebecca set the boy on Benny's lap as Benny straightened. Steadying Eddie with his better arm, Benny took the iced tea Rebecca offered and sipped it greedily.

"Need some sugar with that?" she said, and for once, he kind of laughed. But he looked only at Eddie.

"Hello, son," he said.

But not as if this were his *son,* Rebecca saw now. She'd always seen, but she hadn't comprehended until today. Yet another new thing she now knew.

Eddie slapped at Benny's injured arm. If that hurt, Benny didn't show it. Somehow, he smiled even brighter. "Oh, yeah?"

Eddie cackled, and Benny laughed again, their collective racket almost enough to cover the sigh from the hall.

There wasn't any doubt, this time. That was a sigh.

Whirling, Rebecca ducked out the door, staring toward the banister, the empty staircase, the narrow hallway. The whole space was maybe ten feet square, with Benny's room on this side of the landing and two more doors on the other side of the steps, to the bathroom and the linen closet. Except, how did she know that second door was a linen closet? She'd never once been in there, never seen Jess going in or coming out.

The sigh had come from there.

Hadn't it?

"Rebecca," Benny called, "what are you doing? Come back in here, please."

But Rebecca stayed put. As she watched, the door down there seemed to slip farther back into the shadows that always gathered at that end of the hall like smoke, or the ghost of smoke. She heard no further sound, but that last sigh had snagged on something in her brain, and now it kept sounding. Sighing.

Abruptly, she was across the mouth of the staircase. She heard the alarm in Benny's voice as he snapped, "Hey. Don't go down there."

"Tell me you don't hear that," Rebecca snapped back, moving straight to the shut door, stopping outside it with her right shoulder and leg in light and the rest of her in shadow.

"Rebecca, *stop*."

She twisted the knob and opened the door, which swung back into darkness. As her eyes adjusted, Rebecca made out a window on the far wall with a blackout shade, pulled all the way down. On the low ceiling, she could just see some sort of circular light fixture with no bulb in it. There was nothing else whatsoever in the room.

So what? That was hardly surprising, given the Spartan nature of the rest of Jess's décor. Rebecca almost turned away, then moved forward instead, straight into the middle of the room. The darkness hadn't really shrunk back, that was just her eyes adjusting further. It wasn't holding its breath, either, or freezing on the walls like a watched spider.

Nope. This was just darkness, plain old emptiness, no matter how long she stood in it.

Why was she still standing in it, then? She just was, and that's why this time, when the sigh came, she heard it loud and clear. It wasn't just a sigh, either. There was a word in it, stretched all out of shape, barely recognizable as language, except that it was.

Not only that, but Rebecca had heard it before, though she couldn't place where. Not yet.

"Colllldddd," it said. Right above her.

Rebecca's head flew back on her neck, and she finally saw the outline, unmistakable now that her eyes had accustomed themselves, carved into the flaking paint up there: a drop-down door. To an attic, no doubt. There was even a stub of rope to pull it open, but that had been clipped off and was just out of her reach. Retreating across the hall to the bathroom, she grabbed the stepstool she'd always seen tucked behind the door, there, without ever wondering what it was for.

Benny was shouting, now. "Goddammit, Rebecca! Rebecc—hold on, Eddie, wait—Rebecca, *stop.*"

But she didn't stop. She marched the stepstool into the dark room, planted it under the drop-down door, climbed up, and put her hand on the string.

Only then, and just for one moment, she did pause. She wasn't waiting so much as processing, making sure.

She was sure. Whatever she'd always heard in this house, it was up there. Not only that, but she now realized where she'd heard that voice before. That icy, stretched-out, chopped-up, alien murmur. In truth she'd been hearing it repeatedly, all day long. She'd heard it in Amanda's kitchen, in the Halfmoon House yard, in the woods. Anywhere Joel went with his Bluetooth speaker.

Expecting resistance, she yanked hard on the drop-down cord, but the door seemed to leap from its casing, flakes of plaster flying around it, the folded-up ladder on its other side almost cutting Rebecca in half as it plunged downward. She caught just enough of it with her hand and shoulder to keep it from driving her off the stool. Then she half-stepped, half-staggered down, the stool clattering away as she stabilized herself, eased the ladder to the floor, and stared up.

There was no blackness up there, just yellow, ordinary, electric light. It wasn't even flickering.

"Rebecca, goddammit, *get out of there*!" Benny yelled.

But Rebecca went right on staring at the hole in the ceiling. "Hello?" she called, and waited, and waited some more. Whoever was up there was holding still, maybe even holding his or her breath, as though that person, too, were making sure.

Then came rustling. Person-in-bedsheets rustling. And that was followed by a click, and the chopped-up voice stuttering to life once more.

"Hear you . . . KNOCK . . . can't come in . . ."

"Oh, I'm coming in," Rebecca said.

Up she went.

17

Much to her surprise, by the time Kaylene finished her shift at Healing Together Women's Sanctuary, she actually felt a whole lot better. Despite her stabbing hangover headache, her epic fail of a pass at Jack, and the fact that she'd never even gotten her eyes closed this morning, let alone slept—because every time she lowered her lids, she saw the Sombrero-Man, tasted his dead-rat-and-whiskey breath, felt his fingers around her windpipe, the cold of them as dangerous as the pressure they exerted—today had proved weirdly successful. Kelly Kandace, who until this afternoon had taken every single meal since her arrival at Healing Together in her room, and removed her bathrobe only to layer still more rumpled, filthy sweatshirts atop her bruised body, had actually let Kaylene fold her laundry. She'd still eaten alone, but then she'd come out to the Common Room to join the other two ladies to whom Kaylene had been assigned as companion, laundry folder, checkbook balancer, conversation initiator, and cry-shoulder. Two hours later, Kaylene had left them all sitting together on the paisley Common Room couch alongside her boss, Mrs. Groch, each of the four of them clutching Sanctuary-owned iPads, failing epically and profanely at Butterfly Gauntlet, to which Kaylene had just introduced them.

"I warned you," Kaylene called over her shoulder as she made her way down the hall toward the front door.

"Fuck you, Kaylene, *damn it,*" Mrs. Groch snarled, as yet another of her digital butterflies caught a windshield and splattered across her screen.

"A game worse than men," Kaylene said.

"Worse than men," muttered Kelly Kandace, and one of the other ladies laughed a furious, frustrated Butterfly Gauntlet–laugh.

Then Kaylene was out in the sweet summer twilight, the sinking sun a streak of too-bright gold across Halfmoon Lake, the trees and everything that lived in them awakening in what passed for a breeze. Somewhere across the water, over by Halfmoon House, a single loon let loose. Kaylene winced, felt her head throb, whispered, "Ssh," as if that would shut that wild thing up. She was at the end of the drive, stepping onto the sidewalk, when she stopped, turned around, and stared at the white, shingled triplex that housed Healing Together. She put a hand up to her neck, felt the ring of cold the Sombrero-Man had left there, although she couldn't quite reach or locate the exact spot. Somehow, he'd gotten that cold *inside* her.

Dazed, she gazed at the *Sanctuary* sign over the door, with its crudely painted hands clasped around an even cruder candle. Only then did the thought finally come to her:

Holy shit. I'm one of you. I am a battered woman. Assaulted woman, anyway.

How strange, given everything she did with her time, that the idea that such a thing could happen in her own life had literally never occurred to her. She was Kaylene, mighty daughter of Laughing Dad on Skis and Mom of Perpetual Warm Bao and Sunday Crosswords, A– student without even trying, two-time Southwestern New England Dig Dug Champion, founding member of Jack and the 'Lenes, future nonprofit director of Something Useful, Human Curling magician. The fact that she was also, now, a *victim* seemed ridiculous. Impossible. Unreal. Infuriating.

Rat-breath, bad-hat fuckball. Whistling weirdo, who'd kissed *Jack. Who'd held Jack's eyes, reached up to her throat, and . . .*

No. Nope. She stood her ground, made herself stare at the house where she worked, the lake where she swam, the sidewalks she *owned,* as though together they formed a mandala. Her personal mandala.

No. Not me. Not here. Not us.

Jesus Christ, the police. Why hadn't any of them called the police?

Partly, she hadn't called them because even now, none of it made any sense. Where had the whistling weirdo even come from? Where had he gone? What, exactly, had he done or been trying to do? Strangle her? Sort of? Probably, yes. *Intentionally?* Yes, definitely, but to kill her? He could easily have done that. But he hadn't. So he'd meant to . . . *tease* her?

The only thing Kaylene was completely sure of was that he'd kissed Jack. And of course, he wasn't the only one who'd done that.

"Fuck," she muttered. A shiver kicked up and fluttered over her, and not just her: the whole landscape rippled, especially the edge of the woods, as though all the wood rats in one of those astounding wood-rat pueblos in there had erupted from their holes at exactly the same time. As though something in there had rousted them.

Kaylene squinted into the gloom. She saw branches, branch shadows, ripples of movement already going still. Just her woods. The woods that lined her sidewalk. Hers, and Marlene's, and Jack's, and Rebecca's.

Rebecca.

"Fuck," she said again, stepping off the sidewalk toward the woods. She could cut through there, go by Halfmoon House and into town to that creepy house where Rebecca did her nannying, and have this out face-to-face. And by "have this out," she meant throw her arms around Rebecca, squeeze hard, and somehow drag them both kicking and screaming and laughing all the way back to themselves.

Sounded like a plan.

She was maybe five steps from the break in the trees, the dirt path she'd strolled at least a thousand times since arriving in East Dunham three years ago, when the wind stirred again, galloping straight past her into the forest like a living thing, like something riding the wind more than wind itself. She literally *saw* it vanish into the wall of leaves.

Abruptly, she turned around, not because of any weird wind, and not because of Dead-Rat Sombrero-Dude, and not because she felt cowed, or scared, at least not by that guy. But Jack, on the other hand . . . Maybe she needed to deal with Jack first. Because however strange she felt, how on earth must *he* be feeling?

She could still picture—would never forget—the expression on his face as Sombrero-Man took hold of her. Really, though, it had been more an *absence* of expression. And then he'd just sat there, watching her assaulter. And he'd done nothing.

The fucking bastard. Coward, weakling, asshole . . .

She was kicking the ground more than walking, now. She was also back on the sidewalk, circling the woods to stop by Jack's place. Despite what he'd done, or hadn't done . . . despite what she'd seen or hadn't on his face . . . she was somehow sure that all it would take, tonight, was a single glance, a kind word, to reassure them both. Whatever the hell had happened, it was not what it had seemed, could not have been. Sure, Jack could be a coward. Actually, Jack *was* a coward, always had been, reluctant to confront, unable just to come out and say.

But mostly, that was because he himself got angry so rarely that he was too slow to recognize anger in others. And that was because he was Jack, her lovely too-soft, dart-sporting, bowling-shirt-wearing friend, who made the world sparkle, and understood what board games and brooms and ice rinks were for.

Jack, whom she loved.

She was almost back to Starkey's Pizza, half a block from the edge of town proper and the end of the woods, when she stopped in mid-stride and swung toward the trees again. Then she held still, staring again through the laced branches. The sun hung so low that it seemed to have lodged in the heart of those massed pines, like a fire in a woodstove. Or a firefly in a jar.

And yet, the day hadn't cooled any. Everything about Kaylene felt sticky-August-New-Hampshire hot, except her throat. *That* felt cold.

There's nothing in the trees, she told herself, and watched the woods a little longer. But she didn't see anything in there except twilight, or hear anything but birds and just-awakening bats. And maybe one thing more. She couldn't even sort what it was, but it was there: a bit of extra movement, maybe, a rustling right along the edge of shadows, just out of sight behind the branches. As though someone on the other side of that first row of pines was pacing.

You did this to me, she let herself think. *You fucking bastard.* For an astonishing second, she felt she might cry out.

Don't let me see you again, she thought. Then she said that aloud, to the sidewalk and the trees. "I mean it. Don't let me see you again. Bub." And with that, she wrenched herself around and stalked into town, leaving the woods behind her.

To her relief—at first, it was relief—she didn't even have to ring the clown-nose doorbell on Jack's door. As soon as she'd turned onto his block, she saw him emerging up the stairs from his tiny basement apartment—*as though out of the ground,* she thought stupidly, crazily—and then he was free of the shadow of the ramshackle blue house he lived in, moving over the grass, Operation game under his arm and what looked like a brand-new thrift store bowling shirt—where did he *find* them all?—buttoned crisply to his neck. In the instant before he saw her, she wondered what the name on the shirt would be tonight. All Jack's shirts had names on the pockets, none of them his. *Herman. Jimenez. Kennedy. Bill.*

He saw her and stopped.

For Kaylene, the worst moment—not including the actual choking—came right then, as she realized that her first instinct was to spin on her heels and *run*. The Jack in front of her was her Jack, the one she'd always known. But hovering in the air between them, forming and re-forming over his face like a mask made of mist, was the face she'd seen on him this morning, in the too-clear dawn light, on the bus stop bench:

Jack-minus-Jack. Jack, watching her die.

She came so close to spinning and running. But her stride barely hitched. And as she moved forward, that mask-face superimposed over her friend's seemed to burst beneath the heat of her glare, glitter in the air like firecracker smoke as she strode through it, and stream away. She walked right up to him.

"Kaylene, I don't even know what to—"

She threw her arms around him, eskimo-kissed his nose (only a little harder than she meant to, with just a bit of head butt), and said, "Come Curling."

He blinked as she released him, blushed, ran a hand through his Persian-cat poof of brown hair—his *combed* Persian-cat poof, which made Kaylene realize, with just a tiny twinge of hurt, where he'd been heading just now—

and looked at the ground, then back up. "I'm really glad you're here."

"Of course I'm here. Come Curling." Kaylene reached for his hand, ignoring the last shudder of watcher-from-the-woods crawling up her back. At least, she hoped it was the last.

"I can't. I mean . . . you know I love you."

"I know you love me." She held his hand, feeling neither twinge nor shudder; she really did know.

"But—"

"And I know you love Rebecca more."

"Not more."

"Okay. Different." She watched him smile shyly, his little-boy-with-a-sled, little-boy-let-out-of-his-room-after-being-grounded smile. It rankled her, but less than she'd feared it would. "Human Curling. One round. You're the stone. I get to shove. You owe me."

Then he just up and said it, went right at it, because he wasn't such a coward, after all. "To get rid of last night? This morning, I mean? Bury it, once and for all? Can we . . . I mean, is that poss . . . ? Can we, Kaylene? Please?"

"I'm . . ." Kaylene started, and realized that she was at least as uncertain of what to say as he was. "I'm not even sure what I remember about last night. Or this morning."

"Really?" said Jack, with no smile whatsoever. "Because I'm pretty sure I do." A single sob wracked him, right there in front of her.

"Okay, that's just wrong. That's all wrong. Jacks don't cry." Yanking him by the wrist, ignoring the catching as he got control of his breath, Kaylene tugged him around the corner toward the triplex where she lived with Marlene.

They'd reached her front stoop, Kaylene dragging Jack up the tilting porch steps she and Marlene couldn't get Smoker Harris or his crazy wife to let them fix, when Jack caught the edge of the railing and dragged them still. He pulled Kaylene around to face him, though he wasn't quite looking at her. At least he wasn't crying anymore, either.

"Really?" he said. "We're okay?"

"We are Jack and the 'Lenes," Kaylene said, and was relieved to hear how certain she sounded. "'Okay' doesn't enter into it." She made herself smile at him until she didn't have to make herself anymore. Then she called into the triplex, "Marlene, put down that orgo chem book."

At the front screen door, in his permanent, private Pig-Pen cloud, Smoker Harris appeared, saw Kaylene, and stepped into the evening. When he saw Jack, he held up his hands so Jack could see his nails. This was how Smoker always greeted Jack. "Full yellow," he said.

It was true, though hardly a revelation. The guy smoked so much that his hair, nails, irises, even his gums had clouded.

"Smoker, you are magnificent," said Jack. "*Those* are magnificent."

"Always appreciate a kid who can appreciate," said Smoker, coughed, and shook his ash-gray hair like an ancient dog rousing itself off a mat. "I think Marlene's studying."

"Not anymore," Kaylene said. "Mar*lene*!"

Marlene appeared, coughed as she brushed past Smoker, but also patted him on the back. He had been their landlord ever since they'd come, together, to East Dunham. He would be their landlord, Kaylene knew, until the day they left, even if he stopped leaving bourbon-flavored beignets outside their upstairs apartment door every single Sunday morning, an act he still called their "move-in special." On the day they'd first come to see the place, Kaylene had told him, "Sorry, I can't handle the smoke."

"What smoke?" Smoker had said. "No one smokes in my house." And no one had, from that day forward. Smoker didn't even do it on the balcony anymore, even though Kaylene had never asked him to move away. He went all the way to the back of his yard and stood under the hickory tree, even in winter, even when it was snowing.

"I'm studying," Marlene said, though Kaylene noted that she hadn't even bothered to bring out her orgo book.

I have broken you, Kaylene thought, and grinned. "Human Curling."

"At . . ." Marlene checked her pocket for her phone, but it wasn't there. "This early?"

"What, you think Mrs. Starkey refreezes the rink at midnight?"

"I think school starts in sixteen days."

"I know. And you're only eleven weeks ahead in the reading."

"Thirteen."

"Move it. We're going to Human Curl. See you, Smoker."

Then they were all moving together, slipping into formation, Jack in the center, a 'Lene on each arm. When Rebecca was with them, they really were a humming combine of good days, harvesting the fun from mucky lakes and mini-forests and too-long lectures and crisis centers and hundred-year-old pizza barns. Mulching Dead-Rat Sombrero-Men wherever they sprouted. Down the block, there were kids playing kick the can, ghost in the graveyard, one of those in-come-free games. They moved through midge clouds as thick as Smoker's smoke, which blurred their edges against the deepening dark, made them look like kid-shaped smudges, their voices wild and shrill as loons'. Every one of them was someone Kaylene knew.

Marlene, annoyingly, kept falling half a step behind, as though considering retreating to the triplex, but then Kaylene glanced over and saw the look on her face, registered the concern there. She hadn't told Marlene a thing about last night. She'd told Rebecca, because Rebecca needed to know. Even now, Kaylene wasn't sure whether to tell Marlene, or exactly what she *would* tell her if and when she did.

Yeah, no biggie, Jack probably wasn't actually *going to let me die.*

Their eyes met. Marlene's were wide, so green behind her glasses, teeming with all the things Marlene always knew. She was more than a little like Rebecca, in that way. So completely and permanently her friend.

That was enough. It was all Kaylene needed. She tilted out her arms, ski-jumper style, and leaned into the oncoming night. Marlene matched her.

They didn't even bother stopping into Starkey's proper, just swooped down the dumpster alley toward the giant barn out back, bumping each other as usual, laughing. That's why they didn't notice Mrs. Starkey at the bottom of her back stoop until she whirled on them.

"*Hah!*" she shouted, lashing out with a ladle and waving it back and forth in the air between them. The ladle still had cannellini beans and bits of stewed tomato in it. Even after she'd clearly realized who was standing in front of her, she kept the ladle raised, jabbed it toward them a few more times.

For a moment, none of the trio moved except Jack, who'd jumped back in surprise. Marlene had flinched hardest, and now she just stood there, processing. Kaylene allowed herself a moment of that, too. She took in Mrs. Starkey's lumpy, veiny bare feet in the grass, heavy as old stones, the apron only half on, twisted about her neck and one shoulder, her hair out of its hairnet for once, and—surprisingly—*not* white, not all the way, and also *long,* with lots of lustrous uncolored brown still threaded through the heavy braid that switched on her back like a horse's tail. Mrs. Starkey's warm, brown widow's eyes positively leapt from face to face. She kept the ladle out in front of her chest, bulbed end pointed at them.

"Mrs. Starkey?" Kaylene said. "Are you okay?"

It should have been funny, and would have been if this were some other day, and also if the woman weren't trembling. Actually, she *wasn't* trembling, now that Kaylene looked closer. But she looked as though she had been, just a few seconds ago.

Jack had laid the Operation game he'd been carrying on the stoop and stepped back into line with his 'Lenes. Kaylene felt more than saw his careful smile. "You wave that thing like you mean it," he said. It really was masterful, the way he did that. He was so good in other people's crises, the best she'd ever seen, until she'd seen Rebecca.

"I'll put your eye out," Mrs. Starkey said, waving the ladle one last time, but less like she meant it, more like she was threatening to withhold pineapple from their pizza.

"Probably be more 'scooping' than 'putting' with that thing, really," Jack said. "Right?"

Mrs. Starkey scowled. From long experience, Kaylene knew that was Mrs. Starkey's version of laughing. The woman's shoulders came down, though not the ladle. She seemed to notice her disheveled apron, reached up with her free hand to pull it all the way off or maybe on, then patted the top of her head instead, where her hairnet wasn't.

"You have beautiful hair," Marlene said.

Sighing, Mrs. Starkey twisted fingers through her braid, yanked it once, let it go. "I do," she said. "I did. Some days, you kind of forget it's there, you know? No, you don't know. May you never. The fucking foxes are back." She gestured at the woods across the yard, behind the barn.

"Foxes?" Marlene asked.

"Last summer, they ate my cats. *Both* of my cats. This time . . ." Instead of waving the ladle, she leveled her gaze at the trees, which seemed, to Kaylene, considerably more intimidating. *If I were a fox . . .* she thought. Then she said, "Can we use the rink? We really need to Curl."

Mrs. Starkey turned back to them, raising an eyebrow. "At this hour?"

"See?" said Marlene.

"Just one round?" Kaylene nodded toward Jack. "If there's no hockey or lessons going on in there? I really need to shove him."

"Oh. That's different. Why didn't you say so?" Fumbling in the folds of her apron, Mrs. Starkey produced a set of keys and handed them to Kaylene. "Make sure the damn door's all the way shut, please. Don't let out the cold.

Biggest waste of my money . . ." She moved off toward her kitchen, muttering, almost as if she didn't collect half the leisure cash spent in this town on either her rink or her food.

"Is it even really possible to shut that door all the way?" Jack said.

"She never locks it, either," said Kaylene.

Marlene was still gazing at the back door to the pizzeria, looking nervous, though no more than usual. "That's because we're usually still in there when she closes."

"I'm shoving," Kaylene said to her. "You're sweeping."

Across the unmown grass, the barn hummed. In the last of the daylight, the hum seemed unusually loud, and not only because, as usual, the door hadn't been completely closed and therefore wasn't locked. The noise carved through the evening cricket-cheep like a Jet Ski motor. Yet again, the incongruity of this place struck home to Kaylene: a 150-year-old, hulking, red-roofed structure, re-sided with sheet metal to keep in the chill and protect the shadowed wonderland inside it, where an entire regional subculture of small-college and tiny-town hockey teams and teen figure-skating academies and birthday party traditions had sprouted and flourished. And also where the future Olympic sport of Human Curling had been born. How fragile it all seemed, right then: a whole world that could melt off the earth with a flick of a switch, or a couple of students' graduations, or a widow's passing.

"It really must cost her a fortune," she murmured as they slid the steel door sideways on its rustless runners. Chilled air gushed over them, carrying that smell that Kaylene had never been able to pinpoint: lake water without muck;

sweat without stink; the smell of whiteness. Whatever that odor was, Kaylene had loved it from the first time she'd set foot in there.

"I really, no joke, think she's loaded," Jack said. He stepped back in the weeds, lifted the heel of his front foot so that only his toes touched earth, and positioned his arms just so, like a speed skater on his mark, completing his traditional Jack-entrance routine.

"If she was that rich, why would she still be in East Dunham serving pizza and passing out Human Curling brooms to peons like us?" Marlene asked, and Jack let his mouth fall open in mock-astonishment.

"If you were that rich," he said, "what would *you* do?" Then he exploded past them and through the door, dropping to his knees and skidding, with a whoop, onto the ice, into the dark.

As usual, it took the single track of overhead bulbs several minutes to spasm awake, even after Kaylene found and flipped the switch along the far-side wall. The lights flickered and slowly warmed to a gauzy gray over the nearest third of the rink. Yet another bulb had apparently blown up there, leaving maybe five functioning ones, as far as she could make out through the spiderwebs layered in the eaves like dense, low clouds. Not once in Kaylene's whole college career had any of those bulbs been changed or webs disturbed. Every time she and her gang came through this door, they talked about bugging Mrs. Starkey to get new bulbs, or just bringing some themselves. She wondered why none of the hockey teams that practiced here or instructors who coached local skating prodigies all day Saturday and Sunday ever demanded an upgrade.

In a way, though, she already knew: the murk was part of the magic, for everyone. With the sliding door closed (to the extent that it could close) and the rink humming, this really was somewhere far from New Hampshire, or anywhere, really, especially in summer, the closest any of them would ever get to Neverland. Maybe it was their own Neverland, where everyone did grow up, get old, but they did so sliding.

"Jack, please?" Marlene said, still struggling with the door.

But by now, Jack had already gone full-stomach, was sliding headfirst across the strip of light into the shadows over center ice. When he glided to a stop and stood, he was on the blue line two-thirds of the way to the far end, balancing on one foot. Despite his ridiculousness, he looked remarkably graceful at that moment, like an ice dancer frozen in mid-spin, or Peter Pan himself. A Lost Boy, glowing and grinning, limned against the blacker shadows behind him.

"Get back here," Kaylene ordered. "Get the saucer. Assume the position."

"Ma'am," said Jack, saluted, and slid-skidded back toward them to collect one of the scuffed plastic flying saucers out of the closet in the door-side corner.

By the time Jack had selected a saucer—the green one, his favorite, so shaved down and waxed up that it didn't so much slide as skim across the ice like a hovercraft—and settled at their traditional starting point in the red box that served as a goalie crease when goals were placed there, Kaylene had helped Marlene fix the door as nearly into place as it would go. It was just so rare, so perfect and necessary for this particular session of the game they'd pioneered together, that they had the rink completely to themselves. Collecting the Shoving Implement—it had once been a snow shovel before its promotion to Curling duties—she surveyed the slowly lightening ice, standing shoulder to shoulder with Marlene against the plexiglass and white wooden boards that rimmed the ring. The hum of the motors that kept this place frozen really did seem louder tonight, completely drowning out the world out there, which was exactly what Kaylene wanted: just her and her friends, ice to play on, lights that would last at least a little longer. Not so bad a Neverland to spend forever in.

"Right," she said, lowering her eyes to Jack, seated obediently in his saucer. She gave a few practice shoves at the air with the Implement. "Bastard," she said.

"Hey," said Marlene.

"Ssh. Get your broom." Stepping forward, Kaylene took up her mark behind Jack's saucer, prodding his feet into proper cross-legged position. She avoided looking into his eyes, then looked. There he was, not laughing, still silently asking her the question: *were they really okay?*

The question itself was its own answer. "Better hold tight," she said, and didn't smile, didn't have to. She wasn't kidding, anyway. "Turn around. All the way facing me."

Jack did as he was told. At the nearer blue line, Marlene had taken up post with her broom. None of them had ever figured out what the sweeping was supposed to do, exactly. But they all agreed that this activity simply wasn't Human Curling without it.

"Ready?" Kaylene murmured, fitting the curve of the Implement against the side of the saucer.

"Would it be better for you if I said no?" Jack asked.

She didn't grin, let him continue seeing the hurt he'd caused her. She wanted him to know she didn't understand, knew he didn't, either, and loved him anyway. "It doesn't matter what you say," she told him, hunched over her hips, settled her weight over her feet, and shoved.

It was a perfect shove. Kaylene knew it even before the saucer lost contact with the shovel. The ice slid away at just the right speed, the saucer not even spinning, shooting straight out toward the center. Beyond the blue line, Marlene took a series of dutiful sweeps in the saucer's path and got out of the way. Off it sailed toward the darkness at the far end, where Kaylene already knew it would come to rest, right in the goalie box, without so much as grazing the boards. Right at the feet of the Sombrero-Man, who had just this second taken shape down there as the shadows slid back to reveal him.

Kaylene dropped the shovel. Her mouth fell open to shriek.

But she didn't shriek. Couldn't. She was strangling, instead, on the very sight of that man. He wore the same scuffed work boots as this morning, same tatty jeans, checked shirt: Huck Finn gone old without getting old, and dead-rat sour, mouth pursed as if he were whistling (because he *was* whistling, Kaylene realized, she could hear it now, even over the hum of the motors under the ice, now that she knew what was making the noise), arms outstretched as Jack—still facing Kaylene, still with no idea what she'd shoved him toward—glided over the far-end blue line into what was left of the dark.

18

From her first moment in the attic—the second the blond woman in the cot, propped up on pillows against the sloped, ash-blackened wall, started talking—Rebecca had wanted to leave. She also knew she *should* leave. And yet she didn't, or couldn't. Partly, she was mesmerized by the awful, impossible things the woman in the cot was telling her, some of which had started to seem all too real, or at least less impossible, even before the woman had flipped up the blankets just long enough for Rebecca to see her legs. But partly, it was simply this woman's voice, which . . . *lulled,* like her caller's from last night's, but also sang, almost. Come to think of it, so had her caller's. But this woman's singing sounded more natural, more like singing someone might actually do, to herself, to a baby.

And so instead of leaving, Rebecca found herself first leaning, then stepping deeper into the dimly lit room, away from the gaping opening to the drop-down stairs that led back to the world she'd climbed out of and now seemed to be floating above, as though in a gondola in a balloon on its way to Oz, or nowhere. Certainly not toward home, wherever that had ever been.

Instinctively, though, she'd kept her eyes away from the blonde's. She kept gazing around the room instead, though there wasn't much to see. Above the cot was a single window draped completely by a heavy black blanket. On the floor lay half a dozen open cardboard boxes. On the nightstand, Rebecca saw open cassette cases and a lone picture frame, but she couldn't make out what was in it. On the bed was a laptop, lots of cables.

All the while, that voice lapped at her ears, slipped inside them, murmuring, lulling. Also, it got quieter, by slow degrees. And so, without even realizing it had happened, Rebecca edged all the way over to the bed, until abruptly, here she was, practically brushing the cot with her thighs, and there was nowhere else to look except down at this pale-faced, tangle-haired creature with the bruised flower petal for a mouth and the breasts that loomed at the wilting lip of her nightdress. The voice grated and soothed all at once like beehive buzz, mingling in Rebecca's head with Jack's voice (*"I'm too into you"*), and Amanda's voice, and also that other's, her caller's, from the night before. With a sigh, Rebecca gave in, let her eyes slide all the way up to meet the woman's.

And that was when Sophie rose from the sheets, rocking upright with her whole face yawning open and her arms flung over her head like a *Scooby-Doo* phantom's. Gasping, Rebecca tumbled backward, banged her own head on the top of the drop-down ladder, thought she might drop straight through the trapdoor, and dug her fingers into the floor, driving splinters deep under her nails. She bit back a yelp, closed her eyes, and—crazily—kicked up her legs to batter whatever came for her. Then she opened her eyes.

The woman—thing—Sophie—just sat there, a gorgeous person-shaped stump seated fully on top of her pillows, as though the pillows were a dolly she could wheel. She still had her arms raised over her head. Her legs, of course, had stayed under the blankets.

"Boo," Sophie said, and grinned.

For the briefest second, Rebecca thought she'd been punked, told a Joel-style campfire story, starred in yet another episode of The Orphan Who Really Will Believe *Any*thing.

But she already knew she hadn't been. She'd been in this house for the better part of a month, after all. She'd seen Benny's injuries, and Jess with Eddie, and the photograph in the drawer downstairs. She'd taken in this room, Sophie up here alone under the blanketed window with her computer and cables and cassette deck and tape cases arrayed around her. And somehow, in this last little while, Rebecca's whole world hadn't so much tilted out of true as *finished* tilting, because everything Sophie had told her fit a little too snugly into the jigsaw Rebecca had only now begun piecing together. It all made a certain, terrible sort of sense, or *not*-sense.

All of it formed a single picture: the way Jess seemed to have just been crying every single time she turned around (because, Rebecca now knew, she *had* been); the noises in the ceiling, which had never been rats or squirrels or ghosts, and which Jess had never shown the slightest interest in checking (because she already knew what they were); the fact that Jess and Benny had rented this charred shell of a house that no one else wanted (because that way, fewer neighbors would come visiting or inquiring); the panic in Benny's voice, scant minutes ago, when he'd realized where Rebecca was heading; the phone calls neither he nor Jess ever seemed to make or receive; the photographs they didn't put up or even seem to have, except for that one in the drawer, of a black-haired, shark-eyed beauty stumbling soaking wet, fully clothed, out of the surf, arm in arm and smile in smile with the blonde on this bed.

Once more, Rebecca wanted to leap to her feet, dive down the ladder, grab Eddie, and run. Maybe she would, and soon. Maybe this would all seem funny, ridiculous, as soon as she climbed back down.

But she already knew it wouldn't. And anyway, Sophie's eyes were on her again, and Rebecca didn't seem quite able to move just yet. And her caller from last night really had called, and he hadn't jumped, which meant . . .

Sophie had settled back onto—*into?*—her legs and tucked the sheets and heavy coverlet around herself. Her eyes remained on Rebecca as she tilted her head, her expression as blankly curious and threatening as a snow owl's.

"Huh," Sophie said.

Rebecca pushed up to a sitting position and edged away from the trapdoor opening. She could feel the cooler air down there, again fought the impulse to flee, and simultaneously wondered why that impulse wasn't stronger.

"What?" she said.

"You're the orphan. Jess told me about you. On one of the very rare occasions she has deigned to come up here."

And there it was, the other reason Rebecca couldn't bring herself to leave this room: the hint of mournfulness—or everyday loneliness—in this woman's voice. Just a hint. But it was there, surely. *Wasn't it?* Rebecca, after all, had spent years training herself to recognize that tone, or, rather, to name it, since she already knew it, had practically been born with it.

"I'm . . . *an* orphan. Yeah." Rebecca met Sophie's eyes, felt them grab her, forced herself to look away.

"Yep," said Sophie, hollowly.

"*Yep* what?"

"It's just, I can feel it. There's no doubt about it. Natalie would have dug you."

"Natalie, your best friend."

"Natalie, my dead best friend." The hollowness never left Sophie's voice. Maybe it had always been there, even . . . before. Assuming any of what she'd been saying really was true. But now, it was unmistakable. "I wonder if that's why."

Instinctively, Rebecca ignored that. Whatever Sophie was asking, it seemed to float in the air between them like a beckoning finger. And Rebecca didn't want to go over there again. But she did stand up. "Natalie was Jess's daughter, right? And she's . . . *actually* dead?" She heard herself say that, almost laughed, realized she actually had no inclination to laugh whatsoever.

Sophie cocked her head the other way, slid down a little in the sheets. One of the legs under there—the nearer one—

bumped lower. Sophie reached beneath the blankets and pulled it up, making a face Rebecca couldn't read. There was something so private in the movement, and in the sound Sophie made, that for a moment, Rebecca felt embarrassed to be there.

Then the photo from the downstairs drawer flashed yet again in front of her eyes: the streaked glass, the faces fading under the streaks as though disappearing into seaspray. Those girls with their wet clothes, their smiles so bright, Rebecca half-believed she could hear the echoes of their laughter.

This woman—creature—is so much more alone than I am.

Before she could stop herself, Rebecca heard her own voice saying, "Your legs."

"What about them?" Sophie was busy stroking under the sheets, down her thighs and up them.

"So, I guess they haven't . . ."

"Oh. Yeah. No, they haven't. Serious bummer, too. They still kind of work. I mean, I can feel them. And—this is the really cool part—they feel *me*. Do you understand? No, you don't, stop nodding."

"I wasn't nodding."

"Good. Keep not doing that." Under the sheets, the hands still moved. Each long caress triggered a shudder that seemed to trail up Sophie like a little flare.

"What *is* it like?"

Sophie clucked. "Now, see, Natalie would have known better than to ask that." She brought one of her hands out from under the sheets, opened the nearest cassette, and held the cassette in front of her face. "Wouldn't you?" she cooed to the tape, as though it were a kitten or a stuffed bear. "Yes, you would. Because you would have known you'd get an answer."

Laying down the tape, Sophie nodded. "It's like . . ." Behind her blank bird-gaze, something stirred, then slipped away. "Nope. Damn it, I got nothin'. Even I have not one single thing to compare this feeling to. It's like, when I connect to them—plug them in, that's the closest I can get—I can feel the current. It's like all of me's still down there. Like the drawbridge is still lowered, and I can cross to Castle Leg and visit whenever I want, and Castle Leg's inhabitants can wave out their windows to me. But we can't quite meet. We can . . . talk to each other. Note each other. But. Hey, you know what's cool? Or, weird? I almost feel like, now that we're separate, me and my legs? If my legs had mouths?" She drummed her thighs.

Again, Rebecca felt herself leaning forward. And again, she couldn't resist the silence. She needed to know. And this woman needed to tell her. "Yeah?"

"If my legs had mouths," Sophie said, all but whispering, "you'd be running. Because they can't do anything about it, but they are *hungry.*" Then she burst out laughing. Grabbing the cassette again, she waved it over her stumps like a lamp or a wand. "That-a-girl, Nat Queen Cold. *Scowl.*"

Nat. Queen Cold. Old.

Rebecca stared anew at the cables, the laptop on the blankets, the little black box connected via USB cable, the headset microphone on Sophie's pillow.

Buh— . . . cat-dah. TONGUE.

"It's *you,*" Rebecca said. "That voice. That Internet radio station. It's—

"See, here's what I don't get." Sophie looked up, hands in her lap, hair a wild nimbus of yellow around her too-pale, almost childlike face. Her eyes drank Rebecca in.

Like Miss Havisham, Rebecca thought, *only young. Not young Miss Havisham of the doomed, blind love, but old, vengeful Miss Havisham, younger.*

"What I don't get," Sophie said, "is what you just did."

"What? You mean, figure out that—"

"Don't get me wrong, I'm glad about it. I like you, I mean it. And anyway, it's kind of intriguing for me, too. Also, honestly, when I jumped up at you back there? And when I said that about my legs? I was just playing. Really. So maybe that's it? Although I really *am* hungry; it definitely is getting near that time. Maybe that's why, and it has nothing to do with you at all." Somehow, Sophie's gaze, which had never quite left Rebecca's, seized her fully now. She lifted a finger, waved it in the air between them, and her voice dropped back into its almost-whisper. "But I don't think so. I'm new to all this, I admit it. And I'm a little beat up just now. And pretty fucking confused, or sad, or something. But still. I'm pretty certain you shouldn't have been able to do that."

For a baffling, then frightening second, Rebecca couldn't remember how to speak. She literally couldn't locate her voice. Then, somehow, she did. "Do what?"

"Jump back. Get yourself away from me." Sophie stopped whispering. "Not that it would have mattered, if

I'd really wanted you. I know, I know what you're thinking, my legs. But you will be surprised."

"You *will,*" Rebecca noted, somehow controlling a shiver of her own. Not, "you *would.*" She forced her eyes away from Sophie's—which wasn't hard this time, *she let me go*—and back to the cassettes and the headset microphone. "You're the girl on the radio. The voice."

Surprised again, Sophie grinned. "You've heard my show! Do you like it?"

"I . . . What's it . . ."

"Well"—Sophie patted the cassette cases—"that's Nat."

"Nat."

"-alie."

"Natalie. Your best friend."

"Would you cut that out? Wound, salt, wound, salt. I thought Jess said you worked at some kind of crisis center or something, and knew how to be sensitive to people in pain."

"But you . . . said she was dead."

Sophie's grin hardened. Her head swung to the window. She pulled back the blanket curtain an inch or two, letting in just a little of the gathering dark out there. "That isn't the right question. But the answer is, with great care. With fucking painstaking labor, actually. See, Jess—you wouldn't peg her as sentimental, would you, but she's a goddamn *baseball* fan, if that tells you anything—when she fled Charlotte? When the thought of ever seeing her daughter or me again chased her clean out of town? Practically all she brought with her was this bag of cassettes. Tapes and tapes and tapes of Natalie talking, at all different ages. God knows what she thought she was going to do with them.

But I'm sure glad she has them, because I've had three weeks of ten thousand hours each of *nothing better to do*. So I've been . . . cataloging. Grabbing snippets. Conjuring up my Nat." Once more, she lifted her eyes to Rebecca's. "Baiting my hook."

"Baiting. For what?"

Sophie sighed. "Again, with the wrong ques—"

"You're just keeping yourself company."

Even before the blonde rocked upright again, leaned out over the space between them—which wasn't nearly space enough—Rebecca wanted that comment back. Her feet edged backward, felt for the top step, the opening of the trapdoor. But she already knew Sophie was right: there was no way she'd be fast enough.

Sophie didn't leap at her, though. She seemed, instead, to push herself back into herself, as though stuffing one of those spring-coil snakes back into a can. Abruptly—amazingly—she smiled, not her nasty grin but the smile from the picture in Jess's drawer downstairs. *Exactly* that smile, just for a second. A sweet and shimmering thing.

"You really do remind me of her. Actually, you completely don't. But I'm serious, and it's a compliment: Natalie would have dug you. Probably a lot more than she dug me, in the end." And Sophie laughed, but *not* the laugh of the girl in the photograph.

How did Rebecca know that? She just did. Even so, there was something so close to gentle in Sophie's expression, something so much like affection without *being* that, that Rebecca heard herself say, "Thank you." Even though she had no idea what she meant.

"There are ironies," Sophie said. "Like this one: if I was

the one gone, and Natalie had wound up stashed forever in this attic? She would have been just fine. She'd have had her baby to be with, her music to play, silences to fill, or actually, *not* fill, Jesus Christ, that girl could *not* talk when she wanted not to."

Yet again, Rebecca had an opening. And yet again, her curiosity, her sense of the creature in the bed's barely acknowledged desperation, and her nagging sense that there was something else, something more, kept her where she was. What came out of her mouth was a Crisis Center question, a conversation extender. "Natalie didn't like people?"

Sophie shrugged, petting the tape in her hands. "*I* liked people. And I don't even get to have my son."

Every question Rebecca could think of next seemed cruel, suicidal, or both. Except, just maybe, the most important one.

"Do you still like people, Sophie?"

It took a long time. But in the end, Sophie laid the tape in her lap, resting her palms atop it. "I guess we'll find out when the time comes. When *he* comes."

"When—"

"The whistling asshole. I told you, you keep asking the wrong questions. I said, *baiting*. What you *should* have asked is, 'Baiting what, Sophie?' And my answer, thank you for asking, is, my trap. Because I am betting my boredom—which is all I have left, it is all that motherfucking fucker left me—that whatever he decided he felt for my *dead best friend Natalie,* his motherfuckedup 'Destiny,' he still feels it. And he's a social-networking, music-obsessed, whistling, wanking fuckball. And sooner or later, I don't know how or when but I'm betting sooner, he's going to hear my radio show. He's going to hear these songs. He's going to hear his Destiny's voice. And when he does . . . I don't know what he's going to do. But I know he'll come for her. And when he comes, you and anyone you've ever loved better get out of the way, unless you have a bazooka handy. Because you can't stop him. You have no chance.

"But me? Do you see? He doesn't know I'm still here. I'm sure he hasn't expended a single thought on me since the moment he ripped me in half. I'm pretty sure he wasn't expending any thought on me, then, any more than he does on stairs he climbs or roads he crosses.

"And that means he won't be expecting me. And I'm thinking it's just possible that I'm just enough like *him* that if I get a jump, catch him by surprise . . ."

At no point, Rebecca realized, through her own swelling panic, the voices echoing in her head—the *one* voice, now, that had crept, in the middle of last night, out of the Crisis Center receiver and straight down her eustachian tube into her brain, murmuring, '*My Destiny killed my mother*' and '*My Destiny's mother killed her*'—had she seen Sophie breathe. She certainly wasn't breathing now.

But she did stop talking long enough for Rebecca to ask one last question. It was the one, she realized, she'd been waiting all this time to ask. The one on which so much hinged:

"Are you sure you're still enough like *us* to want to?" she said.

This time, when Sophie's eyes grabbed Rebecca's, they snagged her completely. Rebecca tried turning her head, lowering her lids, forcing a shudder. Then she gave up, gave in, gazed back.

"If you stick around long enough," Sophie murmured, "I think *I* might even decide I like you."

"I hope so," Rebecca said as her phone went off in her pocket and goose bumps erupted all at once, all over her skin, as though she were a lake bombarded by a rainstorm. "Because he's already here."

19

In an ordinary month—any *other month—Caribou would never have done it.* Not *consciously. He had, in fact, spent the past forty years avoiding precisely this action, burying even the possibility of this action.*

Forty years.

Most of those years he'd whiled away by candlelight at this cherrywood desk in this tent, while the rest of the monsters, whoever was in camp, did whatever they did to waste their decades: whittle or whistle or recount slights or swap hunting stories; play card games, board games; fuck, smoke, dance, vanish; talk or sing so convincingly about missing someone or other, you'd almost believe they were capable of it, that anyone or anything on this planet was truly capable of feeling another's absence.

Sometimes, working here in the desktop candlelight, Caribou thought that that was the world's cruelest trick of all, and its greatest gift: the longing for longing. For those fleeting, heart-hurt moments when life had taste.

These were his thoughts now as he sat at the desk Aunt Sally had somehow caused to appear right here, one miraculous night, so long ago. For reasons he had never fully understood, she had chosen him—lanky Caribou of the long, long hands—out of so many others, and so he considered this desk the symbol of his Office and the significance of his duties. When he sat here, with the others down the bank or in their tents or gone and Aunt Sally in her rocking chair outside or in her own tent, dreaming her unimaginable dreams, Caribou sometimes imagined himself her greatest vassal, her Walter Raleigh, mapping the world for the woman he knew would one day behead him. And sometimes—just occasionally, on star-soaked, tingling, dangerous nights like this one—he felt like an artist, a monster-Faulkner, drunk and driven, not just mapping the world but creating it.

Only, Caribou was never drunk. And instead of a Yoknapatawpha County, he made charts.

Here they all were, cataloged and coded in their labeled folders in his cherrywood drawers. Some of them were nothing more than hand-drawn maps. Some were lists, some sketches. But all were constantly updated, their details and demarcations shaded and sharpened. Mother's Whistling fool could keep his iPhone and laptop, his GPS and Google Earth. No program and no satellite would ever see the few thousand square miles of his world—the haunted, disappearing Delta, which Aunt Sally had dreamed and Policy had purposed—in the way Caribou could. In the sheer variety of ways he could.

And so tonight, for a single moment, as he prepared to do what he had never once, in forty years, done, Caribou leaned out of his chair, in the sticky summer night that never, even on the hottest days, made him warm, held his candle over the open drawer, and marveled at what he had accomplished. Here was his own contribution to Aunt Sally's Creation: the jacket folders, numbered and lettered; the unlined papers inside those folders covered with notations and sketches but free of flourish or calligraphic design, smooth in their vellum sleeves, clean and flat as test pressings. They really were like record albums, every one, ready to sing as soon as he dropped his eyes into their grooves.

The monster's Mississippi, Mother had once scoffed, but in admiration. Even she had admired this: the whole of the territory they roamed and hunted, cataloged (and, more importantly, counted) by freeway exit, by distance (miles), by distance (travel time), by number of streets and alphabetical order of street names, family names, businesses, by numbers of magnolia trees or junipers, by address and phone prefix, by births and deaths (current year), births and deaths (historical), by town and county, by times any of Aunt Sally's denizens had passed through or set foot near or in them. A thousand charts, all compiled and rigorously maintained for the sole and express purpose of keeping Aunt Sally's children's actions un-chartable, even by the children themselves, thus ensuring that their orbit—for orbit it was and must inevitably stay, Aunt Sally too great and massive a star ever to release them, fully—remained as elliptical and mysterious as a comet's.

Even more, the charts were meant to ensure that no one, not one of them, ever did what Caribou was going to do tonight. He'd known he must from the moment Aunt Sally had told him what she needed. Even now, he could barely calm himself enough to hear, again, that word in her voice, which sent a shudder through him so bone-deep, so pleasurable and painful, it seemed to emanate from his very center, thundering down the dead, echoing arteries of his entire being like a heartbeat.

Children.

For just a moment, in his excitement and unease, he tried to pretend that he wasn't *doing what he knew he must, knew he was. What violation, after all, was he actually committing? Aunt Sally had tasked him, and him alone, with selecting and procuring the guests for this special, special Party. The numbers he had used to guide the selection of the file in his drawer, then the chart in that file, then the entry on that chart, were precisely the numbers Aunt Sally had suggested his dreams indicated, and she had arrived at those numbers by using the ever-growing, interpretive key she had devised long before there had ever* been *a Caribou.*

In other words, she'd gotten the numbers from Policy, same as always. All he had done was shuffle the order in which the numbers would be applied. He'd had to skip one, it was true, but he often had to skip, even on ordinary nights, if a particular digit in a sequence proved inapplicable to the section or chart the previous number had directed him to consult. He wasn't changing or subverting Policy, just applying it. And that had always been his job.

He wasn't altering the formula by which they had all agreed, for so very long, to make these particular choices.

He was simply shaping it, so that when his hands slid into the drawer, gliding over the tops of the files like birds in formation, they alighted atop the 117th file, then held there, as though settling on a branch. A hum buzzed in his throat. A shiver rocked him, almost as if he were surprised, as if his very skin were playing along, maintaining the illusion that this was just another Policy decision. Chance, not Caribou.

As if he didn't already know which chart he was going to pull, and what the 28th entry on it would be, and where he would be getting their guests for this momentous night.

He withdrew the file, staring as if in amazement at the neat heading across the top: INSTITUTIONAL, ISSAQUENA, SHILOH VALE, WASHINGON, EAST. *Below the heading was just another brief list: schools and civic centers, two libraries, a YMCA camp center, long abandoned.*

An orphanage.

He allowed himself a single sigh so deep, it felt like breath, or like he remembered breath feeling. Was this Policy guiding him, after all? Or Aunt Sally? Was he *guiding Policy (and there it was again, that tiny tremor of unease)? But even if he was—if* they *were, he and Sally together—she had* made *Policy, after all. She had given it to Caribou, to all of the others, like God giving his Commandments to Moses.*

Which made him Moses?

He was actually laughing as he slid into Aunt Sally's blue LeSabre and started down the muddy track out of camp. No one, as far as he knew, had used this car in months, but Aunt Sally always made him keep it gassed and primed and ready, even though she never went anywhere. When, Caribou wondered, was the last time he had driven? He'd forgotten how much he liked it, and he laughed again, watching his reflection in the windshield gliding along the edge of the river like an otter. Then the river was gone, and he angled the LeSabre through the bottomlands, past soybean fields rimmed far to the east by that miles-long furrow of wild-flowers that blossomed blue out of the buckshot soil every single summer, appearing all together, overnight, as though they'd fallen from the sky more than sprung from the earth. Then came the cotton rows where Aunt Sally's shyer monsters sometimes liked to lead their Party guests, on the nights of Aunt Sally's Parties, when the tent got loud and the music rumbled in the ground and rippled the river. Next, the swamp where one night, not too long ago—the night, Caribou realized, that Mother had finally left for good, chasing her Whistling fool—Aunt Sally had let him canoe her, mile after slow mile, through snarls of reeds that always crept closer yet somehow never reached them, pods of sleeping alligators that stirred as they passed like the scaled skin of the swamp itself, clouds so low and heavy that they clung to the earth like wet cotton, and, close on to morning, lightened just a little as the moon settled in behind them. Aunt Sally hadn't said anything about going back, and then it was too late to go back, so they'd sheltered in the crisscross shade of a sycamore grove, and she'd started to allow him to make love to her and then sung to him instead, cradling him like the roots of a tree, rocking him—and herself, it seemed, for that one, magical night—like a baby. Lay down, Sally.

Was this, Caribou wondered, why all the not-monsters—all those pathetic creatures out there roaming or sleeping away their pallid nights beyond the Delta—loved driving so much? Was this why Mother's jabberer sang and whistled so many songs about it? Because every single trip away from home was a passage through everything that made a place home to begin with?

Especially if you knew, as he knew, that this would be the last time? That after tonight, he really might not be back? That this was home no longer?

So many places had resonance, for him, it turned out, a surprising number, given how infrequently he had stirred from the tents by the riverbank. There: *the ruins of the juke joint where Mother's Whistler had learned so many of the songs he sang. And,* there, *just as the gravel turned to macadam and the first streetlights lowered themselves over the glowing, clayey dirt in the fields and baked it ordinary: the bus stop where he and Mother had broken down together, in this very car, and had had to walk the long miles back to camp, not talking to each other, but also not minding or being jealous of each other, for once. Where had they even been going?*

The miles unspooled down the hours, down the charts in his head. Here it all was: gas stations; nighttime barbecue stands with their furtive customers packed around picnic benches in the shadows like moonshiners; a trailer park; a single subdivision, developed years ago but never populated; little towns, Brattleford, West Brattleford; the abandoned shacks of Grace Holler—the former lynching capital of the Delta—all sinking now beneath their kudzu shrouds as they melted into the ground. That was the only place, in all these decades, that Policy had ever directed Aunt Sally's children to visit twice. At the time, that had seemed cruel to Caribou—only right, maybe, but also cruel—until years and years later, when the Whistler had returned to camp one day with the ballad that had surfaced about it all, out there in their world.

Such a beautiful, haunting song, a terrible thing, especially in the Whistler's greedy, reedy voice, in his Whistle that penetrated skin like teeth.

They had ripped out the heart of a cursed town, Aunt Sally's children, and replaced it with a nightmare, a myth for the ages, a fresh Crotoan. Grace Holler, where no one plays, and none dare go. The heart of a town seemed a small price to pay, in the end, for that.

So fast, too fast, his Mississippi fell away in the rearview mirrors and vanished behind him. He would have stopped or slowed to watch it go. But Aunt Sally was awaiting her guests. And there was never enough dark.

Even he was surprised at how little trouble he had spotting the turnoff, which he'd used exactly once before, on the night he'd found this place. It came up right where remembered, a little opening in the longleaf pines, deeper into the Piney Woods than he should ever have had reason to venture in the first place. How had *he found it originally? Caribou couldn't remember. What did it matter, anyway?*

More important, why was he stopping the car now, switching it off and just sitting, despite his time concerns, half a mile down this barely rutted track that hardly qualified as a lane, amid these skeletal, towering trunks that looked more like dock pilings than forest, the foundations for some massive, unimaginable ruin? Moonlight rolled between them, pouring over the ground cover, turn-

ing it that glowing, perfect Piney Woods green, that green of nowhere else.

And what was this stinging sensation, all of a sudden? This stab of . . . something about this place. These trees, this light. The crumbling white plantation house he knew was back there, a mile or so farther down the lane.

The fact that it was all too beautiful for what it was, perhaps? Or maybe that that house, and the people who inhabited it, had been out here so long that the world had all but forgotten they existed, which made them and it more than a little like Aunt Sally's camp full of monsters?

That last thought startled him, made him sit up straight and touch his own cheeks with his fingertips. And then he had another thought: what if this place was reminding him not just of his home now, but his home before*? His birthplace? Was that even possible? Or did it just feel possible tonight, because tonight promised to be so momentous?*

All at once, he gasped, actually sucked in air, an old and meaningless reflex. Apparently, there was magic in Policy, still. Oh, yes, there was. So much more than Aunt Sally professed to believe, maybe more than she knew. Because the only reason he had stopped just here was that he'd been seized by these feelings, and by the moonlight. And they had seized and transfixed him in this precise, Piney spot, at this exact moment. And that was the only reason he saw her.

Actually, all he saw at first was her eyes, little green pinpricks in the new dark, just there behind the trunk of a pine five feet or so to the left of his driver's-side window, blinking closed-and-open, closed-and-open. As soon as whatever was back there saw him looking, it skittered off, low to the ground, like an armadillo burrowing through the needles and leaves, away and farther left, deeper into the pines: a wood creature, surely, a squirrel or badger or wolverine, except he knew it wasn't any of those things even before he stepped out of the car. Silently, leaving the car door open, he glided over the ground cover into the woods, never quite losing sight of the movement, the little figure barely stirring branches as it ducked between and beneath them. He tracked her less by her movements than by those eyes that glanced back from time to time, greener even than the piney green dark, opening-closing.

He finally cornered her against the bark of a lightning-blackened stump, and she froze as he approached, as he stopped and stood staring at her, this miraculous barefoot apparition: a girl, maybe seven, eight years old, brunette hair heavy on her shoulders and down her back like moss, hanging to her waist, bestrewn with wood chips, pinecones. Her feet were bare, her blue jeans smeared with forest, green sweater hanging lopsided almost to her knees. She stared back at him—not at his eyes, but his hands, his mouth—shyly, not quite fearfully enough, like a kitten peering out the top of a bag. A kitten someone had meant to drown.

Kneeling, Caribou hooked his gaze to the girl's. Hers slid instinctively away at first. Then he had her.

"You're from the house," he said, nodding to his right, into the dark.

"Ju," she said. Or, Jew?

Caribou blinked, had to conquer an impulse to edge backward. He had her—knew he had her, he could feel it—but she hadn't answered what he'd asked.

"Short for June," she said.

At least that made sense of the word. And now, even more strangely, Caribou felt himself smile. "I didn't know there was a short for June."

"Are you here to take me back? I don't want to go back, yet."

"Well, all right, Miss Ju. Why don't you come with me? Let's go tell them we're going. Do you want to come on an adventure? You can even . . . invite a few friends. If you like."

Moments later, she was in his car. The thrill of that was almost overwhelming, and Caribou had no idea why. Part of it was simply the eyes on this girl, the bits of tree and ground cover all over her, as if she were ground cover itself, walking. She was afraid of him, yes, hunched against the passenger-side door, and when he smiled at her, she shuddered the whole grass-blade-length of her frame. But then—tentatively, as though trying it out, as though this was her very first time—she smiled back.

He stopped the LeSabre in the lane twenty feet or so from the house, just outside the halo of glowing green and red cast by the strings of Christmas lights that drooped from the cracked, leaf-engorged gutters above the veranda like old skin off older bones. Of course those lights would never be taken down, Caribou realized, probably hadn't come down in years. Who, in that house, could do such work? And of course they would be lit, every night, for as long as at least a few of the bulbs worked, because there were children in there who would want them lit.

Because this *girl lived there, and would want them lit.*

Oh, yes. Aunt Sally was going to like this one. Aunt Sally was going to take this one herself. The thought of presenting Ju to Sally set off shock waves in Caribou's skin and loins and throat, made his tongue tingle. What a present she would make, this Piney-green-eyed girl, who was still smiling at him.

He smiled back and let her go, and she danced through the droplets of light toward the already-open front doors, the old-woman caretakers, the other children emerging from behind them in their Spider-Man pajamas, their pigtails and braids, opening together into the dark like night-blooms on a single, ancient Delta plant. Grinning, still tingling, Caribou eased out of his car and gathered them to him.

20

Kaylene had been conscious for some time before she realized she was holding her breath. What alerted her, finally, was the squeezing in her cold, constricted chest, the involuntary clawing of her hands against the dark. Also, despite the fact that she could see absolutely nothing, her eyes were open; she could tell because she'd just felt herself blink.

So she was already dead?

Then she inhaled, and pain exploded all over her face, shooting firework-ribbons of red and yellow across the blackness around her without illuminating anything. She heard herself gasp, instinctively smashed her teeth shut to cut off the sound, but there wasn't much sound, anyway. Because after he'd finished with her face, the bastard had got hold of her throat again. And now she couldn't get it uncrumpled.

This time, when she breathed, she did so through her mouth, between clenched teeth, sucking air over the blood on her gums. That worked better.

She was thinking clearly enough by this point to know that the room was spinning. *How* she knew that, she had no idea, since she couldn't see a goddamn thing. But it was, around and around. Kaylene's stomach lurched, lurched again, and fluid bubbled out of her mouth and forced her to breathe once more through her shattered nose. Shards of bone pricked her mucous membranes like broken glass.

At least this time she didn't even try to make a noise. She just went on grabbing uselessly at the ice.

The ice.

So she was still in Mrs. Starkey's barn, and therefore not dead. Whatever dead was, Kaylene was pretty sure it wouldn't hurt this much. Not in this many places. And she wouldn't be listening this hard, and she wouldn't be this cold. Or this scared.

Breath sluiced through her teeth as the room slowly, slowly steadied. The rush of air seemed thunderous in her ears. Abruptly, she curled into a ball, everything in her body screaming at her to *hide, play dead.* She lay there a long time, feeling like a roly-poly waiting to be squashed.

Then she'd had enough of that. *Kaylene,* she ordered herself, *MOVE.*

But she didn't move, couldn't even imagine moving. She listened instead, heard nothing. Was it really possible that he had gone? The asshat in the hat?

Memory surfaced, set her clawing at the ice and gasping all over again. And then she remembered Marlene.

She opened her mouth to scream, didn't scream, somehow held both the impulse and the memory back just far enough, just for this second. She waited, curled up, frozen and still. If her attacker was still in the barn, he had to know where she was by now, given the racket she was making while trying to stay silent, even if he hadn't known before. Even if he *couldn't* somehow see in the dark like a cat. Like the fucking monster he was.

But all she heard was the hum of the rink, and she didn't so much hear that as feel it in her ribs, like a murmur in her heart, which was still beating. Still beating. The ice kept tilting under her hands as the room seesawed. But she thought she might sit up.

The whisper was out of her mouth before she could stop it. "*Jack?*"

Again, she curled into herself, clutched the ice as best she could, waited to be torn apart, or for Jack to call back if he could. If he was still here.

Nothing.

And because there was nothing, more memory swelled to fill the empty space. *His* voice, this time. The monster's voice, whispering right in her ear as he smashed her face again and again into the door she'd been trying, with all her trembling, shrieking might, to drag open.

Except he hadn't been whispering, was mostly singing. He'd been singing her a nonsense-song as he held her off her feet by her hair, swung her like a doll.

"*Tell your friend . . .* (SLAM) *. . . your sweet operator* *friend . . .* (SLAM) *. . . I'm overcoming the blow. Learning to take it well. And this won't be the way it feels."*

And even as he'd hurled her one last time into the steel door, driven the bridge of her nose up into her forehead and dumped her on the ice and dragged or kicked her across it until she lost consciousness, Kaylene had realized he'd meant Rebecca.

Who had never seen the Sombrero-Man, and had no idea what was coming.

Too fast, Kaylene scrambled to her knees, shoving her hands into her pockets in search of her cell phone. The wave of nausea almost pummeled her prone again. But she stayed up, somehow. Gagging, she thrust her hands deeper into pockets, patted herself all over, but found nothing.

He'd taken her phone. Or—just as likely—it had flown from her pocket and was probably lying all the way at the other end of the ice (from whichever end she was on, whichever way she was facing), or maybe it was right beside her but completely invisible in the smothering dark. Sweating, shivering, still nauseous, Kaylene freed her hands from her jeans and dropped them to the ice. That felt surprisingly good, like caressing a bumpy, stubbled face. A face she knew. Plus, the cold was clarifying.

She had no idea which way to point herself. But she realized, woozily, that it didn't matter. Any direction she crawled, she would eventually reach a wall. Any turn she took from there would lead her, sooner or later, back to the door. And even if Sombrero-Man had managed to lock that, and even if she still couldn't stand, by then, she would raise such a ruckus that someone from Starkey's would have to hear, sooner or later.

Assuming Sombrero-Man hadn't gone in there, too. And that he wasn't still here, right behind her.

This time, as she ducked, Kaylene actually punched the ice. She'd moved too fast again, and the room spun some more, churning the slosh in her stomach. But she managed to stay up on her hands and knees instead of curling into a ball, and she held on, and nothing jumped on her.

There was *no point,* whatsoever, in thoughts like the ones she'd just had. She was still here. Sealed in the dark, smashed to shit, but *here,* and therefore a threat to Sombrero-Men, wherever they lurked. Oh, yes, she was. All she had to do was figure out how to move.

Like a Dig Dug, she decided, and somehow she scraped up a sort of laugh that hurt all kinds of everywhere. If the monster really was still here, and if he hadn't heard her before, he'd heard her now. So be it.

"Come on," she hissed to the dark, the Sombrero-Man, her own limbs.

Then she was moving. And that went fine, at first. Better than fine. The icy wetness on her palms, seeping through her pants legs, restored more everyday sensation with every sideways slide she took. *I am just a little Dig Dug in the dark, eating a path to the surface, to all my other fellow Dig Dugs prowling right nearby, so close.* The movement itself calmed her stomach, smothered her thoughts, at least until she put her hand down in pulp.

Splinter of jawbone. Shank of hair.

Marlene.

Or Jack? Or both of them? It could easily be. Was this his *hair, here? And this his flappy Jack-earlobe?*

She could hear—*feel*—her brain screaming at her hands

to *STOP,* lift away. But her hands ignored the command, went right on pawing through the slop, all these stringy, shardy bits that might or might not be all that was left of both of her friends. They were definitely Marlene, because Kaylene had seen that happen.

Marlene hadn't frozen, the way Kaylene had (*because Marlene hadn't yet had the Sombrero-Man's hands on her*). Marlene hadn't panicked (*because she didn't yet understand how useless absolutely anything she might do would turn out to be*). Marlene hadn't whirled for the door to run.

Or rather, Marlene had run, all right, at full tilt, straight down the ice, skidding out of the cone of light into the dark, to save Jack, while Kaylene had turned and fled, and failed even to do that successfully.

Apparently, to her own astonishment, *she* was the coward.

Or maybe—simply because she'd already had the Sombrero-Man's hands on her—she already understood what actions might be possible, which movements had the potential to distract that guy, at least, or bring help, and thereby save at least one or two of them. And so she'd reached the door, yanked it, turned around to scream a warning, and seen. Watched.

She still couldn't see anything, now. But she was looking down at her hands, anyway. They were still smearing around on the ice. Her right forefinger and thumb were rolling something slick between them, painting her palm with whatever they'd found.

Get up, she screamed inside her own head. *GET. UP.*

She got up, or started to, coaxing her hands back toward

her sides. She put her right palm down again to push all the way to her feet and caught the edge of the flying saucer, Jack's flying saucer, which tilted up and set the roundish, heavy things resting inside it rolling toward her like apples in a bowl, and she burst out weeping, burst out screaming, felt her brain dive back inside itself again, and she was falling even as the dark swarmed her.

21

Even as she fought it, grabbed hold inside herself of everything she could call up about Natalie—the blue eyes under long black bangs at age seven, and under short black bangs at twenty-one, the smell of Waffle House that clung to her hair, her sweet Natalie-skin—Jess could feel it happening. Really, it had happened, or finished happening, an hour or so ago, right as she left her horrible, crumbling house and turned and saw Rebecca, sweet and lost, needing someone, just standing there in the doorway holding Eddie. It had *been* happening, really, from the second Jess had pulled the trigger on that nightmare beach. There was nothing she could do, it turned out, to stop it from happening or, at least, nothing she *would* do.

The world was coming to get her, to suck her back out

into it. And there was no memory she could grab that was strong or stable enough to keep her where she was, no matter how much she wanted to stay.

And so here she stood, folding the sheets and towels at Amanda's long table in the Halfmoon House kitchen, because Amanda needed help upstairs taking care of the girls, who needed a hell of a lot more help. When Jess was done with this task, she would go straight up to those girls and spend some time with them. She'd concentrate especially on the older one, Danni, whom Amanda didn't seem to know how to reach, since Rebecca was already well on her way to saving Trudi, the little one. When that was done, Jess would come back down and finish the dinner dishes and sweep and clean until her time here was up. And then she would go home *(what a stupid word for that splintery, cindery place)* to her baby *(who wasn't her baby)* and her broken man *(who was indeed her man, maybe more so than her husband had ever really been)* and her grief *(that would never leave her or lessen)* and demand that Rebecca clear out her pathetic apartment. She'd tell Rebecca to bring her ridiculous, clueless guy—who had no idea what he had, yet, but would before Jess was through with him—and move in.

As . . . what? Governess? Surrogate daughter, to the extent that such a thing was even possible? How about *different* daughter?

Or just friend? When was the last time Jess had allowed herself one of those?

Whichever, it was going to happen. Because no matter what Jess wanted—and what she wanted most was still just to *stop*, drop to her knees in the middle of the street in the middle of this town, throw back her head, and wail until her voice gave out, forever—she couldn't seem to shut out everything else for long enough. For fifteen years, she'd walled herself up in a trailer and a Walgreens after losing her husband; then she'd lost her daughter and fled the only town she'd ever lived in, leaving not so much as a working phone number. And she'd still wound up surrounded by people who needed her, and whom she could help, and whom she loved, or knew she would love, given time: Eddie, of course, and Benny, too, but also wounded, wooden Amanda and funny-lonely Joel. And Rebecca, almost more than any of them.

How had that happened? When would it stop? That's what she was thinking as her hands went on folding and smoothing the still-warm sheets in their basket and her voice hummed some song Natalie had loved about not singing this song, *no-nnnn-no-no-no-no, no-no,* when the phone rang.

Jess looked up, stopped humming. As a general rule, the phone, like everything else in Amanda's house, obeyed the routine Amanda had set for it; it rang at occasional and specifically appointed hours but no others. And this wasn't one of them.

Amanda appeared at the other end of the room in her work apron, pushing away whatever single stray hair had dared slip free of her headband. With a glance at Jess, she lifted the receiver. "Hello?" she said. "What? Rebecca, for God's sake, slow down." Then she just stood there.

Freeing her hands from the blankets, Jess peeled off her own apron, feeling herself coil. Amanda was shaking her head and sighing. "Rebecca, what are you even . . . what do you mean, lock up the . . . you're not making . . . *Who?* Who's going to—"

Jess hadn't meant to hip-check Amanda, certainly hadn't meant to send her flying. That's just what happened when she swooped in and grabbed the phone.

"Rebecca, it's Jess."

"Oh. Jess. Good. That guy. The one. Your . . . Jess. Listen, I'm so sorry. I think—"

"It's him, isn't it?"

And there it was, Jess thought: the secret source of the calm she knew she exuded, and really did almost always feel. She hadn't been born with it. It was nothing she'd cultivated or summoned. She had simply learned, very early in her life, exactly how much good wishing or pretending or praying would do. Or fighting, either, for that matter. And then she'd gone on fighting anyway.

And now he was here: the whistling freak who'd driven her daughter out of Charlotte and then back home, so Jess could murder her.

"Rebecca, I'm coming right now. Hold on, kiddo."

She started to hang up, then jammed the phone back against her ear and yelled, "*Wait!*"

"Jess, Sophie thinks he—"

"Don't listen to what Sophie thinks. Jesus Christ, even before she was . . . what do you mean, *Sophie thinks*? How do you know what—"

"I went in the attic."

"You went in the attic. Of course you did."

"I'm sorry. Jess. She's . . . it's real, isn't it . . . and—"

"There's no time for that." Jess punched the wall so hard that Amanda's butcher knives jumped in their block on the countertop. A glass fell and broke. Jess stared down at her hand. Her small, useless hand, good only for folding diapers, pulling triggers. "There's no time. Rebecca, listen. *Shit.* Listen. You have to get it together. Do you hear me? You have to—"

"I am together," Rebecca said.

She was; it was true. And Jess loved her.

"I know. Good. Okay. Understand, please. There's *no time.* Get Eddie out of there. You hear me? That's your one and only job, Rebecca. *Get Eddie out!*"

The pause lasted a split second. Less. "Okay. You get Trudi out," Rebecca said.

Slamming down the phone, Jess stared past Amanda at the back wall of this hopeless, indefensible house with its warped window casings, its falling-off doors. Then she felt herself laugh, just once, savagely, as the world gushed in and filled her once more.

Amanda had stayed sprawled against the cabinets where Jess had knocked her, staring up in confusion or maybe amazement. She stirred, now, but Jess held up a forefinger, gave her a look she could only hope Amanda understood.

But of course, she couldn't. How could she? She'd never seen the man in the sombrero, never heard him speak or whistle or sing, never felt his bobcat eyes on—*in*—hers, probing and perusing. Amanda had no idea what was coming, or how much Jess regretted having brought him here, to this tragic, magical place where people really did occasionally save each other, however briefly.

Damn it. This woman's house had seen more than enough loss already. Like most houses, Jess supposed.

"I'm sorry," she said. From the butcher block, she grabbed the carving knife and the bread knife. She slid the bread knife toward Amanda. "Get up. Lock everything. Get Joel inside."

"Jess—"

"Get up!"

Amanda was on her feet by the time Jess hurtled past her and flew for the stairs, shouting, *"GIRLS?"* Amanda yelled for Joel, and Joel answered from somewhere outside, in his gentle, gravelly voice that always seemed to rise like smoke off the ashy embers of his heart, because it really was—had been—a father's heart. The back door opened, and then came the satisfying, useless sound of windows lowering, latches getting twisted, bolts shooting home. None of which would matter when the bastard came.

But he'll be sorry, Jess thought, grinding her teeth, clenching her fists as she soared up the stairs, knowing he wouldn't be.

Right at the landing, Jess stopped, not knowing why. She stared down the hall at the closed bedroom doors, out the window toward the woods, the massed green leaves at its border, which were surging, folding over and around themselves. *Birnam Wood, to Dunsinane,* Jess thought crazily, shouting yet again, "Trudi! Girls!"

Then she stopped again, realizing what she'd just seen out there, barely glimpsed vanishing into the trees, and refused at first to accept or acknowledge.

"Girls," she said once more, whimpered, really, and moved the last few steps to the bedroom doors, already knowing. She threw open Danni's door first. Trudi's she opened more gently, as though doing that could change what she knew she would find, and found:

The girls were gone.

22

The truth was, the Whistler almost didn't want the conversation to end. All the way through town, he'd chattered, laughed, pointed past both his companions out the rolled-down windows at the little white houses and shops he'd already come to feel were his, now: his pizza place, where he'd lurked outside to watch his new, Still One's companions; his bench, where he'd first introduced himself to them; the Clocktower, where he'd first heard his Still One's voice, which was indeed still, so unlike his Destiny's. His Destiny had spoken like whipped-up water, her inflections full of waves and crests and flashing, reflected light. But this new woman was, in her way, even more *inviting or, at least, the right kind of inviting for the days after his Destiny's death: a lake rather than an ocean, mysteriously deep underneath, but on the surface, almost preternaturally still. A surface that motionless, that peaceful and glassy and quiet: what living creature could possibly resist diving in and shattering it?*

Not him.

"Not you guys, either, huh?" he asked his companions, glancing sideways to see their faces. They nodded along to the hum of the truck, the buzz of his iPod in the truck's speakers. Yes, indeed. They'd all *had too much to dream last night.*

Past them out the passenger window, he saw the forest, all those pines linking branches like worshippers at a service. A service he *was leading. In his mouth and nostrils, the wet, muddy* odor of *leaves and lake mixed with the after-tang of* blood—bloods!*—and the dry-mouth burn of his hunger, which he hadn't allowed himself to sate. Oh, no. Not yet. He'd barely whetted his appetite, which was* huge, *tonight, as though he were brand-new, a still-growing Whistler.*

On impulse, he rolled his window down, waved and Whistled at two college girls in summer running Ts as they jogged past, practically begging them to glance right into the cab of this creaking wreck of a truck. It was the performer in him. And the girls, both of them, they did it, *looked right at him, right past him, and then away, fast, without quite seeing. "Don't Gild the Lily, Lily" burbled out of the Bluetooth speaker linked to his phone, and he supposed he might be guilty of exactly that. Mother had always chided him for going too far, giving too much of himself when he set out to perform, to affect the people he encountered, even the ones he wasn't going to eat. Change and haunt them; give them dreams.*

But that's who he was, after all: a Whistler all the way down, heartbroken heartbreaker. And he'd allowed Mother to deny this part of his nature—let himself deny it—for way too long. Or maybe it had simply taken the deaths of Mother and his Destiny to uncover it.

He turned onto the street where he'd followed his Still One earlier this evening. So bravely early he'd set out and done that, with the world still alight, the light scalding. But he had been strong, and anyway, there'd been no prospect of returning to sleep. Not after his Destiny herself had called to him from out of the trees.

He'd almost introduced himself to his Still One a couple hours ago, as she'd lingered for one of her strange, still moments outside that scorched house. But he'd experienced yet another of those tingles of Destiny, of Aunt Sally's Policy, something, *because he already knew this house, of course. He'd spent his first several nights just mooning around outside it, looking in the windows at the all but empty rooms, at the mother-murderer of his Destiny moving blankly from kitchen to staircase to single couch, where she sat for hours on end, staring at nothing, or sometimes at a photograph she pulled from a drawer.*

Undeniably fascinating, that woman. Frightening, even. But not nearly as compelling as this new, still one, if only because she was already broken.

That didn't mean she couldn't be useful, though. Yes, it was true: he'd finally found a use and a place for his Destiny's murdering mother. "This'll be the day-ay-ay," he said-sang to his companions, waited for them to join in as he parked the truck just a few houses down the block from Jess's house.

"Wait here," he told them. "She won't be long." And he giggled as he popped open his door and hopped down.

A child skateboarded past, not even glancing up. Across the street, kneeling amid her drooping late-summer flowers, an old woman nudged at and sang to a tomato plant in its cage. Oh, yes, she was singing, though with hardly any tune, not even enough voice for the Whistler to make out the song. So often, he'd seen the solitary ones do that, thinking music would comfort them, not realizing that the songs themselves were tearing them to pieces. Because music, in the end, was just a tease, even for him, a come-on, not an action. The greatest tease, greatest come-on, closest anyone might ever come to expressing, or using, what they'd forgotten they had while they had it. But a come-on, all the same.

The Whistler waited until the old woman looked up, and then he waved, freezing her there in the dirt with her dried-up heart flooding. What wondrous playthings people made. Aunt Sally would never realize what she was missing, just sitting in her tent down there in the Delta, sedentary as a bullfrog on a lily pad sucking flies out of the air.

The Whistler so much wanted to stay where he was. His companions wanted him to stay, too; that way, they could all surprise his Still One together, see the look on her face. "I know," he said into the cab of the truck, reached in, and straightened them there against each other, like a florist finishing a bouquet, arranging the last baby's breath around it. "There. You're beautiful." He patted each of them on the legs, shut them in, allowed himself one last glance toward that house.

"Ohh," he sighed.

But he had promises to keep: to his Destiny, who'd come back for him after all, to point the way, to guide and care for him; to Mother and Aunt Sally, who had given him the world and all the creatures in it to play with; to his new, Still One. Most of all, to himself. Never again would he *forget what he had in him.*

And besides. He didn't want to gild the lily, Lily. Turning, Whistling, all but skipping, he lit out back up the block through the evening toward the woods.

23

By the time she'd finished talking to Jess, Rebecca had somehow gotten herself quiet and located her Crisis Center self inside the seething rest of her. At least that made her feel as though she was still the person she'd willed herself to be, even if the world beyond Halfmoon House had proved even more terrifying than experience had trained her to expect. Snapping her phone shut, she stood for just a few breaths in the empty bedroom beneath the attic, staring out the fly-specked, spider-cracked window at the dogwoods and hemlocks across the street sagging with the weight of their own living, drooping toward autumn.

"Okay," she murmured, whirled toward the hallway to go get Eddie, and stopped in her tracks. She clung to the splintery sides of the fold-down attic stairs, and she stared.

How had Sophie even gotten down the stairs? Never mind silently, without Rebecca noticing. How had she done it at all? Rebecca had no idea. But there Sophie was, blocking the doorway to the hall, head cocked, corn-straw hair spilling past her shoulders. More than anything, she looked like a matryoshka doll: dead-faced, pale, draped in a hideous yellow T-shirt from some bar somewhere. The shirt had a drooling, foaming smiley face on it, and the words *Halfway Out!* emblazoned across the chest.

She was holding Eddie in her arms.

"What are you doing?" Rebecca said.

Against the drooling smiley face, in his blanket, Eddie squirmed and fussed. *Because he's cold,* Rebecca knew, without knowing how she knew. *Because it's freezing cold in those arms.*

"How's our Jess? Jessie Supermom?" Sophie chirped. Something snapped in her mouth, and Rebecca shuddered, hunched to throw herself across the room, then realized it was gum.

"Sophie, when did . . . how did you . . . ?"

The next snap from Sophie's teeth triggered louder fussing from Eddie. Rebecca started forward, but stopped as Eddie settled.

Because her spell could hold him, too? Or—and was this worse?—because he knew *those arms, cold as they were? He knew their weight, had no doubt felt them around him, heard that chirping voice almost every single day of his life.*

"What?" said Sophie. "You mean this?" She leaned over Eddie, crushed him against her breasts, and warbled. To

Rebecca, it sounded like pigeon-cooing, less comforting than *wild*. Or hungry.

"Give him to me," Rebecca said. "Jess wants me to get him out of here."

Without looking up, Sophie hugged Eddie tighter, lowered her head farther. "In a sec," she murmured. And she stood—if that was the word—in the doorway on the stumps of her legs in her yellow drooly-face shirt, holding her dead best friend's son. After a while, she put her nose in Eddie's hair, her mouth against his scalp; Rebecca made herself wait. And that's when she realized Sophie wasn't cooing, but singing. Rebecca could even make out some of the words, this time.

"Armless . . . boneless . . . chickenless egg . . . Georgie I hardly . . ."

The singing stopped, but Sophie stayed put, her nose in Eddie's hair. Eddie stirred again, and this time he laughed, or maybe burped. Finally, Sophie lifted her head. She wasn't crying, not like Rebecca had thought, or hoped, she might be. She was grinning.

"Tang!" she said, half-sang. "It's lime Tang. *That's* what that smell is. Is there lime Tang? There should be. They should make something we can drink that smells and tastes exactly like this." One more time, she buried her face in Eddie's hair.

He's here, Rebecca screamed inside herself, to wake herself up, shred this haze that Sophie seemed to generate just by being in the room. *And he's met my friends.* Her half trance shattered, and she fumbled her phone out of her pocket, woke it up. But no one had called. *Why had no one called?*

"Give him to me." Rebecca stepped forward, arms outstretched.

Sophie snapped her gum and swung Eddie farther out of Rebecca's reach, though still cuddled against her chest.

"No problem," she said. "As long as you're leaving."

"Obviously, I'm leaving. Give—"

"As long as you're not going where Jess is. Or to your . . . caretakers? Is that the word for them? Or your friends, either."

"Why shouldn't I? What do you care?"

"I don't. Except." She glanced sidelong at Eddie, touched his face with a purple polka-dot fingernail. He shrieked. With a shrug, Sophie looked back at Rebecca. "You need to understand this, girlfriend. You need to believe it. You need to *know* it. There is nothing you can do out there. If he really has come, and if he's with your friends, you can't help. The best thing you can do—the *only* thing you can do—is run."

"Give me Eddie."

"Tell me you're running."

"*Give him to me.*"

"Tell me you'll let them all die. Say it. Say, 'Sophie, I understand, I will let everyone I have ever loved die to save this kid I barely know who isn't mine.' Say those words, and he's yours."

Growling in exasperation, Rebecca grabbed her phone again and speed-dialed Jack, but got his idiot voice mail: "*Up the beanstalk. Take care of my cow.*"

"Jack, where are you? I need you," she snapped, clicked End, watched Eddie wriggle and Sophie quiet (or mesmerize) him with a wave of her fingers across his tiny eyelids. Rebecca dialed Kaylene.

This time, she got nothing, not even a ring. "*The number you have reached is not available* . . . " And that was just plain ridiculous. Impossible. Kaylene not available was like saying . . . was like Kaylene not breathing . . . was . . .

"Looks like you've got a choice to make," Sophie said, stroking Eddie's hair. The action looked surprisingly comfortable, casual, automatic. Motherly. And all the more disturbing for that.

"How about a compromise? Let's give him to Benny," Rebecca said.

Sophie burst out laughing. " 'Cause he was so good at keeping him away from *me* five minutes ago, for starters? Wasn't he, little man? Little Nat-man." She did it again, dropped her head like a chicken pecking feed and nipped Eddie's cheeks. She might have been kissing them.

The effort of *not* flinging herself at Sophie—bowling her over, grabbing the baby, and bolting downstairs, out of this horrible house and through the woods to reach her friends—was causing Rebecca physical pain. She felt as though her skin might split, unleashing her skeleton from its straitjacket of brain and membrane so it could just get out there and *do something*.

"What did you do to Benny?" she whispered.

Again, Sophie laughed. "Nothing he didn't enjoy. Much as he hates himself for it."

Rebecca gaped. A little more of whatever she had inside her—of the woman she had been, an hour ago—escaped through her mouth.

"Oh, don't be such a prude." Sophie tickled Eddie, smiled at him. "It wouldn't have been the first time. And he can't really help it when I come for him, after all. It's our secret, and it can stay that way as far as I'm concerned. It's been good for both of us: relief, for him; practice, for me."

The image solidified in front of Rebecca's eyes, as clearly as if she had been in the bedroom closet, watching stump-Sophie—like the incubus in that *Nightmare* painting—climbing astride Benny. Crawling up his broken legs.

"Also," Sophie continued, "it's my little private revenge on Jess, for being such a black-and-white, hell-on-wheels bitch half the time."

"For not killing you, you mean. For saving your life."

"I said half the time." Sophie caught Rebecca's eye. Or—no—Rebecca caught *hers,* this time. Sophie blinked, looked away. "When she's not being the mom I didn't have, and really thought I was going to be."

For a single moment, Rebecca wavered. The scene in front of her kept shifting, then shifting again, as if she were looking through a pinhole at a kaleidoscope. She shook her head, closed and opened her eyes, her fists. None of that helped. And there was no time.

"Nope. I'm sorry, Sophie. I'm taking him."

"Only if—"

"You said you'd give him to me if I run. I'll run."

In Sophie's arms, in his blanket, in the sleep she'd somehow caressed him into, Eddie shivered. And Sophie looked up, dead-eyed or maybe just tired. She certainly wasn't grinning. "Really? You think you can make yourself do that?"

"Look at me," Rebecca said, and Sophie did. "You said

you liked me. You told me why you liked me. What do *you* think?"

"I think I'm impressed," Sophie murmured. "I couldn't have done it. And neither—despite what she would have claimed—could Natalie. But then, I guess, you're not really a . . . Not like we were . . ." She lowered her own head to Eddie's one more time. She was holding him out toward Rebecca when Rebecca's phone blared.

Rebecca's reaction was immediate, instinctive, multipurpose. So much in her life—her parents' death, her years at Halfmoon House, the Crisis Center—had trained her for this moment, to somehow do everything that needed doing at the same time in one unbroken movement. She swept the phone to her ear with one hand and flung up a warning finger to Sophie with the other, along with a glance that said, *Don't move,* and also, *hold on*. And, *I'm still running*.

"Where the hell have you—" she started, and the giggling cut her off.

"Guess where we are?" Trudi said.

Rebecca heard more giggling, accompanied, in the background, by outright cackling, which was louder and nastier.

"*I saw what you did!*" the nastier voice taunted. Danni's voice. "Ooh, Amanda's mad at you."

In an instant, Rebecca understood, knew what had happened so precisely, it was as though some of her really had slipped out of her skin, but hours ago, and stayed behind at Halfmoon House to see the whole ridiculous, utterly predictable episode unfold. She could perfectly imagine the reaction to her phone call of just a few minutes prior: it had triggered Jess, who had launched Amanda into action mode, set both of them sprinting through the house, slamming doors, locking windows, shouting for Joel, for the children upstairs.

Shouting. The thing that almost never happened at Halfmoon House, and that pretty much every girl who had ever lived there hated most. And Danni—who could be so mean—hated shouting even more than most, because she'd heard so much of it wherever she'd been before she came to Amanda's.

She'd have been lurking on the landing, probably; that's where she generally lurked. She'd have seen everything that happened. And when the shouting had started, and Jess and Amanda started whirling around and Joel yelled from outside to see what was wrong, Danni would have stood up and crept down the hall to Trudi's room, not to torment—not this time—but to enlist.

To cling to. Like a sister.

Because that was the only relationship—the one person—Danni was absolutely sure she understood, Trudi the only living creature Danni was absolutely certain would respond to her, would neither judge nor fail her. *Like* I've *failed her,* Rebecca thought. And of course, Trudi would indeed come when Danni beckoned, for most of the same reasons.

So Trudi had come, and she and Danni had fled together out the patio door none of the kids was supposed to have a key to, down the back steps of Halfmoon House, across the lawn into the woods to escape the shouting. Once there, they'd chuck pinecones at wood rats and rip bark off birches, or else head to the lake to shriek with the loons, just to prove, once and for all, to anyone who would notice, that they were free.

"Trudi." Rebecca cleared her throat, punching her finger

toward Sophie again to nail her in place. "Trudi, listen. This is no jok—"

"Amanda's mad at you," Danni sang in the background. "Amanda's mad at you."

"Guess where we're going?" Trudi said.

Not to the lake, Rebecca realized, as her stomach rolled all the way over. *The lake wasn't forbidden enough. Oh, Trudi, no.* She sucked in air, thought she might throw it up, commanded herself not to. "You can't go there," she said. "Trudi, don't go there. Not the clearing. Not those trailers. Trudi, please. You have to listen. Go back to the house. No, wait. Put Danni on. Or, come here, to town. I need you. I need you both. We can—"

The phone shrieked in her ears, three short bursts, like laser-fire in one of Kaylene's idiot arcade games. Rebecca knew what she'd see even before she looked at the screen. She'd lost the call. She started to hit Redial but froze with her thumb over the button, watching as Sophie slowly drew Eddie back to her chest.

"Looks like you've got a choice to make," Sophie said.

And no time. Tears came. Rebecca let them, ignored them, stared at the creature in front of her, and made her decision. In the instant—and the only thing she forgot, she would realize later, was how long Sophie had said it had been since the night Jess's daughter had died, and what that would have to mean about Sophie's hunger—she was as confident as she could possibly be that it was the right one.

And even if it wasn't, the Crisis Center had trained her to keep acting, doing something, instead of wasting time regretting.

"You'll protect him?" she whispered.

Sophie shrugged. "Better than you can. You do understand that if he's there—the Whistler—and you go to him, you're not going to be able to do anything except die, right? I've made that clear?"

Rebecca was already moving. Sophie somehow scooted out of the way on her stumps.

"You don't know that."

"Sure," Sophie said, cradling Eddie. "I don't know that."

"If anything happens to this baby—"

Sophie shot out a hand, grabbing Rebecca's wrist as she tried to pass and swinging her viciously around, pinning her to the very air with her gaze. "I can't promise, girlfriend. No one can. But if you really thought *I* was your problem—if you thought *I* was Eddie's problem—you wouldn't be going. Would you?"

That was true, of course. All of it. But what amazed Rebecca most was that Sophie apparently wanted her to say so. Needed to hear it.

"Okay," she said.

"Is she right, little man?" Sophie said, releasing Rebecca, returning her full attention to the bundle in her arms. "Do you think she's read the situation correctly, little Nat-man?"

"Keep him safe, Sophie. Please."

Down the hall, Benny started shouting, pleading, "Rebecca, don't go. Don't leave Eddie with *that.*"

But Rebecca was already flying down the stairs, out the front door onto the crumbling porch, into the surprising darkness, where she stopped in amazement, staring across the street at the battered blue truck parked there. She recognized it instantly, of course, even though she'd only ridden in it once, a few months ago, when she'd come off her late shift feverish and flu-ridden, started across campus, and met Oscar, as usual—sad, sweating, coated in leaves—under the black gum trees. With hardly a word, he'd parked his rake against a tree, left his bags in the grass, and driven her the five blocks home.

If she considered what she was seeing at all, now, she thought maybe he'd taken handyman work in the neighborhood: cleaning gutters, painting fences. No matter what he was doing, Rebecca knew, he would take one look at her face and then take her wherever she needed to go, without asking.

"*Oscar!*" she shouted, and sprinted straight for the truck.

24

In the backseat of the LeSabre, the children Caribou had selected—only three, it was enough, Miss Ju and the dark-haired, gray-eyed brother and sister in matching Spider-Man pajamas—bounced up and down in their seats, played cat's cradle, squirmed around and leaned over one another to point at telephone poles, black horses in long grass, glimpses of moon: the world they'd barely even heard tell of popping up around them as though from the pages of a children's book, as though the world were the fairy-tale place, not their crumbling, hidden, parentless house way back in the woods, or Aunt Sally's camp, tucked away in the last expanse of lost Delta.

In the front, meanwhile, leaning half out of her seat belt toward him, one alabaster hand splayed on the vinyl like a sliver of moon marbled with beautiful blue, sat the children's caretaker. Again, he'd brought only one, left the others; it was enough. And by the time the women he'd allowed to stay behind stirred from the dreams he'd draped over them, realized it was morning, and understood that their companions weren't coming back, the Party would be over, the partygoers dispersed. The camp itself, which had been his and Aunt Sally's home for more than thirty years, would be dismantled, drowned in the river, buried in the fertile Mississippi mud, where it would sprout stories, someday.

The caretaker had white hair streaked with blond, or lighter white. Whatever those colors were, they were natural, their pattern as unmistakable and un-creatable as sediment lines in a riverbank. Beautiful. She'd told him her name more than once, but Caribou had been distracted. He kept thinking about Aunt Sally's voice—the hint of trembling in it, Aunt Sally trembling*!—at the moment she'd tasked him, sent him forth to bring back children. Also, every time he glanced in the mirror, he found Miss Ju's eyes staring back, bright green, unblinking, as though painted on the glass or hovering in the air. She was playing with the other two. He could hear them all giggling, slapping hands, calling out,* "Pizza!" *when they passed a pathetic little strip mall in some disintegrating town. And yet, she was always looking at him. At first, he'd thought it was her stillness that captivated him so. But she wasn't ever really still. So it was something else.*

"Hon?" the caretaker cooed, like a mourning dove, like a lover. "You all right? You want me to drive?"

Ann, Caribou decided. He'd call her Ann. Or think of her as Ann.

In the back, the Spider-Man-sister, too, kept darting glances at him, snatching at his *glances. Her gaze held no mystery whatsoever. Almost, Caribou had left her behind, precisely because she'd started grabbing at his gaze from the moment he'd appeared out of the night and the woods, as if he were some white knight in his dark chariot, come to spirit her away. Her eyes winked with little-girl mischief, but also with longings and loneliness and hungers she barely even realized she felt, let alone had names for, yet. And that, he knew—though even he couldn't have said how, and Aunt Sally certainly hadn't specified—made her not quite the sort of guest he'd been commanded to fetch.*

But she'd wanted so to come, this girl, had twined her arms in Ju's, wrapped herself around Ju like kudzu. And it had seemed easier, somehow, to bring her, and also merciful. For Ju, at least. At least she'd have companions.

And now that the Spider-Man-sister was here, Caribou knew it was also merciful, at occasional intervals, to look away from Ju or the road and actually give this girl a glimpse of what she thought she wanted. He did it only in flashes, only for a moment at a time, long enough to stir her, to let her know that he knew, and saw. But not long enough to set her climbing over the seat to get at him.

And there it was. The girl couldn't help it, of course. If what was happening to her was anyone's fault, it was his. She gave a little wriggle of her tiny shoulders, a near-wink. A smile twitched, too wide, across her heart-shaped face. All wrong. Aunt Sally would not want this one, not tonight. She was too close to conscious maturity, to the woman she would one day be.

Would have been.

To his own surprise, Caribou had a fleeting but powerful urge to turn the wheel. He actually had to fight, for a second, to keep the LeSabre pointing forward toward camp, to keep from spinning them around and speeding straight back past the shuttered pizza joints, the useless towns, through the woods to the orphanage, where he could eject them all from the car and vanish from their lives. Of course, if he did that, he'd have to vanish from Aunt Sally's life, too—oh, yes, he'd have no choice—and from his own, the only one he could remember, and evaporate into the Delta night.

How delicious this feeling was. How startling. Almost new.

It was Ann's hand, sliding over his on the steering wheel, pressing gently down, that brought him back to himself, settled him inside his glowing, ageless skin. She was singing, too, now, just like the children, though not along with them: some old, old song Caribou might have recognized, thought he did, though songs always blurred together for him. Ann's voice proved surprisingly supple beneath the crackles, like a voice on a record; she was singing about tears in vain, regrets absurd. It was that sort of song. Turning his palm gently beneath hers, he shot a quick glance in the mirror and saw Ju, green-eyed Ju, just staring, not stirring. On impulse, Caribou winked. Then, squeezing Ann's hand, he turned his attention fully on the older woman.

She rocked back without letting go. In fact, she clung harder, just as he'd known she would. And despite the fact that he knew it, he found himself marveling all over again. The monsters—the buffoons who stayed close to Aunt Sally's camp, even Mother and her Fool, when they'd been around—always read that reaction as a purely sexual response: primal, ravenous, ungovernable. For them (or, more accurately, their respondents), maybe it was. But though Caribou remembered virtually nothing and no one from the life he'd had before this one, he had held on to this: the idea, for some reason, of anyone other than Aunt Sally responding to him sexually was either absurd or perverse. And Aunt Sally, after all, was like God, and therefore loved and was bored by all other living creatures in equal measure. Her arousals were her own.

And yet here were these girls and this woman, enthralled, mesmerized, anesthetized, just as he needed them to be, but maybe by something even more elemental than lust. It was in the way they stared at him, which was the same way he himself stared down the Delta some long, summer evenings at a thunderhead, a funnel cloud, an incoming storm: with awe, in other words. With terror, certainly.

But most of all, with wonder.

That *was the way Ann watched him now. The irony, of course, lay in the effect that look had on* him, *the tingle it produced inside, all over, where so little else tingled. Surprising, impossible, delicious, tinged with an ache very like what he imagined melancholy to be, plus something else even more hurtful, even more luscious. Maybe that was regret.*

But it was definitely the sensation of himself *stirring, and not in awe, or wonder, either. He gazed openly at this woman, his Ann: the shades of white in her hair; the lines crisscrossing as they funneled sideways over her face, over skin she had actually lived in, ballooning into beautiful blue veins that plunged down her neck, over her breasts, which he imagined suspended in their support cabling under her red zip jumper, heavy and lopsided, each its own individual shape, a shape only this person's particular life could have left as it moved over and through her, filled her, and devoured her.*

So beautiful.

The moon caught her, lit her up, and Caribou couldn't help it. He laughed. And Ann, delighted, dazed, tilted her white head sideways and laughed with him. Such tingling, that caused. What a wonder life still was, just now and then, on rare, charged nights like this one when something—anything—changed.

"Grace Holler!" Ju called from the back, planting her hand against the window glass, lighting the dark with the green in her eyes.

Caribou shuddered and felt it again, whatever this was. Arousal, regret, tingling, wonder. Joy.

That was it, he suddenly knew. That was the secret of Ju's magic, that intoxicating, impossible, and impossibly rare combination, even in children: real curiosity married to unpracticed joy.

"You know that story?" he said, couldn't help saying, as they hurtled through this place that was now no place, with its sideways shacks slumping into the night-shadows of the magnolia trees, its gas station with no building, no pumps, no lights, just an arch and a cracked cement platform threaded with spiky weeds.

"It's a terrible story," Ann said, shuddering. And then—oh, wondrous night—she grinned. "We tell it every Halloween."

The Spider-siblings laughed. Ann laughed. And Ju stared

back at Caribou out of the rearview mirror like a will-o'-the-wisp, a fairy thing. They had the windows open so the night could pour in. And so, from fully half a mile down the dirt track to camp, Caribou heard the music.

Cretins, *he thought.* Buffoons. *Thudding bass drums shook the grasses like dinosaur footsteps while guitars buzzed, deafening and ineffectual as chain saws waved in the air, and some cartoon-yowlerman grunted about his cat-fever, something. Why was Aunt Sally even allowing this? She usually didn't. And why did they even bother, the monster-morons, with this non-music, this sludge of sound that could neither stoke nor accompany an Aunt Sally Party, because it was nowhere near wild enough?*

Just as they reached the turn in the dried-mud track that would lead them into camp, Ju leaned forward and put a hand on Caribou's shoulder, not to stroke him, not to communicate anything at all, but just to get a better look, take in more world. And that really did almost do it. Caribou felt his foot hit the brake, and he glanced around at Ann, the Spider-siblings, his Ju. He was remembering a story Aunt Sally had read him, once, her favorite, she claimed, about some doomed idiot family, the Misfit they met when their car broke down, the fates they had always deserved. That no one deserved. He was actually turning the wheel, starting to spin them around and away from this place, when the camp came into view, and he saw what the monsters had done.

It had been so very long, before tonight, since Caribou had been surprised. But tonight, the surprise seemed never to end. As though of its own volition, the car bumped forward over the dirt into the ring of glittering, sparking torches planted like flags in the ground, and juddered to a stop in precisely the place marked out for it.

"It's beautiful," Ann murmured, her voice audible because even the chain-saw-music had vanished abruptly. And in its place . . . a calliope? Was that what that was?

The tents—both the giant Party tent and Aunt Sally's white pavilion—were festooned, everywhere, with red and white balloons, the balloons and tent fabric spangled all over with glitter. The glitter caught the torchlight and showered it all over the grass, creating firefly-sparks amid the fireflies, as though the stars themselves had accepted Aunt Sally's invitation, come for the Party, and scattered over the Delta to dance. Between the tents, metal poles had been erected and red ribbon strung between them, creating a sort of gestural labyrinth. Off to the left, down near the bank, Caribou saw a new, gigantic, leaning structure that billowed and breathed in the barely-there night wind.

A bounce house? Bouncy castle? Whatever it was, there were monsters in it already. And they were bouncing, all right.

Leaning out his window, Caribou took it all in. Aunt Sally had even had them tend to the smells: the Styrofoam-sweet of circus peanuts; that newfangled sugarsalt popcorn; something else, too, acrid and fairgroundy, that he couldn't identify; and underneath all of that, yet another odor, this one . . . animal? As though Aunt Sally had directed her monsters to rent tigers, just for the night. Or elephants?

At that moment, it seemed entirely possible that an elephant, or a great-maned lion, would surface in the river, part the reeds, wander out of myth into camp. All of this, just for a Party, intended not so much to disguise this night as to make it festive, like a birthday. To render the world new, or less old, or at least aglitter with firefly light, one more time.

The Spider-kids were already out of the car, and Ann, too, stumbling over the dirt toward . . . God, that idiot, Caribou couldn't even remember his name, the stubbly, constantly leering one who'd just come lurching out of the bouncy house, his pocked face obliterated by clown makeup, complete with lit-up red nose, giant rainbow-lips so outsized that Caribou half-expected them to free themselves of that mouth entirely and hang in the air like the Cheshire Cat's smile. But Ju, Caribou realized, was still behind him, still with her hand on his shoulder, her shallow breath at his ear. She was watching it all, this miracle he'd brought her and her housemates and her caretaker-mother to. On impulse, solely—moments later, Caribou wouldn't even be certain when *he had done it, let alone why—Caribou put his cold hand over Ju's warm one, held her there against his skin through his white jacket. To his own amazement, he started to weep.*

Together, they watched the others stream from the flap of the giant tent, arms outstretched, painted faces wild and wide with their smiling. They wore top hats, tailcoats, leotards. One of them called, "Step right up," and then they were all doing it, sweeping around the children, around Ann, linking hands, elbows. "Step right up!" The Spider-sister was whisked—swung, really, her feet barely touching ground as the monsters dangled and tickled her, passed her around—toward the red-ribbon labyrinth. Her brother they took the other way, toward the bounce house. Ann, too, they led that way. There was a moment when she seemed to know, when she glanced back toward the Spider-girl amid her monsters and looked as though she might scream.

Maybe she'd known all along. They sometimes did, despite the spell Caribou worked so hard to cast on them.

Then he looked up, and there were Ju's eyes on his eyes in the mirror, again, watching him, still. And that was too much.

"Ssh," he said. "Sit back. Scrunch down." And with his eyes closed—as though that would hide him, would somehow make the LeSabre's engine quieter—he turned the key and started the car, which purred like a cat, seemed to stretch underneath him, ready to run.

Not one of the monsters turned. No one so much as glanced his way. Why would they? "Stay down," he hissed, swung his head around to reverse out of the clearing, and saw Aunt Sally standing behind them.

The dress she wore was something new, or very old, thin and colorless as a rag, but spotless, clean as a hospital sheet for wrapping newborns. It clung to her like a coating. Like white tar, *Caribou thought crazily, his foot poised above the accelerator, above the brake, touching neither. Like tar that had been feathered, and then* ironed, *the feathers into the tar, the whole dress into Aunt Sally's glistening skin.*

She was looking into the LeSabre, but not at him. She was looking at the mirror, Caribou realized. At Ju. And Ju was looking right back, and not at Caribou at all.

It was that—not the sight of Aunt Sally—that made Caribou's decision for him. His foot drooped toward the brake as his fingers twisted the key, shutting down the car while the bloodless, beatless weight in his chest that passed for his heart folded in on itself, fell to pieces.

Aunt Sally had both hands at her mouth. She was moving forward, now, peering into the backseat, craning her head like one of those ancient dinosaur-birds. Terror-birds. That was something, anyway, Caribou thought. After all these decades, all their lovemakings, all the Policies and chartings and plans. At least, tonight, he'd finally amazed her.

"Oh," she was saying through her fingers as she reached the car, stood at Ju's door. "Oh, 'Bou. Look *what you've brought me."*

"No," said Caribou. Even he had no idea what he meant, what he was denying. Nor did he know whether Ju opened her door or Aunt Sally did. Whether Aunt Sally had seized Ju already and directed the child, or Ju had acted on her own. Ju the green-eyed and curious and marveling. Her expression seemed almost like Aunt Sally's, in that way. But in no other way.

Laughter and screaming giggles erupted from the ribbon-labyrinth, and shouting and laughter from the bounce house. Aunt Sally knelt in front of Ju and reached out slowly, threading piney-green needles out of the little girl's hair and winding them into her own.

"Get along," Aunt Sally said to Caribou, after some time, having seemingly just realized he was still standing there.

"Let me stay," he croaked. He was pleading, hadn't meant to.

Her eyes left Ju's, just for a moment. "Poor 'Bou," she said. "So sweet. So conscientious. So hungry."

"I'm not hungry."

"Always seeing to the rest of us first. Never admitting your own needs."

"I'm not hungry."

Behind him, the giggles and shouts and laughter converged. The labyrinth-dwellers were already spinning the Spider-girl toward the big tent and the food they'd apparently laid out in there and the winking mirror-ball light reflecting down the canvas and the music from the calliope or whatever it was. The bouncers, too, were out of the bouncy house with the Spider-boy on their shoulders, waltzing him, and Ann along with him. They, too, moved toward the big tent.

"Go on, now," Aunt Sally said.

She meant to sound kind, he knew. She tried to, sometimes. But she didn't sound kind. Because she wasn't. Whatever "kind" was, it could never be her.

Again, though, what set him stumbling toward the tent wasn't Aunt Sally but the little girl. She did it by the way she turned, looked up, clearly saw the inexplicable tears he could feel massing once more in his eyes. And waved.

In a daze, Caribou moved away across the grass, following the others. The monsters, like him. They were just like him. Torchlight flickered all around, the Delta sounds still whirring and ticking and hooting and shuffling, still audible under the din everyone in camp was making. All that life, just continuing, no matter what he and Aunt Sally and her pathetic Policy-slaves did to it. It was more powerful, more awake than any of them would ever be, no matter how many flickering seconds of waking they got.

For the third time tonight, quite possibly the first three times since Aunt Sally had found—had made—him, Caribou wanted to leave this place. He could just slip past the tent while all the rest, even Aunt Sally, were busy, and disappear out of the Delta into the world, where he had been alone long before he was a monster. He could blend in, somehow, or hide out alone, become . . . not what he'd been, whatever that was, he had virtually no memory of that. Not one of them, *the ones the monsters preyed on, either. The idea of that was too frightening, too pathetic.*

But maybe he could be something else. Someone else. If there was—could be—such a thing. Could he?

Then he turned, not wanting to see, the air thick around him even though he wasn't breathing, the smells permeating his pores: popcorn, peanuts, greasepaint, that acrid, awful something else, which was even stronger here by the tent. Much stronger.

There they were, right where he'd left them: Aunt Sally and Ju. Except that now, Aunt Sally was seated on the dirt in her spotless rag-dress, and Ju was on her lap like a cat. Were they talking? Just looking at each other? Ju reached up and smoothed a tendril of Aunt Sally's hair against her forehead. Once more, Caribou wanted to run to her, to Aunt Sally, screaming, Don't. Wait! *Because somehow, Ju was still in there. Too aware. She would feel it all, everything that was about to happen to her.*

How was that possible? Because she was a child, maybe? Because she was an orphan? Because she was whatever kind of orphan she was?

This time, it was Aunt Sally, not Ju, who saw him. And Caribou realized that whatever was happening over there—or might be happening—it wasn't Ju's doing, or might not be. Of their own volition, his eyes fell into Aunt Sally's. His whole body went rigid, as though he'd been hit by lightning, singed forever into this moment, this place, this very air.

She held him paralyzed a few seconds, then let him go.

Where was *there for him to go? Certainly not over there, where Aunt Sally and Ju were. There was no place for him there.*

And anyway, he didn't want to see. Not *that. Not what came next.*

And so, as always, he went where Aunt Sally sent him. With a last glance at the shining, twisty-haired creature on Aunt Sally's lap—who was neither fairy nor wood nymph, just a green-eyed girl who'd strayed off the path in her woods—he turned and stumbled between the billowing canvas flaps into the tent, where the carnage had already begun.

25

How had she gotten out?

Even now, stumbling in the sudden moonlight down the bike alley between Starkey's and the bank toward the trees, Kaylene couldn't remember. She had no fucking idea. Had the rink door ever actually been locked? Had someone opened it, finally, and seen inside? Had she been conscious for that?

The truth was, she couldn't remember a single second of the past . . . however long it had been. She wasn't even sure whether she'd staggered into Starkey's first, and gotten someone to call the cops before dragging herself toward Halfmoon House. The only plan in her head was to find Rebecca, warn her, huddle beneath that canopy of kindness Rebecca had draped over all of them for so long, now.

Maybe then she could start to try, somehow, to stop remembering the *other* moments—the ones right before the ones she'd forgotten—or at least stop picturing them in such vivid detail.

Jack and his smile sliding through the light over center ice, on the saucer she'd shoved, straight into the arms of the thing in the sombrero.

And then the sounds. Not snarling, not spitting or roaring or hissing, just grunts here and there as the Sombrero-Man tore and raked and ripped, a sigh as he bit through, snapped off, slurped. He hadn't sounded like an animal; the noises and shadowy movements were too practiced, specific, methodical. Artful.

That's what those movements had reminded her of, she realized now: glassblowers, loom-weavers. It had been like watching a master craftsman at work. She'd thought that even before he started singing, and long before he'd killed Marlene.

Killed Marlene. Her beautiful, brave, brilliant best friend, roommate, partner in 'Lene-ing, who had gone stupid right at the end, had dropped her broom and taken off down the ice. The Sombrero-Man had barely looked up as he gathered her in. He hadn't even stopped singing, that Johnny Cash song Kaylene already knew she could never listen to again, would never stop hearing, about getting a rhythm. That same rhythm buzzed in Kaylene's head now, chopping up her thoughts, her *self,* everything she had ever been, like a table saw he'd set spinning inside her, leaving just the one coherent thought: get to Rebecca.

Right as she reached the trees, the ground tilted up on her, and the world yawed sideways. Kaylene had to grab for the nearest trunk, a birch, its bark slippery and useless, flaking away the second she touched it, like onionskin. *Like people skin,* she thought, picturing Marlene, Jack. She sobbed, felt the moon on her own skin, a cold laser that burned her clean through, froze her solid. Overhead, something leapt from the branches, and Kaylene ducked, yelled, banged her jaw against the trunk, which wasn't so slippery after all, not underneath. She sat down hard in the baked and bristly summer grass at the edge of her woods.

Squirrel, she realized, somewhere in her chopped and chattering thoughts. It sat up straight in the leaves and gave her a look. If she'd had a spirit animal, Kaylene had always thought it might be one of these twitching, leaping, playing things. She was either a squirrel or a Dig Dug, burrowing forever, never sleeping, finding others.

Using the tree to steady herself, Kaylene started to push upright but stopped. She stared at the caked blood on her arms, black and glistening in the moonlight, like scales. She *had* gone to Starkey's first, because she'd noticed her arms there, just like this, clutching the pizza parlor's glass door. She'd gotten a glimpse of her reflection in that door, too, dripping dirt and blood and earth, hair sticking to her lips and cheeks, which were frozen through from lying on the ice, clothes cloying everywhere as they thawed, unleashing shudders that wracked her, flickered her in and out of conscious awareness, like buzzing in a fluorescent light.

Her only hope, as she had stumbled through that door, was that she looked as messed up as she felt. From the expression on Mrs. Starkey's ageless Mt. Rushmore of a face, she'd been pretty sure she did.

"Cops," she'd managed, her voice not just breaking but

mangled, as though playing through a smashed speaker. "Don't go in the rink."

Before anyone could stop her, she'd headed right back out, through the alley toward these woods, the lake, Halfmoon House, so she could warn Rebecca, and then die alongside her.

"Shit!" Danni snapped, smacking at the branch Trudi had just let rubber-band back into her face. "Turd-i, slow down."

"*Tru*di," the little girl sang and sped up, burrowing through brambles, trampling pinecones and fallen branches like a puppy let off a leash.

"Not to me," mumbled Danni, and stopped. The woods in the dark were almost shadowless back here. There was moonlight, but it got caught in the shivering branches surprisingly far overhead, which made Danni feel like she was standing not on the forest floor but the bottom of Halfmoon Lake. Knotting her long blond hair behind her head, Danni closed her eyes, went still, and just listened. What she heard was no-one-yelling, and what she felt was no-one-near-her. Both feelings lasted until the Tasmanian devil up ahead realized she wasn't being followed and came whirling back.

And now, here she was, pine needles crisscrossing her arms like porcupine spines, a caterpillar crawling over one cupped palm. "Look," Trudi said, and then, "Here's your phone."

Danni cringed, thinking of Rebecca: self-righteous mini-Amanda, pretend-grown-up, Goody Two-shoes. She wished she hadn't lent the phone to Trudi, and sighed. "We shouldn't have called her."

"I wanted to."

"Yeah, but now she'll come after us."

"I want her to come."

"Well, I don't."

"Well, you should," said Trudi. Then she said, "Look," again as the caterpillar inched all the way up her arm, inside the droopy mouth of her sleeve.

What Trudi had said was true, Danni realized. She *should* want Rebecca here. No one in recent memory, maybe no one Danni had ever met, had tried harder to be her friend—not take care of her or teach her, just be her friend—than that girl had.

Well, she thought, *maybe someday. But not today.*

"It tickles," Trudi said, wriggling.

Danni put a hand on the little girl's head, held her still. "Listen."

As if on command, the woods erupted. A pair of barred owls, somewhere close, burst out barking and trilling, which set off all kinds of movement in the bushes and low branches as little things scurried and burrowed and leapt. Mosquitoes seemed to pour out of the ground, buzzing into each other and alighting on the girls' skin. On the lake, a loon laughed, calling up a breeze that feathered the leaves and stirred the pines, which somehow settled everything else again, almost completely. Only the needles on the ground still rustled, as though something underneath had shrugged off the surface of the world like a blanket and sat up.

And whatever that *was,* Danni thought, swatting at

mosquitoes, allowing herself a single shiver and a half-breathed curse, she had always known it was there. She had sensed it even before her parents died, lurking underground, inside tree trunks and cumulus clouds. She could feel it even now, every waking second, behind Amanda's businesslike commands and Joel's jokes, just biding its time. With a jolt, she realized—was absolutely certain—that Rebecca sensed it, too, and always had. It was obvious in everything that girl did, the way she kept coming over, kept talking to Danni no matter how rudely Danni talked back.

Yep. Rebecca sensed it, too. Danni just hadn't noticed, before. Because whatever it was, it didn't seem to scare Rebecca. And it didn't make her anywhere near as angry.

"Come on," Danni told Trudi. "Let's go to the lake."

"Should we go back? They'll be worried."

They'll be shouting, Danni thought. *At each other, until we appear. Then at us.*

"Lake."

"Trailers!"

"Ugh. Gross. Why do you like that place?"

But Trudi was already ducking between pines in the direction of that clearing, the needles enfolding her as one of the owls unleashed its awful, taunting call. *Whocooks-foryou . . .*

"You invited me, Danni," she called from somewhere in the trees. "You wanted me to come."

"That's because I'm stupid," Danni murmured. She started to follow, wishing, nonsensically, that Trudi would lower her voice. "Shut—"

"That's what Rebecca says."

Mid-tree, needles jabbing at her arms and neck, Danni

stopped. The question was out of her mouth before she could stop herself. "She says I'm stupid?"

But Trudi was out of earshot as well as sight, now, racing down the overgrown path. Even the ripples of movement she'd stirred had gone still in her wake.

Rebecca had been comforting Trudi, Danni realized. *That's why she'd said that.* If *she had.*

Then she thought of what she'd seen and overheard this afternoon. Was Rebecca *trying* to destroy Halfmoon House? After all, she was already safely out of it, the thoughtless, two-faced . . .

"Yeah. Well, she's stupider," Danni said to the trees, to whatever that thing was behind and beneath them that had followed her for so long. A shrew stuck its head out of the roots, scampered right over her foot. Down the hill, the lake, stirred by something, smacked against the boat pier. "Trudi, wait up," she yelled, pushing through the branches toward the path. Abruptly, instinctively, she broke into a run.

Even before she reached the trailers, she smelled them, as usual. They reeked of the leaves and dirt and spores that blew through them all day and all night, the worms and insects that wriggled up through their rotting floorboards and spawned in their wheel wells and rusting walls. And yet, despite the life they housed, they also smelled dead, like the forest but minus light and air. Forest-in-a-casket. Trudi was not just babbling as usual but whooping now, the noise way too much for the place, and Danni was *shushing* her furiously as she burst out of the deep-shadow shade into the clearing and stopped, and saw.

Just at first, and just for a second, Danni started to laugh.

Here was Crazy Trudi, sock-puppet whisperer, sometime-sister, in her natural habitat: limned in moonlight, rampaging around and around the clearing, past the tilted-over trailer with its front door hanging down, the American flag trailer (rust, not-white, and blue), the yellow trailer with the bullet holes, the black Sierra back there in the trees that hadn't ever been there before. In the baggy, thrift store flower-dress Amanda had bought her, with her corn-row pigtails flying, Trudi looked like a child ripped out of time, hollering like a marauding Sioux, or—no—like a wagon-train girl, a pioneer kid *playing* marauding Sioux.

And that seemed like bad luck to Danni, downright ill-advised. She'd stopped laughing even before the man in the sombrero stepped out of the Sierra into the clearing.

26

The second that Sophie appeared in the doorway, with Eddie lodged in the sling she'd jerry-rigged from her sheet so she could swing herself along—Benny jackknifed upright. And that surprised her so much—as far as she knew, he'd just lain in that bed for three weeks straight—that it actually froze her momentarily. If he'd thought to untwist the sheets before he made his move, he might even have made it out of them.

Not that that would have mattered, in the end, but maybe he would have felt less weak, more of a man, something. Regardless, she had him, now. She could actually see *the wave she'd unleashed with her gaze slam into him, so powerful it could have flung him against the wall if she'd wanted it to. She really was getting the hang of that, and after just a few weeks. Although she had to admit, it had barely registered on Rebecca. Go figure.*

She watched Benny's mouth round, his breath spurt out, as though she'd punched him, punctured him. She smiled slow, pursed her lips. Even with Natalie's kid squawking away against her—and even without her legs—she was way too much for Jess's fuzzy little man.

He did manage to speak this time, at least. Eventually. And that was undeniably cute, even impressive, given how much of himself he was fighting. But all he said was, "No."

Sophie burst out laughing. "You're a sweetie, Benny. Always were."

"Sophie. Please."

"You always had a peach pie slice for me. I'll never forget that, I mean it. Every single time I came in to your Waffle House. Almost like you were saving one for me." Sophie felt her smile widen, all on its own. She was glad to know it could still do that.

Abruptly, she cocked her head, studying fuzzy Benny as he cowered before her. Her skin prickled, and her dead lungs seemed to spasm in her chest. "Almost like you hoped I'd come," she murmured, only now realizing, when it was way too late.

In a single movement, she deposited Eddie at the end of the bed and vaulted one-handed onto Benny. Clearly, the hours of practice up in the attic and the hundred thousand pull-ups had paid off, and oh, she was getting good. She lowered herself onto Benny's lap and stared down into his face, and that was the moment she knew she was right, understood the reason that the power she wielded seemed to devastate this man more than anyone else she'd met since she'd met the Whistler.

Benny had loved her then. *Before. Not desired, at least not seriously, not consciously, but he'd loved her. Like a father, maybe. Was that what father-love was like?*

Whatever. He'd loved her, and more than he ever realized, and definitely more than she *had realized. Maybe even more than he'd loved Natalie, and wouldn't that have been a first?*

With a wink—which felt mean, forced, and actually broke her spell momentarily, so that he cried out as though she'd bitten him—she dropped her full weight atop him. She ground herself there, just once, and felt him stiffen pitifully beneath her. Jess's fuzzy little man, who loved her, or had, once.

So why was she doing this?

Because it infuriated her that he'd felt that way and yet never said anything or even figured it out. That she had never known. Because that, *of all things, really might have made a difference. It wouldn't have changed the ending, maybe, or changed anything, really. Except maybe the feel of all those wandering nights* before *the ending . . .*

"And anyway," she whispered, returning her gaze to his face, "you loved her more." Those words felt thick, almost suffocating in her mouth, like a peach pit.

"Sophie," Benny whimpered, "what on earth are you—"

"Jess." Gathering Eddie to her, she lifted him to her face, blocking her view, because she didn't want to look at Benny's face right then. "Yes he did, little Nat-man. He loved her—loves her—more than anyone loved me, ever. Except your mom."

Eddie wriggled, squawked, started to flail. She crushed him again against her chest, held on, whispered, "Both of you. Just stop." Then she closed her eyes for one blessed second.

That was a mistake, of course. Immediately—so fast!—Benny jackknifed again, got all the way sitting up, grabbed her hard around the elbows and locked her in place. His face hovered inches from hers, now, but he kept his eyes averted. His whole body coiled, she could feel it. It was almost as though he really thought he had a move to make.

Sophie stayed still, let him carry out whatever it was he thought he'd planned, which turned out to be locking her arms to her sides and pinning Eddie between them. He shook her a couple times. The child screamed. She could have bitten Benny's Adam's apple out of his neck with a single dart of her head.

But he'd loved her. And that wasn't her *plan.*

Benny tightened his grip on her arms, but he also sagged back slightly to give Eddie room. Then he just sat there.

"It's a problem, huh?" she murmured, right in his ear, which set his whole body trembling. Even those million white hairs sticking out of him quivered like twisted-up chicken wire in a wind. "You've got me. And well done, by the way. But now what?"

"Shut up."

"Want to head-butt me, Benny? Hurl me off the bed? Of course, there's the Eddie problem." She gestured with her chin at the squirming, screechy bundle between them, which wouldn't stop screeching, now, and she couldn't catch his eyes to quiet or comfort him. That was annoying. "You could grab Eddie, I suppose. But then I'd be free."

In the end, he couldn't help it. He looked up. There he was: the walking toilet brush, exploded pillow. Benny Peach Pie, who could have been a father to her, if either one of them had understood themselves sooner. She watched him melt under her gaze, his eyes flashing hatred.

"Oh," Sophie said. "I see. I guess you could try and rape me."

"You raped me!*" Benny shouted, hands popping open like handcuffs he'd slipped. He sank all the way backward into his pillows.*

It was strange, but until he said that, Sophie hadn't thought of what she'd done to him that way. She rolled her head around her neck, tapped her fingers on his stomach through the sheets. "Huh. I . . . Well, kind of. I guess I did. Ugh, quiet, *little Nat-man. Jesus, you're getting as grumpy as your mom." She lifted the baby and settled him against her breast and rocked him. He kept hiccupping and squirming, but he stopped screeching. Sophie returned her attention to Benny. Her smile felt ugly, even to her. "And you know what? I think I'm sorry. Not that you seemed to mind at the time."*

She felt bad about that last bit even before Benny teared up. He stared pathetically back. "The part of me that's me *minded."*

Yet again, something inside Sophie flinched, while something else reared up. The sensation was brand-new, and it was awful. "Yeah. Well. As far as I've seen, that's the way it mostly is with sex, isn't it? The part of us that's us always minds, for one stupid reason or another."

"That's because you didn't get to see enough," Benny whispered.

And that was such a perfect—almost loving—thing to say, that Sophie considered handing him the kid, right then. If she'd done it, she would also have broken down crying.

Outside, on the street, something else shrieked, and it went on shrieking. Sirens? Were those sirens?

Sloppy, sloppy Whistler-prick . . .

"You see?" she said quietly, rocking Eddie but gazing at Benny's eyes, through Benny's eyes, all the way down into Benny. "We kind of have the same problem, you and me, Benji-boy. We can't do it all. We have to make choices. I could just . . . but then there's Jess . . . and . . . him, *the fucking monster who . . . You just can't do it all. I mean, not just you, none of us can. And also . . . I hate to say it, Benny, but I'm getting more than a little . . . peckish . . ."*

She withdrew her gaze from him, like a needle from a vein, the poison already delivered, pouring into his bloodstream. She saw him watching, watched him understand. And then—astonishingly, even sweetly—he nodded. He . . . accepted. *Just let go of her arms and settled back.*

"Okay," he whispered. "Go ahead. Take me. Just . . . afterward . . ." He wasn't lecturing or pleading, knew there was no point, but he was going to ask. "Tell me you'll save—"

Abruptly, still cuddling Eddie with one hand, she dropped the other hand over his mouth to shut him up. Then she brushed the white whiskers smooth along the curve of his face. She felt herself smile at him, one more time. "Does Jess, do you think, know what she had? What you gave her?"

Whiskers quivering, eyes overflowing, Benny . . . smiled? Was he smiling?

"A man worthy of her?" he said, as Sophie's palm lifted. "I hope I was. Save that boy, Sophie. Tell me that when you're done, you'll save the boy."

For answer, Sophie swept Eddie to her open mouth, clamped her lips to his skin at the open zipper of his onesie, and farted against his neck. He jerked, laughing his surprise. That laugh! Along with her Roo's laugh, it had once—not so long ago—formed a river of laughter right down the middle of Sophie's life, one that promised to carry both her and Natalie everyplace they'd always heard those rivers really might run. Without thinking, looking, giving herself a single second to reconsider, she dropped Eddie onto Benny's chest and vaulted off the bed, scuttling straight down the hall, down the stairs, and out the front door into the shrieking summer night.

The hardest part for Rebecca, as she tore through the woods, wasn't deciding whether to sprint straight for the trailers—because she already knew that's where Trudi and Danni would be—or to Halfmoon House to get help. The hardest part was keeping from turning around. Because that was what she most wanted to do. It was, in fact, the only thing she wanted to do.

She didn't want to escape, but to return to Oscar's truck, throw open the door once more, and stand there. She wouldn't shout or even cry. Eventually, she'd climb into the cab, slide into the space between her guys, and sit amid the ruins of them: Oscar and Jack, who had supported more of the life she'd barely begun staking out than either of them had ever imagined, because she'd never managed to communicate it, hadn't even realized it, really. And now that it was too late—which, apparently, would always be her cue—the only acknowledgment she could think to make was to be there, sit among them, wind her hands through their knotted, ripped-out entrails, untangle what she could, tuck in what was possible, and when that was done, slip her arms around their shoulders and pull them to her. Then she would hold them until every last trace of heat, of the magnificent people both of them had been, had streamed, softly, away.

That was her proper place, as far as she could see, possibly the one role her whole life had prepared her for.

Unless it was to keep running, get to the clearing or Halfmoon House, dangle her whole self over the lip of the void that she'd always known was there, and pull anything that was still living back out of it.

And that was why she didn't turn around. She tore down the forest path, hurtling past startled scurrying things underfoot and overhead, the birches with their individual mottlings, the oaks with their mosses, each pattern on each trunk as familiar to her as faces in wood grain on a bedroom closet door. These tree trunks *were* her closet-door faces, this woods her bedroom, those loons—*oh, hello, loons!*—her overheard, downstairs, grown-up conversations.

Was that her voice, shouting? Was she shouting?

Flinging aside the fronds of the weeping willow at the bottom of the lane, Rebecca burst onto the grounds of Halfmoon House, hurtled across the yard, and yes, that was definitely her voice, she really was shouting. But she stopped short of the porch and stood in the too-long grass, panting, sweating, weeping—-how long had she been doing *that*?—until she felt like herself again, detached, almost calm: Crisis Center Rebecca, on the scene, for whatever the hell good that was going to do.

Jess came out first, flying down the little porch stairs, all five feet of her, eyes blazing. She had a steak knife in one hand and what looked like a pinking shears in the other. Behind her, at the door of the house they had built—which hadn't even quite become *their* home, either, Rebecca realized—stood Amanda and Joel. Amanda had Joel's broken-toothed rake and Joel a shovel, which made them look, for one second, like younger versions of the couple from that *American Gothic* painting. Like that couple's children, except that the second they saw her, they smiled, *both* of them, the smiles relieved, frightened, fleeting. But they'd been there, and Rebecca had seen them.

"Oh, good, you're here," Amanda said.

"I know where the girls are," said Rebecca, already turning, knowing the rest of them would follow. She hadn't even made it back to the willow before the screaming started.

27

In the dappled moonlight, on the low, leaning stump between the tipped-over trailer and the American flag trailer, with his hat pushed back and one hand in the air, the Whistler stood like a fly fisherman on a bank, and he waited. Ooh, he waited, watching the two girls across the clearing—the little one in the braids with the sock on one hand, and the blond, reedy one with the shards of broken glass for eyes—as they fought him, tried to fight him. So much *fight in them. The reedy one radiated so much fury that she distracted, even mesmerized him momentarily, and that allowed the little one to get off a scream.*

So exciting.

Even now—after the tall one had finally started to give, he could feel it—the little one wriggled, almost as if she still thought she could run. Such a mighty little hooked thing. The Whistler thought she might even be the stronger of the two.

Then a new thought burst over him, bright and brilliant as a holiday firework: maybe the struggle wasn't being caused by these girls at all! Was it possible that he himself had lost something when he lost his Destiny? Or even Mother? Had his grief—and he had *grieved, hadn't he?—weakened him, somehow, made him less? Was that what grief did? Left him lonesome, orn'ry, even meaner?*

From somewhere close, off in the trees, his new, Still One's voice sang out. "Truuuueeee," she was calling, in her blue, hollow tone. "Truuuu."

And with a shiver in his shoulders—another spasm of his boundless grief—the Whistler understood, or rather remembered: his Still One was no replacement for his Destiny, never had been, never could be. No. She was for something else entirely. And grief, it turned out, hadn't weakened him at all.

Grinning wider as the girls fought him, the Whistler bore down, lowered his arms. Using only his will, he gave a little tug, and watched as Shards-for-Eyes staggered toward him. She was still fighting, but not even trying to hang on to anyone or anything. This one wasn't scared or sad; she was simply enraged.

Delicious.

He watched her get her head turned even as she continued stumbling toward him. Her clawed fingers scratched at the moonlight her eyes and hair reflected. How very like people, really, to resist the very things that lit them up, the desires that made them who they were. They spent their entire existences battling the engine they called "life," whose only actual function was to drive them toward death. The girl snarled something over her shoulder at her little braided companion.

"*I* can't," *the braided one said.*

"She really can't," said the *Whistler to Shards-for-Eyes, and he sat down on his stump and raised his arms to greet her.*

And then he made himself wait, poised right at the most ravishing moment, his favorite moment: the split-second silence between verse and swelling chorus; the breath (theirs, of course) between kiss and bite. He did not move again, nor did he direct the girl to move again, until everyone else—the others he'd heard coming—poured out of the trees into the so-bright clearing, which he had transformed into this perfect, glorious stage.

How he had missed performing for them. He really was going to have to go back to doing that.

First out of the trees was the tall black man who had been here this afternoon, waking him to (or from?) his dream of his Destiny's voice; behind him, a pale, once-pretty blond woman with a frown etched so deeply into her face that it looked carved, seemed almost driven through *her face, like a jack-o'-lantern's mouth. Such a face!*

Then came his new, Still One, her mouth still rounded around her last "Truuu," brown eyes churning like just-turned soil. Nothing about her seemed still, now. And just when he thought it couldn't get any better, be any more perfect, his Destiny's mother stepped clear of the trees. Call it Destiny, Policy, God, whatever, but it really did seem as though something had guided him here, landing him exactly where he needed to be.

He smiled at the assembled as he hooked and quieted them, like a pastor settling his congregation. He did love them in his way, every one. Especially, he loved and smiled at his new, Still One. Really, this was all about her, now, all for *her. He watched her take in the tableaux he had created. And yes, oh, yes, she knew what was about to happen. He could see it in her face. The sight sent a shock through his bones. And that was exactly right,* her *destiny, the very reason she'd been born: to be his very own doe-eyed pincushion, sin-eater, the thing he could hurt, over and over, until he stopped hurting.*

He watched her wriggle, fight him, but not like Shards-for-Eyes, or even the girl with the sock puppet. Not as though she thought she could win; her life had already taught her better.

When he was sure she saw, and knew, and was watching—when he'd drunk deeply from all of that—he returned his gaze to the furious child in front of him. This one still exhibited so much rage, he almost felt like singing as he pulled her to him. He was tempted simply to Whistle her to sweet, sweet sleep.

He broke her back over his knee instead.

The *crack* rattled through Rebecca so forcefully, it might as well have come from her own bones. In disbelief—or, worse, belief—she watched Danni's broken body spill off the Whistler's lap and fall at his feet, all her fire and fury doused, just like that, without even smoke to suggest it had ever been there. Yet another piece of Rebecca's world—the one she'd assembled from the box of discarded pieces of other people's worlds that life had given her—swept away.

Like Oscar.

Like Jack.

All of them, gone, in less than an hour.

The Sombrero-Man wouldn't stop staring at her. He looked thin, had so many leaves sticking to his denim jacket and the outsides of his raggedy boots that he looked more like a stick insect than a person, except that he had even less expressive eyes. He watched her watching. A smile spread over his face, and his lips puckered, and that sound came out. Partially, it was whistling, but also it was nightingale's mating cry, owl's murder-song, all in one. He opened his arms, and somehow, she sensed immediately what he wanted from her: a cry of anguish, then a useless charge across the clearing.

Of course, that's what she wanted, too. It was the only thing left to do, except the thing she did.

With a gasp—it was like she'd imagined tearing out an IV would be, and it *hurt*—Rebecca lunged not forward but sideways, not toward the Whistler but Trudi. She didn't exactly see the Sombrero-Man twitch, but she heard the hiccup in his whistle, knew she'd surprised him. He lurched off the stump, and that sudden movement freed everyone else, too, just momentarily, but long enough for Jess to shout, "Rebecca, *yes*!"

Grabbing Trudi around the waist, Rebecca uprooted her, yelled "*Run!*" to the rest of them, and bolted between trailers toward the woods. Trudi startled awake, started squirming and screaming. Rebecca kept hold, kept running, expecting the Sombrero-Man to land on her back any second: the moon, with claws, come to lift her away and away.

But he didn't come, and she made the trees, and then she was in them, crashing through roots and whipping branches, rattling the world the way loons did when they reared at last, at the end of their summers, flapped their desperate wings, rose out of Halfmoon Lake into the air, and vanished.

A split second after Rebecca made her move—*brilliant girl, good girl, nothing like Natalie except in the way she was exactly like Natalie*—Jess made hers. It was almost as though she and Rebecca had planned it beforehand. As if *they* were the ones who had shared a past, and still hoped to have a future.

And you will have one, Jess thought. *Run, Rebecca.* She threw herself right into the bastard's path, between him and the fleeing girls, pinking shears raised. They wouldn't do enough, she knew, even if she drove them through the fucker's eye. Whatever she was doing now, it wasn't about surviving or even stopping the monster in front of her; it was about Natalie. About what the good girl Jess had raised had done to save *her* son. About hurling herself under the wheels of this careening truck and maybe puncturing just one as it crushed and released her. Maybe that would buy Rebecca and Trudi a little more time. Maybe even enough time.

She was in midair, stabbing the pinking shears forward, when she realized the Whistler wasn't chasing Rebecca, hadn't moved from his spot near the trailer. He'd stood up, all right, but that was it, and now he was just gazing after Rebecca with what looked like the same admiration and affection Jess was feeling.

Of course, it wasn't the same. Not in the end.

Shears still raised, Jess stared at the creature that had shredded what was left of her life. He wasn't even paying attention to her. Again. He wasn't interested in her. Again. Because he couldn't hurt her enough, she realized instinctively. He had already suffused every atom of Jess's being with hurt, and that made her no longer interesting or useful to him.

Instead, he'd zeroed in on Rebecca, on Amanda and Joel. He gazed at them now like a little boy at birthday presents.

"No," she said, because she saw what was going to happen next. It was as clear to her as memory, as if it had already happened.

Then it happened.

Late. I'm late. For a most important date.

That's what Sophie was thinking as she swung-scuttled through the rustling, chattering night-woods. Eventually, she started chanting those words, and that helped, some, distracted her from the sticks jabbing up into her stumps, the snarled, ground-level branches that smacked and scratched her as she plowed through them. After tonight, she really was going to need a pants plan. Or some stilts.

After tonight. And there was *going to* be *an after, once she had seen the Whistler again, poked his stupid hat off his head so she could see his heartless, gorgeous face, and so he could see her. She wasn't sure he'd even really noticed her before. He would now.*

The Whistler and *Jess. Oh, yes. They'd both see her. She was about to see them both together. Ignoring the scratches and smacks the forest inflicted on her, she dug harder into the earth, swung forward faster. She was moving so fast, darting across streaks of moon from shadow to shadow, that she actually hit an armadillo, pitched forward across it, lurched upright, and found it tipped over on its back, waving its scaly legs in the air.*

It was . . . meowing? Was that what armadillos did? Or maybe this really was *the Wonderland forest.*

Her mouth filled, abruptly, with the taste of just-dead deer, the deer she and Natalie had tried devouring after Natalie had plowed into it with her GTO. Ah, yes, *Sophie thought.* Another magical night, that one. The one where my best friend tore my jugular vein in half and drank from it.

As though giving CPR—or, negative-CPR, whatever the opposite of CPR was—Sophie leaned over the screaming armadillo, clamped one hand over the other on the soft spot on its chest, and crushed the scream out of it. She pushed a little too hard, wound up shooting half its insides out its mouth like toothpaste through a tube.

"Sorry, dude," she murmured, and she was, some. "You're too loud."

After that, she followed the racket. And she was so focused on that that she almost barreled right into Rebecca, fleeing toward *Sophie down the path. Sophie had to throw herself sidelong, right into a pricker bush, to avoid getting run over. The only reason she didn't get seen was that Rebecca, too, was riveted on the noise from the clearing behind her—the shouting, the snapping and breaking—and was therefore looking that way, over her shoulder. She wasn't even glancing at the wild, wriggling thing yowling in her arms.*

Yet another screeching kid that girl could hold in her arms. How, Sophie wondered, did she do it?

Same way I did, *she realized, surprising herself. She went on thinking about that—about her Roo—while she waited for Rebecca to pound away down the trail. Then she eased herself off the thorns that had impaled her, brushed the burrs from her skin, and edged back out of the bush.*

There was less sound now from the clearing, which probably wasn't a great sign for the people in *the clearing. A bat fluttered madly in the leaves over Sophie's head, and then the leaves went silent.*

Glancing just once after Rebecca, Sophie was startled to see another figure stagger out of the woods. This one was black-haired, bloodied, broken. And it was calling Rebecca's name.

Whoever that was, Sophie figured Rebecca would come back for her. And that would keep her close by. And that was all to the good.

I'm late, *Sophie murmured to herself, thinking of the Whistler, of Jess. She let herself smile, fingered the phone, the little Bluetooth speaker in her pocket. Then she slipped away once more into the shadows.*

There was a moment—several, actually—right after Rebecca snatched up Trudi and fled, when no one in the clearing seemed to know what to do. Gripping the rake, trying to resist jabbing it into her own face in the hopes of waking herself up, freeing herself of *whatever this feeling was,* Amanda stared at the monster in the sombrero. But he just stood there, preternaturally quiet, staring after Rebecca, almost precisely in the way Joel had taught so many of the girls who'd passed through Halfmoon House to watch the night-woods for owls.

Only, this guy was even quieter. He didn't even seem to breathe.

Jess had made some crazy leap, cried out, stabbed absolutely nothing with the pinking shears, and now she was just standing there, too, looking dazed, and also small: a tiny, grief-wracked widow, shapeless in her gray sweatshirt but transfixed by moonlight, ablaze with it. She looked reared up, somehow, like a little gopher at the mouth of its den, waving uselessly at the fox that had come for her young.

And then there was Joel. He, of course, had broken completely with the snap of Danni's spine. Because, as always, he'd gone and done exactly what they'd both set out to do with Halfmoon House, right from the beginning. He'd done the one thing Amanda had never quite let herself do.

He'd let himself love them. Even—especially—the furious and fucked-up ones. And until ten seconds ago, he'd actually believed he could save them all, and that they would save him in turn.

By saving me, Amanda realized abruptly. *By waking me up. As if I were only sleeping, all this time.*

She looked at him, her mad, broken, no-longer-laughing husband, arms wrapped around his shovel, mouth open, eyes overflowing, and not just with tears but also everything he'd shared with these children who were not his children: his crazy songs, his dreamed-up-in-the-instant games, his ridiculous theme-picnic plans. All the things she'd loved about him, once. She still loved them. Sometimes.

All the life he still believed—or maybe had believed, until just a few seconds ago—he might one day have. *With me,* she thought.

"Joel," she said, hating the sound of her voice, as she had for years, now, because even she couldn't read the emotion in it. "Go live."

He didn't even stir, of course. His attention remained riveted to the heap at the Sombrero-Man's feet. The heap that had been Danni.

But Jess heard. And Jess understood, immediately. Of course she did.

"Amanda, *no,*" she said.

"Save the girls," said Amanda, feeling herself finally, finally tear free of whatever it was that had held her in place. In truth, it had held her long before today. And now, just like that, it was gone. And here she was, after all this time, unfolding inside herself.

Hello, me, she thought, trembling, letting life flood in. *Long time no see.* Then she leapt.

She died so fast—so much of her flying in so many

directions—that neither Joel nor Jess would ever be sure exactly what it was the Whistler had done to her.

A split second too late, freed by the movement his wife had made (or else by the momentary distraction that movement had caused the Sombrero-Man), Joel leapt, too. He didn't think, hadn't planned, hardly even raised the shovel, but suddenly, he was sailing through a winking red haze that hung in the air, a corona of Amanda—of what had been his wife—around the summer moon.

Like flying through the forest, he thought, *in the seconds after a tornado hits.*

The Whistler smashed him to the ground, knocked the shovel flying, seemed to swirl down on him like a tornado.

The Whistler hardly felt what he was doing, he simply did, *set the air screaming and the night whistling just by whirling his arms. Sounds spilled from him—from everywhere, really—as he stepped on the neck of the guy with the shovel. The guy* formerly *with the shovel. Unless that was a root he'd leaned down on to crack?*

Who cared?! Not him. He flung his wet, red arms wide, bathed them with world, which was there for him to Whistle to, sing to, swallow whole, snap. It existed only to make noise under his feet, come apart in his grasp, experience.

He was Whistling now, a proper whistle, his first in ages, weeks. He hadn't Whistled this way since his Destiny died. What a truly wonderful world, *he thought, watching and feeling the blood and flying skin-bits coat and mottle his own skin, become him as he hummed.*

Don't know much about . . . biology . . .

The movement alerted him, but not quite in time. He shivered back into himself, into the moment, and glanced around.

The other woman—his Destiny's murderer-mother—was gone.

Marvelous!

"Ready or not," he said-sang to the moon and stars, the trees and trailers, the shredded and snapped things at his feet. "Here I come."

Trudi hadn't stopped screaming "*STOP!*" since Rebecca had spirited her out of the clearing. But when Rebecca pulled up momentarily and set her down, tried to spin so she could see who or what had just called her name, Trudi somehow screamed louder.

She kept repeating the same word, howling it at everything and nothing, and who could blame her? Right now, Trudi wanted the whole world to stop.

Let me know if you get a response, kiddo, Rebecca thought, and squeezed her arms tight around Trudi's back, though not nearly as hard as Trudi was squeezing—clinging to—Rebecca's leg. She should have been more afraid. But whatever had just stepped out of the woods, it could have her if it wanted her. Rebecca was too tired, too heartbroken to run from anything else. Using her knee as a nudge, letting Trudi cling, Rebecca eased herself around and saw Kaylene.

She was swaying, leaning sideways in the center of the path—*Jack and the 'Lenes,* Rebecca thought, as she clutched Trudi harder—with her beautiful nose smashed flat on her face and pearls of blood strung like beads through her long, matted hair. There was so much red all over her, even in the shadowed forest dark, that she looked as though she'd been turned inside out.

Rebecca tried to ease Trudi back, just enough so they could move toward Kaylene. But Trudi grabbed tight and dug her nails into Rebecca's shoulders, clinging and kneading like a cat caught in a screen. She was also pleading, without language, just pure, anguished sound. "*Nnnnnnn . . .* "

"Okay," Rebecca whispered down to her, while looking at Kaylene through a veil of tears that already—had always—felt permanent and part of her. "It's okay, it's okay, it's . . ."

Then Kaylene's eyes met hers. For one moment, Rebecca almost smiled. "You're okay."

"He killed Jack." Kaylene's voice came out metallic, a digital sample of Kaylene's voice. "The guy in the sombrero."

"I know. I've seen. He killed Oscar, too," said Rebecca. "The grounds-crew guy I always . . . my friend from campus."

From deep in Kaylene's throat came a grating sound, scraped and awful: bottom-of-the-tear-barrel tears, the kind that come after crying. Rebecca knew those tears well.

Kaylene wiped at her face, even though there was no new wetness there. "And Marlene."

"No," Rebecca whimpered, although she realized she had already assumed that.

Marlene.

Standing there amid the shuddering trees, fighting to hold position as Trudi pressed into her, Rebecca could feel herself shredding. She was a little sapling, peeling apart, its buds and blossoms plucked away, one by one.

"I saw it happen, Rebecca. I *watched* it happen."

Another sound scraped from Kaylene's throat. That one was familiar to Rebecca, too, though not so much from her own life. She recognized it from Crisis Center phone calls. That terrible, guilty tremor.

"It wasn't your fault, Kaylene. You couldn't have done anything. I've seen him, too. There's nothing you—"

"You're wrong about that," Kaylene muttered. Behind her, the pines started shaking.

Run, Rebecca thought, stirring inside herself. *We have to run.* And then she thought again of Marlene. Twinkies in her bag, squashed under her chem books.

Somehow, without letting Trudi go, Rebecca grabbed Kaylene and pulled her close. Kaylene was still shuddering even harder than the trees, in abrupt, violent gusts. Instantly, her hands were in Rebecca's hair, and she was clinging, too, like a drowning person dragged from the water.

But onto nothing, Rebecca thought. *There's no life raft here. I have nothing, for anyone.*

"Kaylene, we've got to go. *Kaylene!* Help me. We've got to *go.*"

"I could have saved her. Rebecca. I could have saved her."

"Then save *her,*" Rebecca snapped, and ripped free of both Kaylene and Trudi, left them clutching each other. "Kaylene. Save this girl. Save Trudi."

"*NNNNNN,*" Trudi grunted, wriggling awake. She almost bit Kaylene's arm as she tried to squirm back to Rebecca. At least that finally stirred Kaylene. She held tight, tugged Trudi close, glanced up at the rustling in the trees around them.

"It's okay," Rebecca said, though she had no idea to whom. She watched Kaylene surface again behind her face. There she was: Dig Dug Girl.

"Rebecca. What are you doing? Where are you going?"

"I'll be right back."

In the trees—not too close, from the direction of the clearing with the trailers, and maybe not even headed this way—footsteps sounded amid the scurries and rustling. For a moment, the sound seemed as deceptively peaceful as bubbles on the surface of Halfmoon Lake. The ones that told you something living was lurking underneath.

"You can't fight that guy," Kaylene said. "We've got to go. You said it yourself. Please. I can't lose you, too."

Rebecca nodded, knew Kaylene was right. But what she said was, "I can't let them die."

"They're already dead. *All* of them. And if they're not, and they live, it won't be because of anything you do."

That was right, of course. Rebecca reached out abruptly and touched her friend's hair. This was very possibly her *last* living friend, she realized. Then she looked down at the little girl in Kaylene's arms, who suddenly—it had literally just happened—wasn't little anymore. Trudi was simply staring up at her.

"I'm going back anyway," Rebecca said, and went.

In his excitement—in the sheer, slippery, wildwoods glee of the moment—the Whistler almost didn't notice, almost didn't hear, as he leapt off the neck of the tall guy (like a little boy jumping from a tree stump into leaves or a lake), the telltale tap of a single finger against one of the trailers. That almost-soft-enough not-quite-sound of a barely lifted toe sliding over tiny twigs.

Coming from . . .

Yes. The sounds came from around the side of that tilted-over trailer, with its screen door dangling like a torn-out rib cage.

He didn't stop running after his new, Still One, didn't even break his stride. He was far, far too clever a Whistler for that. Instead, he ducked into the trees, all the way into the shadows, and continued quite a ways down the path. Only then did he stop, turn, and listen. He lifted his own foot, in what he was sure was a precise parody of the movement his Destiny's mother must be making at this very moment, just back there on the other side of that trailer, scant moments away from her *destiny, though she did not know it yet.*

Anything you can do, *he thought. He threw his hands up in front of his face, sucked in the smell, licked up the taste. Then he started back the way he had come, quietly, quietly, like a cat, only quieter, like a wind with nothing to resist it, and so nothing to sound it. He was trying to decide if, right at the end, he would prefer if his Destiny's mother did or did not feel him coming.*

Rebecca had slipped well off the path, forcing herself to move slowly. Now, approaching the clearing and the trailers, she slowed even more. She stayed way back amid the bristling, prickling ground cover, not exactly picking her way, not bothering to try *not* making sound, because she suspected that would only give her away. She had some vague notion of trying to make *natural* sound, becoming just one more forest-noise amid all the stirred-up chirring and hooting and crackling and rustling all around her.

What she had no notion about was what she would do when she actually reached the clearing. If she did. She had heard, all too well, the sounds behind her as she'd fled with Trudi a few minutes earlier: the sounds of something—someone—being sucked into an industrial fan.

Someone she had loved. Very possibly several someones. Or all of them.

Or not. Not yet.

When had she dropped to her hands and knees? And why was she crouching lower still, now, into the dirt, the broken bits of branch and honeycomb and seed and soil, all of it so cool and crawly and soft against her stomach as she slithered slowly, steadily forward? She could see the side and roof of one of the trailers straight ahead: the American flag trailer, hulking, dark, and sad, as always, about as haunted as a toy truck left out in long grass.

Beyond that, she could see the fire pit, now, and curled flat on the ground against it—and *moving*!—Joel. His body seemed to push up against itself, uncoil, push together, uncoil, like a caterpillar pulsing over a leaf, except he wasn't going anywhere. Rebecca couldn't see his face. That was probably for the best. Less chance of either one of them calling out.

But the sight, awful as it was, steadied her, made her feel as though there might be something left to do, after all, just maybe. Something other than die. And dying had never been her plan, just a possibility.

Like it always is, she thought. She had always thought that, always known it. She kept crawling, eyes fixed on the fire pit and away from the tipped-over trailer, not because she was scared of it, but because of what she feared—almost knew—she would see beside or inside it. Those bodies, she knew, would *not* be moving.

Then she was at the edge of the clearing, and she had no choice but to look.

At first, what she saw looked less like bodies than a collection of raked-together bits: Danni's surprisingly thin arm flung out toward the fire pit; Danni's blond hair splayed across the dirt, almost artistically, like a child's drawing of the rays of a fallen star, still glinting; Joel's curled back, pulsing, without any appearance of volition or consciousness, his jeans and work shirt spattered with what Rebecca thought was dirt and only slowly—as shapes coalesced out of shadows, became shapes once more—realized was pieces of Amanda.

How did she know it was Amanda? By the stubbiness of the lobe on that section of ear atop Joel's hip. By the pale pallor of the shreds of skin everywhere, like rind from a peeled orange. The blue of the eye leaning out of that smashed-apart skull against the stump where the Whistler had stood. Somehow, that eye was like a whole face all by itself, a face at the window of a collapsing building. The eye of someone considering jumping. Which was how Amanda's eyes had always looked.

I'm so sorry, Rebecca was murmuring without actually speaking, exploding into tears but moving only her mouth, nothing else. *Amanda.* The words swelled inside her, filled her throat, ballooned toward her mouth, where she would have no choice but to scream them, sing them. She glanced to her left and saw Jess.

Jess—upright, still moving—was crouching low, creeping around the side of the tipped-over trailer toward that dangling door. Rebecca watched her gather Joel's discarded shovel to her, peer around the clearing. For one moment, Rebecca almost forgot the Whistler entirely, transformed back into her kid-self, terrified only of this trailer and the creature she'd always imagined coiled inside it like an eel, all face and mouth.

Jess, she was thinking, wanting to scream. *Don't turn your back.*

Jess seemed to sense something, too. She stopped in her tracks, glanced sideways, hunched even lower. And that was why she didn't see the Whistler—grinning, arms extended, legs lifting high as he tiptoed, his every movement a parody of a child sneaking up on a parent—when he appeared behind her.

Shoving to her knees, rattling branches, Rebecca threw out her hands, sucked in breath to shout one last useless warning, and stopped once more, this time in disbelief: *another* face had appeared, not inside the tipped-over trailer but atop it, on what had once been its side wall and was now its roof. This face leered as it leaned, not more than two feet above Jess, who still hadn't seen it or the Whistler, either. The Whistler, too, seemed oblivious; he was too intent on his prey, on the *play* he was making of preying,

But that face noticed Rebecca, glanced toward her. And so Rebecca got a full blast of Sophie's excitement, her flat-out, fascinated glee as she pulled herself to the edge of the tipped-over roof, gazing back and forth between Jess's head and the Whistler's like a little girl watching an ant farm. Her excitement was way too much like the Whistler's, Rebecca thought, shuddering through her sorrow and her fury. For Sophie, too, this was far too much like play.

And then Rebecca realized she had a choice to make: she could shout a warning, and so save Jess for a little longer, give her a fighting chance or at least one good swing of the spade; or she could stay silent, trust Sophie to choose correctly between the woman who had cared for her all her life and never loved her enough—and would never, ever love her now—and the Sombrero-Thing that didn't love anyone, but was now more like her than anyone else in this world.

Rebecca's whole life, it turned out, had been preparation for this moment. All that practice on Crisis Center phone calls and in grief-counseling groups and foster homes full of resentful not-siblings and not-parents, all those years of reading people, knowing whom to trust and when to stay and when to run, intuiting whether someone was really jumping, really going to hurt someone else, all this time sorting monsters from mothers, had led her to this. Because everything she had left in her world depended on who Sophie was, right this second, and what she wanted, and whether Rebecca read that correctly, and guessed right.

She guessed.

He almost didn't want it to end. A few weeks ago, he had met his Destiny, courted her, abandoned his Mother for her, and lost them both. So tragic. Tonight, he had taken his revenge—that's what it had been, surely, there'd been such marvelous intensity *in his actions, such ferocity—on his Destiny's murderer-mother's minions. That, after all, was what they were. And now, at last, he would have his revenge on the murderer herself.*

And just when he thought the whole experience could not get any more exquisite, any more inspiring, *he realized he had an audience, a proper one. His new, Still One had popped up in the bushes as though he'd planted her there, sprung her at just this precise moment, so she could watch. That was her job, her very purpose on this earth, after all.*

He didn't look at her, not directly. She mustn't know that he knew. He wanted her right where she was, in her place, on her knees with her mouth open, unable to speak, poor thing, unable to do anything but marvel. She had been born to be audience, his *audience, like all of them. The ones he let live, anyway.*

The Whistle inside him roared up his windpipe, uncontainable, as irresistible to him as it was to them. But it was for *them, all his poor, pitiful little creatures.*

He coiled to strike, opened his mouth to unleash his Whistle. And right at that moment, out of the very air, came . . .

Came . . .

Jess heard it too, of course. She jolted, quivered, stood shuddering in place as though she'd been hit by lightning, She couldn't move, couldn't speak or do anything but listen as her daughter's voice—*Natalie's voice*—filled the clearing.

"*HEY bay-beee . . .*" it was saying. Chanting. "*You look . . . GOOOOOD . . .*"

Almost, Sophie waited too long, held the moment too tightly, couldn't stop savoring: Jess the Righteous at the instant of her extinguishing, and the Whistling Fuck, oblivious to the end, both of them rooted so firmly in place, it was as though she'd bewitched them, turned them to stone.

And because she waited so long, and also got startled—though she shouldn't have been—by the sheer speed with which the Whistler snapped back to himself, snarled like a rabid thing, and threw himself forward, she had no choice, in the end; she couldn't think, only lunge. And so she got her timing exactly right.

At the very instant the Whistler's hands gripped Jess's shoulders, Sophie slammed down on his back. The impact sent Jess and her steak knife flying and drove the Whistler's sombrero into the air but the Whistler himself toward the ground. By the time he hit it, Sophie had her teeth in the back of his neck. She snapped her jaws all the way shut. Given that the blood in there didn't actually circulate, the explosion in her mouth was remarkable, viscous and cold—which, again, shouldn't have surprised her, and did—like the gel in the middle of that gum she'd always hated and chewed anyway, made Natalie chew anyway, just so she could watch Natalie's face.

Freshen-Up. That was it.

She ground her teeth harder, drove her whole head into the hole she'd made at the base of the Whistler's skull while he flailed, trying to punch or rip at her. He was whistling out both sides of his face, now. Kind of cool, that. Bits of vein-thread sliced up between Sophie's teeth like dental floss, straight into her gums. Every inch of this asshole was sharp, spiky, horrible.

And I, *she thought,* am the tick on your back. The thing you cannot shake. You ripped away my body, killed my son, tore out my heart. And so, here I am, burrowing into you.

Rebecca kept thinking it would stop, had to stop. But it didn't. It just kept going. The Sombrero-Man—stripped of his sombrero—flailed and bucked but couldn't get up, jerked around like a chicken with its head cut off, only his head wasn't all the way off. Sophie stayed clamped to his shoulders, ears-deep in the back of his skull, a cartoon badger gnawing out a tree trunk. Both of them just went on screaming, whistling, howling, roaring.

Like cats in heat, Rebecca thought, swaying in the bushes. *Like wild things, mating.*

Some of the screaming, she realized, was her own. There was a whispering from somewhere, too. Her own name, in whispers. That was coming from Jess, she realized, from over where Jess had crumpled after slamming her head against the side of the tipped-over trailer.

Then, with a screech that seemed to shoot up the surrounding pines like lightning in reverse, the Sombrero-Man suddenly humped up and flipped over, slamming Sophie to the ground underneath him, both of them faceup. Rebecca got a momentary glimpse of his eyes, which seemed to be draining into the bones underneath as Sophie sucked out everything behind them. But his smile . . .

That stayed put.

This time, Rebecca's decision was immediate, instinctive; it was also the only choice. Darting forward, eyes never leaving the Whistler as he humped up, slammed down, humped up, slammed down, and, *Jesus Christ,* started to sing, Rebecca grabbed the shovel that had flown out of Jess's hands and landed right by Joel. He, too, had rolled over and regained some sort of consciousness. Enough, apparently, to remember what had happened to his wife. He was blinking, bloody, staring up through a well of tears, and he had his mouth open as though he were about to call something ridiculous up the stairs of Halfmoon House, something to wake his orphans up laughing one more time.

"Hang on," she told him.

In two steps, she was over the Sombrero-Man and Sophie. Both of them stared straight up, too, but not at her, not at anyone, as they yowled and slammed and bit and wrecked. She watched the Sombrero-Man register her, saw that awful smile spread. He never stopped singing, high and keening. Birdsong. "*The cuckoo . . . she's a pretty bird . . .* " The words rang her, the voice itself roaring down her veins straight for her heart.

As she swung the spade over her head, Rebecca saw Sophie register her, too, from *inside* the Sombrero-Man's head. Her eyes were sticking out the side of his skull like extra eyes, one creature's eyes, filmed over with red. There was nothing in them but hunger.

At least, that was all Rebecca saw. That's what she would tell herself, later. *And even if it wasn't. Even if that twitch in Sophie's eyes really had been . . . a* wink *. . . which was what it had looked like . . . there really was no other choice.*

With a shriek, Rebecca slammed down the spade. When she lifted it, the singing started again immediately, only it was mostly whistling, this time, like a teakettle gone mad. She slammed down again, onto—*into*—both faces. The one on top splintered, with nothing left to support it. The one beneath gave way. Rebecca kept smashing until all the screaming and singing and whistling stopped, until the spade seemed to be smashing dirt, not bone, not skin.

Then she slammed some more.

When she stopped, staggered back, and looked up, she found Joel and Jess standing together by the fire pit. They were leaning into each other, staring at her in amazement.

"I've got to go find Trudi and Kaylene," Rebecca said.

Without so much as a glance at the mess she'd made, she dropped the spade and started into the woods to do just that.

"Sit *still,*" Jess said, leaning in again with her gauze and washcloths while Rebecca slumped back against Amanda's worktable. Gently, Jess probed, pressed, wiped away. Beyond her, Rebecca could see Joel and Benny seated on the stairs, Joel holding Trudi, Benny rocking Eddie.

"And *you,*" Jess snapped, not even looking at Kaylene but sensing Kaylene's bandaged, still-bloodied head drooping again toward the tabletop. "I told you. You can't sleep."

"Isn't that just in case you have a concussion?" Kaylene murmured, shaking herself. Jess had gone at her, first. Most of the blood had been wiped away, though there was still a dried, crusted trickle on her forehead.

"Honey, you have a concussion."

"Right. So now we know. So I might as well sleep." A guttural moan spilled from her throat. Rebecca started to her feet, and Jess shoved her back again.

"Sit."

"Jess, I told you. He never even touched me."

"There are scratches all over you."

"From branches. From running."

And then, abruptly, Rebecca was crying again. She looked at Jess, who raised a cloth to mop the tears but didn't use it. Instead, she held Rebecca's gaze. After a while, she cupped Rebecca's chin in her hand. They stayed that way a long time. Their sorrows were shared, familiar, instantly recognizable to one another, though their losses were their own.

At some point, Rebecca glanced across the room and saw Joel and Benny leaning together, too. Jess followed her gaze. The sight seemed to brace her. She straightened, and Rebecca watched her fight for—and almost get—control of her face. But that just brought the sight of Sophie's face—Sophie's last wink—swimming up into Rebecca's vision. Instantly, that song went off again in her ears, the one the Sombrero-Man had unleashed on her at the moment she'd smashed the life completely out of him.

"She sucks all . . . the sweet flowers . . ."

Then Jess grabbed her hand and tugged her to her feet. They stood in Amanda's kitchen among their remaining loved ones: Kaylene at the end of the table with Trudi's sock puppet pulled down over one of her hands, Joel and Trudi on the stairs, Benny and Eddie on the stair below them.

"Look at us," Jess said, wiping, uselessly at her own tears.

They looked together, Rebecca and Jess. They held on to each other. It would be a long time, Rebecca thought, before she let go of this woman.

"Jess," she said, after a long, merciful silence while just holding Jess's hand, leaning into her, while Jess leaned back. "What . . . I mean. What do we do now?"

And Jess stirred, looked around the room. Then she was looking only at Rebecca. The faintest, ghostliest smile flickered, just once, on her mouth. "I don't know, hon. I think . . . I guess we eat."

So they got up together, and set about making that happen.

From underneath—from the protective tortoiseshell she'd somehow made from the Whistler's shattered skull, the bike helmet she'd created, in the instant, out of what had been his brainpan, while Jess's new substitute-daughter rained down blow after blow with her shovel—Sophie listened and waited, lying still, until long after everyone had gone. Her own head buzzed with aches, rang with the blows that hadn't quite broken it and might or might not have been meant to.

You had to give it to that girl, *Sophie thought.* She had made her decision. And then she'd followed through on it.

Like Natalie would have.

Except that Natalie would have checked, afterward, to see if Sophie was still under there or not. Then she would have faced that *murderous decision, and made that one, too, one way or the other.*

Pushing Whistler-bits aside, crying out as the wrist Rebecca had apparently broken bent all the way back on its joint, Sophie pulled herself free. She kept having to spit, over and over, gag and spit, even though it didn't help. At least she had now confirmed for herself what Natalie had learned, on the night Natalie had indeed tried to kill her: we taste like shit, *she thought.*

She spit again, coughed, and at least dislodged a gob of Whistler-brain from the back of her throat, vomiting that onto the dirt like a cat with a hairball. When she was all the way out of the Whistler's body, standing on her stumps in the dirt in the center of the clearing, in dark that had gone moonless, now, in woods that were small-hour quiet, Sophie put her hands on her hips and gazed around, taking stock. She'd discovered one advantage of being a stump tonight, anyway: there was less of her to break.

But her face ached. And her wrist . . . that was going to take days *to heal, even the way she healed, now. She was sure her eyes were black, her nose pummeled. Also, her teeth ached from sawing through so much skull to all that cold, sloshy Whistler-pudding.*

Which was Whistler no longer, because she really had done it. She'd avenged Natalie, and herself, for whatever that was worth, to anyone.

Bad guys, 1,000, *she thought.* Good girls, 1.

Dragging herself to the other side of the fire pit, through wet spots in the dirt—some of which were dew—she collected the little speaker she'd set up. The tiny black box where Natalie lived, now. In her pocket, Sophie found her phone, still intact. She couldn't resist hitting Send, setting off the Bluetooth speaker one last time.

"HEY bay-beee . . ." said the speaker, in Natalie's voice.

"Hey baby," Sophie said. She started to hum, but a different song, an older one. One of Natalie's all-time faves. "We're walkin'. Yes indeed."

Then the speaker was in her hand, the phone in her pocket. She was all but out of the clearing when she heard the moan.

At another time—in another life—Sophie might have mistaken the sound for an owl, or the soughing of wind.

But not this time. Spinning on her stumps, crying out each time she had to lean on her broken wrist, she swung around and across the ground; she reached the side of the whimpering girl in no time.

"Oh, sugar," she said, gazing down at the blond, broken thing, bent backward, splayed against the fire pit. Some of her spine poked through the back of her shredded shirt, propping her against the side of the pit like a kickstand. "My goodness. Look what he did to you."

Danni gazed helplessly up, eyes wild with terror, unless that was pain. Mostly terror, Sophie suspected. She doubted this girl was feeling pain or anything else, at this point. She could still cry, though, apparently. And she looked furious. Good for her.

"It's okay," Sophie said. If she'd still had a lap, she would have laid the girl's head in it. As it was, she simply settled herself against her. She stroked the long blond hair. Presumably, the girl could still feel that; at least, it seemed she could. She stopped moaning. Her panic didn't so much abate as level.

"It's okay," Sophie said again, stroking the girl's hair. She thought of Natalie, safely in her pocket, now, and then of Jess, who had probably loved Sophie once. Certainly, Jess would never love her again. "It's okay." She looked down at this new girl. This fierce, fighting thing. Oh, yes. Sophie could still see the fight in there. "Look at you," she said.

Then she struck, so fast and hard that she was sure the girl never saw—never even imagined—what was coming.

And that's something, *Sophie thought as she drank.* And I'm sorry.

But after all. A girl had to eat.

28

Almost until the very last moment, Caribou attributed his unease, his sense of dislocation, to the strangeness of this entire day: Aunt Sally's break with Policy, and the discovery of Ju in the woods, and the drive back to camp with her and the laughing Spider-kids and his loving Ann; the impulse to run, for the first time in his life or afterlife, and then the calliope and the bouncy castle, the circus tent and the games, the screaming and spatters of color as the Party started in earnest, while Aunt Sally sat outside in the dust in the Delta moonlight with Ju on her lap, just stroking the child's hair. Instead of creating that giddiness, that rush of heightened reality that Aunt Sally's Parties usually did, this one had left Caribou . . . actually, he didn't even know what. He wasn't sad, *what-*

ever that was, and he wasn't bored, either. He just . . . wasn't here. Even as he sucked the last meat off the few fingers he had dutifully salvaged from the fray—the Spider-girl's, he suspected, judging by their length, their surprising tenderness—he marveled, distantly, at the lack of any taste.

And then, right as the tent walls erupted in flame, the flames shooting across the floor and up the legs of all the feasting monsters, setting them dancing all over again, screaming and dancing, Caribou rocked to his feet and realized exactly what had happened. The detachment he'd been feeling—like everything he had ever felt—wasn't actually his own. And it wasn't really detachment. It was absence. Aunt Sally's absence. Her *detachment, from all of them. Because she had reached a crossroads, and chosen.*

As for the meat's lack of taste, that wasn't any emotional side effect, but a physical one, the result of the kerosene—or turpentine, or whatever concoction Aunt Sally had soaked every shred of this tent with before erecting it while the monsters were out fetching supplies—that now filled his nostrils, burning out his sense of smell. That's *what that odor was.*

Or rather, had been. Now, the only odor was flesh, burning. The reek of that seared away all others.

The reek of his own flesh, burning.

In disbelief, Caribou stared down at his pants legs. Vines of twisting white-red light shot up them, entwining at his waist, engulfing him. Fire-kudzu, *he thought, swaying, unable, even now, to drag himself all the way back inside his own body.*

Then, with a shriek—as the others collided, careened, bellowed like alligators, squealed like pigs, exploded, melted into each other—he hurled himself at the tiny gap between canvas and earth at the bottom of the nearest tent wall, the little thread of night just visible there. It was like diving through a waterfall of fire, or into fire's mouth; the heat somehow intensified *as he hit the dirt and rolled, screaming. The giant tent behind him billowed, spitting plumes of eerily transparent smoke skyward, and there were shapes in that smoke, souls shredding. Caribou rolled and screamed, felt his legs flare, his shoulders, his chest, but he just kept rolling, listening to his skin hissing and whispering, as though everyone he'd ever known—or eaten—was pouring through his pores, escaping up the smoke toward oblivion.*

He rolled to a stop, let himself sizzle. For a while, he had no idea how long, he lay there in the wet and loamy Delta earth. Behind him, the screaming reached a crescendo. Then it stopped, and in its place came a crackling, a hissing and sighing as the fire—Aunt Sally's surprise guest, the one she'd told no one was coming—subsided out of its frenzy, settled down to feasting.

Caribou opened his eyes.

Aunt Sally stood over him, holding a hose, her white dress streaked with ash. There was a single streaked handprint, right at her hip, where one of the monsters must have tried to grab hold of her to pull himself free of the flames. Before she'd pushed him back in.

He tried lifting a hand, found he didn't dare. He thought he might not have enough hand left, might just melt away into the ground if he so much as stirred. He wanted to look elsewhere, too, didn't want to be staring into Aunt Sally's face. But he was no longer sure he had eyelids. And anyway, she didn't seem to want him to look away. She seemed to want him to ask.

So he did, as best he could, by lying there and looking up at her face as his flesh blackened and his bones flaked toward ash.

"You're wondering why?" she said. "Oh, 'Bou. Poor, poor 'Bou."

She glanced over her shoulder in the direction of her car, where Ju, Caribou realized, must already be strapped in, might even be sleeping, all tucked up and ready to go.

To go! *Despite the horrific pain, and the even more devastating hurt—because she'd left him with* them, *with the other monsters, had in fact ordered him to join them—his blackened body filled with longing. He looked up at Aunt Sally, hoped she understood.*

And she did, *he thought. She might even have reconsidered, briefly. But after a while, she said, "No. I think not. I'm sorry. I did mull that, 'Bou. You were the only one I thought about taking. But sometimes, it's best just to clean house, you know? I believe in a clean house. Actually, I believe in* no *house. A cataclysmic burn, then a new road. It's just"—very slowly, even regretfully, Aunt Sally smiled—"Policy."*

She waved the hose at something. At the night. The liquid at the end caught the moonlight, flashed purple. Aunt Sally was still talking, but not to him, anymore, or even to herself; she was talking to the stars, the Delta, all the years she had survived before Mother, with Mother, after Mother but with Caribou. She was talking to the years coming.

"We are all creatures of cataclysm," she was saying.

"Accidental aftermath, ignited into darkness with nowhere near enough light or oxygen or love to sustain us . . ."

Caribou watched Aunt Sally murmur, her voice trailing away, her mouth still moving as she gazed over her shoulder toward the LeSabre. And abruptly—despite the pain, despite what she'd done—amazement flashed through him. And not just amazement. If he could have gotten up, if he'd been sure his skin and skeleton wouldn't stick to the ground when he rose, he would have risen. He would have approached, carefully. He would have put his arms around Aunt Sally and held her. Because he understood, and he was amazed.

Aunt Sally was afraid. She was afraid, because she wanted a companion, a permanent one. A daughter: Ju. And she did not know—any more than any of them ever had—how to make that happen, how to make Ju one of them instead of dead when the moment came and Aunt Sally, inevitably, struck. Whether the impossible, flickering, miraculous something *that was Ju would just wink out and bleed away, or else rise up—like Mother had; like* he *had—and ignite in the dark.*

And Caribou realized that he wanted to see what happened, too. He wanted to know. Desperately, he wanted that, so desperately that actual tears swelled in his singed ducts, sliding out of his eyes and down the char of his face. How astounding to understand, at the last, how much life—any life, even the one he'd lived—matters to the living.

Of course, Aunt Sally noticed. She always did. She raised the hose, put her hand on the nozzle to douse him, purify him, baptize *him. Droplets hung at the hose's mouth, slick, purple-black. Not water, Caribou saw. Too late, he saw that. Not that seeing or knowing would have mattered.*

"A clean burn," Aunt Sally said. "A new start. A little more cleaning up to do. A bit more erasing. And then my little girl and I, we'll just . . ."

She did finish that sentence. But Caribou couldn't hear her over the spray of the hose. He couldn't scream, didn't even want to, as she slipped a match from her pocket, lit it against the pack, and dropped it on him.